THE WRONG HANDS

THE
WRONG
HANDS

A NEW DETECTIVE MILLER NOVEL

MARK
BILLINGHAM

Atlantic Monthly Press

New York

First published in Great Britain in 2024 by Sphere, an imprint of Little, Brown Book Group UK.

Printed in the United States of America

First Grove Atlantic hardcover edition: July 2024

Typeset in Plantin by M Rules.

Library of Congress Cataloging-in-Publication data is available for this title.

ISBN 978-0-8021-6309-7
eISBN 978-0-8021-6310-3

Atlantic Monthly Press
an imprint of Grove Atlantic
154 West 14th Street
New York, NY 10011

Distributed by Publishers Group West

groveatlantic.com

24 25 26 27   10 9 8 7 6 5 4 3 2 1

For Claire, Katie and Jack

THE
WRONG
HANDS

He was a stone-cold mechanic out of Miami with a job to do. Just a regular killing. Just some punk who was going to get what was coming to him. It would be a snip.

'The train now standing at platform two is the 08.37 to York calling at Poulton-le-Fylde, Preston, Blackburn, Accrington ...'

He downed two fingers of Beam and checked the Glock strapped beneath his left arm. The weight of it felt good. Like an old friend.

'Burnley Manchester Road, Hebden Bridge ...'

He slapped a five on a ten for the bartender and slid off the barstool. It was time for work.

'Travellers are reminded that there is no buffet service available on this train. We apologise again—'

'Oi, Andy!'

'Oh, sorry, Keith. I was—'

'Yeah, miles away, course you were. Where the heck have you been? I said half-eight under the clock. It's nearly twenty to!' Slack stared and shook his head. 'Bloody hell, what have you come as?'

Andy Bagnall self-consciously pulled his shirt down over his beer gut and adjusted his ponytail.

'We're supposed to be inconspicuous, you dozy twonk.'

'I am inconspicuous.'

'In a Hawaiian shirt? You look like you've puked up on it.'

'This is from Florida. My auntie got it for me when she went to Disneyworld last Christmas.'

Slack wasn't listening. He was staring across the busy station concourse towards the public toilets. Bagnall watched him, and then, for want of anything better to do, he stared as well.

Keith Slack thought this was definitely his best plan ever. Businessmen carried all sorts of valuables in their brief-cases. Laptop computers, mobile phones, wallets, iFags. Businessmen had to pee. Businessmen had to pee with two hands. Nobody kept one hand on their briefcase and tried to wrestle out their old feller with the other, and no businessman wanted wee on the bottom of their briefcase, so they put it down a reasonable distance away from the urinal. Slack knew all this because he'd done the research.

Create a diversion. Away with the briefcase. Piece of piss.

'So, you know what you're doing, Andy?'

'When?'

'In the toilets, mate.' Slack tried to stay calm. 'In the bloody bogs.'

'Oh, yeah. I'm creating a diversion.'

Slack saw a worrying glint in Bagnall's eye and the flaw in his otherwise perfect plan became glaringly obvious.

'Now, when I say "diversion" I don't mean throw a bleedin' fit or anything. When you see somebody put their bag down, just talk to them. Ask them to help you find a contact lens or summat.'

'I don't wear contact lenses, Keith.'

Slack sighed and rubbed his tired eyes.

'I could ask them to help me find my sunglasses.'

'It was just an example, Andy. Oh, and make sure it's a decent briefcase or summat like that. I'm not doing this for some poxy Adidas bag full of rancid football socks, OK? OK, Andy?'

'Yeah, got it. No socks.'

'Right, off you go. Just hang about and wash your hands or whatever. I'll be in in a bit.'

Bagnall ran his fingers through his bleached blond hair and strode off across the concourse, the heels of his cowboy boots clack-clacking on the polished stone. He stopped at the entrance to the toilets and after a moment turned back to look at Slack.

Slack held out his hands and mouthed at him. 'What?'

Bagnall mouthed back. 'Can you lend me twenty p?'

Slack knew he was the brains of the outfit, but didn't that at least *imply* the other bloke was the muscle? Andy Bagnall was thick as mince and that was all there was to it. They'd do a few more stations after this and then Slack would tell Bagnall he was branching out on his own. OK, so they'd been mates at school, but playing footie and dicking around with Bunsen burners was one thing; when it came to basic thieving, Bagnall was a liability. If he hadn't actually got his head stuck in some stupid thriller or was pretending he was American, he'd be staring off into space with a gormless expression like someone had sprinkled Mogadon on his cornflakes. Well, sod him, because Keith Slack was moving up. Bagnall could go back to cut-and-shutting Ford Sierras.

Slack ambled towards the toilets. It was time to go and see just how much of a balls-up Bagnall had made of his beautiful plan.

He'd spotted the mark straight away. It was all going down like the Man said. Time to make his play. He was cool, like always. Look nobody in the eye. Mr Invisible. After the hits went down, it was like he'd never been there. Ice cold and no bad dreams. Waste 'em, then go look for the nearest cold beer or hot woman.

Time to roll the dice.

Bagnall reached for his weapon . . .

*

Bloody Nora, thought Slack, he's talking to some bloke at the pisser.

Bagnall was indeed calmly urinating while chatting amiably to a tall dark-haired man who, similarly engaged, was standing next to him. Slack saw the abandoned briefcase and strolled towards it, taking in every detail in a matter of seconds.

Nice and chunky, good quality leather.

He began to pick up speed.

Combination locks. He'd have those off with a decent screwdriver.

As he picked up the case, he became aware that Bagnall's new chum was turning towards him. Slack started to run. As he vaulted the turnstile, the swinging briefcase laid out a middle-aged bloke blithely inserting his 20p on the way in. A hideous scream came from the toilets behind him and rang across the concourse as Slack sprinted away.

Its echo was hot on his heels as he legged it towards the exit and away into Blackpool town centre.

Detective Chief Inspector Bob Perks nursed half a shandy in Scruffy Murphy's and sat wishing he was more interesting. He didn't want to be a cliché, like all those coppers on the telly, with broken marriages and drink problems, he just fancied . . . livening his lot up a little. He'd given quirks a go, but the truth was, he just wasn't cut out for them. He wasn't religious, he didn't have any strange hobbies (or normal ones, come to that) and with the exception of Michael Bublé (who he adored) he thought most music was rubbish.

He wasn't like some coppers he could mention. Rats and ballroom dancing, for pity's sake.

Bob Perks's life was comfortable and ordered, if a little on the dull side.

An unemployed good-for-nothing from Woodplumpton and an over-imaginative grease monkey from Mereside were about to change things.

When his mobile phone rang, Perks froze. He kept meaning to change the Bublé ringtone ('Everything' – his signature song), but could never bring himself to, because Bublé was the business. He shrugged at the pinched faces of the lunchtime regulars as if to say, *I'm not an idiot, I'm a high-ranking police officer, so get over it.*

'Sir?' DS Dominic Baxter was trying to sound efficient, but Perks could hear laughter in the background.

'Better be good, Dom. I'm having my lunch.'

'There's been a robbery at the station, sir.'

'So? Let Robbery handle it. We're watching Draper.'

'That's just it, sir. It was Draper that got robbed.'

Perks put down his drink. 'I'm listening, DS Baxter ... '

'Well, Draper was talking to some bloke in the toilets.'

'Of course he was.'

'He puts the case down and a second bloke grabs it and legs it out the bogs. This other bloke hurdles over the turnstile, whacks somebody in the face with the briefcase while he's at it, and ... ' Baxter hesitated.

Perks took another sip of beer. At least things were livening up. 'Sounds like our luck's in, Dominic. Now we can have a look in the case without blowing the surveillance. Not that we don't have a pretty good idea what's in it.'

'We haven't got the case, sir. The bloke who nicked it got away.'

There was more laughter in the background. Perks hissed into the phone. 'What about Draper? Lost him as well?'

'No, sir, we know exactly where he is. Fact is he had a little accident ... zipped up in a bit of a hurry. He's in Victoria Hospital.'

'Let me get this straight, Baxter. Draper is about to meet Wayne Cutler and hand over the briefcase. After a three-month operation, we're about to tie the Cutlers to George Panaides's murder and you watch some tuppenny ha'penny tea leaf waltz off with the evidence while Draper's eyeing up some bloke's todger?'

'That's about the size of it.'

'Are you trying to be funny, Baxter?'

'We didn't want to blow our cover, sir.'

Perks took a deep breath. He *seriously* needed that quirk. A decent amphetamine habit, say.

'This bloke that Draper was trying to pick up, you *did* work out that he might have been in on the briefcase snatch?'

'We didn't actually work that out, no, sir.'

'Right.'

'He sort of melted away in the melee.'

'*Melee?*'

'It means a confused fight or a scuffle—'

'I know what it means, Baxter.'

'Yes, sir.'

'And Cutler never showed?'

'Oh yeah, he showed.'

'That's something. You get pictures?'

'Well, no. Actually it was him who got whacked in the face with the briefcase.'

Better make that a crack habit, Perks decided. A serious one.

'He's on his way to the Vic as well,' Baxter said. 'Concussion and a suspected broken collar bone.'

Perks recognised the laughter in the background now. DC Stuart Knight. He'd have the jumped-up little tit for breakfast. He stood and wedged the phone between ear and shoulder as he struggled to put on his coat.

'Nobody move, I'm coming in. And tell Knight to start ironing his uniform.'

'We've got Draper, sir!'

'Got him, *how* exactly?'

'Well, we know where he is, at least.'

Perks was gobsmacked at the note of triumph in the DS's voice. 'And what do you propose to hold him on, Baxter? Indecent exposure?'

'It's a thought, sir.'

'He was in a public toilet, you idiot.'

Perks's growl rendered the entire saloon bar silent. He couldn't be arsed with more apologetic shrugging because he had work to do. He had to find the poor bugger who'd stolen that briefcase before Wayne Cutler did.

Within half an hour they were back at Slack's place. Bagnall sat slurping Fanta as Slack set about the briefcase with a rusty screwdriver.

'I have to say, Andy, that was cracking. You did really well, mate.'

The Man wasn't telling him anything he didn't know. The Mechanic shrugged and took another hit of bourbon. He knew he was the best.

'Oh . . . cheers, Keith. I didn't actually do anything, really. I was just a bit nervous, you know, so I went for a wazz and this bloke just came up and started talking to me. He was dead friendly.'

Slack smirked at him. 'Probably your shirt, mate.'

Bagnall smiled. He'd known the shirt was a good idea. Then he got it. 'I don't think I like your insinuations there, Keith—'

And the briefcase flew open.

He'd seen dough before. Lots of it. And it always looked great. It looked like freedom. It looked like—

'Jesus H. Christ on a bike, Keith!'

There were rings; four *massive* signet rings. Two gold sovereigns, one that looked like it had a ruby set into it and a huge square one embossed with the letters *GP*. But it wasn't so much the rings that caught Andy Bagnall's attention, as the fact that they were still in place on the waxy, swollen fingers of two neatly severed hands.

STEP ONE

SAMBAS & SAUSAGES

ONE

If it looked – to the casual observer – as though Detective Sergeant Declan Miller's mind was not on his job, that was almost certainly because it wasn't. Miller had a butterfly mind (if you were being generous) or was just easily distracted (if you weren't, which meant you had the misfortune to be working with him). In an interview room, while a colleague pressed a suspect hard in search of a confession, Miller might well be wondering why one or other of his pet rats (Fred and Ginger) was looking a bit peaky, or weighing up the various merits of assorted crisp flavours before deciding that pork scratchings were the superior snack anyway. On the witness stand in court, as he solemnly swore to tell the truth, the whole truth and nothing but the truth, he could easily be trying to remember the names of the actors in *The Magnificent Seven* or thinking through the tricky steps at the climax of a Viennese waltz (speed *and* rotation could still trip him up).

Or trying to decide which was the best fish.

Or what it would be like to wrestle a chimp.

Or why those idiots who couldn't find San José or Amarillo didn't just buy maps.

Right that minute, waiting for the inappropriately named Goody brothers to emerge in handcuffs from a two-up-two-down he couldn't imagine generating much excitement on *Homes Under the Hammer*, Miller was thinking about how much Adolf Hitler had loved Blackpool.

Miller's partner – DS Sara Xiu – wandered across to join him and they stared at the house. It boasted a garden that would have given Monty Don the heebie-jeebies, several boarded-up windows, and a front door which had been somewhat forcefully 'distressed' by a metal battering ram half an hour earlier.

'I like what they've done to the place,' Xiu said. She looked to Miller, waiting for a reaction. It was about as close as she was willing to get to a pithy remark; to the use of pith in any context. As someone she could imagine making a similar remark himself, she was sure Miller would appreciate it, but he didn't appear to. She shrugged, said, 'Suit yourself.'

Miller turned to her. 'Here's something I bet you didn't know.'

Xiu steeled herself. She was, by now, well used to Miller's tangential observations or the inexplicable delight he took in passing on information neither she nor anyone else needed to know.

'Blackpool was a legitimate military target during the Second World War,' Miller said. 'It was right up there.'

'Was it?'

'Too bloody right it was, Posh . . .'

Xiu didn't mind the nickname any more, though she still wasn't quite sure why Miller persisted in using it.

'Because when it's pronounced correctly, *Xiu* sounds like

jus,' he'd told her, the last time she'd raised the issue. '*Jus*. Which is basically just posh gravy, right?'

'Yes, I do understand the reasoning—'

'Hence "Posh". It's a daft nickname, that's all.'

'I understand that, too. I'm just not sure what nicknames are *for*.'

'Well, they're not *for* anything,' Miller had said. 'But if someone's got an unusual name, or a name that sounds like something else, it's only natural to . . . adapt it.'

'Is it, though?'

'If you were German, say, and your name was Koch . . . well, the temptation to turn that into an amusing nickname would be irresistible. Actually, I'd say it would be pretty much compulsory.'

'Because Koch sounds a bit like cock.'

'Because it sounds *exactly* like cock.'

'It actually means cook.'

'Not the point. I'm simply pointing out that nicknames are a thing, especially with coppers, and that almost everyone has one at some point. Actually, I'm not sure *I've* got one . . . unless I just haven't heard it.'

'People call you all sorts of things.' Xiu had smiled then and turned away. 'But I'm not sure you want me to tell you what they are.'

Now, for reasons that Xiu was still unable to fathom, Miller was continuing to blather on about the Second World War.

'They made Wellington bombers here *and* they used the place to house thousands of troops on leave. Like I said, a legitimate target. But Hitler specifically told the Luftwaffe not to bomb the place, because it turns out he was a bit of a fan. No doodlebugs on Blackpool! *Nein!* When the Germans won – which, spoiler alert, they didn't – Adolf was planning to make Blackpool the holiday destination of choice for Nazis in need of a bit of R&R. Maybe there were a lot of Nazis who liked donkey-rides and rollercoasters, I don't know the ins and outs of it, but by all accounts he was all set to stick a massive swastika on top of the Tower.' He nodded to where the tip of the tower was just visible in the distance. 'Maybe a revolving one or something. As I said, I don't know the details.'

'Right,' Xiu said. 'Thanks for sharing.'

They both turned at the commotion near the front door and watched as half a dozen uniformed officers escorted Josh and Jason Goody from their home and attempted – amid a barrage of vituperative effing and jeffing – to get them into the back of a police van.

Miller turned to see an old woman watching from next door's garden, shaking her head, arms firmly folded. 'I'm sorry about the language,' he said.

The old woman shrugged, then waved at the prisoners – who had presumably not been the loveliest of neighbours – before letting the pair know exactly what she thought of them with a torrent of shouty filth that made Josh and Jason sound like children's TV presenters.

'Glad to be of service,' Miller said.

Just before being bundled into the van, the younger Goody brother leaned back and launched a healthy gobbet of spittle in the direction of the two detectives responsible for his appre-hension and arrest.

'Disgusting,' Xiu said.

'Agreed,' Miller said. 'But I can't help admiring the distance and elevation. That gob must have travelled twenty feet.'

They walked towards their car.

'We should celebrate,' Miller said.

The obvious charge was assault with a deadly weapon,

but Miller thought they could push to do each Goody for attempted murder, considering that the attack appeared to have been well planned and the deadly weapons in question were machetes. It was a good result, though not for the lad who'd undergone four hours of emergency surgery three days before and might well lose the use of his right arm.

'A couple after work?'

'I've got something on tonight,' Xiu said.

'Ah.' Miller nodded. 'King's Arms, is it?'

Xiu unlocked the car and climbed into the driver's seat.

Once a week, the pub in question hosted a heavy metal night in a room upstairs. Bands with names like Blood Whores and Goatkillaz would do serious damage to the hearing of a hundred or so sweaty metalheads and, while Miller didn't know if Xiu actually liked the music, she was awfully fond – in a 'take them home for the night and get even more sweaty' kind of way – of some of those who did.

Male, female, whatever. Xiu did not seem particularly fussy.

Miller fastened his safety belt. 'There's no need to be embarrassed.'

Xiu put her foot down. 'Says the bloke who dances tangos with old age pensioners.'

'Fair point,' Miller said. 'A fair point, well made.'

TWO

Reading a room was not always Miller's strong suit, but it was obvious enough that something was going on; had been ever since he and Xiu had got back to the station. Clusters of staff were gathered in corners, whispering. There were murmured comments and knowing looks.

There was an *atmosphere*.

Basing his assumption on similar situations in the past, Miller concluded that, whatever had happened or was still happening, chances were it had something to do with him. There had certainly been a comparable *frisson* when he'd returned to work a few months previously. He was as surprised as anyone at the time to find himself working a case again so soon, but bar a few sideways looks (and he was always going to attract those) the awkwardness had largely died down.

Fellow officers still laid a hand on his arm now and then.

An anonymous colleague had left a couple of inspirational (and helpfully laminated) messages on his desk:

*You will survive and you will
find purpose in the chaos.*

Moving on doesn't mean letting go.

Miller had binned them immediately.

Now, sitting at his desk, trying and largely failing to lob scrunched-up memos about 'workforce wellbeing' and 'innovations in the effective reviewing of CCTV footage' into a wastepaper basket, Miller racked his brains. Had he upset anyone recently? He decided he'd better narrow it down and think about anyone he might have upset that day.

He'd called DI Tim Sullivan a 'premier league shit-gibbon', but that was par for the course. He'd had what some might have perceived as a heated debate with DS Andrea Fuller about whether it would be better to have hands for feet or feet for hands, but they were still friends at the end of it (even though she was entirely wrong). He'd told Tony Clough that his new haircut made him look like a paedophile, because it did.

None of those exchanges could really explain what was going on.

Eventually, curiosity got the better of him and Miller collared Xiu as she walked past. 'Wagwan?'

'Sorry?'

'It's what young people say, Grandma. It means "what's going on?"'

'So, why didn't you just say that?'

'I'm down with the kids, what can I tell you? Well . . . ?'

Xiu shrugged, like there was nothing to get excited about. 'Some kind of S&O cock-up yesterday afternoon. A major cock-up by the sound of it.'

'Ah.'

That would explain why so many of the funny looks had been thrown in Miller's direction. S&O. Serious and Organised. The unit responsible for investigating gangland activity in the town and, crucially, the one for which Miller's wife Alex had been working when she'd been murdered five months before.

'Details,' Miller said. 'I need details.'

'I don't have any.' Xiu took a step away from Miller's desk, then turned. 'Somebody said something about a briefcase. Oh, and toilets . . .'

To call Miller's knock at the door of DCI Susan Akers *cursory* would have been generous. He did not wait to be invited in. Or to close the door behind him and sit down.

'Come on then, Susan. Spill! What have Serious and Disorganised been getting up to in the bogs?'

Akers looked up from her paperwork, her half-smile making it clear that she was pretending not to have heard him.

Miller was well used to it.

'Nice job with the Goodys this morning,' she said.

'Yeah, well.' Miller sat back, frustrated, but guessing he'd have to be patient. 'It was hardly the most taxing piece of detective work I've ever been involved with. They were bragging about it in the pub, Josh Goody left his wallet at the scene and there were two blood-stained machetes poking out from under the settee. A monkey could have put it together.'

'All the same—'

'Or even Tim Sullivan.'

Akers said, 'Declan,' but the half-smile was still there.

'Please, Susan.' Miller could not wait any longer. He leaned forward, his hands pressed together. 'Tell me the story and I'll buy you and your missus dinner. You can't say fairer than that. I pick the restaurant, though . . .'

He waited, watching his boss weigh up the offer.

S&O might have been Alex's old unit, but it was extremely unlikely that whatever had happened could have anything to do with her murder. That case was being investigated by a homicide squad based on the floor directly above them, though *investigated* might be to overstate the effort they appeared to be putting in. Five months on and they were precisely nowhere. There was virtually nothing in the way of evidence, zero credible suspects had been identified and the investigation's 'murder book' would be more accurately described as a pamphlet, its contents typed in a very large font.

'I'm really not sure that we should be wasting our time with tittle-tattle,' Akers said.

'So, don't waste time and tell me quickly,' Miller said.

Susan Akers was an honest and loyal officer, not one given to scabrous comment on the activities of colleagues. Unity was important and the maintenance of decorum was part of that.

But good gossip was good gossip.

'It was a sting operation at the railway station,' Akers said. 'They'd been tracking a man named Draper who was a prime suspect in a murder they believe to have been sanctioned and paid for by Wayne Cutler.'

Miller tried not to react, but could not control the sharp breath he sucked in or the muscle that worked in his jaw for a few seconds afterwards. Wayne Cutler's ... organisation was one of those being investigated by Miller's wife at the time of her death. Miller remained convinced that Cutler – like his main rival Ralph Massey – knew more about Alex's murder than they were letting on.

If Akers noticed, she didn't say anything.

'According to their intel, Cutler was set to hand a sizeable amount of cash to Draper in return for a briefcase. Nobody's letting on what its contents were.'

'I'm guessing it wasn't a copy of the *Financial Times* and a big bag of boiled sweets.'

'Well, whatever was in it, the briefcase has gone missing and Cutler ended up in hospital.'

'Please tell me it was nothing trivial.'

'Well, they're keeping him in overnight, but I don't think it's particularly serious.'

'Shame,' Miller said. 'So, how did this operation go so tits up, then?'

'By all accounts there was some kind of incident in the Gents.'

'Yeah, I heard.' Now Miller was trying not to smirk, but not very hard.

'The briefcase was pinched by a couple of lads who I very much doubt had any idea what was in it. So there we are: the transaction between Cutler and Draper never actually happened, which is why no arrests were made and why there's a lot of red faces on the top floor. Actually, this bloke Draper ended up in hospital as well. Tried to chase the lad who pinched his case and got his penis caught in his zip.' Akers saw that Miller was about to chip in. 'Yes, I know . . . shame that wasn't what happened to Wayne Cutler.'

'Oh, I've imagined far worse things,' Miller said. 'Lots of them.'

Akers took off her glasses and leaned back. 'How are you doing, Declan? We haven't really caught up for a while. You look a bit tired.'

'Yeah, things are . . . good,' Miller said, eventually.

They weren't.

'I'm moving on.'

He wasn't.

Whether Akers believed him or not, she seemed content not to dig any further. 'You'd best go and write up the Goody arrest ...'

Miller stood and stretched. He bent to check that the plant on the DCI's desk had been given enough water.

'I *will* take you up on that promise of dinner, you know.'

'Why wouldn't you?' Miller trudged to the door and opened it. 'Oh, and just to avoid any embarrassment on the night, it's a fifteen pounds a head maximum and that does include wine.'

THREE

Wayne Cutler had a splitting headache. The truth was, he couldn't remember when he *hadn't* had one, what with some of the halfwits he had working for him, Justin – his eldest – acting up and his wife Jacqui crying and moaning all the time. To be fair, there'd been a lot more crying and moaning since Adrian – his younger son (and his favourite, what was the point in pretending otherwise?) – had been shot and killed a few months before.

He closed his eyes. Muttered, 'Rest in peace, son.'

Problem was, he hadn't been able to deal with all that the way he might usually have done. He hadn't been able to react ... appropriately. If that slimy sod Ralph Massey or anyone else had been responsible for what had happened to Adrian, Wayne would have known exactly what to do and someone would have suffered, big time. As it turned out, it hadn't been business at all and his silly bugger of a son had been killed just because he was playing hide the sausage with someone else's wife.

So, Wayne just had to suck it up.

Grieve, like any normal father.

Now, on top of all that grief – as in proper 'waking up in the night and weeping' grief, plus bog-standard 'people are bloody useless, pain in the arse' grief – he had an *actual* headache to contend with. A right royal, blinding, buggering headache.

He reached up and gingerly fingered the lump behind his ear. He couldn't actually remember anything between walking into Blackpool North station that morning and waking up in hospital (quite normal with concussion, according to one of the nurses), but one of the coppers he was 'friendly' with had popped by to visit and filled him in on exactly what had happened in those toilets and at the turnstile immediately afterwards.

It was downright embarrassing.

Wayne Cutler had been swung at with a crowbar and been hit twice with a baseball bat and he'd not come off as badly as he had after being smacked in the head with a sodding briefcase. There certainly hadn't been any need for chuffing hospital. Once he was out, he would do everything in his power to make sure this was kept as quiet as possible.

He had an image to maintain, after all.

At least his collarbone wasn't broken. It was flipping sore, though, and they'd put his arm in a sling just to keep him comfortable. He closed his eyes again, dog-tired, feeling heartily sorry for himself and trying his best to zone out the sound of the old man whimpering in the next bed. If he'd been able to move without feeling sick, Wayne would have been over there to give the old git something to whimper about.

He settled for shouting.

'Keep it down, would you, pal?'

Jacqui would be in a bit later, which he supposed was

something to look forward to. Not that he particularly needed her fussing and jabbering at him when all he really wanted was to go home, but she had promised to bring in his favourite pillow from home and a couple of Creme Eggs.

'Time like this, you need a bit of pampering, love . . .'

He shifted himself a little higher in the bed and it felt like there was a small person clog-dancing inside his head. He thought for a second or two that he might chuck up his lumps, but thankfully the feeling passed.

A few minutes later, just when Cutler had begun drifting towards sleep and things seemed a bit better, the nurse pulled back the curtain to announce that he had a visitor and things suddenly got very much worse.

Dennis Draper (or whatever his real name was) stepped into the cubicle brandishing a brown paper bag. He sniffed and whipped out a bunch of grapes, like a magician pulling a rabbit out of a hat.

'Grapes,' he said.

'Over there.' Cutler nodded towards the cupboard by his bed-side. He watched as Draper walked across and reached down to open the cupboard itself. '*No.* Just leave them on the top.'

Draper did as he was told, moved back to the other side of Cutler's bed and pulled up a chair. He was extremely tall with long dark hair that hung in greasy curtains on either side of his face. Cutler decided that anything that masked the man's wholly unappealing features even a bit was to be applauded. The man had a gob like a depressed greyhound.

'I thought you were being treated in here as well,' Cutler said.

Draper had his coat on. 'I was, and I'm all sorted, but I thought I'd pop in to see how you were before I left.'

'Well, you've done that, and how I am is knackered, so now you can just pop away again.'

'Righto,' Draper said.

Cutler closed his eyes for a few seconds, but when he opened them again Draper hadn't moved. 'Why are you still here?'

'Why d'you think?'

'I haven't got the foggiest.'

'I'm waiting for you to pay me what I'm owed.'

Cutler stared at the man's unsettling display of teeth. He definitely preferred the depressed greyhound to the smiling one. 'I don't think I follow you.'

'Come on, Mr Cutler. The money for the job. Ten thousand pounds which, seeing as you were brought straight here from the railway station, I'm guessing you still have on you.' Draper glanced across at the bedside cupboard. 'Or somewhere nearby, anyway.'

'If you're talking about any previous arrangement we might have had,' Cutler said, 'I'm really not sure it applies any more.'

Draper inched his chair forward. 'But I *did* him, Mr Cutler. You know I did him.'

Cutler reached to plump his pillow, at least as much as the half-arsed excuse for a pillow *could* be plumped. 'Do I, though, Dennis? I know George Panaides is dead, but how do I know that's down to you? He might have been hit by a bus.'

'But I blew the back of his bleedin' head off, Mr Cutler. It was in the *Gazette*.'

'We had a deal, Dennis. I was there with the money in good faith and now look where I am.' He gently lifted his sling. 'See? I'm not going to be playing table tennis any time soon, am I?'

'I didn't know you played table tennis.'

'It's just an expression.' Cutler groaned and laid his arm back across his chest.

'Yeah, well I'm sorry about your injury and that.' Draper looked depressed again. 'But it weren't really my fault—'

Cutler leaned forward fast, then took a few deep breaths until he was sure he wasn't going to throw up again. 'Not your fault? I wouldn't sodding well be in hospital at all if you could keep your chopper in your pants.'

Draper winced, his hand absently moving to cradle his crotch.

Cutler smiled. 'How is it *down there*, by the way?'

'Stitches come out next week.'

Cutler winced. 'Look, it's all very unfortunate, Dennis, but without the agreed proof, I don't cough up. Get the briefcase back and then we'll talk. Fair enough?'

The look on Draper's face told him that he didn't think it was very fair at all.

'It's your own fault, Dennis. You've got to put your . . . tendencies on hold when you're working.'

'My tendencies aren't any of your business.'

'Under normal circumstances, definitely not. Under normal circumstances, I couldn't give a monkey's what you get up to or where or with who, but bearing in mind our current situation, I reckon you've *made* them my business. Wouldn't you say?'

Draper had clearly heard enough. He stood up, threw back the curtain and strode away, grumbling. Striding was evidently not wholly straightforward given his delicate condition genital-wise, but he did the best he could.

Cutler shouted after him. 'I wasn't sure you were the right man for this in the first place, but a mate recommended you. When he said you were a whizz at a hand job, I thought he was on about how good you were with a hacksaw!'

The old man in the next bed began whimpering again.

'And you can pipe down an' all . . .'

*

Draper slammed the car door, put both hands on the wheel and took a deep breath. The Cutlers were on the slide, everybody said so. When he'd got this briefcase business sorted out, he'd be back for them. For the top man, at least. He put the car in gear and rolled away towards the car park barrier and out on to the main road. A tosspot in a Cavalier cut him up, but Draper decided to leave it.

He had some serious thinking to do.

He thought about the bloke who'd been standing next to him at the urinal a few hours before. The one in the Hawaiian shirt. He'd clearly been in on it. Draper gently adjusted his trousers and smiled, because he thought he knew where to start looking for him. Back in those toilets, he'd obviously had an eyeful of the bloke's tackle, but he'd also got a good look at his hands.

Draper knew all about hands and he knew that what he'd seen under that lad's fingernails had been motor oil.

FOUR

Once he'd fed Fred and Ginger, Miller sat in the kitchen, eating poached eggs on toast and listening to a phone-in show on the radio. Listening . . . up to the point he felt compelled to join in. Engaging with the discussion in a way that, for Miller, was both cathartic and emotionally uplifting.

'I tell you one of the questions that I can never get my head round, Steve . . . keeps me awake at night, this one.'

'I'm listening, Jason.'

'We evolved from monkeys, right? So why are there still monkeys?'

Miller growled, his mouth full. 'When you say *we* evolved . . .'

'You know, chimps and that.'

'Well, to begin with, chimps aren't actually monkeys, Jason.'

'Ha, suck on that, you dipstick!'

'Be that as it may though, you're not actually thinking about evolution in the right way. It's more that we shared a common ancestor.'

'So, like my great, great, great, great, great ... whatever grandad was a chimp—?'

'No, not a chimp. Try thinking more in terms of cousins ... '

'Yeah, think about cousins, Jason. Think about what happens when they marry. Like your mum and dad ... '

Miller loaded the dishwasher then ambled into the living room. He caught sight of himself in the mirror and thought about what Akers had said about him looking tired. He stood for a minute, peering at his reflection and was forced to concede that she had a point. His gaze dropped down to the picture of Alex next to the TV, looking amazing in one of the competition frocks her sister had made.

'I don't think you look tired.'

Miller turned to see Alex perched on the edge of the sofa. 'Obviously not, because you love me to bits and think I'm devastatingly handsome.'

'You are devastatingly handsome.'

'Who am I to argue?'

'But also because I'm not actually here and you're just imagining me saying nice things to you.'

Miller walked across and dropped onto the sofa next to her. He reached for the TV remote. 'Yeah ... it's very much a minor perk, but you being dead is doing wonders for my ego.' He flicked through the TV channels and settled for an episode of *Gogglebox* because, if there was one thing more satisfying than shouting at the telly, it was shouting at people on the telly who were shouting at the telly themselves.

'I did say nice things to you *before* I was dead,' Alex said.

'Yeah,' Miller said. 'You did.'

Miller watched for a while. The posh, middle-aged couple who had silly nicknames for each other were suitably disturbed by an episode of *Embarrassing Bodies*.

He said, 'I wonder how your old boss is coping with today's disaster.'

Alex shrugged. 'Bob Perks is old enough and ugly enough to handle it, and it's not like there haven't been cock-ups before. Not when *I* was working there, obviously.'

'Course not,' Miller said. 'Unthinkable.'

'Besides which, it *is* pretty funny.' Alex laughed. 'Toiletgate . . . '

It had been funny to begin with, the details at least. Like a bad Benny Hill sketch (which wasn't to suggest there had ever been any good ones). A few hours on, though, Miller was less inclined to see the lighter side of a botched operation which had seen Wayne Cutler escape what sounded like an iron-clad 'conspiracy to murder' charge with nothing worse than a bang on the head.

'Did Bob Perks know who you were meeting that night?' Miller turned to look at his wife. The man who'd called her from an untraceable number a few minutes before she fled a dance competition. The man who had almost certainly shot her dead shortly afterwards.

Alex said nothing.

It was usually the way it went when they were discussing anything remotely . . . difficult. When Miller was asking questions he didn't already know the answer to. 'I mean, I've got to presume not, because otherwise he'd definitely have said something to the investigation. Right?'

Alex looked at the floor.

DCI Lindsey Forgeham, who was leading the investigation into Alex's murder, had certainly spoken to everyone Alex worked with. Miller remained deeply irritated that many of Alex's old colleagues at S&O seemed to know more about what Forgeham's team was up to than he did. It wasn't altogether surprising considering that, because of his close personal connection to the victim, he was not allowed anywhere near the investigation himself. Being told to stay away still rankled nevertheless.

It had to be said that Miller was rankled by a great many things (snotty doctor's receptionists, the bloke next door who always used the wrong bin, people starting a sentence with 'So,') but being warned off *anything* was number one in a carefully curated list of things that seriously cheesed him off.

Top of the rankle-rankings.

'Are you ever going to hand over those photos?' Alex asked.

Now it was Miller's turn to study the carpet.

'The video . . . ?'

Miller's mobile rang.

'Hey, Miller . . . '

'Hey, Finn . . . '

Miller turned, but Alex was gone, which wasn't much of a shock. Finn was Alex's daughter, the child of a marriage that had ended when Finn's father – a violent, hardcore drug addict – had overdosed. When Finn was sixteen and showing the same addictive and disruptive tendencies as her father, Alex had kicked her out of the house. It had, without question, been an extremely difficult decision and Alex had been haunted by the choice she'd made until the day she died.

'I'm a good copper and a terrible mother.'

'No you're not.'

'Not what? Which one aren't I?'

'Give me a minute . . . '

Bad jokes, comfort, whatever. Miller had done his best to help his wife cope with the ravages of the guilt.

Finn had lived on the streets of Blackpool for more than ten years now, begging for the money she needed to feed herself in every sense. Through all that time – the decade of Miller's marriage to Finn's mother and the months since Miller had become a widower – she had been Miller's eyes and ears on the streets. The information she provided was not always useful, but it gave Miller a reason to hand over money and it gave Finn a reason to take it.

He tried to give her advice which was more often than not ignored.

He asked her to move in with him, but she always refused.

He would never dream of saying as much to the girl herself, but it didn't take a genius to figure out he was trying to be the father she'd never really had.

'I need a favour,' Finn said.

'You been nicked again?' There'd been a fair bit of that over the years. A quiet word with a beat officer or two; a nod and a wink and a couple of pints to smooth things over.

'It's for a friend, actually.'

Miller could hear the buzzes and bells of an arcade, the screams of the fairground. The Pleasure Beach was a good place to scrounge up enough for dinner if you were lucky. 'What friend?'

'He's just a lad I get a bit of weed from sometimes.'

'You're asking me to do a favour for a drug dealer? You do know that's frowned upon in my line of work?'

'He's not a dealer, he just lends me a bit now and again. He's a good bloke, I swear, but he's got himself into a bit of a mess and when I told him I was close to a detective, he asked if you might be able to help him. That's all.'

'Close?'

'Don't get soppy, Miller.'

Miller smiled. 'What kind of a mess?'

'He wouldn't tell me, but he's seriously scared.'

Finn sounded rattled herself and that didn't happen often. Whatever state her friend was in, it was clearly upsetting her.

'Yeah, all right. I can't promise to help him, but I don't suppose it can hurt to find out what's—'

'Great, because he's outside your place right now.'

'What?'

Finn hung up and, thirty seconds later, Miller's doorbell rang.

FIVE

The young man skulking on Miller's doorstep was in his mid-twenties; the same sort of age as Finn. He was a big lad, though there was rather more fat than muscle and it appeared to weigh heavily on him in more ways than one. The essentially harmless type, Miller decided, who'd have been the bully's mate at school, as opposed to actually being the bully himself.

'I'm Andy,' he said, proffering a hand. 'Bagnall.' A broad Lancashire accent.

Looking at the nervous smile that broke across the boy's soft, round face, Miller decided that he was wrong and that his visitor was far more likely to have been the one getting bullied. Miller knew a little about that. During his own schooldays, his best friend Imran had been on the receiving end often enough. To this day, Miller wished he'd done a bit more to protect him.

'Right.' Miller shook the boy's hand. 'You'd best come in, then.'

If the lad was as scared as Finn had said, he certainly wasn't keeping a low profile appearance-wise. The baseball cap did little to hide the bleached-blond ponytail, and skin-tight jeans with cowboy boots were not the wisest choice if you wanted to be inconspicuous. He was wearing a shirt that wasn't as much loud as deafening and a denim waistcoat which – Miller saw when the boy moved past him into the house – had an enormous stars-and-stripes-coloured eagle embroidered on the back.

He was probably visible from Huddersfield.

Having processed the boy's fashion choices, Miller couldn't fail to clock the black briefcase he was clutching. He thought about the story Akers had told him a few hours earlier and began to understand what was making Andy Bagnall so nervous. Miller watched him set the case down gently on the carpet once he'd perched on the edge of the sofa and taken a deep breath.

'You want some tea?'

'No, I'm good, thanks.' The boy was staring at the play-pen that took up nearly half of Miller's front room. Fred was standing on her hind legs pushing her nose through the bars while Ginger scampered around in the wheel. 'Rats,' Andy said. 'Nice ... '

Miller sat down opposite him. 'Yeah, *I* think so. Not everyone's quite so keen.'

'Remember that old Michael Jackson song, "Ben"? That was about a rat, did you know that? It's from a movie, I think. Back when he was good, you know, before all the plastic surgery.'

'And the business with the kids.'

'So, what ... you're Finn's stepdad or something?'

'Something,' Miller said. He looked at the briefcase, then saw Andy look at it. It was clearly what the boy had come to talk about, but Miller sensed that he might need easing into it a little. 'Finn's obviously told you what a top-notch detective I am—'

'Well, she said you were a detective.'

'Which means you won't be surprised to hear I'm getting the distinct impression that you're a fan of all things American. Baseball and doughnuts and whatever.'

'Yeah, I love it. Well, I mean, not everything.'

'Quite right,' Miller said. 'The bacon's rubbish *and* the cheese. And they can't do chocolate for toffee. Or toffee come to that. So, what's your favourite part?'

Andy looked a little embarrassed. 'I've never actually been, tell you the truth. I *want* to, like ... and when I've saved up enough money ...' He glanced down at the briefcase, which Miller guessed had been the latest in a long line of failed attempts to get enough cash together for a plane ticket stateside.

'Right, so let's talk about—'

'New York, L.A., Chicago ...' Andy leaned forward, excited; counting off on his fingers the places he wanted to visit. 'Detroit, Miami, San Francisco *obviously* because that's where Sam Spade works. All the places I've seen in the movies or read about.'

'What kind of books do you read?'

'Crime and cops, you know ... thrillers!' Now Andy was warming to his theme. 'Serial killers, gangsters, spies, anything. I don't really mind as long as it's set in America, with all American cars and guns and food and that. Only thing I'm not mad about is cosy stuff.'

'Cosy, like crumpets and slippers?'

'Cats and libraries and vicars and what have you. I prefer a bit more murder and mayhem.'

'Right ...'

'Do you read?'

'Well, not as such.' Miller didn't think that *Why Walk When*

You Can Quickstep? – A Ballroom and Latin Dance Practice Journal would sound very impressive. 'I quite liked that one about the girl on the train, mind you. What was that called?'

'*The Girl on the Train.*'

'Yeah, that's the one. Actually it was my wife who read it, but it *sounded* pretty good ... but I don't think you came round to chat about starting a book club, so let's talk about the briefcase.' Miller nodded down to the case. 'That's what you're so scared about, right?'

Andy sat back and closed his eyes for a few seconds. It was as though his enthusiasm for crime on the page had temporarily taken his mind off the unpleasant ramifications of the real stuff. Now he swallowed hard, and though Miller thought he was trying not to show it, his lively imagination was clearly conjuring up what some of those ramifications might be. 'Well, yeah ... I'm a bit *nervous*, definitely.'

'Does your mate know you're here?'

Andy sniffed. 'What mate?'

Miller sighed. 'Come on, lad. I know there were two of you at the station, so let's not waste any time. What's his name?'

Andy thought about, then shook his head. 'I'd rather not drop him in it, if that's OK. I mean, it doesn't make any difference, does it?'

Without knowing what he was dealing with, it was a question Miller couldn't answer, but he was willing to let it go for the time being. He looked down at the case again, saw the dent in one corner which he knew would match the one in Wayne Cutler's head. 'Is that what you're so worried about? The bloke you brained at the station?' Miller didn't want the lad to be any more terrified than he already was, so he did not bother mentioning the brainee's name. Or the misfortunes that usually befell people who crossed him.

'It's not that,' Andy said. 'Besides, it wasn't me that smacked the bloke in the head, it was Ji—'

The boy had managed to stop himself in time, but he'd almost given away his mate's name. Just the one syllable of it. So, his partner was most likely a Jimmy. A James . . .

'It's not the case, it's what's inside it.' Andy swallowed again and scrunched up his face. He pressed himself back into the sofa. 'You should see for yourself, I reckon.'

Miller moved to pick up the briefcase then sat down again with the case across his lap.

'I'd better warn you,' Andy said. 'It's a bit bloody grim. So, you know . . . best to prepare yourself.'

Miller shook his head as he fingered the locks. 'Listen, I'm a police officer and I don't want to sound like I'm patronising you, but some of the stuff I've seen would make those gory thrillers you're so fond of look like Enid Bly—' He opened the case. 'Holy shit!'

'Told you,' Andy said.

Miller studied the contents of the case for a minute or so before gently closing the lid and setting the case at his feet. 'Right, then.'

'So, what are we going to do?'

'Well, we could put an ad in the local paper's lost and found section. You know, "If you're struggling to wave at friends or having trouble applauding, we might have a couple of things that belong to you", but I doubt the individual to whom these were once attached will be coming forward to claim them any time soon.'

'Because they're . . . dead?'

'That's my best guess,' Miller said.

'Bloody hell.'

'And what *you're* going to do is hand this case straight in to the police station. Come on, I'll take you down there.'

Andy Bagnall stood up, shouting and shaking his head. 'No, *I* can't take it. They'll nick me for something, won't they?'

'Just tell them you found it. Tell them your dog found it. Have you got a dog?'

'They're never going to believe that.' Andy was pacing the carpet and starting to hyperventilate. 'I'm sure they'll find summat to do me for.'

Miller thought the lad was probably right. There was CCTV at the railway station, so they wouldn't have much problem identifying him and at the very least doing him for theft. Even if the individual to whom the case belonged had now vanished and was very unlikely to press charges.

'Right,' he said, eventually. 'You'd best make yourself scarce then.'

Andy stopped and stared. His hands were pressed together like he was saying a prayer. 'Serious?'

'You were never here, fair enough?'

'I was never here, right.' Andy thought for a moment. 'So, where was I, then?'

Miller ushered him towards the door. 'It doesn't matter. Just make yourself scarce. Oh . . . have you ever been nicked before?'

'Well, I've had a few run-ins, like.'

'Properly nicked, I'm talking about,' Miller said. 'Have you ever had your fingerprints taken? They'll be all over this case and if they match up to prints they've taken before, there's not a lot I can do to help you.'

Andy shook his head. 'I had a mugshot taken once. You know, one of those fake ones you can have done at the Pleasure Beach. I put it in my wallet. Thought it would impress girls.'

'Did it?'

'Not so much,' Andy said.

*

Miller watched Andy Bagnall walk quickly away from his front door, stopping only to turn and give Miller a thumbs-up. Miller walked back inside, had another look at what was in the briefcase, then called Sara Xiu.

She sounded distracted, and Miller had a fair idea what or who was doing the distracting. Xiu was shouting above what sounded like three or four jet engines tumbling down a flight of stairs. She told him to wait while she found somewhere quieter, which Miller reckoned would have been just about anywhere. A minute or so later and he guessed she'd gone outside. He still had to raise his voice above the muted yet repetitive thumping, now cut through with a noise that was frankly startling; resembling, as it did, the agonised growls of a laryngitic Alsatian.

Miller thought it would make a good name for a heavy-metal band. 'Good evening, Blackpool! We are Laryngitic Alsatian. One, two, three, four ...'

Xiu's advice, once Miller had told her what he had in front of him, was unambiguous and predictable. She told him to get to the station as quickly as possible and turn the briefcase over to S&O. She wondered why he even needed to ask.

Miller thanked her. She was right, of course, as she usually was.

He closed the briefcase, played with the rats for a while, then went to bed.

SIX

He was glad there was nobody home when he got back to his apartment. It was better that way. Time to think, to plan his next move. Besides, he liked his own company just fine. Just him and a bottle of Jack.

What was not to like?

Palming the case off on that cop had been a smart move, but since when had he made any other kind? Now, it was the cop's problem. The Mechanic was free as a bird. So, he'd maybe have to smooth things over with his partner, but that was no biggie. It was time to move on and wait until the next job came calling. The next mark. He worked better alone, anyway.

Just him.

And that . . . bottle—

Bagnall's phone rang.

'Bugger.'

Andy put down his bottle of Pepsi Max and looked at his phone. It was Keith calling, which wasn't much of a shock, because Keith had been calling constantly ever since the previous evening. When he'd come back and found that the case had gone, presumably. Andy had guessed Keith would be straight round to try and get the case back, so he'd been walking the streets for twenty-four hours, more or less.

Until he'd run into Finn, who'd told him she might be able to help.

He let the phone ring out then listened again to the message Keith had left several hours earlier.

'Hello, mate, it's Keith ... again. Listen, I'm not angry because you took the case, I swear, and I know you're a bit freaked out by everything and I get it ... but don't do anything daft, all right? Just stay calm and let's meet up for a pint or whatever and sort everything out. Obviously we need to get rid of what's in that briefcase, but not all of it, yeah? Just stop and think about how much those rings must be worth. Bloody loads, pal. I'm sure we can find someone to take 'em off our hands and obviously we'll split the dosh fifty-fifty, because that's only fair. Right? I'm betting it'll be more than enough to get you to New York or wherever. Business class, an' all, like as not. So, anyway ... stay calm, like I say, hang on to that briefcase until I see you and give me a call back. Yeah? Call me, Andy ... for God's sake ...'

Andy laid down his phone and slumped back on his sofa. Fine, so he'd got rid of the briefcase and he was fairly sure that the copper was trustworthy because Finn had said so, but it wasn't like that made everything fine and bloody dandy.

He needed to stay clear of Keith, that was the main thing. He didn't believe for one minute that Keith wasn't angry. He'd waltzed off with the case while Keith was down the road getting chips, so Andy knew he'd be sodding furious. He knew Keith had a temper, too. He'd seen him stab a kid in the arse with a compass once, because the kid had said something about Keith's haircut being done by the council, and that was when he was only twelve, for God's sake.

Andy didn't want to get stabbed in the arse.

Or anywhere else, come to that.

He got up and began to pace about, just like he'd done in that copper's front room. Last thing he needed now was another panic attack, so he grabbed one of the empty crisp packets on the table and began breathing into it. He inhaled a gobful of salt and vinegar crumbs for his trouble, so he gave up, and stood there panting for a while, trying to work out what to do.

Keith knew where he lived, obviously – he'd been there often enough when Natalie wasn't around – so the sensible thing to do was to get the hell out of there. Thinking about it, it occurred to him that Keith might be outside already, so Andy rushed to the window, just to make sure he wasn't.

Once he'd established that the coast was clear, he ran into the bedroom and began to chuck pants and socks into a bag. A few of his favourite books. Maybe he could bed down next to Finn for a few nights, but then again he might be better off getting out of Blackpool altogether. He didn't know where to go, though, because he'd never been further than Preston.

It wasn't like he had enough money to get far, anyway . . .

He stopped and, just for a few moments, he thought about the rings in that briefcase and the money Keith had said they could get for them, and he imagined a plane touching down at JFK. He pictured himself strolling down Fifth Avenue in the sunshine. Scoffing a chilli-dog in Central Park or showing his fake mugshot to some girl who would be dead impressed, in one of them booths in a dimly lit bar, with neon signs and jazz and stuff.

Then he remembered the waxy dead fingers those rings had been on and started throwing things in the bag a bit faster.

He stopped again when he thought about Natalie. She'd be worried when she came home and he wasn't there. She always worried about him. He'd call her as soon as he was sorted, let her know he was OK, but he needed to let her know now that there was no reason to panic. He ran back into the front room to grab a pen and a takeaway menu from the drawer.

Andy finished packing his bag and dropped it next to the front door. He chucked some snacks and drinks into a plastic bag. Then he sat down, turned over the menu and began to scribble a note.

SEVEN

Miller took off his crash helmet, removed the elasticated cables he'd used to attach the briefcase to the back of his moped and sauntered into the station. The duty sergeant clocked what Miller was carrying as he walked past the desk and nodded. 'Somebody's going upmarket. Got your sarnies in there, have you, Dec?'

'Just a pair of severed hands,' Miller said.

The officer shook his head, chuckling, like Miller was a caution.

A few minutes later, when Xiu saw what Miller was carrying, her reaction was rather different. She jumped up from her desk, marched across the incident room and manhandled Miller back into the corridor.

'Is that what I think it is?'

'Depends on what you think it is,' Miller said. 'You're tricky to second-guess sometimes.'

Xiu was not in the mood. 'Seriously? You said you were going to bring it in last night.'

'It was late,' Miller said.

'It was nine o'clock.'

'Right, and I'm normally tucked up with a hot milky drink by then. I had my jim-jams laid out and everything.' He tried to move past her, but she blocked his way. 'Come on, a few hours aren't going to make much difference.'

Xiu, who clearly thought they made a great deal of difference, looked as though she was ready to snatch the briefcase off him and hand it in herself. What would have been an unseemly tussle was only prevented when DI Tim Sullivan appeared in the corridor.

'Excellent,' Sullivan said. 'You're together.'

'Who's been spreading rumours?' Miller said.

'We've got a body in a flat behind Kingscote Park.'

'A dead one?' He returned the DI's contemptuous stare. 'No need for evils, Tim, I'm just making sure I've got all the facts.'

'Get yourselves down there.'

'Righto.'

Sullivan was already stabbing at an iPad. 'I'll set up a briefing for this afternoon.'

'Won't be a tick.' Miller held up the case. 'Just need to drop this off at my desk.'

Sullivan was oblivious to Xiu's scowl. 'Quick as you can, Miller.'

'Sir.' Miller winked at Sullivan as he stepped past him, rubbing the case like its contents were precious. 'Cheese and tomato and a blackcurrant Fruit Shoot.'

It was a small, two-bedroomed flat on the top floor of a house on Nethway Road. From the living room window it was possible to see right across the park, but those already working inside – the force photographer, a team of CSIs, the on-call pathologist – had an altogether less pleasant view. Outside in the hallway, as they climbed into plastic bodysuits and got ready to take in the grim scenery themselves, Miller and Xiu were briefed by the uniformed officers who'd been first at the scene.

'The victim was found by his sister,' one of them said. 'She's a nurse, on nights at the Vic. Discovered her brother's body when she got back from work this morning.'

'In bits, obviously,' the second officer said.

'What ... dismembered?' Miller looked horrified.

'No, the *sister's*—' The officer stopped when he realised that Miller was winding him up and looked at his partner, unsure how to react. The first officer – a woman who had worked with Miller before – simply sighed and shook her head before the pair of them wandered away.

'It's always hard, the first time,' she said. 'You'll get used to him ... '

Miller zipped up and followed Xiu into the flat.

It was possible, of course, that the victim and his sister had not been the tidiest of tenants, but Miller doubted that the state of the place was down to lackadaisical housekeeping. Every room had been comprehensively trashed. Mattresses had been turned over and slashed, drawers emptied out and ornaments scattered. Miller and Xiu wandered back into the living room where Prisha Acharya, the pathologist, was examining the body.

'What a mess,' she said.

'The body?'

'Everything.'

The victim lay on the floor in front of a sofa that had been tipped on to its side, his chest and legs strewn with the fluffy white innards of the sofa's disembowelled cushions. A see-through plastic bag was tied around his head, fastened with a belt at the neck.

'Probably asphyxiation,' Acharya said. She pointed. 'Plenty of bruising though, so I'd say the poor lad got a good beating before the killer put the bag over his face.'

Xiu moved to stand next to Miller and looked down at the body. They had barely exchanged a word since leaving the station, but suddenly there was nothing to say.

Miller leaned down to get a closer look. The face was already swollen beneath the plastic, but Miller didn't need to look very hard. He shook his head, said, 'Bloody hell . . . '

Xiu followed him out into the hallway and watched as he stood, ripping off the bodysuit like he was trying to shred it.

'Disturbed a burglar, you think?'

Miller turned and glared. 'Oh, so you're talking to me now?' Seeing the shock on Xiu's face, he quickly raised a hand and shook his head. He hadn't intended to speak to her quite so sharply. 'Sorry . . . '

'It's fine.' Xiu reddened, then shrugged and began removing her own bodysuit. 'What's—?'

'This wasn't a burglar,' Miller said. 'Be a damn sight easier if it was, but this is someone a lot more dangerous, who killed that lad because he felt like it, then tore the place apart looking for something. Something I know he didn't find, because the lad didn't have it any more.'

'Didn't have what?'

Miller kicked out at the crumpled plastic suit gathered around his feet, but it felt childish, besides which, no amount of anger and aggression could shift the picture in his head. That soft, round face; the nervous smile.

'I prefer a bit more murder and mayhem.'

'The victim's name is Andy Bagnall,' Miller said. 'He's the one who gave me the briefcase last night.'

EIGHT

Xiu drove them back towards the station. She swore at a van driver with as much vehemence as one of the Goody brothers, then turned calmly to Miller. 'So, why *didn't* you hand the case in last night? *Really* . . . '

She waited.

Miller stared out of the window, wishing he had an answer; a stupid one, a comical one, anything. Perhaps, the night before, there *had* been some half-baked (and mercifully short-lived) notion that he'd be able to use the briefcase as some kind of leverage against Wayne Cutler. He could have shown up at Cutler's bedside and forced a confession, then marched triumphantly into S&O having single-handedly salvaged their botched operation. Alternatively, he could have quietly suggested to Cutler that the briefcase might 'disappear', if only Cutler could shed some light (any light at all) on who had been responsible for Alex's murder.

Mercifully short-lived . . .

'Was it because it was S&O? Alex's old squad?'

'No,' Miller said. 'What's that got to do with the price of fish?'

'Cutler, then. Because the briefcase is connected to Cutler and you still believe he had something to do with Alex's death.'

Miller grunted, non-committal. No, Xiu didn't laugh at his jokes nearly enough, or even at all, and the heavy metal sex thing was downright weird, but Miller had to admit she was good.

'It's not like you haven't got form, is it?'

'As a top-class thief-taker, you mean?' Miller nodded. 'The scourge of local villainy. As an unorthodox, yet hugely respected detective who'll do whatever it takes to get results?'

Xiu glanced across at him. 'Form for not handing over evidence.'

'Oh, right . . . but that's only because I'd be handing it over to the "elite" unit that's supposed to be investigating Alex's murder and they're not awfully competent. Or they're wilfully *in*competent, depending on what kind of mood I'm in.'

When it came to DCI Lindsey Forgeham and her team of defectives, Miller vacillated between a pent-up fury barely held in check and the overwhelming desire to deposit something unspeakable in Forgeham's desk drawer.

'More than five months now,' he said. 'And they've still got bugger all.'

'All the more reason to hand over potentially helpful evidence, I would have thought.'

'Oh, would you?'

'Yes, I would.'

'Nobody likes a smartarse,' Miller said.

Miller had told Xiu about the photographs he'd been sent by a man named Gary Pope and was still holding on to. Pope – known to everyone except his mum as Chesshead – had himself been murdered shortly afterwards; shot with the same gun that had been used to kill Miller's wife. Miller hadn't told Xiu about the video he'd received a few days later.

Hadn't told her *yet*, because he would.

Alex herself had been banging on at him to do so for a while. Annoyingly, Alex herself wouldn't/couldn't answer the really important questions, like who the man in the video was, or what it was that he appeared to be handing over to her, but she had plenty to say when it came to withholding evidence pertinent to a murder inquiry.

If anything, being dead had made her more talkative.

'You trust her, don't you?' Alex had been standing at the living room window, staring out at the sea which she'd always loved (the smell, the sound, the enchantment) and into which Miller would not so much as dip a toe (the creatures, the whole 'drowning' thing, the floating turds). 'Xiu?'

'Of course I trust her.'

'And you trust *me*, right . . . ?'

Now, Xiu turned on to the prom and Miller stared as they drove past a posse of young women tottering along in heels and pink onesies. One sported a veil while several of her accomplices, who were weaving back and forth across the tramlines, were carrying inflatable sheep. It was, he supposed, a hen party, or else a group of women who had lost their minds. It was quite possibly both.

Why *sheep*? Was the bride-to-be marrying a farmer? Or a shepherd?

Before his train of thought could career off the tracks altogether, he was distracted by the arrival of a text message.

'You are going to hand the briefcase in *now*, though, right?' Keen for exactly that to happen as soon as possible, Xiu leaned on the horn and, behind them, one of the women helpfully waved a sheep.

Miller read his message.

'Because whatever you were thinking last night, it's now connected to a murder inquiry. It's actually the *reason* for the murder, so—'

'We need to stop off somewhere first,' Miller said.

'*What?*'

'We've been summoned by Ralph Massey.'

'Well, *he* can certainly wait.'

'Actually, I think it might be useful.'

'How the hell—?' Xiu braked hard as the lights in front of them turned to red.

It was Miller's turn to swear (a highly creative mash-up of three different curse-words) as he braced himself against the dashboard. Then, as he idly contemplated a whiplash claim, he passed the phone across so that Xiu could read Ralph Massey's message.

I would be ever so grateful if you could pop by for a natter. Haven't seen you for ages and I'm sure you'll find it to your advantage. I know you must be busy, but don't worry, I'll keep it BRIEF if that's the CASE.

🐿 Ralph x

NINE

Performing as Miss Coco Popz ('she'll have you for breakfast'), Ralph Massey had achieved a modest degree of success
in his former career as a cabaret artiste. He was a popular
draw in the local pubs and clubs and had twice won the North
Lancashire and District Drag Queen of the Year award (com-
monly known as the 'Golden Girdle') back when drag was
rather more *niche* and RuPaul was still wearing a training bra.
It was later on, however, as a businessman and entrepreneur
that Ralph had really shone, even if one or two of his business
practices might have seriously upset some viewers of *The
Apprentice*.

The ones who thought Lord Sugar could be a tad harsh.

The ones who didn't have very strong stomachs.

Despite a conviction (personal as opposed to legal) that he
was born to entertain, he was a man who remained perfectly
content with his decision to diversify. His accountant was
thrilled and Massey liked making people happy. At the end of
the day it was all good, because notoriety was a kind of fame,

and he could always get the frocks and feathers down from the loft when he felt the urge or if friends demanded it.

He could be awfully insistent that they demand it.

As the owner of the Majestic Ballroom (and several associated premises), Ralph Massey managed a medium-sized empire that artfully combined popular entertainment and money-laundering. It was generally accepted by both the police and the town's criminal fraternity that he and Wayne Cutler had Blackpool carved up between them and would have no compunction about carving up anyone who threatened to rock that boat.

Miller would happily have taken an axe to the boat, set fire to the pieces, then danced on the ashes in his underpants singing 'Oh What a Beautiful Morning'. It wasn't just because, underpants aside, that was basically his job. It wasn't only because he was a copper and Massey was a serious criminal.

Massey and Miller had history.

He was waiting for them in the main ballroom (there was a smaller one available for hire, plus a 'chill-out' space for rave nights) when Miller and Xiu arrived; artfully reclined in the front row of the faux-velvet purple stalls. He smiled and patted a cushion, sending up a cloud of dust. Miller plonked himself down next to Massey, while Xiu took a place a few seats away.

'Kind of you to drop by.' Massey was wearing shiny black trousers and a bright yellow shirt, his long silver hair arranged into a man-bun which, as far as Miller was concerned, was in itself an arrestable offence. Massey had not taken his eyes from the floor of the ballroom, where his two favourite henchmen – a pair of handsome, identical twin skinheads he called Pixie and Dixie – were busy refocusing lights. They took turns scampering up and down a stepladder, while Massey waved them this way and that.

'Keeping your "nephews" busy?' Miller asked.

'Always.' Massey was smiling again when he turned to look at him. 'Now . . . ' He sat up straight and adjusted his man-bun. 'Much as I love an inconsequential chinwag, we've all got plenty to get on with, so I should probably explain my little message.'

'If you would.' Miller was aware that Xiu was already getting impatient.

Massey nodded towards Pixie and Dixie. 'Ironically, I thought I might be able to shed a little light on a current . . . situation your colleagues are having.'

'A situation?'

'Vis-à-vis some serious, if less than organised, toilet shenanigans.'

'We are currently investigating a murder closely associated with the incident to which you're alluding,' Xiu said.

'Oh, dear.'

'So, if you have any useful information, Mr Massey, we'd appreciate it if you could shit or get off the pot.'

Miller turned to her and nodded, impressed.

'That's very funny.' Massey looked at Miller. 'Oh, wait, your partner doesn't do jokes, does she?'

'Not as such,' Miller said, 'so best crack on.'

'Very well, then, crack on I shall.' He paused to pick at some lint on his shiny trousers. 'So, I know there's a briefcase, whereabouts currently unknown, and I know what's in it—' There was a crash as one of the skinheads dropped a light from halfway up the ladder. Massey glared across at Pixie or perhaps Dixie and shouted, 'That's coming out of your bloody wages!'

'How do you know what's in the case?'

'Well, perhaps I should clarify. I don't know *specifically* what its contents are, but I know what they represent.'

Miller waited. Right now, that briefcase (whose whereabouts he knew exactly) was the reason a lad had been brutally murdered and no more than that. Perhaps he was about to find out precisely why.

'Proof.' There was a note of triumph in Massey's voice. 'That case represents proof of a job well done.'

'A job done for who?'

'Well, I think we all know that, don't we? A man whose initials are rather appropriate, considering from whence the briefcase was stolen.'

Miller glanced at Xiu.

'OK, so who was this job done . . . to?' Xiu was struggling to word the question correctly. 'Done *on*. To whom was it—?'

'You know what she means,' Miller said.

'A man called Panaides,' Massey said.

Miller remembered the name, and the case. A fortnight or so before, it had been initially handled by another homicide team before being snaffled up by Bob Perks at S&O. It made sense, considering that the murder (a bullet to the head behind a nightclub in Fleetwood) could not have looked more gangland if Guy Ritchie had choreographed it and Ray Winstone had been hanging around mumbling about 'shooters'. Miller had read the reports in the paper and there hadn't been any mention of the victim's hands being removed, but maybe Perks had decided not to release that particularly heartwarming detail to the press.

'Panaides worked for a man called Frank Bardsley,' Massey said. 'You know him?'

'Never had the pleasure,' Miller said. 'But I know enough.'

'Why did Cutler want this Panaides killed?' Xiu asked.

'It's an excellent question.' Massey sat back and sighed. 'If it was just a question of sending a message to Bardsley it seems a little over the top, even by Cutler's standards. Yes, Bardsley's a player in Preston, and Blackburn maybe, but aside from one shop and a couple of backstreet pubs, he's *nothing* here. Certainly nothing our friend Wayne couldn't handle rather more quietly.'

Miller thought about it. What Massey was saying made sense. Then again, working out what was going on in Wayne Cutler's head (even *before* it was on the receiving end of a flying briefcase) was a near impossibility; like capturing a moonbeam in your hand or punching Jacob Rees-Mogg just the once.

'Well, that's about all I've got.' Massey bowed his head. 'You are entirely welcome.'

'One more question,' Miller said. 'The big one, really. Why the hell would you be providing us with helpful information?' He craned his head and peered around. 'This isn't some kind of hidden camera show, is it?'

'Because it's potentially damaging to Wayne Cutler, obviously. Anything that makes that man's life more difficult is naturally going to brighten up mine. To be honest, a painful death would be the dream, but until that glorious day dawns ... even a cold sore on that swine's fat mouth puts a spring in my step.'

'Of course,' Miller said. 'Stupid of me.'

'Right then.' Massey stood up and Miller and Xiu did the same. 'Oh, just to say, I'm sure you're every bit as keen as I am to see Wayne Cutler put away, but in case you need an extra incentive ...'

'I don't, but carry on.'

Massey glanced at Xiu, then turned back and stage-whispered

to Miller. 'This might actually be a conversation you and I should have in private.'

Xiu shook her head and began to walk away, but Miller held up a hand. 'Anything you've got to say to me, you can say in front of her.'

Massey thought about it for a second then shrugged. 'Very well. I just wanted to add that if this *does* result in Mr Cutler's removal from all our lives . . . ' he crossed himself, 'and I very much hope that's the case, I may be able to help in identifying the man who murdered your wife.'

Miller stared, the breath punched out of him. To hear that from him, *here* of all places. He closed his eyes and he could still hear the murmurs of confusion; the laughter from the crowd when Alex had failed to appear for the last dance.

The knock on his front door a few hours later . . .

Xiu marched back across to Massey and jabbed a finger at him. 'If you have *any* information that could further the investigation into Alex Miller's death, then you need to tell us. Do you understand? I'll take you in myself right now if I have to.'

Massey stepped back and raised his hands. '*If* is very much the operative word here, detective. I *may* be able to help you, I said. I think you're getting a little ahead of yourself.'

There was a brief and somewhat half-hearted staring match, before Xiu grimaced then turned to leave, grabbing Miller as she went. 'Come on . . . '

Miller followed her for a few steps then veered sharply away on to the dance floor. He ambled across to where Pixie and Dixie were still hard at work; one fiddling with a spotlight, while his doppelganger steadied the ladder. Miller nodded hello, gave the ladder a good, hard kick and watched as the twin holding on to it fought to stop it toppling over.

'Oi!' shouted the one at the foot of the ladder.

'What's your game?' demanded the one who'd nearly fallen off it.

'Sorry,' Miller said.

TEN

Dennis Draper (the latest in a long line of alliterative aliases which had most recently included Desmond Darke, Damien Dangerfield and David Deckham) groaned as he sat back on the lumpy bed in his B&B (he had registered, with uncharacteristic flair and a cod Spanish accent, as Diego Diaz) and considered his next move.

His last one had been straightforward enough.

It had just been a question of making a list and Draper loved lists.

FAVOURITE DRINKS

1. Lager and lime.
2. Lager top.
3. Fizzy wine.
4. 'Sex on the Beach'.
5. Panda Pops (esp. blue raspberry).

THINGS TO DO BEFORE I DIE

1. Have a threesome.
2. Visit Alton Towers.
3. Be on *Pointless*.

THINGS PEOPLE HAVE SAID
BEFORE THEY DIED

1. I swear I'll get the money (yawn).
2. You've got the wrong bloke (yeah, right).
3. Mum/mummy (not clever or funny but always a popular choice).

This one had simply been a bog-standard list of garages in Blackpool, put together after five minutes of googling when he'd come out of the hospital, and it had been pretty much the same routine at the first two places he'd visited.

'I'm looking to get an MOT done sharpish.'

'Sorry, mate, I can't fit you in for at least a couple of days.'

'That's a shame. Actually, it was a lad who works here who told me you'd be able to do it. Big soft sod with a blond ponytail and a loud shirt ... ?'

He'd got a couple of blank looks, said he'd try somewhere else, then struck lucky at the third time of asking.

'Oh, that'll be Andy, the silly sod. I'll be giving him a talking to an' all, because he really shouldn't have told you that.'

'I'll give him one myself if you let me have his address.'

'Well, I don't know about that, mate ... '

Draper had immediately become a bit less friendly and happily the bloke in the overalls had changed his tune, once he'd been kicked into the inspection pit and Draper had started sloshing petrol around. He'd had another bit of luck after that, catching the lad at home just before he legged it, but Draper still hadn't got the result he'd been hoping for.

The result he needed if Cutler was ever going to pay up.

Yeah, so he'd made sure the pillock with the ponytail had paid for taking what didn't belong to him. There'd been no last words worth writing home about, though to be fair the plastic bag had made it tricky to understand what the lad was on about at the end. It was all just shouting and snot. Fun as that had been though, because he always relished the work, Draper knew he'd only done half the job.

There'd been no sign of that sodding briefcase.

Inching carefully across the bed (because things were still a bit tender in the todger department), he reached for the TV remote; attached to the headboard by a curly wire, which was rarely the sign of a top-notch establishment. He turned on the minuscule set, fixed skew-whiff on the wall opposite, and flicked through the channels until he found a repeat of *Midsomer Murders*, which he always enjoyed. Laying the remote down again on the bedside table, he glanced at the mobile he'd taken from the thief's flat. He felt sure it would provide information as to who currently had the briefcase, but he'd need to find someone who could unlock the bloody phone first. Guessing that its owner had not been the sharpest knife in the drawer, he'd tried 1-2-3-4, after which he'd given up, because neither was he. It was no big deal, because it wouldn't take him too long to get into it, and until then, he had the note.

While DCI Barnaby sought justice for a woman murdered with a giant round of cheese (one of Draper's favourites from the post-Nettles era) he reached for the takeaway menu on which the boy had scribbled his last words. There was nothing worthy of making the list in there either, but it did give Draper somewhere to start. A couple of names to start with, anyway.

Judging from the separate bedrooms and a few of the photographs he'd studied before smashing them, Draper guessed that the 'Natalie' for whom the note had been written was a sister as opposed to a girlfriend. A sister the lad 'didn't want to worry'. Maybe he'd given the case to her and, even if he hadn't, she might have an idea who'd got it or where it had been stashed.

She'd certainly be worth keeping an eye on.

He'd start with Andy Bagnall's friend, though. Not the one from the railway station (he guessed that name would be in the phone somewhere) but the one he'd been planning to lay low with. *A couple of nights sleeping rough won't kill me,* that's what he'd said in the note to his sister. *Chuck my sleeping bag down next to hers. I'm sure she won't mind . . .*

He settled back to enjoy the thrilling spectacle of DCI Barnaby ruthlessly hunting down a killer twisted enough to use an oversized dairy product as a weapon. Now, Draper had some hunting of his own to do. Yeah, Blackpool had more than its fair share of druggies and wasters, but there weren't *that* many people dossing down on the streets, so this girl shouldn't be very hard to find.

Finn was an unusual name.

ELEVEN

A few minutes after Miller had unceremoniously plonked it down on his desk, DCI Bob Perks pushed the briefcase away and removed the nitrile gloves he'd snapped on before opening it. He puffed out his cheeks, sat back and sighed.

'You're welcome,' Miller said.

Sitting across from him, Miller could see no reason why Perks should be anything other than delighted that the case had finally turned up, but if he was, the man from S&O certainly wasn't letting his face know about it.

'You'll understand I'm quite keen to know how *you* ended up with it.'

'My dog found it,' Miller said.

'Like that dog who found the World Cup.'

'Exactly like that.' Miller nodded enthusiastically, as if Perks was spot on. 'Aside from the body parts, obviously. And the fact that it's not a cup.'

'What's your dog's name?'

The offices of Serious and Organised were at the top of

the headquarters building, two floors above Homicide, where Miller was based. He stared past Perks at the skyline, barely visible through windows whose cleaning was clearly no longer a priority now that budgets were tighter than a gnat's chuff. They were on the wrong side of the building to have a view of the Tower, but Miller had seen that just about every day of his adult life and the magic had worn off after he'd seen it the first time. He stared out at a crane instead, a concrete pipe suspended beneath it, and wondered what he should call his imaginary dog.

'Have you forgotten?'

'Sorry?'

'Your dog's name?'

'Oh, did I say *dog*? I meant this *lad* found it, then gave it to me. Sorry, I'm a bit all over the shop.'

'This ... lad being one of the ones who nicked it at the station.'

'I can see why they pay you the big bucks, Bob.'

'Why did he give the briefcase to *you*?'

'It doesn't matter,' Miller said. 'Anyway, those lads were just chancers, so there's really no need to worry your pretty little head about them.'

Perks looked as though he was worrying a great deal but chose not to pursue it there and then. 'Did he at least have a name? This chancer.'

'Andy Bagnall.' Miller watched Perks reach for a pen and begin to scribble the name down. 'I can tell you exactly where he is, too, if that helps.' Perks nodded, pen poised. 'He's currently residing at the mortuary, because the poor sod was murdered last night.'

Perks put the pen down. 'Oh, shit.'

'Shit indeed. I'm guessing he was killed by the bloke

responsible for the contents of that briefcase, who clearly wants it even more than you do.'

The DCI sighed heavily and sat back, taking in this disturbing new development. Then something dawned on him and he quickly sat forward again, pointing at the briefcase. 'So, you had this *last night?*'

'Well, Bagnall didn't give it me *after* he was killed, did he?'

'So why the hell am I only getting it now?' Perks immediately raised a hand to ward off an answer, well aware that whatever Miller was about to come up with was only going to make his mood a lot worse. He scowled and lowered his voice. 'I'll tell you this for nothing, Dec . . . if Alex hadn't been one of my team as well as being a bloody good friend, I'd be making damn sure you were up on a serious misconduct charge. As it is . . .'

'Alex always said you were one of the good ones, Bob.' As Miller recalled, her precise words had actually been 'tedious tit', but he decided he'd best keep that to himself, all things considered.

Perks nodded and sighed again. 'God knows how I'm going to explain how the case has suddenly turned up, mind you.'

'Maybe you could say *your* dog found it.'

Perks opened his mouth to speak.

'Roger!' Miller nodded, pleased with himself. '*That's* what I should have called my dog. Roger the dog . . . though that is of course arrestable under the Sexual Offences Act of 2003—'

'Can we please get on with it?'

Miller looked shocked. 'I'm waiting for *you*. So, let's hear it then: what's the story with your super-successful sting at the station?'

'I don't think I need to tell you anything,' Perks said.

'Come on, I told you about Bagnall.'

'Just his bloody name.'

'Quid pro quo, Clarice.' Miller nodded at the case. 'Look, I already know who those hands belonged to.'

'How?'

'A little bird who runs a dancehall told me.'

'Yeah, not surprised *he* knows what's going on.'

'*What*, but not *why*,' Miller said.

The DCI rubbed his eyes, thinking about it. Then he shrugged. 'You ever had a Bardsley Burger?'

'Not as I can remember.'

'You should keep it that way, if you want to do your arteries a favour. Anyway, there's a chain of them in Preston and Blackburn, as well as a few pubs and bars. Frank Bardsley's built himself a decent little empire over there and he's started to make inroads here. Nothing much, and certainly not enough to worry the likes of Wayne Cutler or your friend at the Majestic.'

Miller's face darkened. 'He's not my friend.'

Perks raised a hand, acknowledging the tactless remark. 'Bardsley's certainly not in their league when it comes to criminality, that's what I'm saying. It's strictly Sunday kickabout stuff. The odd kebab shop owner having an unfortunate accident with a skewer, a few burger vans mysteriously catching fire, but nothing terminal.'

'So, what's rattled Cutler's cage?'

'Bardsley's number two was a man called George Panaides, who—'

'Won't be making shadow puppets again any time soon.'

They both stared at the severed hands; the rings adorning the swollen fingers which had now begun to blacken. 'Well, I don't have *all* the details because that murder was handled by a homicide team in Fleetwood, but yes, we have to assume they're Panaides's hands.' Perks pointed at the largest of the rings, the raised letters GP. 'George Panaides.'

'Well, let's not jump to conclusions, Bob. Does Gwyneth Paltrow have big hairy hands? Or maybe they belonged to a doctor with terrible taste in jewellery.'

Perks ignored him. 'It was Panaides who oversaw the opening of Bardsley's first pub here.'

'On Wetherby Avenue?'

'Right. And who, almost certainly unknown to Frank Bardsley, began running a small drugs operation.'

'Ah . . . '

'So, because that definitely *is* stepping on his toes, Cutler hires a man named Dennis Draper – which we don't believe to be his real name, by the way – to sort Panaides out, which he did a couple of weeks back.' Perks opened a drawer, took out a file and removed a selection of photographs. He slid them across the desk. 'These are the only pictures of Draper that we've been able to get.'

Miller picked up the photographs. Unsurprisingly, all had been taken surreptitiously from a distance and none provided any great detail. The subject was tall and stringy with long dark hair and – blurry as it was – the face did not look to be one you would forget in a hurry, however much you wanted to.

'He's a seriously nasty piece of work,' Perks said. 'But I obviously don't need to tell you that.'

'Not really.' Miller blinked and saw Andy Bagnall's face, purplish and bloated beneath that plastic bag. Brutally murdered, and guilty of not much more than dreaming of going to America.

Now, real or not, Miller had a name.

'Cutler was at the station the other day to meet Draper and hand over payment, in return for proof that Draper had done what he was hired to do. Catching Cutler in the act would have given *us* proof that he'd paid to have Panaides killed. Sadly, this lad Bagnall and his mate had other ideas, so ...'

Miller stood up.

'Where are you going?'

'To get you your proof,' Miller said.

Now Perks stood up. 'Hold your horses, Dec—'

'When I get Draper, you'll have what you need, because I can't see him going down without wanting to take Wayne Cutler with him. Blokes like that don't tend to be super loyal.'

'Look, I know you've caught this murder and I can see you're fired up because you had dealings with this lad, but remember, this is my investigation.'

'Well obviously,' Miller said. 'Soon as *I* get anything, *you'll* get it.'

'A bit quicker than I got this sodding briefcase, though, right?'

'Scout's honour. That said, I *was* chucked out of Scouts because I called Akela a bell-end, on top of which I could never say *woggle* without giggling.'

'We'll ... *liaise*, yeah?'

'You can use fancy French words all you like, Bob, but if you mean will I trot up here and tell you, absolutely. This is very much a bisexual arrangement though, right?'

'Excuse me?'

'It goes both ways. If you get any useful forensics off that briefcase or any leads on Dennis Draper, you let me know.'

'Fair enough.' Perks followed Miller to the door. 'This mate of Bagnall's, have you got a name?'

Half a name, Miller thought. 'I'm on it,' he said.

'Best get on it fast,' Perks said.

Miller didn't need reminding why. Until Draper had his

hands on the briefcase containing Panaides's hands and got
the payday it represented, he would remain very dangerous.
Now he'd eliminated Bagnall, chances were he'd go after the
lad Bagnall had been with at the station.

Miller urgently needed to find Andy Bagnall's partner in
half-arsed crime before Draper or Cutler did.

TWELVE

Frank Bardsley owed everything to his prowess at mathematics. Being good at maths at Moorbrook School was a triumph in itself, growing up in an area of Preston where reading a tabloid cover to cover was likely to earn you the nickname 'professor'. Frank had always loved numbers. They did what they were told. Two multiplied by two was always going to sodding well be four with no arguments. So, while his contemporaries signed on or went thieving, Frank waited for his numerical acumen to pay dividends.

One night in a burger joint on Fishergate, it did.

The forty-four (and counting) fast food establishments upon which the Bardsley empire was based grew from a stroke of genius best expressed as a simple mathematical equation.

Lager + Time = Shit Food.

It had dawned on Frank – in a Eureka moment that made that Greek bloke in the bath look like Joey Essex – that these burger bars and kebab houses were wasting their time opening during the day. There was something *in* lager, some secret

additive, he was sure of it. That was the only possible explanation for people wanting to eat greasy reconstituted rubbish
in the first place. And a good few pints as well, not just a quick
half at lunchtime. Nobody in their right mind wanted a kebab
at *lunchtime.*

So, why were these idiots wasting good money on wages,
raw materials, heating and lighting and all that during the
day? Open between 11 p.m. and two in the morning and you
were on to a winner. Obviously there was the small matter of
getting rid of the competition, but that was where Frank's best
mate George had come in.

George Panaides, too, had taken his childhood interests and
successfully exploited them in adulthood. His area of expertise
was more predictable in a school where you were overdressed
with both your ears. At Moorbrook, George had been the
leading exponent of an initiation rite in which first-formers,
in a timeless gesture of warmth and welcome, had their heads
shoved down the toilet. Once he'd put away childish things,
George began to branch out. He used other, more imaginative
combinations of vessels and liquids: a bath full of paraffin; a
septic tank; and, on one occasion of which he was particularly
proud, a deep-fat fryer.

'I don't know which I enjoyed more, Frank,' George had told
him. 'The sound of the bloke squealing or the sizzle when I
shoved his arm in.'

So, through a creative mixture of mathematics and dunk-
ing, the Bardsley empire grew until nobody ate so much as a
battered sausage in Preston without Frank knowing about it.
Soon they branched out into the licensing trade, taking over
a string of pubs on the north side of the city.

Now he had the lager *and* the shit food, Frank truly believed
that he owned men's lives.

Of course there had been pressure, notably from George, to invest in the city's other growth industries – prostitution, gambling and drugs – but Frank had always pushed back, because fast food was where his heart was. Fast food had made him. The sight of a discarded Styrofoam carton bearing the legend Bardsley's Burgers was still enough to bring a tear to his eye. The fact that, in all probability, it still contained the burger was neither here nor there.

Frank had earned the big house in Woodplumpton, the swimming pool and the fleet of flash cars. He'd worked his tits off for the holidays in St Lucia and the private schools for Francesca and Archie. And now it could all turn to doo-doo because stupid bloody George had got greedy.

It had been George's idea to open a Bardsley's Burgers in Blackpool, the pub as well, and even though Frank had briefed him on the perils of encroachment on firmly established turf (after first explaining what encroachment meant) George had insisted on pushing ahead. And for a while, it looked as if they'd got away with it. There had even been a phone conversation with Wayne Cutler, during which Frank had assured his fellow businessman that he had nothing to worry about.

'Burgers are my business, Wayne.'

'I'm glad to hear it.'

'Burgers and nowt else. Well, we also do a blinding saveloy . . . but you get what I'm saying.'

Cutler had said that he did. He said that he might even pop in one night to try a Bardsley quarter-pounder for himself and, as long as burgers *stayed* Frank's only business, they would get on like a house on fire. Which might well be what would happen, he warned, should the situation change.

Well, the situation *had* changed, all because George had decided to moonlight as a bloody drug dealer, knocking out weed and pills and whatever else along with the nuggets and the onion rings. He'd paid the price, too. Left a wife and two kiddies behind.

He'd known the risks, of course he had. Daft sod. Nothing was going to bring him back, though, and whatever else Frank could be accused of, he was not and never had been a man of violence. Not very *much* violence, at any rate.

But . . . George had been his friend.

And then there was the maths problem. The bloody maths didn't work! Frank was now minus one and it niggled him because things needed equalling up. The obvious way to do that was to 'subtract' one of Cutler's crew and, in an ideal world, it would be the one who'd taken George out of the equation.

It couldn't be that hard to find out the bloke's name.

Plenty of gobby coppers were partial to a Bardsley's Big Beefy One.

Frank stood up, poured himself a Campari and soda and knocked off the sound on *Countdown*. The numbers game was a piece of cake anyway. He wandered across to the big windows in his sitting room and looked out at the garden. Archie and Francesca were messing about on their quad bikes.

It was an awful lot to risk, but maths was maths, wasn't it?

Not that any of it would matter if Maureen did what she'd started threatening to do and walked out with the kids. For the life of him, he couldn't work out why his wife had been so miserable lately. It hacked him right off, what with everything Bardsley's Burgers had given her, but once this George situation had been sorted out, he'd do whatever he could to improve the situation and make her happy again.

Some nice jewellery, maybe, or a new car. She'd come round . . .

Standing at the window, Frank was thinking about another lad he'd known back at Moorbrook, one who'd been particularly matey with George, as it happened. Martin Molineux had been rather more ... practical than Frank had, with metalwork lessons being *his* particular favourite. He was a dab hand with rasps and power-tools and stuff, and Frank could still picture the cracking set of coat-hooks he'd knocked up for his mum. Martin had eventually been expelled for nicking equipment but – fair play to him – had gone on to use his skills both professionally as a skilled welder and in rather more creative ways. Once when someone cut him up at traffic lights and, most recently, when someone had looked the wrong way at his girlfriend.

Frank was pretty sure he'd be out of prison by now.

In the garden, Francesca and Archie were tearing around the pool on the bikes. Frank banged on the window, worried that they were getting too close to the edge, but they couldn't hear him.

He thought about George and his innocent glee at that 'sizzle'. About happier days when the two of them stood proudly behind the counter together in that first branch of Bardsley's Burgers. He thought about the simple pleasures of equilibrium.

Then he took out his phone to give 'Torchy' Molineux a call.

THIRTEEN

Miller and Xiu sat with the victim's sister in the corridor outside the viewing suite at the city mortuary. In the street beyond the front door, passers-by were bundled up against a cold snap that was just beginning to bite, and it wasn't a great deal warmer in the hallway. Xiu had fetched tea from a machine, but Natalie Bagnall just sat hunched over on the plain wooden bench, staring into her cup as though it might contain answers and not just horrible tea.

She was in her mid-twenties, Miller reckoned; tall and skinny with short black hair, the tips dyed red. A small stud glittered on the side of her nose and her eyes would almost certainly have been kind, were they not so swollen.

She looked every bit as broken as Miller expected.

He knew that, as a nurse, Natalie Bagnall was well used to seeing a range of the grim and gruesome things that most people were mercifully spared, but not being easily shocked at work would not have made identifying her brother's body any less terrible. Thanks to the skill of the pathologist and her assistants, the body certainly looked a damn sight better now than when Natalie had discovered it first thing that morning, but still.

Miller could sympathise, because although he had seen his fair share of horrors, it had not prepared him for identifying Alex's body in that very same viewing suite five months earlier.

That was when he'd realised he hadn't seen horror at all.

Natalie sniffed and Miller laid both his hands over hers. She looked down at his hands then up at his face and shook her head. 'How is anyone ever supposed to get past this?'

'They're not,' Miller said. 'They can't. You can . . . catch up with it, if you're lucky.'

Xiu leaned across. 'We can put you in touch with a grief counsellor.' She threw Miller a look when he scoffed. 'That can be a big help.'

'Yeah, right,' Miller said. 'If they start talking about "honouring the spirit" or the gift of "sacred silence" feel free to throw up. Oh, and if anyone mentions "moving on", my advice would be to slap them.'

'Miller!' Xiu was shaking her head.

'Actually, a bit of slapping probably works wonders.' Miller nodded, wishing that he'd done a lot more of it himself. He watched Natalie glance back towards the viewing suite. Behind the doors, Andy's body would by now have been eased silently into a chilled steel drawer. Miller had imagined Alex inside one of them so many times; hating it because he knew how much she felt the cold.

'Why would anyone have wanted to hurt Andy?'

'Obviously, investigations are ongoing,' Xiu said.

Miller knew *exactly* why, but knowing wouldn't do Natalie Bagnall any good.

'I mean, who . . . ?' She shook her head again, took a sip of lukewarm tea.

Miller thought he knew the answer to that one, too. Natalie Bagnall would find out soon enough, once Miller had arrested her brother's killer, and sometime after that she would be able to enjoy staring at Dennis Draper in the dock, enjoying his last hours of freedom. Until then, ignorance was . . . well, *bliss* was clearly not the right word considering the circumstances, but it was better than the alternative.

'We're quite keen to trace one of Andy's friends,' Miller said. 'So, we were wondering if you might be able to help with that.'

'He didn't have a lot of friends,' Natalie said.

'Maybe someone he'd been hanging about with recently?'

She thought for a few seconds, considering another sip of tea before deciding against it. 'I know there *was* a lad he was knocking about with. Someone he knew from school, I think. Andy would go round to his place or this lad would come over to ours at night when I was at work.' There was a shrug and a half-smile. 'I knew they were up to something.' She looked at Miller. 'Andy was harmless, he really was . . . but I know he could get himself into scrapes. He was easily led.'

'Do you know what this lad was called?' Xiu asked.

'Sorry, I don't.'

'James, maybe?' Miller waited. 'Jimmy . . . ?'

'Andy never said.'

'Was he at school with anyone named James?'

'I've no idea. I think there's a school photo somewhere, you know, with names on.' She blinked slowly. 'If I can find it. Talking of which, when do you think I might be able to get back into the flat?'

'Sorry, but it'll be another couple of days yet,' Xiu said.

'I want to go back and clear everything up, you know? Get things back to the way they were.'

Miller nodded, though he knew that was never going to happen. 'Is there somewhere you can stay?'

'I think I'll be staying with my mum and dad for a bit.' Natalie stared at the wall opposite, glassy-eyed. 'They're going to need a bit of looking after and there'll be stuff to organise, the funeral and all that.' She turned back to Miller. 'Thinking about it, they might well have that photograph. Up in the loft, you know . . . ?'

Miller told her there was no rush then watched as Fiona Mackie, a family liaison officer he'd known for many years, came through the door. They exchanged nods. Natalie Bagnall's mention of work had reminded him of something: a question it couldn't hurt to ask. 'When you were at work last night, I don't suppose anyone mentioned a man coming in mid-morning with a head injury? Actually, he'd still have been in there for your shift.'

'There were probably several,' Natalie said. 'Nobody I saw, though.'

Miller wasn't sure what he'd have said if she *had* remembered treating a man with a briefcase-shaped head wound. There was little point in revealing that her tender mercies had been squandered on the arsehole who'd kickstarted this whole tragic chain of events.

'Everyone was still talking about the poor so-and-so who'd come in earlier with his wedding tackle caught in his zip. Actually, it was one of my best mates who got the short straw and had to stitch it up.'

Miller and Xiu exchanged a look.

'Ouch,' Miller said, making a mental note that – although there would certainly be important footage from the station and they already had the pictures Perks had handed over – the hospital CCTV would definitely be worth a look. This latest nugget of information had shot straight to the top of a growing list of things the victim's sister didn't need to be told. The fact that not only had the man who'd killed her brother been in her hospital, but her friend had sewn up his pecker.

A few minutes later, Miller and Xiu watched Natalie Bagnall climbing into the back of Fiona Mackie's car. She gave them a small wave before her head dropped and they drove away.

'We should check the cameras at the hospital,' Xiu said.

'I'm way ahead of you,' Miller said. 'That's not a surprise, though, is it? Working with me, every day is a learning experience, right?'

'Not in the way you mean,' Xiu said. 'With luck we'll get a nice close-up of Draper.'

'Hopefully just his face though. Not the . . . injury.'

'If you think he's the bloke we're after.'

'I think that as far as suspects go, he's top of a list of one and we need to get him quickly.' Miller buttoned up his jacket against the cold. 'Not that he can run very fast at the moment.'

They began walking towards the car.

'I was wondering if you fancied popping round to my place later.' Miller smiled when Xiu's mouth actually fell open. 'No need to look quite so keen.'

'Why?'

'I need to show you something. Nine o'clock-ish?'

'That's very late.'

'It won't take long.

'I don't know . . . '

'No funny stuff, I promise.' Miller raised his hands. 'I don't even *like* heavy metal.'

Xiu was still looking somewhat horror-struck, fearful even.

Aside from the occasion a few months before when, in an effort to save his life, she'd burst in with a firearms unit in tow, she had never visited Miller at home. It was an arrangement with which she was perfectly content because, though there were very few things Sara Xiu was afraid of, she knew the kind of pets Miller kept. 'It's just . . .' She grimaced. 'The rats.'

'Oh, I'm sure they won't mind,' Miller said.

FOURTEEN

'I have to say, Declan, your rumba tonight was tip-top.' Mary raised her gin and tonic and took a sip. 'Very . . . *intense*, and as we all know that's down to what your legs and feet are doing and not your hips.'

Mary's husband Howard nodded. 'Bloody good job an' all. State of my hips.'

'Hip, singular,' Mary said. 'There shouldn't be anything wrong with the metal one.' She looked around the group. 'To be fair, you were all on good form this evening, but credit where it's due, Declan's rumba was particularly impressive.'

'I'm not going to argue.' Miller raised his glass, happy to accept the praise. He knew that he'd nailed it. 'Not so sure about my cha-cha-cha, though.'

'Well no, it was a little clumpy. And that's being . . . '

'Cha-cha-charitable?'

'No, it wasn't *that* bad.'

'Cheers.'

'Best not dwell on your foxtrot, though.' She shook her head. 'Where was the swing, where was the sway?'

'Oh, come on, Mary, you know how much I hate the bloody foxtrot. It's basically walking, only not as interesting.' Miller tore open his bag of pork scratchings and began crunching.

'Don't sulk,' Mary said. 'It's constructive criticism.'

'I'm not sulking,' Miller said, spitting half a scratching into Howard's lap.

The group was seated at its usual table in the corner of the Bull's Head; a decidedly mixed bunch, both in terms of dancing ability and vintage. Retired coppers, ballroom veterans and husband and wife team Mary and Howard were well into their seventies. Gloria and Ransford, who ran a florist's shop in town, were not very far behind, though neither had, as far as Miller was aware, had any major body parts replaced. Ruth, who did secretarial work from home, was in her early forties, while Nathan (who was twenty-seven with two left feet and a major crush on Ruth) somehow made a living out of playing computer games.

It had been Alex who'd persuaded Miller to join the group several years earlier, then later to start dancing rather more seriously when it turned out they were pretty good at it. Howard, Mary and the rest of them felt Alex's absence almost as keenly as he did and – though Miller would certainly not be dancing competitively any more – he was happy to be part of it all again. He looked forward to the weekly practice sessions in their glorified scout hut and, when he wasn't getting it in the neck about his sodding foxtrot failings, he very much enjoyed the hour or so in the pub afterwards.

'Oh, before I forget . . .' Mary leaned forward. Howard, as was his wont, leaned forward in sync with her. 'I've been talking to someone who's keen to join us. Some new blood! If everyone's in agreement, obviously.'

'A man or a woman?' Nathan asked.

'Well, a woman, obviously.'

'Fine with me,' Nathan said. There were nods and noises of assent around the table.

Mary looked at Miller.

'We don't need anyone new,' he said.

'No, it's not strictly *necessary*,' Mary said. 'But we're an odd number, so—'

'That doesn't matter.' Miller downed a mouthful of IPA. 'If me or Nathan play the piano, there's an even number.'

'Yes, but I do think four couples would be better.'

'Mary's usually spot on about this stuff,' Howard said.

'Why would it be better?'

Mary hesitated. 'Not . . . *better*, no . . . but it can't hurt to ring the changes, can it? I just think that if everyone had a rather more regular partner, the level of all our routines would improve. Even your foxtrot, Declan!'

Howard snorted, but it didn't raise a smile from Miller.

'Obviously there's me and Howard.' Mary grabbed her husband's hand and nodded across the table. 'Gloria and Ransford always dance together . . .'

'Me and Ruth,' Nathan said.

Ruth patted Nathan on the arm. 'Yes, sometimes.'

Mary nodded. 'Absolutely. So I was only thinking that if you had a more . . . regular partner . . .' Miller was already shaking his head. 'I mean, she might not want to come every week, anyway.' She looked at Howard who was signalling *very* unsubtly that she should change the subject. 'She's ever such a nice woman.'

'I don't care,' Miller said.

'She used to be a traffic warden, so you'd have plenty in common.'

'*What?*'

'I'm just saying—'

'Can we talk about something else?'

For ten or fifteen seconds there was only the garbled conversation of drinkers on nearby tables and the mechanised bleeps of the fruit machine next to the bar. Gloria and Ransford stared at the carpet, while Howard and Mary tried to send messages to one another with looks that neither recipient quite understood.

'OK, what shall we talk about?' Ruth asked.

In turn, Nathan, Howard and even the usually reticent Gloria quickly chipped in with conversational openers.

'The new defender Blackpool just signed looks quite tasty . . .'

'That one way system by the Aquarium's a right bugger, isn't it . . . ?'

'Rap music is basically just shouting, don't you think . . . ?'

'How about two severed hands in a briefcase?' Miller asked.

That got everyone's attention.

He'd been planning to tell them about the investigation anyway, because this diverse bunch had proved to be a useful sounding board in the past, but now seemed like as good a time as any.

He would have the rap discussion with Gloria another day.

Once Miller had given them the basics, he volunteered to get another round in. By the time he was back with the drinks (a G&T, two IPAs, two large glasses of white wine and a bottle of WKD), there were plenty of questions. They weren't all what Miller would consider *searching*.

'How do you cut someone's hands off?' Nathan asked.

'Hacksaw?' Howard suggested. 'Chainsaw if you're pushed for time, like.'

'An axe would be quickest,' Ransford said. 'Got to be sharp, though, to get through the bone.'

'We don't know *how* the hands were removed yet,' Miller said. 'And, if I'm honest, I *was* hoping for a bit more . . . insight from this group of enquiring minds. And Nathan.'

Nathan was about to protest, but Mary didn't give him the chance. 'You think Draper will be going after the victim's friend?'

'He wants that briefcase,' Miller said.

'So, it's the obvious move,' Ruth said.

'But you don't know who this friend is?'

'Not as yet, but hopefully we'll get something from the CCTV at the station. We'll get a picture at least.'

'You think Draper knows who it is?' Howard asked.

'Let's hope not.'

'There'll be something on the victim's phone, right?' Nathan was looking around the table, seeking some reaction to his own enquiring mind. 'Texts between him and his mate or whatever, bound to be.'

'That's right,' Gloria said. 'Youngsters like that have everything on their phones.'

Miller knew they were on to something, but he also knew that a mobile phone had not been anywhere on the list of evidence taken from Andy Bagnall's flat. 'Actually, we didn't find the victim's phone.'

'Ah,' Mary said.

Ah was right. If Draper had Bagnall's phone, he was already several steps ahead of them.

'Sounds like you need to get a shift on,' Ruth said.

'You could try the lad's mobile provider,' Howard said. 'Get them to send records or what have you, but we all know how long that's likely to take.'

THE WRONG HANDS   87

Miller knew he could learn Chinese faster.

'It strikes me that what you need is a two-pronged attack.' Ransford spoke slowly in his Lancastrian-cum-Jamaican lilt. He leaned forward, using his fingers to illustrate what two prongs might look like. 'You must find that young man who helped steal the briefcase, but at the same time you also need to go after the man who killed his friend—'

'And chopped that bloke's hands off.' Nathan leaned quickly across and whispered to Ruth. 'My money's still on a chainsaw.'

'Correct,' Ransford said. 'And if you're lucky you can find *him* before *he* finds this young man you're yet to identify.'

Miller nodded and drank. He couldn't argue with the florist's summing up of the situation but still. It was strange how people trying to be helpful could make things seem so much more bloody difficult.

'So, where do you start?' Howard asked. 'With the first prong, I mean.'

'Which prong's that, love?' Mary asked.

'What?'

'Which prong? Just so I'm clear ... '

'The ... choppy-off hands bloke.' Howard performed an appropriate mime, in case there was any confusion.

'Cutler,' Miller said. 'The one who paid for the ... choppy-off hands. I think I should pay him a visit and see how his poorly head is.'

'You take care then, Declan,' Mary said. She and Howard had retired from the police back when Wayne Cutler was still nicking cars and flogging single spliffs in a paper bag, but they knew well enough what he'd become.

'I don't know how you do it,' Gloria said. 'Deal with hoodlums like that every day.'

Miller grinned, because calling Wayne Cutler a 'hoodlum' was like saying Elon Musk was 'comfortably off'. 'What can I tell you? I'm incredibly brave. Not to mention witty and handsome.' He waited, looking from one member of the group to another. 'You *can* mention it, obviously.'

Mary smiled sympathetically and leaned across to poke Miller's arm.

'Right then,' Howard said. 'I'll get 'em in ... '

FIFTEEN

Knowing that punctuality (alongside a frankly baffling compulsion to tell the truth, a hair-trigger temper and a strange aversion to jokes) was a key facet of Xiu's psychological make-up, Miller wasn't surprised to hear her motorbike pull up at one minute to nine. Now, ten minutes later, she was sitting next to him on his sofa staring at Fred and Ginger's playpen as if they might escape at any moment and go for her throat.

'Why don't I just take one of them out for a bit of a cuddle?' Miller asked.

'I'd rather you didn't.'

'They've got very soft fur, you know.' He made as if to stand up.

Xiu immediately let out an involuntary yelp and pulled her feet up onto the sofa.

'I'm *kidding*. Blimey . . . '

Xiu scowled at him. There was a slight twitch around her right eye, which was rarely a good sign. 'Isn't there anything *you're* afraid of, Miller?'

'Well, not "afraid" as such, but there's plenty of things I'm not awfully fond of. The sea, for a kick-off ... being *in* as opposed to looking *at*.'

'So, there you go—'

'Pan pipes, caravans, baked beans in a ramekin, idiots who say they don't like the Beatles ...' Miller paused for breath. 'Electric scooters, non-electric scooters, that opera singer in the Go Compare adverts, anyone at a call centre who says "yourself" when they mean "you", and people who put little dogs in pushchairs.'

'OK ...'

'Oh, and I do suffer from hippopotomonstrosesquippedaliophobia, which ironically is an irrational fear of long words.'

'Hippo ... *what*?'

Miller put his head in his hands. 'Please don't make me say it again.'

Xiu shook her head, ignoring the joke or not getting it; Miller couldn't always tell the difference. He sat back and chugged at the beer he'd produced when Xiu had arrived. 'Long day.'

Xiu took a drink of her own. 'A damn sight longer for Natalie Bagnall.'

'I know.' Miller glanced across at the photograph of Alex next to the TV. The woman herself hadn't put in an appearance, but that was no surprise because she knew why Miller had asked Xiu to come round. Putting that off for as long as possible, he shared his worry about the likelihood that Draper was in possession of Andy Bagnall's phone. The advantage he had over them.

'Let's see what we get from the hospital's CCTV,' Xiu said. 'See if he still has the advantage then.'

'Positive thinking, I like that.' Miller hoped his partner

would still be thinking positively when she'd seen what he had to show her.

'I know it's a long shot,' Xiu said, 'but if there's no evidence tying Cutler directly to Panaides's murder, might he not just decide to give Draper up?'

'I'd say that wasn't so much positive thinking as pie in the sky. A really massive magic pie made of wishes and dreams. A unicorn pie.'

'I don't see why.' Xiu leaned towards him. 'We'll get enough forensics from the briefcase and from the hands to charge Draper with killing Panaides and there'll be more than enough at the crime scene to do him for Bagnall's murder too.'

'So?'

'So, Cutler might think *he's* safe and decide to do us a favour.'

'Wayne Cutler isn't in the business of doing favours for the likes of us, especially when *us* includes *me*. Besides, even though money never changed hands for the contract he put out on Panaides, Cutler can't be sure Draper doesn't have *something* on him. Messages, recorded phone conversations, whatever. I don't think Draper's stupid, even if he *was* distracted by a dick at a crucial moment.'

'Yeah, well, we've all been there,' Xiu said.

Miller sat up straight. 'Ooh, spill the beans, Posh.'

'No chance.'

'Tell me or I'll set a rat on you!'

Xiu gave him a thin, 'not in a million years' smile. 'Wasn't there something you wanted me to look at?'

Miller sighed and stood up. *Wanted* was putting it a bit strongly.

He led Xiu across to the table where his laptop was already open and asked her to sit down. A video had been lined up and the cursor hovered over the play symbol. 'This arrived not long after those photos that Chesshead sent me. Alex and some bloke.'

'Arrived how?'

'They broke in and trashed the place, but that was all just for show. They wanted me to see this.'

'*They* being . . . ?'

'Chesshead was working for Ralph Massey at the time, so I always presumed he was the one that had the photos taken. He's probably behind this as well, but I can't swear to it.'

'You thinking about what he said this morning? Him knowing something about what happened to your wife.'

'I haven't stopped thinking about it.' Miller leaned down to press *PLAY* then went back to the sofa. 'Just watch it.'

It was no more than fifteen seconds long and Miller had always thought it was a clip from something longer. Alex and the same man she'd been with in the photographs. The man stayed in the shadows as far as possible and Miller had thought it was because he had known he was being filmed, but now he was no longer sure. Whatever had brought Alex and this stranger together, the action was easy enough to follow.

The man handed Alex an envelope, then waited.

Alex opened it.

She took out the money that was inside.

When Xiu had finished watching, she turned to look at Miller.

'Watch it again,' he said.

When she had done as Miller asked, Xiu walked back across and sat down next to him. She thought for a few seconds. She said, 'Your wife was an experienced officer with an impeccable record. She sometimes worked undercover.' She nodded across to the laptop on the table. 'It could be a lot of things.'

'I know all the things it could be.'

'Right, and the thing you *don't* want it to be is only one of them.' She looked at him. 'I take it you've never shown this to Lindsey Forgeham.'

'Just you,' Miller said.

'So you don't think *I'll* go straight to Lindsey Forgeham? You know, the officer who's actually in charge of investigating Alex's death?'

'I'm hoping you don't,' Miller said. 'You know as well as I do that, for whatever reason, that investigation's going backwards.'

Xiu thought about it some more. 'So, when do you think that video was taken?'

Miller turned to look at her. He was as sure as he could be that she was on board, or seriously considering coming on board; that she wouldn't go behind his back, at any rate. 'Alex had her hair cut about a week before she died and you can see how short it is in that video. It can't have been more than a day or two before she was killed.'

'What about the man with the envelope?'

'I haven't got the first idea,' Miller said. 'But there's something about him that's niggling at me. Has done ever since I first saw it. Something that's familiar. Something he *does* . . .'

They sat in silence for a minute or two more while Fred and Ginger chased each other noisily around the playpen. Xiu seemed oddly unconcerned, her mind elsewhere.

'I need to go,' she said eventually.

Miller walked her to the door. 'I didn't mean to put you in an awkward position,' he said.

'It's fine.'

'I was just trying to be upfront with you.'

'My place next time though,' Xiu said.

Miller watched the motorbike roar away, closed the door then turned to see Alex, head down in one of her favourite hidey-holes. The small gap between the edge of the sofa and the wall into which she squeezed herself at awkward moments.

'You trust her, don't you? Xiu?'

'Of course I trust her.'

'And you trust me, right . . . ?'

'I'm going to bed,' Miller said.

Alex looked up with an attempt at a playful expression that she wasn't quite pulling off. 'You don't hate caravans, Miller. Or scooters. You were just showing off.'

Miller turned off the light and walked upstairs.

SIXTEEN

It took DI Tim Sullivan a few minutes to make sure that everything was as it should be for the morning briefing. That the PowerPoint presentation was cued up correctly, that his iPad was fully charged with the appropriate applications ready and that his flies weren't undone. While others around the table looked at their phones or pretended to leaf through the briefing notes in advance, Miller spent the time mentally re-casting James Bond films using actors from the Carry-On series.

Sid James as 007, *obviously*. Babs Windsor as Pussy Galore and Charles Hawtrey as Goldfinger, which Miller decided was a creative stroke of near genius. 'Oh, hellooo, Mr Bond!'

'Right then,' Sullivan said.

Would it be wrong, Miller wondered – in these days of cultural appropriation and gender warfare – to cast Hattie Jacques as Oddjob ...?

Sullivan stabbed at his iPad and a picture of Andy Bagnall appeared on the screen behind him. He spent the next ten minutes running through the basics. Cause and approximate time of death, the ongoing forensic examination of the crime scene and the last known movements of the victim.

'For reasons that will become obvious, I've been liaising closely with DCI Perks from Serious and Organised. He has been able to ascertain that our victim was, in fact, one of the two individuals who stole a briefcase during the abortive S&O operation at the railway station the day before yesterday.'

'Blimey,' Tony Clough said, which for him was a remarkably perceptive comment.

Miller could not resist asking a question to which he himself – though Sullivan could not possibly know that – was the answer. '*How* exactly was DCI Perks able to . . . ascertain this?'

Sullivan produced a thin smile. 'That's a little above my pay grade, DS Miller.'

'Of course.' Miller thought that directing kiddie-cars was above Sullivan's paygrade, but nodded like he was satisfied.

'I do know that DCI Perks has also managed to recover the missing briefcase, but – before DS Miller asks – I have no details on that, either.'

'The whole pay grade thing again?'

'Correct,' Sullivan said.

Miller had no idea how Bob Perks had explained away the sudden reappearance of the stolen briefcase and its grisly contents, which was probably for the best. He also decided, in the interests of muddying the waters a little, that he would nip into TK Maxx first chance he got and buy himself a briefcase as similar to the one in question as he could find. Bringing that into work for a while should stop the desk sergeant and anyone else who'd seen him with the *actual* case the previous day putting two and two together and making a shedload of trouble.

'So, we can leave our colleagues in S&O to get on with their own investigation, while we concentrate on this *homicide.*' Sullivan nodded and brought up another image. 'After all, that's what it says on our door, right?'

One or two newbies actually turned to look. There wasn't anything written on the door to their office. There were one or two things scribbled on the back of the *toilet* door, but Miller didn't think that Tim Sullivan would want to know about them.

'Again, thanks to DCI Perks, we know that as far as the murder of Andrew Bagnall goes, *this* man is most definitely a person of interest.' He turned to point at one of the blurry photographs that Bob Perks had shown Miller the day before. 'Dennis Draper is already wanted in connection to another murder and we have good reason to believe he is a known and recent associate of Wayne Cutler.'

'That's why Cutler was at the railway station.' Andrea Fuller nodded to one or two of her colleagues at the table.

'There's little to be gained by speculating at this stage,' Sullivan said. 'But Mr Cutler *is* definitely someone we should be talking to.' He looked at Miller. 'DS Miller? You've had the most dealings with him, so . . . ?'

'Happy to, sir. Myself and DS Xiu?' He looked across at Xiu. They had not spoken since the night before, but she seemed happy enough.

'Fine with me,' Xiu said.

'No, let's mix things up,' Sullivan said, nodding enthusiastically, like he was Simon Cowell changing the line-up of a boyband. 'Sara, could you get down and have a look at the station CCTV, see what you can find?'

'No problem . . . and then the hospital, right?'

'Oh, are you not feeling OK?'

'Draper was treated at the hospital, sir. Hopefully we can get footage from there, too.'

'Yes, but we still don't really know what Draper looks like,' Sullivan said. 'So how will we know who we're trying to get footage *of*?'

'Well, we know roughly what time he was admitted and there can't be too many people who were taken to hospital by uniformed officers.'

'Certainly not with . . . that kind of injury,' Miller said.

Clough sniggered, then cleared his throat because his moment had come at last. 'I got *my* penis caught in a zip once.' He grinned. 'That's the last time my wife asks me to do her dress up.' It got a big laugh, but only from Clough himself.

'There's every chance we'll finally get a picture of him,' Xiu said.

'Yes, of course.' Sullivan fiddled with his iPad while he gathered what few thoughts he had. 'Get down to the hospital and if you do get a decent picture let's get it sent to every officer in town. This is a *very* dangerous individual.' He turned again, but his fiddling had somehow managed to replace the photo of Draper with one of himself wearing an unwisely tight T-shirt. He quickly rectified his error.

'You been working out, sir?' Fuller asked.

Sullivan pointed to her. 'Why don't you go with DS Miller to interview Wayne Cutler?'

'Really, sir?'

'If he's that keen for some company.'

'I'm not,' Miller said.

Fuller shrugged. 'Well, I *can*, but there's plenty of other things I could do with getting on with.'

Miller could not understand why Andrea Fuller wasn't gagging to tag along with him. Perhaps she was still smarting after their argument a couple of days earlier. Hands for feet! It was *always* going to be hands for feet.

'I'm sure DS Miller will be fine on his own.' Fuller looked across at him and winked. 'I know you like to think of yourself as a bit of a lone wolf, Dec.'

Miller saw Xiu smile but chose to ignore it. 'I don't care either way, Andrea,' he said. 'I actually prefer to think of myself more as a curious and free-thinking wolf with a small group of close friends, but it's up to you.'

Sullivan clapped his hands. 'OK, *whatever*, people ... let's just get on with it.'

Miller left the room in an upbeat mood. He decided he would take the moped. It was a nice enough day, chilly but mercifully dry, and the ride across to Cutler's place wasn't unpleasant. He might also have just enough time to scribble something else on that toilet door before he left.

SEVENTEEN

To say that Jacqui Cutler welcomed Miller into her home would have been an overstatement, but at least she wasn't abusive. She certainly didn't question the marital status of his parents, which she'd done on many previous occasions. Hell, since Miller had caught the person responsible for the death of her son Adrian a few months earlier, they were virtually besties.

She showed him through to a living room which was a shrine to Swarovski and Leatherworld, where her husband sat staring at a TV screen that would not have disgraced a small cinema. On her way out she asked if anyone wanted tea. Miller was about to say, 'Yes please, and a biscuit would be nice' when Wayne barked a 'No' and the offer swiftly dematerialised.

'I'll be upstairs,' Jacqui said, before she closed the door. Miller presumed the information wasn't meant for him.

They weren't *that* friendly.

Miller dropped into an armchair and nodded at the screen. 'Anything good on?'

Cutler didn't even turn round. '*Police, Camera, Action.*'

'Oh, is it one you're in?'

Cutler pointed the remote and turned the TV off. 'Was there something you actually wanted?' He was wearing tracksuit bottoms and an Armani T-shirt. Miller had worked that out because it said *Armani* in very big letters on the front. His new teeth (rumours suggested many thousands of pounds' worth) still looked as though they didn't fit properly and the dressing on the top of his head was doing a far better job of disguising the hair loss than the combover ever had. He might have been the boss of a feared criminal organisation, but to Miller he always looked rather more like a second-hand car salesman or the manager of a lower league football team.

'Why were you at the railway station three days ago?'

'I haven't got the foggiest,' Cutler said. 'Maybe I fancied an hour or two's trainspotting.'

'In the toilets?'

'I must have been caught short . . . I really can't remember.'

'Seriously?'

Cutler's hand moved towards the dressing on his head. He touched it and winced theatrically. 'Concussion's properly nasty, Miller. You ever had it?'

'Can't say as I have.' Miller gazed up at the enormous chandelier directly above his head. 'Judging by the number of memory lapses you've suffered over the years though, you must have had it loads.'

'I certainly haven't forgotten how funny you are,' Cutler said. 'How funny you *think* you are.'

'Shall I try and fill in some of the gaps for you?' Miller leaned towards him. 'Might help bring some of it back.'

'Fill your boots,' Cutler said.

'You were there to meet a man named Dennis Draper. To

hand over some money in return for a briefcase containing the proof that Draper had murdered a man named George Panaides.'

Cutler nodded and hummed. 'Yes . . . something's coming back to me.'

'It's a miracle,' Miller said.

'Not about being at the station or that first bloke you mentioned . . . what was his name?'

'Dennis Draper.'

Cutler closed his eyes like he was concentrating, then shook his head. 'No, bugger all about him, I'm afraid. Sorry. But I *do* remember the Panaides murder. Bad business that.'

'What, bad as in being shot in the back of the head and having both his hands cut off? Or "bad business" because what Panaides had been up to was bad for your business?'

'Was it?'

'I'll be honest with you, Wayne, I can get a bit jealous when a new detective starts work. I can be a bit tetchy about it, you know?'

'Oh yeah?'

'It's ridiculous, course it is, but we're only human, aren't we? I can only imagine how you must feel when someone comes bowling along and has the barefaced cheek to start selling disco biscuits on your doorstep, because you've had dibs on that for ages! Fair dos, right?'

'Like I said.' Cutler sat back and laced his fingers across his designer-label belly. 'How funny you *think* you are.'

Miller smiled and waved away what he'd said. 'But you'll be glad to know that I don't particularly care about any of that. Well, I care a *bit*, obviously, because it's murder and drug dealing and as a police officer I'm supposed to be, you know . . . *anti* all that. With that in mind, the person I'm really interested in is Dennis Draper.' He raised a hand. 'I know, you've never heard of him, or if you have, you've forgotten. But if that name *should* suddenly start ringing a bell and you were able to point us vaguely in Mr Draper's direction, it would certainly earn you some brownie points.' Miller waited. 'To put that in a context you'll understand, we might not try and arrest you quite so often.'

Cutler leaned forward, eyes narrowed. 'Why are you so interested in Draper?' He hesitated, then corrected himself. 'This bloke Draper, I mean ... whoever he is.'

Miller could see the cogs turning. Wayne Cutler understood very well why Serious and Organised would be keen to get their hands on Draper, as it would ultimately be a way of getting their hands on *him*. But he was evidently a lot less sure why a homicide detective would take such a sudden interest.

Miller very much enjoyed being one step ahead of him; knowing something that he was now certain Cutler didn't.

'Well, because since the incident at the railway station, he's gone on to murder someone else. Making quite the nuisance of himself is our Mr Draper. As it happens, the victim was one of the lads who stole that briefcase that you got whacked across the head with. Is that spooky, or what? Considering that getting whacked is what led to your unfortunate, if convenient amnesia. Never mind "rain on your wedding day" Alanis chuffing Morissette ... *that's* ironic.' He shook his head as though this tragic and easily explicable chain of events was deeply strange. 'Am I right, Wayne?'

Cutler said nothing.

Miller stood up and wandered across to the window. For a second he imagined that he could *hear* the cogs now spinning furiously in Cutler's poisonous little brain, until he realised it was a man working with a strimmer at the bottom of the garden.

'So, anything coming back at all, Wayne?' He turned to look at Cutler. 'Is that Dennis Draper-shaped bell starting to ring yet? The faintest tinkle? Is there perhaps a familiar face starting to emerge from the concussive mist? Or better yet an address and phone number?'

Cutler turned slowly to look at Miller. 'I wish I could help you.'

'Yeah, course you do,' Miller said.

'I wish I could help you with a lot of things.'

Miller waited, something tightening in his stomach because he sensed what was coming.

'Look, I know you're still cut up about your wife and why wouldn't you be? I know how that feels, having lost someone close myself recently, and if I could do something to help catch the person responsible for Alex's death ... if I could do *anything*, I would.'

'I don't want to hear you saying her name.' Miller stared and waited until Cutler could see that he was staring. 'Please don't do it again.'

'I swear I would, though.'

'Right.' Miller turned away and looked around the room, making a swift yet comprehensive inventory of the things he could use to inflict a lot more damage to Wayne Cutler's skull than a briefcase.

'I know you think I had something to do with it,' Cutler said. 'I'm not stupid.'

The poker, just a few feet away, next to the gas fire; the fake-leatherbound encyclopaedia that Miller guessed had never been opened; the plug-ugly glass paperweight he guessed was meant to be a teardrop but looked more like a giant sperm.

'Just because her and I had some cat and mouse thing going on or whatever, because her lot were investigating me . . . but you're barking up the wrong tree, Miller.'

The crystal decanter; the ceramic leopard on the side table; the side table . . .

'It would really be something though, don't you reckon? If I was the one that actually helped you nail your wife's murderer.' Cutler was grinning, bright-eyed. 'Now that really *would* be ironic.'

EIGHTEEN

Jacqui Cutler was seething.

From her bedroom window she watched that weird copper walking back towards his silly scooter and found herself hoping that, for once, he'd got the better of her husband. That he'd be back with a few of his mates and maybe even an arrest warrant.

Bloody hell, she'd never thought *that* before.

She almost laughed.

Hand on heart, she couldn't say that she'd been anything like happy for a good while, but she'd forgotten what happy was even like when Adrian had been killed. Admittedly, in the end it turned out that he hadn't died because of anything Wayne had done, but the fact that they'd all *presumed* it had been to do with the business was enough. It was proof that things had got to change. She wasn't going to let anything happen to the only son she had left, that was for sure.

Then . . .

Now she was seething like she'd never seethed before.

Then . . . there was the incident with the Creme Egg.

For more years than Jacqui cared to remember, she'd been by her old man's side. Through thick and bloody thin. She'd watched him being carted away by coppers on a regular basis and seen him come home covered in blood that wasn't his. She'd heard things whispered on the phone that she'd never be able to forget and had she ever complained? Had she ever once suggested that maybe she'd be happier and a bit more fulfilled doing an Open University degree or going to antique fairs or joining a book club? No, obviously not, because those things were stupid and she'd hate them, but it was the principle of the thing that counted.

She'd been the good and faithful wife, hadn't she? She'd said nothing and looked the other way and done all her crying in private. She'd raised three kids as good as single-handed only to watch the two boys go the same way as their father. She'd cooked and cleaned for the lot of them and entertained all their dodgy friends without a word.

Well, enough was sodding well enough.

The other morning in the hospital had put the tin lid on it.

She was sorry Wayne had been hurt, of course she was, even if she'd seen him in much worse states over the years. Hadn't she rushed up to that hospital? Hadn't she come straight back home to pick up anything she could think of that would make him a bit more comfortable? His favourite squashy pillow and a nice bit of chocolate?

And what had she got for her trouble?

OK, so he hadn't been in the best mood ever because of the whole concussion thing and feeling sick, and his head was obviously giving him serious gip, but *none* of that could excuse what he'd done.

Jacqui Cutler was nothing if not a woman of the world. She

could appreciate the sound business reasons why such and such a bloke might need to have his legs broken. She could see that sledgehammers and battery acid were the only language that some people understood. She could even sympathise with the personal slight that had left Wayne with no other option than to chuck that tax inspector off a multi-storey car park, but there had to be a line in the sand.

There were no excuses for throwing a Creme Egg at someone.

It was scary, even thinking about . . . making a change, but she'd been thinking about very little else since having the chocolatey treat she'd hand delivered out of the goodness of her heart thrown back, quite literally, in her face.

It was the Creme Egg that broke the camel's back.

She'd miss the money, obviously. She'd miss all the nice things that the business had bought for them, but she was increasingly starting to realise that she might not have to. Because while she'd been keeping her mouth shut, Jacqui's ears had been very much open. She'd listened in on phone calls and conversations Wayne had believed were private and if he thought she didn't have the password to his mobile and computer, he was even dafter than she thought he was.

She knew where the bodies were buried.

She knew because she actually had the precise locations written down, on top of which she had the GPS co-ordinates for several others that had been dissolved, dumped or dismembered—

She turned from the window and walked towards the door because Wayne was shouting from downstairs, demanding lunch.

'Coming, sweetheart . . . '

Jacqui was actually feeling quite peckish herself. She

decided that she'd probably just have a sandwich or a bit of salad, but one of these days, when she was feeling just a bit braver, she thought she might nip into town and treat herself to a Bardsley Burger.

Miller had just put his high-vis jacket and crash helmet on when he heard his phone start to ring, so had to quickly take the helmet off again.

'I've got a bit of news,' Bob Perks said.

'Can it just be the funny bit?'

'What?'

'You know, the funny little story they always have at the *end* of the news to stop us all killing ourselves.' Miller turned back to look at Cutler's house and saw Jacqui Cutler stepping away from an upstairs window. 'Five minutes of war, a few violent deaths, a smattering of famine, and now . . . a monkey on the back of a tandem!'

'The hands,' Perks said.

'Right . . . '

'The ones in the briefcase.'

'Yes, they're the ones I presumed you were talking about.'

'They don't belong to George Panaides . . . or rather, they *didn't.*'

'Bloody hell,' Miller said.

'Bloody hell is bang on,' Perks said.

It was certainly news, but being used to a forensic service that usually moved slower than a sloth in a sack race, Miller was as astonished by the speed with which a DNA result had come back as he was by the result itself. He told Perks as much.

'We didn't actually have to go down the DNA route,' Perks said. 'I just spoke to the SIO on the Panaides murder. I told him why I was calling and, when he'd finished laughing, he politely informed me that the late Mr Panaides wasn't actually *missing* any hands.'

'Not even one?'

'When he was buried a week or so ago, he was perfectly intact.'

'Well, I'm not sure the back of his head would have been all there,' Miller said, 'but I'm splitting hairs.'

'So . . .'

'What about the rings?'

'Yes, his widow has confirmed that the rings *were* his. My guess is that Draper took them from the body after he'd killed Panaides and then put them on another pair of hands.'

'Whose?'

'I've no idea,' Perks said. Though never *quite* as perky as his name suggested, the DCI sounded shattered and utterly cheesed off; as if he was on the verge of tears, or early retirement.

'OK, let's park that one,' Miller said. 'How about *why*?'

'I've got a working theory.' Perks said it like what he actually had was terminal piles. 'Panaides's hands were the proof that Cutler demanded specifically, but for whatever reason, Draper didn't have time to remove them at the scene. Maybe he was interrupted or something.'

'Maybe he'd forgotten to bring a saw,' Miller said. 'It's easily done.'

'So he snatches the rings, then finds someone else to kill—'

'Making sure he's got his saw with him this time.'

'Now he's got a usable pair of hands to put the rings on.'

'I tell you what,' Miller said. 'The more I hear about this bloke, the less I like him.'

'We'll run DNA tests on the hands *now*, obviously.' Perks let out a long sigh. 'On the off chance we get a match.'

Miller climbed onto his moped. He glanced back at the house again, and this time he saw Cutler watching him from his front room. 'Well, that's one more very good reason to catch Dennis Draper,' he said. 'Like we don't have enough.'

NINETEEN

Miller had arranged to meet Xiu for lunch in the pub across the road from the station. The menu in the Black Swan (known locally as the Deadly Duck) was more likely to earn its chef a lawsuit for food poisoning than a Michelin star, but he and the landlady (to whom the chef was married) had been friends with Miller for a long time. They had always preferred Alex to Miller, but Miller was fine with that, because nearly everyone had.

The landlady – who was called Janet and was not nearly as fearsome as she pretended to be – came over to take Miller and Xiu's order.

'I'll have the incinerated cottage pie from your ever-popular "fresh from the freezer" range please, Janet,' Miller said. 'With a couple of slices of gravy and some of your delicious bullet peas.'

'Stick it up your arse, Miller.'

'That certainly couldn't make it taste any worse. Oh, and I'll have a glass of tap water an' all. With a twist of lemon.'

Janet turned to Xiu and winked. 'What about you, love?'

'I was thinking about a salad.'

Miller snorted and Janet clicked her pen against her teeth.

'OK ...' Xiu picked up the menu again. 'What are the rissoles like?'

'Blimey, that is a *bold* move,' Miller said.

'Rissoles, right.' Janet scribbled it down without waiting for confirmation. 'I can chuck a bit of coleslaw on as well if you want.'

'Perfect,' Xiu said.

Once Janet had stalked away towards the kitchen, Miller told Xiu about the phone call from Bob Perks. If she was shocked, she appeared to get over it surprisingly quickly.

'It doesn't really change anything,' she said. 'Not materially—'

'Tell that to the poor bugger those hands belonged to.'

She scowled at him. 'I was *going* to say ... other than confirming just how dangerous the man we're after is.'

Miller nodded. 'Oh yeah, he's definitely at the high end of the psycho scumbag spectrum. Which is why I'm hoping that your morning spent trawling through CCTV footage has been a raging success that will get this case wrapped up quickly and see one or other of us promoted immediately to Chief Constable.'

'Well ...'

'Actually, *you* can have the promotion, Posh. I'm happier working the streets, you know? Getting my hands dirty.' Despite the doubt he'd heard in Xiu's voice, watching her remove a laptop from her bag gave Miller cause for cautious optimism.

She clicked and scrolled. 'I don't think promotion is on the cards.'

Miller said 'Shame', because it sounded as if she really meant it.

'I got *something*, though.' There was more clicking and scrolling. 'The CCTV at the station was worse than useless. Only one working camera, but even that was no help. When the two lads first come into the station, the one we're after – the one that *isn't* Andrew Bagnall – keeps his head down, which makes sense when you think about what he and Bagnall were there to do.'

'A pair of determined desperados.'

'Well, not really,' Xiu said. 'Later on, after they've snatched the case, they're running away, so we just get blurry images, no detail at all. Basically, we've still got no idea what he even looks like.'

'*Something*, you said.'

'Yes, better luck at the hospital.' She clicked one last time, then turned the laptop so that Miller could see the screen. 'Here's our psycho scumbag.'

Miller looked at a clear, close-up image of Dennis Draper, which would have served him quite nicely as a publicity shot had there been any sort of glossy hitmen's directory. He wasn't looking happy, but Miller didn't suppose a man like that smiled very much, on top of which he'd just sliced open his penis, which was likely to put a crimp in anyone's morning. Get his old feller stitched up, have a spot of lunch or whatever, then toddle off to murder Andrew Bagnall before the anaesthetic had worn off. Probably just an average day.

'Looks like a charmer, right?'

'We need to get this picture on every copper's phone,' Miller said. 'In all the papers.'

'Already being done,' Xiu said.

'Good.' Miller cocked his head. 'Having said that . . .'

'What?'

Miller had felt Wayne Cutler's eyes on him when he'd pulled away from that house half an hour before and now he remembered them narrowing a few minutes before that. *'Why are you so interested in Draper?'* 'I have a strong suspicion we won't be the only ones looking for him.'

'Cutler?'

'I was right about your unicorn pie, which incidentally you are far more likely to find on the menu in here than salad. There's no way on God's green earth that Wayne Cutler is lifting a finger to help us find Draper. He's far more concerned about getting hold of Mr Draper himself.'

'So that Draper can't incriminate him?'

'Which he definitely will, given half a chance. If Draper's got *anything* to prove it was Cutler who hired him to kill Panaides, he's going to sing like a giant canary on *The Masked Singer*. The problem for us is that, as of now, bearing in mind he actually *knows* the bloke, Cutler's a tad better placed to find Dennis Draper than we are.'

'And Draper's better placed to find that lad from the station.'

Miller let out a long breath and tapped a finger against the edge of the table. 'We're like those people who dress up as Daleks or dinosaurs to run the London Marathon,' he said. 'Everyone who counts is way ahead of us.'

Xiu considered this, then shook her head. 'Marathon's the wrong word.'

'All right then, Snickers.'

'No, I just mean this is more of a sprint. A marathon takes ages and we might not have that long.'

'Well, longer than a few hours. Hopefully.'

'Hopefully.' Xiu sat back and folded her arms. 'So, what's next?'

'Well, if we survive lunch, and it's a big if ... I have no bloody idea.'

Janet brought the two glasses of water over and laid down cutlery and paper serviettes. 'I couldn't find a lemon,' she said. 'I could pop a pickled onion in there if you like.'

When she'd gone, Miller stared at the image on Xiu's laptop. 'I don't think I'd shed a *lot* of tears if Cutler got to him before we did. I'm just saying. It wouldn't be any great loss to humanity.'

Xiu shook her head. 'It's not justice though, is it?'

'Well, sort of. You know ... biblically.'

'Not for Natalie Bagnall or her mum and dad.'

Miller sat up a little straighter. '*That's* what we do next.'

'What?'

Miller took out his phone. 'Have you got a number for Natalie Bagnall?'

Xiu went back to her laptop for a few seconds. She read out the number and Miller dialled. He put the phone on speaker and set the mobile down between them.

'Natalie? It's DS Miller here. I'm with DS Xiu ... '

Xiu leaned towards the phone. 'Hi, Natalie.'

'How are you? Sorry, stupid question.'

'Oh, you know.'

Miller knew very well. 'I'm really sorry to bother you ... '

'Is there news?'

'I'm afraid not, but I wondered if you might be able to help us.' Miller could hear voices in the background. 'You mentioned an old school photo.'

'I was just looking at it ten minutes ago,' Natalie said. 'I'm at my mum and dad's place and we're sitting here going through all the old photos.'

'That can't be easy.'

'I know it sounds a bit mad, but we've actually been laughing,' Natalie said. 'The pictures of Andy as a kid and that. Bad haircuts and wearing shorts at school. That photo you're on about was in a box in the loft like I thought.'

'Have you still got it there?' Miller asked.

'Hang on . . . '

Miller could hear voices again.

'Who is it?'

'It's the police.'

'What do they want? Have they found out who—?'

'It's fine, Mum, I just need to grab . . . ' Natalie came back to the phone. 'OK, I've got it.'

'I seem to remember you saying it was one of those photos that's got the names of all the kids in the class.'

'Yeah, there's names underneath.'

'OK, can you have a look and see if there's a James?'

There was near silence for a few seconds. A few breaths and sniffs. Miller looked across at Xiu, who crossed her fingers.

'Yeah, I've found a James,' Natalie said. 'He's stood right next to our Andy as it happens, pulling a stupid face.'

She gave Miller the full name and Xiu immediately started searching on her laptop.

'Listen, thanks so much, Natalie.'

'Is this who you think killed Andy? This James?'

'I'm afraid not, but it *is* someone we need to locate urgently.' Xiu gave Miller a thumbs-up. She had an address. 'I'll be back in touch as soon as there's any news,' Miller said. 'I promise.' He thought about what he'd said earlier to Bob Perks; his stupid jokes and the reasons for them. He knew that, when it came to news, the likes of him and Natalie Bagnall were people for whom the funny bit at the end would never make the slightest bit of difference.

As Miller put his phone away, Janet arrived with the food. Xiu quickly put her laptop away and snatched at her knife and fork. 'We should get a shift on,' she said, pushing half a rissole into her mouth.

'Shouldn't be a problem,' Miller said. 'You won't finish it.'

TWENTY

Draper didn't know Blackpool *that* well – and he had knocked about in some very dodgy parts of the country with some seriously iffy individuals (several of whom he had later killed) – but even he was surprised by just how many people appeared to be living on the streets. Yeah, there were plenty of so-called 'street artists' or buskers making a racket in the touristy parts of town, but they didn't really count. He reckoned that most of them were actually students or lived at home with their parents and were only hanging about on the streets all day because it was easier than getting a proper job. Because they just happened to juggle a bit or know the chords to 'Wonderwall' or 'Summer of *bloody* '69'.

If someone was willing to stump up the money, he'd happily take on a kill one/kill one free type contract and knock off the lot of them.

The next idiot he heard singing 'Sweet Caroline' he'd do for nothing.

No, he was talking about the great many that were *properly* homeless, that dossed down in doorways with ratty dogs or made their beds out of the cardboard boxes used for fridge-freezers that they nicked from those massive skips behind Currys. The ones that genuinely had nowhere safe to go and slept out in the rain and snow after a day spent begging for enough to get a hot meal.

Those useless, scrounging tossers.

He'd seen a documentary about it once, so he knew that a lot of them had mental health problems or were escaping abusive relationships of one sort or another. If you caught him in a generous mood (you were more likely to win the lottery or see a Yeti in Tesco) he might even shrug and say that was fair enough. But Draper had been around a bit, and he knew that most of them ended up where they were because of drugs. Plain and simple. Ended up where they were supposed to, if you asked him.

There weren't too many people he liked very much, or even at all, but Draper really hated druggies. Obviously, everyone had a sneaky puff of wacky-backy when they were young or popped a pill to see what it was like, but normal people *stopped*. Normal people went 'Well, this is a bit rubbish' and got a life. Those weirdos who went 'Yeah, this is really great, I quite fancy doing something that will end up with me losing my family and all my money and will probably kill me' were people who deserved everything they got, because it wasn't like they didn't know what they were getting into, was it? It was like those morons who climbed into cages with lions or thought they could trot up mountains in a pair of carpet slippers.

It was natural selection in action.

He actually had more sympathy – which is to say *some* sympathy – for the people that sold the stuff, because, honest or not, they were just trying to make a living. They had a work ethic, at least. It hadn't stopped him putting one into the back of George Panaides's head, but that was only because *he* was trying to make a living too, so Dennis Draper wasn't going to feel remotely conflicted about *that*, thank you very much.

Mind you, Draper could say one thing for the town's community of smack-rats and stoners: they did tend to stick together. Credit where it was due and all that. Almost everyone he'd spoken to was very wary when it came to giving out information, especially about one of their own. Wary until Draper had got his wallet out, of course, but he admired that initial effort.

It hadn't taken very long.

He walked quickly along the prom, past the north pier towards the illuminations. He jogged across the tramlines, smiling at the young couple waving from one of the town's ubiquitous horse-drawn carriages, then cut left on to Church Street. There were two branches of Greggs within spitting (or throwing up) distance of the Winter Gardens, and because the zonked-out imbecile he'd spoken to hadn't been very specific, Draper knew he'd need to check out both.

'She loves them veggie sausage rolls, mate, so she's usually hanging about near one or the other.'

He found her in a doorway near the second one, competing with several other beggars working the foot traffic between the seafront and the shopping centre. Some were using kids, which Draper thought was a bloody disgrace, and a couple were shuffling up and down with their hands out and some chat about a 'hostel', which he and anyone else with an ounce of common sense knew meant 'heroin'. The girl herself was just sitting there quietly, head down with a rucksack next to her and a tatty hat on the floor. She looked up at anyone who walked past and muttered something about change, but she didn't push it, and when the passer-by had done exactly what they were supposed to do and passed by, she just nodded and lowered her head again.

Off her face already, Draper guessed.

It was a shame, because underneath all that grime she looked like she might even be quite a pretty little thing. Stupid, really, the things people did to mess their lives up. To piss other people off, to make enemies, to get themselves killed.

He stared into the window of a mobile phone shop for a while, then turned and wandered across. Halfway there, one of the girl's rivals tried her luck, but Draper just glared and the woman scuttled quickly away.

The girl looked up.

Draper smiled and dug into his pockets. He pulled out a handful of coins then bent to drop a fifty pence piece into the girl's hat.

Finn smiled back and raised a thumb.

'Cheers, mate . . . '

TWENTY-ONE

'Schwarzpool!' Miller nodded, pleased with himself.

Xiu looked at him. 'What?'

'That's what this place would have been called,' he said. 'You know, if Hitler had won. If we'd got a spinny-round, lighty-up swastika on top of the Tower and Germans goose-stepping along the prom.'

'But he didn't win,' Xiu said.

'I know he didn't. I'm just saying—'

'And why would the name be half in German and half in English?'

'It wouldn't,' Miller said. 'I just don't know what's German for pool . . .'

They were walking from the car towards a terraced house a few streets back from the front. Xiu took out her phone; swiped and stabbed as they approached the address.

'There are lots of German words for pool,' she said, scrolling through her search results. 'It depends on what sort of pool we're talking about. Swimming pool, typing pool, pool like snooker . . .'

'Well, it's not one of those, is it?'

'I'd go with ... *Tümpel*, then.'

'Schwarztümpel!' Miller began to strum an invisible uku-
lele, then proceeded to startle a passing dog-walker with what
was actually a pretty decent George Formby impression.
'With me little stick of Schwarztümpel rock. Aye up, turned
out shite again ... '

Xiu opened the front gate. They took out their IDs as
they walked up the narrow path, then stopped to stare at
the front door or, more specifically, the metal ramp leading up to it.

'Does he live on his own?' Miller asked.

Xiu said, 'No idea,' and rang the doorbell.

When the door was opened, Miller stared at the property's
occupant as though he'd never seen a man in a wheelchair
before. Or even a wheelchair.

The man in the wheelchair stared back.

Xiu held up her ID and introduced herself and Miller. 'Are
you James Holloway?'

'Yeah,' James Holloway said. 'Is there a problem?'

'Can we come in?'

Miller looked at her. 'Is there any point?'

'Miller!'

'Well, he's clearly not the—'

Xiu smiled at Holloway. 'Can we ... ?'

Holloway moved back to allow them in and they followed
him into a spacious living room. 5 Live Sport was playing on a
radio somewhere; a conversation about curling, of all things, to
which, on any other occasion, Miller might have made one or
two salty contributions – pointing out to no one in particular
that anything which involved sweeping could not possibly be
a sport – but now was probably not the time.

He and Xiu sat together on a small sofa and Holloway wheeled himself into a position directly in front of them.

'What's this about?' he asked.

Miller leaned forward. 'I don't want to pry and I'm sorry if this sounds in any way insensitive, but I don't suppose there's any possibility that whatever happened to put you ... you know ...'

'In a wheelchair.'

'Right.'

'A car accident.'

'Right, thank you. A car accident which I'm guessing didn't happen in the last three days?'

Holloway looked at Xiu. 'Is he really a detective?'

'It was a long shot.' Miller stood up, ready to go. 'Clutching at straws, really. Sorry.'

'Mr Holloway,' Xiu said, 'do you remember a kid you were at school with named Andrew Bagnall?'

Miller sighed and sat down again.

'I remember the name,' Holloway said. 'But not the kid.'

'You were in the same class. Bagnall ...'

Holloway thought about it. 'OK, yeah, I *think* I might know who you mean. Strange lad.'

'So, you weren't a friend of his?'

'If I remember rightly, he didn't have many friends. Like I said, he was a bit strange. Always had his head in a book.'

'What a weirdo,' Miller said.

'Do you remember anyone he hung about with?'

'I don't, no.'

Miller stared pointedly at Xiu, then stood up again. 'Sorry to have wasted your time,' he said. Then rather more quietly, 'And ours.'

'OK, then.' Xiu stood up, too.

'My brother might remember.'

'Why would he remember?' Xiu asked.

'I *think* Andy Bagnall played football and my brother was in the school football team, so . . . it's just a thought.'

'Will you ask him?'

'Yeah, I can call him.' Holloway turned his chair and moved towards the door. 'I'll have to leave a message, mind; he never answers his bloody phone, and he's not always the best at getting back to you.'

'Could you tell him it's urgent?'

Holloway shrugged. 'OK.'

'Not as a ruse to get him to call you back,' Miller said. 'But because it really is urgent.'

'Yeah, I get it.'

'I mean *properly* urgent. Not urgent like a business meeting's urgent or an urgent dash to the chippy before they run out of haddock. Urgent as in murderous psychopaths with guns and people having their hands chopped off for shits and giggles.' Miller nodded and smiled. 'That kind of urgent.'

The colour drained from Holloway's face.

Miller turned to see Xiu staring at him. '*What?* I just want to make sure he knows this is somewhat pressing.'

Walking back to the car, Xiu said, 'What the hell was that all about?'

'Sorry?'

'That . . . performance.'

'Well, like I said—'

'You scared the poor bloke half to death, and I don't know *what* you thought you were doing when he answered the door.'

'OK, so I might have been a little . . . brusque.'

'Brusque?'

'Curt, then. I was curt.'

'You were rude, Miller.'

'Look, I might not be the finest detective in the world – though I'm certainly in the top half-dozen – but it didn't take a genius to work out that he wasn't the lad we're looking for. The wheelchair was the big clue, in case you missed it. I was just trying to keep things moving along because time is not exactly on our side.'

'It was worth talking to him,' Xiu said. 'He might well have known the lad we're after and maybe his brother will come up with something.' She keyed the fob on the car key to unlock the doors.

Miller walked around to the passenger side and nodded back towards the house. 'You talk about *me* being rude . . .'

'Because you were.'

'There wasn't even a suggestion of tea in there. Never mind a biscuit.'

'*What?*' Xiu stared at him across the roof of the car. 'I thought we were pushed for time.'

'We are.' Miller opened the door. 'But politeness costs nothing.'

Xiu struggled to find the words, but the twitch around her eye spoke volumes.

TWENTY-TWO

Miller sat on the sofa with Fred curled against his neck, while Ginger rolled around the room in her plastic ball. Miller had put *Revolver* on, which was just about his favourite Beatles album, even when Ringo's percussive efforts were being subtly undermined by various arrhythmic clatterings and crashes as Ginger's ball careered into chair legs and skirting boards.

Miller guessed that John would have quite liked it.

'You *were* pretty rude,' Alex said, without turning round. She was sitting on a chair by the window. It was dark outside, but she'd always liked staring out at the beacons on the distant trawlers and cruise ships; the flickers of light from North Wales and the Isle of Man on a clear night.

'Was I?'

'Not as rude as you can be, but yes, I think so.'

'I didn't mean to be,' Miller said.

'I know you didn't.' There was a smile in her voice. 'You never do.'

Miller rubbed his cheek against Ginger's fur and thought about it. Yes, the fact that James Holloway was in a wheelchair so had clearly not been the James they were looking for was the reason Miller had been frustrated and impatient and – he was willing to concede – a bit rude. But did the fact that the man was in a wheelchair make what Miller had said any *ruder*? He wasn't convinced that it did. He'd once been *very* rude to a man with no legs and had got into an ugly slanging match a few months earlier with a blind bloke (involving a number of unpleasant and thankfully unseen gestures) who Miller thought had been a bit shouty with his guide dog. In point of fact, Miller could and *would* proudly state that, at one time or another, he'd upset people of every shape, size, race, creed, colour and sexual persuasion. There were many things Miller knew he could be accused of – though he didn't like to dwell on them – but when it came to falling out with folk, he was an equal opportunities offender.

Did that make what he'd said to Holloway all right?

He wasn't sure . . .

'It's hard,' he said. 'Without you around to keep me in check.'

'Well, you've got Posh to do that now.'

Miller grunted, trying to sound non-committal, but knowing he was fooling nobody; least of all Alex. The truth was that he'd grown to like Xiu's blank stares and twitches of disapproval. He valued her professional opinion more than anyone else's and, despite all evidence to the contrary, he wanted her to think well of him.

He wasn't sure that was exactly working out.

He needed to go easy with the jokes and the heavy-metal comments.

'You need to go easy with the jokes and the heavy-metal comments,' Alex said.

'I *know*.' Miller sighed and eased himself up. He carried Ginger back to the playpen and laid her gently back on her bed of straw, then chased after a runaway Fred and did the same. 'I showed her the video,' he said. 'Posh.'

Now, Alex turned round.

'"It could be a lot of things." That's what she said.'

Alex nodded. She walked past him and sat down.

'She's right, obviously, but it was definitely money in that envelope, wasn't it?' Miller waited. He knew there was next to no chance that Alex would respond, not to questions like this, but he always waited. 'I'm saying, it wasn't raffle tickets that bloke was giving you, was it?'

Alex looked . . . defiant, suddenly. Defiant like she'd been that night at Accrington Town Hall when they were leading with one dance to go and Sue Dixon had tried to psych her out by saying she was going to mess up her quickstep. Like when she turned her ankle during a salsa at the Palace in Wigan and they won anyway. Defiant like she'd been when her arse of a DCI had told her she was never going to make inspector.

They stared at each other and the seconds ticked by . . .

The doorbell rang.

'Saved by the bell,' Miller said.

'Saved from what?'

Miller shrugged. 'I don't know. It just always sounds dramatic.' He walked towards the front door, turning when he was halfway there to see that Alex had gone. He said, 'Suit yourself,' but something about the speed with which she'd absented herself made Miller apprehensive. He moved a lot faster towards the door, anxious suddenly without knowing why.

Until he opened it.

Finn was panting heavily, as though she'd been running. When she lifted her head, one hand was pressed to her face and there was blood running through her fingers.

Miller said, 'Christ,' and reached out, but she ducked under his arm and ran into the house. He called after her as she hurried into the toilet and could do nothing but wait, pacing and jittery, until she emerged a few minutes later with a wad of tissue pressed to her nose.

'Are you OK?'

She walked past him and dropped onto the sofa, lowered her head and sobbed for a minute or so. Miller sat down next to her and rubbed her arm, but she didn't seem to notice.

'Some bloke,' she said, eventually.

'What bloke?'

'I'd seen him this afternoon, in the precinct. He gave me some money. Then . . .'

Miller's hand clenched into a fist. 'Then *what*?'

'I was just mooching around behind the aquarium, looking for somewhere to sleep and he came out of nowhere.' She was staring at the carpet as she spoke, shaky suddenly, as if she was going into shock. 'He grabbed me and turned me round and smashed my face against a wall. He had hold of my hair and he just kept pushing. Talking about some brief-case . . . did I have it, did I know where it was, had I hidden it somewhere?'

Now Miller knew *exactly* what bloke.

'I told him I didn't know what he was talking about, but he kept pushing even harder and whispering all the things he was going to do to me. So I kept telling him, *screaming* at him, until he just stopped and when I turned round he'd gone.'

Why had Draper targeted Finn?

It didn't matter why.

'He mentioned Andy's name, too.' She turned to look at him. 'Is this something to do with why Andy was so frightened?' She saw Miller hesitate and her eyes widened. 'Was this the bloke that killed Andy?'

Miller nodded. 'His name's Draper and I'm going to find him. OK? I promise he'll never hurt you again—'

'Why haven't you caught him *already*?'

'It's complicated.' He reached out in vain as Finn jumped to her feet and picked up her rucksack. 'Where are you going?'

'I'm going back ... *out*.'

Miller jumped up too and moved to stand between her and the door. 'Oh no you're not.'

Finn hoisted her rucksack on to her shoulder and sniffed. There was still a clot of blood caked beneath her nose. 'You think I'm scared?'

Miller recognised that fierceness, or her attempt at projecting it. She could be tough when she needed to be and he knew that she *often* needed to be, but he saw what was underneath, too.

She was so like her mother.

Alex had been every bit as strong as *she* needed to be, but Miller had seen the tears often enough at the end of a difficult day.

'You need to stay here,' Miller said.

Finn shook her head.

'You really think I'm letting you go back out on the streets tonight?'

'You can't make me do anything.'

'I'll arrest you if I have to.' Miller pointed. 'You've got drugs in that rucksack, right?'

She began to cry again, silently this time, and the rucksack slipped from her shoulder. 'I can't stay here.' She looked around the room as though she'd never seen it before, wringing her hands, then raising them to claw at her hair. '*Please,* Miller. Don't make me stay here.'

TWENTY-THREE

The woman who ran the guesthouse of which Dennis Draper was unlucky enough to be a resident had collared him on his way back in. Her name was Isla (it was written on a badge in felt-tip) and she'd stepped out from her room on the ground floor just as Draper was about to head up the stairs. She'd dolled herself up since he'd last seen her – bright red lippy, a flowery headscarf and some bizarre neckerchief-type thing – and had smiled at Draper in a way which frankly put the wind up him a bit.

'Hola, Señor Diaz.'

Draper had blinked, then said 'Hola' right back at her, desperately hoping that it was as much Spanish as the woman knew, because it was certainly as much as he did.

She had then switched – thankfully – to English, speaking slowly and loudly, confusing – as so many people did – being foreign with being an idiot. 'I just wanted to check that everything is satisfactory with your room.'

Draper had been standing there, wishing he knew the

Spanish for 'satisfactory my arse', when it had finally dawned on him that Isla was flirting. That it was a lot more than just a late-night conversation she was after. He could hardly blame her – even if she was very much barking up the wrong tree – because she was only flesh and blood after all and maybe he'd overdone the mean and moody Latin thing. She was giving him the 'concerned landlady' bit when all the time she wanted nothing more than to follow him upstairs, get her posh frock off and fiddle about like his knackers were maracas.

Well, he couldn't be having that, obviously. Not with a *woman*, no thank you very much, and not with anyone when he was working.

So, he had just smiled right back at the fruity landlady, given it his best Julio Iglesias – 'Ees very nice, gracias, señora' – then legged it up to his room three stairs at a time.

Now, lying on the bed, thumbing the TV remote and bemoaning the fact that cheap digs never had any porno channels, 'Diego Diaz' tried to come up with an alias for whatever job came next. Something French, he thought: Didier, maybe? Or he could just pronounce David the French way, as if it was spelled Daveed? It was fun pretending to be foreign; it spiced things up a bit, but then again the language thing might catch him out one day, as it had nearly done with Up For It Isla, so in the end he decided it was probably best to avoid the whole foreigner thing from now on.

Spirit of Brexit and all that.

Besides, he wouldn't need another name until he had another job and he wasn't going *anywhere* until this one was put to bed and he got paid. Until he had hold of that effing briefcase.

Draper quickly lost interest in the TV and lay there, restless and more than a little confused, asking himself why he hadn't killed the homeless girl. He wondered if it was down to the fact that he'd met her earlier in the day, when he'd given her money and she'd smiled at him. Was it because they'd made a connection?

Whatever the hell a *connection* was.

In the end, he decided it was just because he'd reckoned the girl had been telling the truth and it would have been a bit over the top – even for him – to kill her because she *didn't* have the briefcase. Of course, Bagnall hadn't had it either, but he'd got what was coming because he was the one who'd caused all the trouble in the first place. Pretending he was interested in those toilets while his mate was pinching the sodding case.

His elusive bloody mate.

That was who Draper would be going after next.

He'd found some backstreet scally who promised to unlock Bagnall's phone for fifty quid (Draper had beaten him down from seventy-five) so by tomorrow afternoon, with a bit of luck, he'd have all the information he needed and it would all be over soon enough after that. For Bagnall's mate, anyway, because case or no case there was only one way that bit of business would be ending up.

Half an hour later, as he was drifting off to sleep, the perfect name popped into his head, and he wondered why he'd never thought of it before.

De'Ath.

That was an actual name, wasn't it?

Daniel or Desmond or whatever, but more importantly he'd have the perfect nickname too. 'Sudden', because of the way he struck without warning, coming at his targets out of nowhere.

So he'd be 'Sudden De'Ath'. Like sudden death. It was funny.

He didn't laugh, nothing like that. Draper almost never laughed out loud and, when he did, it was always because of something bad happening to someone else. Something fatal more often than not. He was smiling though, satisfied as he turned over and closed his eyes again, because that poxy briefcase thief, whose name he would know soon enough, was definitely not going to find it remotely amusing.

TWENTY-FOUR

It was a stupidly early hour to be knocking on someone's front door, but Miller knew the occupants of the house well enough to be certain they would already be up and about. Bright-eyed (cataracts notwithstanding), bushy-tailed and breakfasted already. Standing on the freshly blackened doorstep, admiring the hanging baskets and perfectly kept pots, he couldn't help but wonder why people, when they reached old age, got up earlier and earlier, when they had less and less to do? Was there really much point in kicking off your duvet at six in the morning only to get dressed, toddle downstairs for a boiled egg, then fall asleep in front of a television that was turned up far too loud?

Well yes, of course there was.

The reason was obvious, if somewhat depressing. It might even have been subconscious, Miller decided, but most people inevitably made adjustments once booking a holiday or buying green bananas became a gamble; when time was no longer on their side (if it had ever been) and it would be a terrible waste to sleep what was left of it away.

They seized the day.

It made perfect sense, he supposed, even if for many of them the actual seizing involved a trip to the garden centre before hurrying home in time for *Bargain Hunt*.

Miller was thinking about his mother, wondering when he might next get up to Manchester to see her, when Mary answered the door. She said, 'Good morning, Declan,' then leaned forward to peer at him. 'You're looking ever so tired.'

'I didn't get a lot of sleep,' Miller said.

'Of course you didn't, love.'

'How's she doing?'

'Still dead to the world,' Mary said. 'We thought we should let her sleep as long as she can.'

Howard lumbered up the hallway behind her, dressed in a jacket and tie as if he was all set to go to work. He gave Miller a thumbs-up. 'No need to fret, lad. She's tough as old boots that girl. She'll be right as ninepence.'

'Do you want to come in?' Mary asked. 'We've got kippers in the fridge.'

'I need to crack on, but thanks. And thanks for coming to the rescue last night.'

'Don't be daft,' Howard said.

It had been Howard who had driven over as soon as Miller had called. He was actually a terrible driver who pranged their Vauxhall Corsa on a regular basis, but Mary had already downed a couple of gins by the time Miller rang, so there wasn't a lot of choice in the matter. Miller hoped that Finn's journey back to Howard and Mary's place had been less traumatic than the assault she'd suffered a few hours before, but there probably hadn't been a great deal in it.

'Right, then.' Miller took a step back and put his crash helmet on, but Mary moved forward to join him.

'I meant to say sorry.' She laid a hand on his arm. 'For being a bit insensitive the other night at practice and banging on about that woman who wants to join. I really don't know what I was thinking.'

Miller lifted his visor.

'The woman who used to be a traffic warden, remember? I won't make any arrangements until you're good and ready.'

'Actually, I think *I* was being *over*-sensitive,' Miller said. 'So go right ahead and ask Lovely Rita Meter Maid to come along.'

'Her name's Veronica,' Mary said.

Miller smiled and shrugged. 'Fresh blood is always good, right? Well, it can be a bit icky at a crime scene, but you know what I mean.'

Now, Howard stepped forward, grinning. 'What with her being an ex-traffic warden, maybe she can hand out fixed penalty notices if one of us messes up a dance or whatever. Foxtrot fines or . . . tango tickets!'

'You silly old sod,' Mary said. She moved back to punch her husband on the arm, shaking her head and giggling like a girl.

Miller walked back to his moped, leaving the pair of them laughing. He guessed that however you chose to seize the day, if you could spend it with someone you still found hilarious after forty-odd years of marriage, it was going to be a good one.

The desk sergeant nodded down at the briefcase (£31.99 from TK Maxx) that Miller was carrying somewhat showily as he walked into the station. Miller held it up, said, 'Tuna mayonnaise, a bag of Quavers and a can of Vimto,' and hurried on through to the incident room. He made sure everyone in there got a good look at the case too, and was still carrying it fifteen minutes later when he walked into the briefing room.

He saw Xiu clock it and winked.

Tim Sullivan raised a hand to call those around the table to attention, a clear message that made everyone immediately fall silent, all except a member of the team's civilian staff who had obviously been deep in private conversation with a colleague.

'Hashtag, *Sex-God . . .*' He looked up to see everyone staring and mumbled an apology.

'Right . . . so, where are we with Dennis Draper?' Sullivan asked. The photograph from the hospital's CCTV was on the screen behind him.

'Not a sniff of him,' Clough said. 'Gone to ground, looks like.'

'Wrong,' Miller said. 'He assaulted a young homeless girl last night, on waste ground behind the aquarium.'

'That's great!' Sullivan said.

'*What?*'

'Well, not great, obviously, I just mean . . . let's get her in and get a statement.'

'Not going to happen,' Miller said.

'What's this girl's name?'

Miller waved Sullivan's question away. 'She came to me because she's one of my confidential informants and she would rather that her name is kept out of the investigation. I promised her that we'd respect that.'

Miller saw that Xiu was staring at him. She knew exactly who he was talking about even if nobody else did.

'She made a verbal statement, which is all we're going to get, but I don't think it much matters one way or another. When we catch Draper, slapping an extra assault charge on top of umpteen murders isn't going to make a great deal of differ-ence, is it? Life, or life plus six months . . . either way he's not going to be around to pick up his pension.'

Sullivan thought about it, then nodded as if he'd already come to the same conclusion himself. 'Right, so we move forward. Obviously a terrible experience for the girl concerned, but at least we know now that our prime suspect hasn't gone anywhere.'

'Of course he hasn't,' Miller said. 'He wants that briefcase back. Cutler's denying all knowledge, obviously, and even if they aren't actually Panaides's hands, Cutler doesn't know that, does he? Either way, that case is the proof that Draper carried out a murder on Cutler's behalf and Draper won't get paid until he produces it.'

Sullivan nodded again. This was solid stuff and the team was making progress. A team that could only ever be as good as the officer in charge.

It was Andrea Fuller who asked the obvious question.

'Why attack a homeless girl, though?'

'It turns out that she knew Andrew Bagnall,' Miller said. 'Smoked a bit of weed with him now and again. My guess is that he found something at Bagnall's flat after he killed him that made him think the girl might have the briefcase. Or know who did.'

'So, what's our next move?' Clough asked.

Miller was fairly sure that Clough's next move would involve a trip to the pie shop or a nice lie down, but said nothing. Instead, he looked to their esteemed leader for guidance.

'We flush him out.' Sullivan pointed to the picture behind him. 'This photograph is on the front page of today's *Gazette*, the *Lancashire Evening Post* and the *Pendle Express*, on top of which it will be shown on all today's local news bulletins. Draper can't stay hidden for ever, not with that kind of media saturation.'

'Where's he staying?' Fuller asked.

Sullivan pointed. 'Is the correct question! With a mate? Let's work through all known associates. A hotel? Let's check them all out.'

'The bloke's a sleazebag,' Miller said. 'He stinks of it and I don't think he'd risk drawing attention to himself by staying anywhere half decent. I reckon he'd go somewhere a bit more downmarket, where he's more likely to fit in. A scuzzy guesthouse, maybe ...'

'So, maybe we focus on the scuzzy guesthouses,' Sullivan said.

Clough puffed out his cheeks. 'Have you any idea how many of them there are in this town?'

'Seven hundred and thirty-four,' Miller said.

'Seriously?'

'How the bloody hell should I know?'

Sullivan was pacing now, fired up and buzzing at the way his team was gelling and working together, but even a machine as finely oiled as this one needed someone to press the buttons. He pointed at Fuller again. 'Andrea, draw up a list and organise teams. Get Clough to give you a hand ...'

As soon as the briefing had finished, Xiu drew Miller into a corner.

'Is Finn OK?'

'She was upset,' Miller said. 'Scared and a bit battered and bruised, but no major damage, thank God. Staying with some friends.'

Xiu nodded, obviously relieved to hear it. They walked out of the incident room into the lobby. 'Are *you* OK?'

'Yeah, I'm grand.' Miller could see the concern on her face. She knew that he and Finn were close, though not quite how close. Or why.

It was something else he should get around to telling her one of these days.

'That photo of Draper being everywhere.' Xiu looked worried. 'Now he's going to know we're after him.'

'Oh, I think he's figured that out,' Miller said.

'Of course, but now he's going to have to speed things up, isn't he? He knows Finn hasn't got the case, so the only other option is Bagnall's friend.'

'Let's hope he's no closer to identifying him than we are.'

'He's got Bagnall's phone,' Xiu said. 'Remember?'

'You're a little ray of sunshine,' Miller said.

They stood together in silence for a minute, until Xiu said, 'We've got that photo, though. The school photo.' She began to nod, excited. 'We just need to trace everyone in it and ...' She stopped when she saw Miller's expression, like she'd suggested the earth might be flat.

'So we trace then interview another thirty-odd people as quickly as possible, on top of popping round to every one-star hotel and flophouse in Schwarztümpel? How many people do you think there are on this team? We could barely organise a five-a-side game.' Miller shook his head, then raised it to stare up the steep staircase leading to the first floor.

Xiu was watching him. 'What Draper did to Finn ...'

'What about it?'

'You're not going to make this personal, are you?'

'Me?' Miller tried to look offended. 'How could you even—?'

'You have to promise me that, Miller. If you make it personal you won't do a good job, and ...' She shook her head as though this was painful to admit. 'I need you at your best.'

'You *need* me, Posh?' He sniffed. 'I may just shed a tear.'

'Oh, grow up, Miller.'

'It goes without saying that my worst is probably far better than most people's best,' Miller said. 'Nonetheless, I promise not to make this personal. OK?' He looked up at those hard, steep stairs again. He was planning to visit a team on the second floor anyway, but he couldn't help thinking that, once he had the man they were after in custody, it would be the ideal staircase down which Dennis Draper might accidentally tumble.

TWENTY-FIVE

Frank Bardsley had a lot to think about.

In an ideal world, he'd be spending the day on the phone to his distribution team to confirm that adequate supplies of foot-long spicy sausages reached every branch in time for the launch of his brand new 'Bardsley's Bangers' range. At the same time, to guarantee the launch went smoothly, he'd be checking in with other 'associates' to ensure that the proprietors of certain rival businesses – A Turn For the Würst in Preston and The Weiner Takes It All in Clitheroe – were busy dealing with the theft of two delivery vans and the mysterious fires at their meat suppliers' warehouses. As it was, he had all this to deal with on top of his ongoing mathematics conundrum.

The George Panaides problem.

It was a problem he had already taken steps to solve, of course, but now it appeared that a different and altogether less satisfactory solution might be on the cards.

Frank dropped his copy of that morning's *Gazette* onto the

table and stared down at the photograph of Dennis Draper on the front page; a photograph that sat, somewhat ironically, above a half-page full-colour advert for today's Bardsley's Bangers bonanza.

FREE CHEESY CHIPS WITH EVERY BANGER – FOR ONE DAY ONLY!

A hundred and fifty quid that ad had cost him, but even so, all Frank could think about was the photo of the man he was sure had shot George. The man whose face was now plastered all over the media and who was obviously being hunted by every copper in the county.

Draper being arrested would not be a terrible result (even if Draper himself would not be overly thrilled), but it would not make things equal.

Frank had spoken to Martin Molineux first thing. Torchy had seen the picture too – it was on Granada news apparently – and had assured him that he was on the case, that he would get the job done. Frank had tried to stay calm while stressing the urgency of the situation.

'This is for George, remember.'

'I know it's for George. Why do you think I've already bought a new twenty-one-inch cutting torch with a built-in flashback arrestor?'

'Well, I hope you get to use it sooner than later.'

'Calm down, Frank, I'm on it . . .'

It had already crossed Frank's mind that Wayne Cutler might be on it, too, because Frank had read about the murder of that lad in Blackpool a few days before. He'd put two and two together and the answer to that simple sum was that the likes of Cutler would not want a loose cannon like Draper causing havoc all over the shop, getting himself nicked and naming names.

If Cutler got to Draper before Molineux did, that wouldn't be the worst outcome in the world either, but it still wouldn't feel right. It wouldn't add up, simple as that. On top of which, Frank had already paid Torchy a hefty deposit and he really didn't fancy asking for his money back.

Why was everything so buggering complicated?

Like all *that* wasn't enough to give Frank an ulcer and make him wish he'd stuck to doling out burger and chips from the back of a transit van, Maureen was really starting to kick off. The truth was, she'd been a bit funny even before George was killed, but since then there'd been no dealing with her.

She certainly wasn't the woman he'd married.

Even as he thought it, Frank could hear her complaining that *he* wasn't the man *she'd* married. No, he bloody well wasn't, because he was a lot richer and a damn sight more successful. He was the Fast-Food King of Preston (and the surrounding area), so what was she moaning about?

Perfectly on cue, the door to Frank's office opened and Maureen marched in with her hat and coat on. She had her bag over her arm and a face on her that Frank did not like the look of at all.

'We're going out for the day,' she said.

'We're *what*?'

'Come on, look lively. We're going for an adventure.'

'Going where?'

'I don't much care, Frank. We could drive out to a nice country pub, maybe, go for a walk, then get a ploughman's. Or we could nip down the Fishergate, see what's in the sales and there's that falconry centre on the A59, we've been saying we'd give that a go for ages.'

'Have we?'

'It doesn't matter. Let's just *do* something.'

'But . . .' For the second time that day Frank was trying to stay calm. 'This is a big day. It's the Bardsley's Bangers launch.'

'I know very well what day it is,' Maureen said. 'But you've got a team, haven't you? You can *delegate*.'

'I need to be on top of things, Maureen. I need to be here.'

'And what about what I need, Frank?'

'I hear you, love. Just not today.'

'I don't think you're hearing me at all.'

'We'll do something tomorrow, I promise. Anything you fancy—'

Maureen was already on her way out. She slammed the door behind her then shouted through it, stifling a sob. 'What about what *I* need?'

Frank sat back and shut his eyes. When he opened them again, Dennis Draper was still staring up from the front page of the paper, there were five thousand foot-long sausages waiting to be distributed the length and breadth of Lancashire and his wife was still angry with him. She clearly needed *something* and lately that was all she seemed to be saying in one way or another, but he didn't actually know what the something was. He was damn sure it wasn't a ploughman's lunch or a chuffing falconry display, but beyond that, Frank was clueless.

What was he doing wrong?

He let out a long-suffering sigh and picked up the phone, because it was time to get back to business. Halfway through his call to a vacuum-packing plant in Ribchester, Frank decided that, when he wasn't marshalling several dozen delivery drivers or transferring funds to a pair of local arsonists, he'd try and find ten minutes to get online and book himself and Maureen a fortnight in Mauritius.

TWENTY-SIX

The officers and civilian staff who worked in the homicide unit based two floors above Miller's were well used to the sight of Miller bowling in like he owned the place. Though Miller knew full well that he was *persona non grata* with the squad investigating his wife's murder, he could never stay away very long. He was like a moth drawn inexorably to the white-hot flame of their investigation, though a more suitable analogy – considering how little he thought of said investigation – would have been a dog returning to its own vomit. A dog whose tail was usually wagging because, however frustrated and enraged Miller felt about what DCI Lindsey Forgeham's team were actually doing – or rather not doing – to catch Alex's killer, he'd begun to get a perverse kick out of being made to feel so hugely unwelcome.

It put a spring in his step that even Mary would have applauded.

Though she would then have asked why he couldn't apply the same sort of jauntiness to his foxtrot, so ... swings and roundabouts.

Whistling as he ambled across the incident room towards Forgeham's office at the end of the day, Miller was greeted by the same gallery of horror-struck expressions and barrage of muttered curses as usual. He felt like he'd gate-crashed a funeral wearing a Grim Reaper costume, and decided that should any of these halfwits get hit by a bus on the way home he would immediately go out and buy one for the occasion.

He walked up to Forgeham's door.

'Oh no you don't . . . '

A young detective he'd had the misfortune of encountering several times before stepped in front of him. The skinny, job-pissed idiot had tried to prevent Miller getting into Forgeham's office on at least one previous occasion, like some kind of sentinel in a cheap suit.

'What are you then?' Miller asked. 'The early warning system?'

The detective shook his head and barked out a laugh. 'I was here before you, that's all. I need a quick word with the boss.' He knocked on the door, then held up a file as if it contained answers to all the mysteries of the universe, though it was probably just an expenses claim.

They stood awkwardly for a few seconds, waiting for the door to be opened.

'Urgent, is it?' Miller nodded down at the file.

'I just need a signature.'

'Oh, right.' Miller smiled. 'Getting approval for all the overtime you've been working on the Alex Miller murder.' He reached across to pat the man on the shoulder. 'Yeah, you go right ahead, mate, because you've earned it. You and the rest of Lancashire's finest must be absolutely knackered.'

The detective had the good grace to redden a little and was

momentarily lost for words when Lindsey Forgeham opened her door and stared at the two of them, confused.

'Ma'am,' the detective said eventually. He held up the file. 'I just need you to sign off on this.'

Forgeham nodded then looked at Miller. 'Right ... let me just deal with DC Palmer's paperwork.' Her tone darkened. 'Then I'll deal with you.'

With the door still open, Miller watched Palmer follow Forgeham back into the office. He saw the DCI take papers from the file and flick through them, while the young DC waited, shifting from foot to foot, clearly impatient because the work he needed to get back to was *so* important.

For a few ridiculous moments, Miller wondered if any of the paperwork *might* relate to Alex's murder. Then he remembered where he was and who he was dealing with and reminded himself that it was more likely to contain a confession from the Zodiac Killer or a break in the Jack the Ripper case.

As soon as Palmer had emerged, head down, and walked quickly away towards his desk, Forgeham beckoned Miller in and told him to close the door behind him.

'You can't keep doing this,' she said.

Miller sat down. 'I know.'

'So why are you doing it? Why do you keep coming up here when you know you can't be anywhere near this investigation?'

'I can't help myself.'

Forgeham nodded, took off her glasses. 'Look, I know you're still grieving, and I *do* understand—'

'I can't help myself ... because I think I'm in love with you.'

'*What?*'

'I've tried to fight it ... my God, I've tried. I keep telling myself it's wrong, but it doesn't do any good. It's like this terrible, wonderful sickness and the fact is that I don't care that it's wrong any more. I know what people will say about us, but I don't care about that either. I don't care about anything but you, DCI Forgeham. Oh, I've tried to stay professional, but I've examined this case thoroughly and all the evidence points to the fact that I'm madly in love with you, ma'am. Stupidly, insanely—'

Forgeham held up a hand and put her glasses back on. Now *she* was blushing, but she lowered her head and spent a few seconds adjusting papers on her desk until she'd recovered herself. 'Have you finished?'

'Yes.' Miller lowered his head for a moment or two, then raised it and began to declaim again. 'I'm finished with lying to myself and denying my feelings when the truth is—'

'That's enough, DS Miller.'

Miller shrugged and smiled. 'Let me down gently, why don't you?'

'We've got nothing.' Forgeham said it matter-of-factly. 'On your wife's murder. That's what you came up here for, right?'

'*Still* got nothing, you mean.'

'No new witness statements, no fresh leads, no new forensic evidence. I wish I could tell you that we have and I *really* wish you'd believe that I'm every bit as frustrated about it as you are.'

Miller nodded, thinking about the new evidence that was sitting in his front room. The photographs and the video. He told himself again that he was doing the right thing by not handing them over. He needed to keep telling himself.

'Actually, I got some fresh information the other day,' he said.

'From who?'

'Ralph Massey.'

'Right,' Forgeham said. 'Well, because you're a good detective you'll obviously have taken that with more than a pinch of salt.'

'Not really,' Miller said. 'He implied that he knew something and I believed him.'

'Do you not think we've looked at Massey? And at Cutler?'

'I'm not sure you've looked hard enough.'

Forgeham stood up. 'I think we're about done.'

'Just answer me this, Lindsey.' Miller stared up at her. 'Can you look me in the eye and promise me that Alex's case is still ongoing? I mean, *really* ongoing? That she hasn't been ... shoved on the back burner.'

Forgeham sat down again and took a few seconds. 'I never worked with your wife, but I understand she was a good detective and that still counts for something. Now, whatever you think of me, so am I ... so I really don't think I need to dignify your question with an answer. Are we clear, DS Miller?'

Forgeham waited.

'We're clear,' Miller said.

'Good. So you know what happens now, yes?'

'Of course I do. You entertain a few wistful thoughts about my declaration of love, then you get on the phone and make a complaint to my DCI, which you subsequently put in writing.'

'That's right, and because Susan Akers is also a good detective, she'll do what she's supposed to and take that complaint higher up. That will add another black mark to your force disciplinary record which, if it gets any blacker, might eventually cost you your job.' She looked at him and shook her head. 'And you really don't care, do you?'

'Not even a little bit,' Miller said.

TWENTY-SEVEN

Draper thought it was gobsmacking and frankly ridiculous – the stuff these youngsters kept on their phones. He'd heard people say that losing their phone, or even being without it for a couple of days, would be 'like, the worst thing in the world' because their whole life was on there and, looking through the mobile he'd paid to have unlocked, he could well believe it.

Bloody idiots.

It wasn't as if Draper didn't have a phone himself (he had at least half a dozen) but they just did what phones were supposed to do. They made and received calls and (occasionally) texts, but that was about it. He had a computer for all the other important stuff: emails and googling and porn. He also had a diary and a wristwatch and a brain that could hold several bits of information in it at once, because he wasn't an imbecile.

Clearly, Andy Bagnall wouldn't be too worried right now about not having his phone, but judging by all the stuff Draper had found on there, at any other time he'd have been frantic with worry. You know, if Draper hadn't put that bag over his head.

There were endless screens crammed with different apps and games, plus photos, videos and more music than anyone would ever have a chance to listen to. There were dozens of books (entire novels, for heaven's sake) with links to hundreds of articles about movies and TV shows. There were stories he'd written himself about being some sort of super-cool secret agent or something (Draper was unable to get past the first few lines). There were gizmos to monitor weight loss and heart rate and recipes for healthy eating and ... Draper gave up ploughing through it all in the end.

Crucially, there were contacts and there were voice messages.

Listening to the most recent message – left just a few hours before Draper had paid Bagnall a visit three nights earlier – confirmed his theory that Bagnall's friend could easily have gone round there and retrieved the case before Draper had got there himself. Draper might only have missed the jammy beggar by a matter of minutes.

Well, now he had most of the details he needed and the jammy beggar was about to run out of jam. Draper might have a *bit* more work to do to get the lad's address, but before he went down that road he reckoned the obvious option was simply to ask for it. It couldn't hurt, could it?

He could be perfectly reasonable, if he needed to be.

Having managed to nip up to his room without encountering his landlady, Draper lay back on the bed and made the call.

It went unanswered, so he waited a minute and rang again.

'Hello ... ?' There'd been fifteen seconds of breathing and gulping before Keith Slack had actually said anything. 'Who's this?'

'Well, seeing as I'm calling from your dead friend's phone, why don't you take a wild stab in the dark?'

'Christ.'

'Not even close, Keith.'

There was more gulping. 'What do you want?'

'Nothing too complicated,' Draper said. 'Just the briefcase. The one you stole.'

'I haven't got it,' Slack spluttered. 'Andy had it.'

'Well, he certainly hadn't got it when I called round. So, if he didn't have it and you haven't got it, who the hell *has* got it?'

'I don't know,' Slack said. 'I swear I don't know.'

'I don't believe you.'

'Please—'

'Last chance, Keith. Look, I'll make it nice and easy for you. We'll agree a place and you just pop out and leave it there, OK? Then I can collect it and you'll never hear from me again.' Draper wasn't being strictly up front, obviously. He fully intended to kill Slack at some point later on, just for all the trouble he'd been put to, but that was by the by. 'How's that sound?'

'I can't give you the case, because I haven't got it.'

'Oh, bugger,' Draper said. 'I was hoping this might be easy.'

Draper didn't do social media, anything like that; Facebook and all the rest of it wasn't something he engaged with. To be fair, it would be tricky having any sort of online presence when there were arrest warrants out for him in every county in the UK, several American states and a number of European countries, on top of which it was a proper time suck. He knew what it was, though, and he made it his business to know (sort of) how it all worked. He'd learned how reasonably straightforward it was – if you knew what you were doing – to trace people through their Ticky-Tocks and Twittering.

'What are you talking about?' Slack had started to cry a bit. 'What are you going to do?'

'I'm just saying, Keith. Looks like we'll have to do things the hard way.'

He already had a name and number, so finding an address would be a piece of cake, and even if *he* didn't know where to begin, Draper reckoned that lowlife who'd unlocked the phone for him would crack it in ten minutes.

'What are you going to do . . . ?'

Draper hung up.

He didn't mind too much, because a lot of the time, the hard way was a lot more fun.

TWENTY-EIGHT

Once he'd left Forgeham's incident room, waving its occupants a cheery if unorthodox goodbye which only involved one finger, Miller stopped in the hallway to gather his thoughts. It didn't take very long. He needed something to calm him down and, in the absence of strong drugs and with nothing handy that he could punch repeatedly, he reached for his phone and dialled his dead wife's number.

He'd been doing it a lot less, lately. Sometimes, though, the imagined voice of his wife during their conversations at home was no substitute for the real thing. Even if the words were always the same.

He smiled, listening to the call ring out, knowing that Fred and Ginger's ears would now be pricking up at the sound of the *Strictly* ringtone. He pictured the phone in its sparkly red case, charging on a table near the door where he always left it, when he wasn't scrolling through it late at night in search of answers he never found.

The phone Alex had left behind in the dressing room at the Majestic.

The phone her killer had called that night, luring her to her death.

'This is Alex and I can't talk right now, because I'm out some-where fighting crime, or doing serious damage to a bottle of red. Either way, beep, message, you know . . . '

Once he'd hung up, Miller took a minute, then made a second call, keen to find out how Finn was doing. Mary told him that she'd left straight after breakfast. 'We couldn't stop her,' Mary said. 'She wouldn't even let me put something on those bruises. She's so stubborn, Declan.'

Miller did not need telling. He thanked her again and trudged the two flights back down to find Xiu waiting for him at the bottom of the stairs. He could tell that she knew exactly where he'd been.

'Are you OK?'

She could also see that he'd been crying.

'Allergies,' he said.

'What are you allergic to?'

'Where do you want to start? My wife being dead. The fact that the people charged with finding her killer are about as useful as a sniffer dog with a heavy cold. Oh, and also several varieties of soft fruit, but unless you've got any gooseberries in your pocket I doubt that's the problem.'

'Right . . . '

'So.' Miller rubbed his hands together. 'Any major progress?' He waited. 'Any *minor* progress? Has what DI Sullivan laughably calls media saturation yielded any-thing useful?'

'Well, there's a woman who wants to see you in reception.'

'Ooh, is it Anneka Rice?'

'I didn't get her name,' Xiu said. 'She's got something she wants to show you on her phone.'

'I hope it's a funny dog video,' Miller said. 'Or one of those with lots of people falling over.'

Xiu was about to ask the obvious question when her phone rang and she stepped away to take the call.

'Because I could do with cheering up.'

The woman sitting patiently opposite the reception desk was, he reckoned, somewhere in her mid-thirties, though she could also have been ten years older than that. Miller could usually tell when a suspect was lying and it was a matter of pride that, more often than not, he could spot the one thing that was out of place at a crime scene, but he was about as skilled at guessing a person's age as he was at quantum physics or conjuring.

'I gather you've got something to show me,' he said.

'I certainly have.' The woman stood up and thrust out a hand, which Miller dutifully shook. 'I hope it's useful . . . only I saw the piece on *That's Lancashire* – you know, after the national news – and they showed a picture of this man you're after.' She grimaced. 'He doesn't look the sort you'd want to take home to meet your mother, does he?'

'No, he doesn't,' Miller said. *Not unless you wanted her bumped off.*

'And I know it was mainly about some dreadful murder . . . *in connection with*, that's what the newsreader said, but it also mentioned an incident at the railway station and that's when it clicked.'

'What clicked?'

'I was *there*, you see. A few days back, when there was all that commotion.'

'You were at the station?'

'I was meeting my sister who was coming in from Hebden Bridge. I was just hanging about because the train was delayed, as per usual, and when it all started I filmed the whole thing. That's what you do these days, isn't it? These lads were running like billy-o, so I just pointed my phone, like you do . . . and I was right there when one of them jumped over the barrier outside the toilets and conked this other poor bloke on the head with a briefcase. A right nasty whack he gave him.'

Miller stepped closer. 'Can I see?'

The woman pressed a button and raised the phone so that Miller had a good view. To begin with, the footage was a little chaotic and blurry. He heard the shouting and saw Bagnall racing through shot, but then the focus shifted to the second lad. Miller leaned in to get an even better look as the lad ran towards the barrier and vaulted it, the swinging briefcase smacking (with a satisfying *clunk*) into the head of a man he knew to be Wayne Cutler. Sadly, there was no close-up of an injured Cutler to enjoy, but there *was* a nice clear close-up of Andrew Bagnall's friend.

Miller hit pause and stared at the young man that he, Draper and probably Cutler were all looking for.

He saw the mistake he'd made.

'Is it any use?' the woman asked.

'Oh yes,' Miller said. '*I'm* an idiot . . . but *you've* been incredibly helpful.'

'Well, just doing my bit.'

Miller took out his phone and began to search for a number. 'Thank you so much . . . and thank you to your sister.'

'I'll give the man at the desk my name, shall I?'

As the woman was walking away towards the desk sergeant, Miller was already talking to Natalie Bagnall. He apologised for bothering her again and for the fact that he wasn't calling with any real news. Then he asked if she possibly still had that school photograph to hand. She told him that she did and went to fetch it.

While Miller was waiting, he watched the woman giving her details to the desk sergeant. He was trying not to get overly excited, knowing that there was still one major hurdle to negotiate.

'Got it,' Natalie said.

'OK, sixty-four-thousand-dollar question,' Miller said. 'Is the photo in colour?'

'Yeah, but why—?'

'Is there a kid with red hair?'

'What?'

'I mean, there's usually a carrot-top in every class, right? There was certainly one in mine, so fingers crossed.' Miller waited.

'Yeah, there *is*. Big daft grin on his face an' all.'

'What's his name, Natalie?'

Half a minute later, when Miller had hung up, Xiu came charging into reception. 'I know the name of Bagnall's friend.' She was waving her phone. 'That was James Holloway. His brother got back to him and—'

'Keith Slack,' Miller said. 'That's the name of the lad we've been looking for. Yes, I know you're tempted to bow down and pay homage, but there's really no need. I'd've got it a lot quicker if I hadn't jumped to conclusions.'

Xiu just stared.

'I thought Andy Bagnall almost said the name, when he came round to my place that night with the briefcase. It was a *nick*name, though, you see?'

'Not really.'

'I should have borne that possibility in mind. Remember

what I said to you about nicknames? I told you they were important.'

'That's not exactly what you said—'

'So, not *Ji*— as in short for Jimmy. *Gi*— as in short for Ginger!' He shook his head. 'An easy mistake to make, I suppose, but I'm still cross with myself—'

'It doesn't matter, Miller—'

'Now we just need an address—'

'I've already *got* it.'

'Oh ... OK then.' Miller looked at her. 'Top stuff, Posh.'

'It wasn't difficult.'

'Right, then. To the Batmobile!'

They moved towards the exit. Xiu caught the woman's eye on their way out and smiled, a little embarrassed. 'It's actually a Honda Civic,' she said.

TWENTY-NINE

Keith Slack had been sick twice already since the man had called and it felt as though he could make it a hat-trick at any moment.

It wasn't like he hadn't been scared before. He'd actually been scared plenty of times. He was scared when he nicked the briefcase for a kick-off and that was *before* he knew what was in it. He'd even been a bit scared when he was stabbing that kid in the arse with a compass and, now that he thought about it, he'd been scared most of the time when he was at school. And a lot of the time since he'd left, come to that, even when he'd been acting the big man.

It was just a question of how well you hid the fear.

This was different, though. This was ... oh, God ...

He ran into the toilet and chucked up again, but by now it was just liquid. He wiped his face and came back into his front room. He fell onto the sofa, pulled his knees up to his chest and lay there close to tears.

People talked about being 'scared to death' when they saw

a spider or a zombie film or whatever, but this was actually the real thing. Well, scared *of* death if you were being picky, but either way, that man on the phone had sounded like he meant business and, seeing what had happened to Andy, death suddenly felt like a real possibility.

Slack closed his eyes and tried to decide what to do.

He'd already double-locked the front door and made sure the back door was bolted, but he wasn't sure that would be enough if the man really wanted to get in. He had Slack's name and his phone number, so it was only a matter of time before he found out where he lived. Andy would have locked the door too and look what good it had done him.

He lay there and ran through his (limited) options.

He'd thought about legging it to his parents' but the last thing he wanted to do was put his mum and dad in danger. The man on the phone might think *they* had the stupid brief-case, and Slack didn't reckon he'd have much compunction about hurting them. Hurting anybody, come to that, so it wasn't like Slack could ask anyone else to put him up either.

He thought about just jumping on a train, but he didn't have enough money to get him very far. A bus then, to . . . wherever.

It didn't make a blind bit of difference, Slack knew that, because the man would find him. Would hunt him down. He'd heard it in his voice and, if it was the man he thought it was, he'd seen it in that face on the front of the *Gazette*.

Looks like we'll have to do things the hard way.

There was really only one option. It had been the very first thing Slack had thought to do, of course, but he'd hesitated because that's what the likes of him did. The bad lads and the scallies. When you were already in the system and, more likely than not, would end up getting done for something yourself, even if you were the one in danger. In the end, he decided it was more than worth the risk. Yeah, so he might end up going down for what had happened at the station, but a few months inside was a price well worth paying. At least he'd be safe. Well, *safer* . . .

He jumped off the sofa, grabbed his phone and rang the police.

A few minutes later, when he'd hung up, having been assured that officers were on their way, he sat down again and began to breathe a little more easily.

He might not have been quite as scared any more, but he suddenly began to feel horribly guilty, because it struck him that Andy had only taken that briefcase to protect him. They had both understood the trouble they were in the moment they'd opened the bloody thing, and even if Slack had been quick with the big talk about flogging those rings, Andy had known all along they were out of their depth. Who the hell had Slack ever thought he was kidding? Nicking money out of fruit machines was out of their sodding depth.

Slack was close to tears again.

Andy had taken that briefcase to make sure *he* was safe. He'd done something brave and daft, like one of those characters he was always pretending to be and had wound up being killed for it.

It might have been two minutes later, or it might have been twenty when he finally heard the knocking.

He crept down the hallway and leaned close to the door. 'Who is it?'

'Police.'

'I didn't hear a siren.'

'I've got ID if you're concerned, sir. I can slide it under the door . . .'

Slack waited and, a few seconds later, a laminated

Lancashire Police ID card attached to a lanyard appeared. He bent to pick it up, examined it, then began to unlock the door. 'OK, sorry.' He fumbled with the key, beginning to jabber as the relief flooded through him. 'I just thought there'd be a siren or blue lights or something, that's all . . . '

He was just reaching to release the chain when the door was shouldered open, knocking him off his feet. He looked up to see a man step in and move quickly to stand over him.

'Woo-woo-woo,' Draper said. 'That do you, mate?'

THIRTY

It was already dark and had begun to rain heavily and this, together with the rush-hour traffic, meant it had taken them forty minutes to get there from the station. Xiu received a call just as they were finally turning into the road where Keith Slack lived. She parked up fast and turned to Miller.

'That was the control room on the phone. Keith Slack made a 999 call five minutes ago from this address. He told them he was in danger.'

Miller was shaking his head as he opened his door. 'So why are we sitting here like idiots then?' He didn't see the twitch around Xiu's right eye as she reached to open the driver's side door.

They closed both doors gently and ran across the road though the rain.

It was a three-storey house divided into several flats, one up from the end of a terrace. Miller and Xiu moved quickly but quietly up to the front door. Xiu checked the numbers and pointed to the concrete steps leading down to their left. 'Basement flat.'

Miller nodded and they began to walk down.

The curtains were drawn in what he guessed was the front room. There was no light creeping around the edges though, and none visible through the frosted glass in the front door. 'Maybe a beat patrol's already been,' Miller whispered. 'Taken Slack out of here.'

'In the last five minutes?'

'Yeah, fair point.' Miller knew that uniformed officers did a difficult job and he still had unpleasant memories of his own time in a pointy hat. He also knew there simply weren't enough of them, and that of those who might be free to attend an emergency call there wouldn't be too many in a massive rush to venture out and get soaked; not for a caller whose name would more than likely have come up on the police computer for all the wrong reasons.

'Maybe we should wait,' Xiu said. 'We know they're on their way.'

'I'm not sure we've got time.' Miller nodded towards the front door which had not been closed properly. He leaned forward and ran his fingers up and down the jamb until they found the holes where the safety chain had been forced. 'No, we definitely haven't.'

'Miller—'

He pushed the door open with his boot and shouted. 'Mr Slack?' He waited. 'Keith . . . ?'

Miller and Xiu looked at one another, then the two of them stepped into the darkened hallway. They stopped and Miller shouted again, but there was no response. Xiu pushed open a door to their left and switched on a light to reveal a front room that, although it would hardly have graced a show-home, showed no signs of disturbance. The light that now spilled out into the narrow hallway revealed that something *had* gone on just inside the front door. A thin rug was scrunched up against a wall. A low table lay on its side and a collection of junk mail and magazines, which Miller guessed had been piled on it, now lay scattered across the grubby linoleum tiles.

'A struggle,' Xiu whispered.

'That, or a protest against unsolicited mail,' Miller said. 'But let's go with your theory for now.'

Xiu rolled her eyes and they crept forward, moving slowly past an empty bedroom and a small bathroom. She pointed to a closed door at the end of the hallway, a light on beyond it, in what was probably the kitchen.

She shouted Slack's name again.

There was a groan from the other side of the door, then the noise of what sounded like a bolt being drawn back.

'Ah,' Miller said.

'I think Draper's got Slack in there,' Xiu said. 'We should—'

'Maybe he's making them both a sandwich,' Miller said.

There were more noises from the kitchen, feet against the floor.

'Even a nut-job like Draper needs to eat, right?' Miller was already walking towards the door, asking himself serious questions like how much longer it would take for a squad car to arrive, what he was planning to do if Draper was armed (which he almost certainly was), and why they hadn't searched the Civic for some kind of weapon. There was bound to be a tyre jack in the boot or a really heavy service manual in the glove compartment.

'Miller, wait . . . '

He opened the door like he was simply wandering in to make himself a cheese toastie, then stopped as though embarrassed to be interrupting the people who were already in there. He said, 'Oh.'

Dennis Draper stood with his back to the kitchen worktop, no more than two steps away from an open back door. He had his hand over Keith Slack's mouth and the blade of a kitchen knife pressed against his throat. The lad looked as though he'd already taken a fair beating. The one eye that wasn't swollen and discoloured had widened when Miller walked in and now he groaned against Draper's hand, coughing and spluttering blood through the killer's fingers.

Draper stared at Miller, then at Xiu when she arrived at his shoulder.

'Well, this is awkward.'

'Not really,' Miller said. 'I'm Detective Sergeant Miller and this is my colleague Detective Sergeant Xiu and, while I would never dream of speaking for her – because she can be quite touchy about that – I think it's safe to say that we're both in favour of keeping things nice and simple.'

'Simple works for me,' Draper said.

'We're all on the same page then, which is excellent. So, bearing that in mind, why don't you just let Mr Slack go, toddle off into the night and we'll say no more about it?'

'Yeah, I thought you might suggest something like that.' Draper spoke with a thick West Midlands accent that made whatever he said sound a little depressing, which in this instance it was. 'Not a goer, I'm afraid. The letting him go bit, I mean.'

'There are more officers on their way,' Xiu said.

'Is that right?'

'Slack called the police before you got here.'

Draper leaned close to Slack's ear. 'Did you, Keith?'

Slack eventually managed to nod, a sweaty tangle of red hair falling across his forehead.

'Well, that's a shame,' Draper said. 'But they're not here yet, so we don't need to do anything hasty. I doubt you've had time to tell them to go round the back anyway.' He nodded to the open doorway, the rain battering down just outside. 'I reckon that's the way I'll be headed.'

'OK, sounds like a plan,' Miller said. 'What's out the back?'

'Buggered if I know.' Draper removed his hand from Slack's mouth and leaned down to his ear. 'What's out the back, Keith?'

'Garden.' Slack swallowed and spluttered. 'Back gate ... alleyway leading to the next street.'

'That'll do.' Draper put his hand back. 'But I think I'd best take Keith along to show me the way.'

Slack shook his head and instantly regretted it, crying out as a thin line of blood appeared behind the knife.

'Steady on, Ginger Nuts, that's very sharp,' Draper said.

'He hasn't got the briefcase,' Miller said.

'Yeah, that's what he said.' Draper sighed, then narrowed his eyes at Miller. 'How do *you* know what he's got and what he hasn't?'

Miller said nothing.

They watched as Draper dragged Slack across to the doorway and stepped out backwards into the rain.

'Just leave him here and go,' Xiu said. 'We won't follow you.'

'Why should I believe you?'

'Because it would be stupid and dangerous. Because you've got a knife and we're unarmed.'

Miller walked towards the open door, thinking that the fact something was stupid had not stopped him doing it before. That perhaps, this time, it should. Then thinking that even one of those hefty cans of de-icer would have been better than nothing ...

'Don't come too close.' Draper shouted at him through the rain. 'I'm very protective of my personal space.'

'Don't worry, Dennis.' Miller kept walking, out into the garden and following Draper at a distance towards the back gate. Even though it was dark and the rain was coming down like stair-rods, he could see the terror on Keith Slack's face. 'I respect that.'

'I seriously hope so, for the lad's sake.'

Draper pulled Slack back towards the gate, reached behind to open it then stepped into the alleyway. He glared a final warning at Miller, then raised the knife to show it again before he and Slack disappeared from view.

Miller was aware of distant sirens and of Xiu shouting at him from the kitchen doorway as he ran to the back gate, losing his footing several times on the mud and wet grass. He wasn't surprised when he felt his knee pop, cursing Mary for making him dance that sodding lindy hop at their last session. When he finally moved through the gateway, he could see Draper and Slack at the end of the alleyway.

The shapes of them, at least.

Drenched and swearing, he could only stand and watch as Draper pushed the young man to his knees then, just when it looked as if Draper was all set to cut the boy's throat, he saw him turn and sprint away into the darkness. Miller ran/hobbled/staggered to the end of the alleyway, pausing just for a second or two to give Keith Slack a thumbs-up, and looked both ways along the street.

There was no sign of Dennis Draper.

Five minutes later, when Miller finally stumbled back into the kitchen like a drowned rat with only three good legs, Xiu was comforting a sobbing Keith Slack. She had found a blanket from somewhere to wrap around his shoulders and was wiping the blood from his face with a flannel. Looking back down the hallway, Miller could see blue lights beyond the frosted glass in the front door.

'There's paramedics on the way too,' Xiu said.

Miller nodded then looked across at Slack. 'You're welcome.' He flicked on the kettle and grabbed milk from the fridge; then, drying his hair with a tea towel, he limped around the kitchen, opening and closing cupboards. 'Have you not got *any* biscuits at all ...?'

STEP TWO

FOXTROTS & FRIDGES

THIRTY-ONE

As Miller had tried (and failed) to point out to Mary, even with the addition of a new member the group still had an odd number of dancers. At least it did if those dancers wanted any music to dance *to*. As it was, with his knee still painful after going arse-over-tit in Keith Slack's back garden, Miller was perfectly happy to sit the dancing out and restrict himself to ivory-tickling duties, at least until such time as he could cock up a foxtrot with two fully functioning legs.

Of course, the numbers issue had not been the real reason Miller had objected to the addition of a new dancer. He hadn't felt ready to see someone taking Alex's place, simple and stupid as that. As it turned out, Lovely Rita Meter Maid – or more accurately Perfectly Pleasant Veronica, Erstwhile Parking Enforcement Officer – had slotted into the group very nicely, although Miller was quietly relieved that she chose not to join them all in the pub afterwards for drinks and shared savoury snacks.

He wasn't ready for that level of intimacy just yet.

'I think that all went very well.' Mary was looking at Miller as she raised her glass of gin, as though to toast their new member in absentia. 'Her dancing is certainly of an acceptable standard, her waltz most especially, I thought . . . but thankfully not *so* high that she'll make any of us look bad.'

'Well, that's got to be a bonus,' Howard said.

'God, yes,' Ruth said.

Nathan nodded enthusiastically. 'Definitely a plus.'

Miller raised his glass to signal his agreement, despite thinking that a chimp with two left feet and no sense of rhythm might make one or two of Nathan's moves look a tad iffy.

'So, come on then.' Howard leaned towards Miller. 'Let's hear it.'

With Ransford and Gloria having hurried home to attend to the lamb casserole they'd left in a slow cooker, there were five of them around the corner table in the Bull's Head and they were all keen to hear exactly how Miller had done his leg in. His response to their initial enquiries when he'd rocked up at the hall had been deliberately vague, while equally as demanding of further explanation.

Howard and Ruth had been doing rudimentary warm-up exercises while the others changed into their dancewear: chiffon training dress and high heels for Mary; a loose skirt and pumps for Veronica; trackies, trainers and a *World of Warcraft* T-shirt for Nathan.

Carrying a mug of tea and a large plate of custard creams across to the piano, 'line of duty' was as much as Miller had been prepared to say about his mysterious injury.

'Did you knacker your knee kicking the bad guy's door in?' Nathan asked now. 'Draper, was it?'

'Yeah, Draper,' Howard said. 'The bloke who was after the briefcase.'

'Bloody hell, he didn't shoot you, did he?'

Miller raised a hand to calm everyone down, then told them exactly what had happened two nights earlier at Slack's place. Well, more or less. He chose to leave out one or two of those more prosaic details – the lack of any sort of weapon while approaching an armed suspect, the failure to call for backup, etc. – that might imply his actions had been a trifle cavalier at best or at worst downright idiotic. Miller never forgot that there were two former police officers around the table. He guessed that Mary would have been as much a stickler for operational protocol when she was on the Job as she now was about dancers always travelling anti-clockwise, never walking backwards onto the dance floor, not talking or chewing gum while dancing (Nathan) and never forgetting to thank your partner once a routine had been completed.

'Bloody hell,' Nathan said, when Miller had finished his tale. 'You're a hero, mate.'

'Not sure I could have done that,' Howard said.

'I wouldn't have let you,' Mary said, before turning back to Miller. 'It was certainly very brave, Declan.' She was nodding, though something told Miller that she knew very well they hadn't been given the full story.

'I don't know about that.'

'You saved that lad's life,' Ruth said.

Miller said nothing, knowing all too well that things could easily have turned out very differently. Standing in that alleyway, it had felt like they might be about to. Draper could have decided to use that knife on Keith Slack just for the hell of it and Miller would now be dealing with something a damn sight more painful than a gippy knee.

He took a welcome slug of IPA and tried not to think about it.

'So, where's Slack now?' Ruth asked.

'He's in protective custody,' Miller said. 'A safe house, but we're just covering our backsides really, because I don't think he's in danger any more.'

'Thanks to you,' Nathan said.

'Well, he certainly shouldn't be.' Howard looked at Mary who nodded her agreement. 'Draper will have scarpered, right?'

Miller stared down into his pint. 'Let's hope so.'

'Why wouldn't he?'

'Right.'

'No reason for him to stick around, is there? Not now he knows—'

'So, Veronica fits right in,' Miller announced suddenly. He smiled and looked around the table. 'Don't you reckon?'

Mary looked at him. 'Yes, I just said so.'

'Yeah, I know. Just ... agreeing with you.'

'Well, I'm glad.'

'Don't know why I was so worried about it, really.'

Ruth reached across and patted him on the arm. 'It's understandable.'

'Absolutely,' Mary said. 'But looking ahead, I was thinking that I'd bring in a proper accompanist.'

Miller snorted and tried to look offended.

'Oh, don't be silly, Declan. We all know how good you are and we're grateful for you stepping in. I'm talking about when you're fit and ready to dance again. We need you out on the floor rather than sitting at the piano, and having someone who could accompany the group full time would solve any issues about even numbers and partners and so on.'

'It's a cracking idea, love,' Howard said.

'There would be a small increase in subs to cover the cost, but if nobody has any objections ... ?'

Nobody did.

'Excellent,' Mary said. 'There's a gentleman who plays for the Thistleton community choir who's supposed to be *very* good. I'll put out feelers.'

'Right then.' Howard stood up. 'Who's for another one?'

It turned out that everyone was and, while Howard was at the bar, Nathan shuffled his chair a little closer to Miller's. He leaned in to whisper. 'Were you scared? That bloke waving a knife around?'

More than once, Nathan had talked about becoming a police officer himself, claiming that he had what he thought it took. Miller saw no reason now to sugar-coat what the job might occasionally involve. The danger, the fear. 'Yes, I was scared.'

Nathan shook his head. 'I think I'd've wet myself.'

'Well, course you would.'

'What, you saying you *did*?'

'No—'

'Did you wet yourself?'

'No, Nathan, I didn't. I'm *saying* I'm not surprised that's what *you'd* do because you've got a certain amount of form in the involuntary wee-wee department. As I recall, there was a small ... accident a couple of months back during that Latin medley. When you stretched, remember?'

'*One* time,' Nathan said. 'It was one time and only because Mary kept telling me I could get my leg out further.'

'I'm just saying, if that's what can happen when you're doing an over-exuberant samba, you might want to reconsider your future as one of Lancashire's finest.'

'That's not fair, Dec,' Nathan said. 'I'd had four cups of tea.' He stared down at the table and muttered, sulkily, '*And* a big bottle of Lucozade Sport ... '

*

Back at home and not yet ready for bed, Miller watered his plants while listening to the radio – a particularly irksome phone-in about climate change. Just as he was ready to chip in and point out to one misguided caller that raging forest fires and catastrophic floods were not simply 'unseasonable weather', Alex hijacked his train of thought with a few well-chosen remarks of her own.

'That was about as subtle as a flying sledgehammer,' she said.

Miller looked round. Alex was sitting on the sofa flicking through a magazine. 'What was?'

'Your grinding change of subject in the pub. *Suddenly* talking about that new woman . . . Veronica or whatever her name is, when Howard was steering the conversation somewhere you didn't want it to go.'

'I don't know what you're on about,' Miller said.

She sighed and put her magazine down. 'Of course you do, because I'm only saying what you're thinking. Remember, Miller, that's how this whole "chit-chat with a dead person" business works?'

'I was just getting fed up talking about what had happened at Slack's.'

'No, what you didn't want to talk about was why Dennis Draper almost certainly *hasn't* scarpered. Why he's probably still around.'

Miller leaned down to prod at the soil in a spider plant.

'Howard was about to say it and you didn't want him to, because you're ashamed about what you didn't tell Draper. The one key bit of information you decided to keep to yourself the other night.'

Miller dribbled water into the plant. He didn't need reminding.

'He hasn't got the briefcase.'

'How do you know what he's got and what he hasn't?'

Draper had asked Miller how he'd known Slack didn't have the case and Miller had said nothing.

'You didn't tell Draper because if he knew that the police already have the briefcase and that he's never going to get it, he *would* have scarpered and you'd never have a chance to catch him.'

'He might have scarpered anyway,' Miller said. 'We came close to getting him the other night, so he might have decided to cut his losses.'

'You know that's not true, Miller. You want him around so you can get him, simple as that. So that when you do, it might give you some leverage with the likes of Cutler and Massey.' Alex pointed. 'Oh, I think that bromeliad's looking a bit thirsty.'

Miller stepped across to give the plant a drink.

'So, now you feel rubbish because rather than put an end to this by simply telling Draper he's wasting his time, you've left him out there thinking someone else might have the case.'

'Like who?'

She shrugged. 'Don't ask me, but while he thinks someone's got it, that someone's life is at risk. And that's down to you. That's the choice you made.'

'I wasn't thinking very clearly,' Miller said. 'These were split-second decisions. He did have a knife, remember?'

'Yes, I know he did and you were an idiot going in there in the first place.'

'Mary said I was brave.'

'OK, a brave idiot, but still an idiot. And while I remember, that was a bit mean, reminding Nathan about his samba accident.'

'Funny though, right?'

They looked at each other, Miller pulling the stupid face that usually eased the tension and made Alex smile. It worked and, for the first time in days, he felt like smiling himself, if only briefly.

'FYI,' Alex said, 'she seems nice and all that, but I was a way better dancer than this Veronica will ever be.'

'Don't be daft,' Miller said. 'Obviously you were.'

She had said it quietly and it had sounded more sorrowful than anything, a plea rather than a boast, and for all that these conversations had often brought him a degree of comfort, now Miller wanted to do the one thing that was quite impossible. He wanted to pull his wife to him, hold her close and assure her that she could never be replaced.

Not on a dance floor and never in his heart.

He turned to water the umbrella plant they'd bought one Saturday from Ormskirk market and when he looked back, Alex had gone.

'She *is* pretty good, though,' he said. 'Veronica. Her Viennese waltz was seriously tasty.' He waited, wondering if Alex would pop back to tell him what an annoying arse he was, but there was only the space where she'd been.

Miller knew that she'd been right – the idiotic way he'd handled things at Slack's and more importantly the stupid and selfish decision he'd taken when talking to Dennis Draper.

If anyone else got hurt, it would be down to him.

With Alex no longer around, Miller took out his frustration at the radio instead; shouting loudly enough to wake several neighbours, put the wind up a passing dog-walker and to send Fred and Ginger scuttling straight into their straw-stuffed shoebox.

THIRTY-TWO

Two mornings earlier, Miller had limped into the briefing room to be greeted with the hearty applause of his colleagues. Even DI Tim Sullivan had managed a congratulatory if somewhat grudging nod. It was the sort of reception normally reserved for those occasions when a confession had been obtained or a guilty verdict delivered, but everyone was well aware that rescuing Keith Slack from the clutches of a ruthless killer had been a major result.

Whatever the operational irregularities.

Miller had accepted the plaudits with his customary modesty: holding both arms aloft and punching the air like he'd just snogged a supermodel or scored the winner in the dying seconds of the FA Cup final. Then he'd clocked Xiu eyeballing him ferociously and dialled it down a little.

'Obviously, DS Xiu was there as well,' he'd said.

Sullivan had nodded in Xiu's direction. 'Yes, of course. Good work, Sara.'

'But I was the one who chased him. *And* I hurt my leg . . .'

Now, as soon as Sullivan had called the briefing to order, he made sure everyone understood that the time for backslapping had passed. That despite the sterling efforts of two of his officers, said ruthless killer was still out there and that their investigation was very much ongoing.

'Absolutely, sir,' Xiu said.

'Bang on,' Clough said.

'The knee's a bit better today,' Miller said. 'Thanks for asking.'

Sullivan looked to DS Andrea Fuller. 'So, where are we *vis-à-vis* the sweep of local guesthouses and the like?'

'Well, we're still ... sweeping,' Fuller said. 'But it's quite a job. There are nearly three thousand bed spaces in local three- and four-star hotels—'

Miller cut in. 'Like I said before, Draper will have gone for something a bit more cheap and not very cheerful. Somewhere scuzzy, so he doesn't stick out.'

'Agreed, but there's another ninety-odd thousand beds available in the small guesthouses and B&Bs and that's presuming he isn't staying somewhere a bit further out.'

'We're going to need a bigger brush,' Clough said.

Everyone stared at him.

'For sweeping, you know, like in *Jaws*.' Clough loosened his tie. 'Only that was a boat, so ... '

Sullivan glared at the one member of the team who made him feel better about his own capabilities, then turned back to Fuller. 'So, how are you and Tony going about it?'

'Well, we started by compiling a list,' Clough said, quickly. 'Like you said, sir. Then we emailed every establishment on it, with a photograph of Draper and an urgent request for an immediate response, whether they recognised Draper or not, so we could cross them off the list.'

'We didn't get many responses,' Fuller said.

'No.' Clough looked sheepish. 'Not many.'

Xiu nodded. 'Spam folders.'

'Right.' Fuller stared at Clough. 'I did *say* that's what would happen, didn't I? A lot of email clients will automatically divert mass mailings into a spam folder … so, we *then* sent every email again, individually.' She rolled her eyes. 'That's a day I'm never going to get back.'

'We still didn't get replies from everyone, though,' Clough said.

'Not even close,' Fuller said.

Xiu looked horrified. 'Why wouldn't members of the public reply to an urgent request from the police?'

'Because they can't be arsed,' Miller said. 'You'd be amazed how many people can't be arsed. Some might not have seen it, granted, or just forgotten to reply … but my money's on not being arsed.'

Xiu was thinking about it. 'I think a more likely explanation is that a lot of them will have thought it was bogus. Doesn't matter how official it looks, a lot of people will see something asking them to call a number and presume it's a phishing email.'

'Bang on.' Clough nodded. 'I got one from the FBI once saying I was being investigated because I'd accessed "illegal websites". It looked kosher but when I called the number it turned out to be a scam.'

Everyone looked at him.

'You called the number?' Miller was grinning.

'I just wanted to make sure, didn't I?'

'*Anyway* …' Fuller sighed. 'There are still hundreds of places we haven't had a response from and bearing in mind the number of properties we're dealing with, we don't have enough manpower to go knocking on doors. So it's phone calls initially, and if there *is* anything that sounds like a possibility and the proprietor in question hasn't already seen Draper's photograph in one of the local papers, we send them one. No luck so far, but we've barely scratched the surface.'

Sullivan sighed, staring down at his iPad as though it might provide some much-needed inspiration. Or perhaps he just had a cheery screensaver of some flowers or a nice kitten. 'Well, until someone comes up with a better idea … keep scratching.'

'Sir?' Xiu raised a hand.

'You don't have to put your hand up, Sara,' Sullivan said. 'This isn't a classroom.'

Miller thought that if it had been, Sullivan would be a supply teacher at best, a PE teacher at that, but it always amused him that Xiu stuck her arm in the air like that. He'd have put money on her being head girl at school, a prefect for sure. They did have prefects at Miller's school – not that he was ever in the running – but they were no better than adolescent gangland enforcers, demanding dinner money with menaces on behalf of feared head prefect Graham Trotter. Thanks to a winning combination of slyness and funny voices, Miller had managed largely to avoid the painful attentions of Trotter's bum-fluffed henchmen, but his friend Imran had been on the receiving end of a great many dead legs and Chinese burns.

Miller guessed that Xiu would have been a rather more wise and benevolent dictator.

'Could we not draft in some extra officers?' she asked. 'This is a major inquiry, after all.'

'I have been trying,' Sullivan said. 'DCI Akers is doing her best, but as of now we'll have to manage with the officers we've got.'

'Maybe we could suggest some kind of transfer scenario with another team,' Miller said. 'We give them DC Clough and they give us ... I don't know, a couple of cadets or a lollipop lady.'

'You cheeky sod,' Clough said.

'Better yet, we just ... give them DC Clough.'

'This isn't helping,' Sullivan said.

Miller nodded upwards. 'What about DCI Forgeham's team? They *must* have a few spare officers knocking about, because they're doing less than nothing with their own investigation.' He looked around the table, but with the exception of Xiu nobody would meet his eye, all well aware exactly which investigation he was referring to.

Sullivan cleared his throat and stabbed at his iPad. 'Right, well, let's get back to it. Goes without saying, but anyone who's free to give Andrea and Tony a hand phone-bashing, please muck in. The apprehension of Dennis Draper remains this team's number one priority. Is that understood? Before anyone else is harmed.'

There were murmurs of assent and words of determination and commitment from almost everyone gathered.

This time, it was Miller who stared down at the table.

Half an hour later and Miller could well understand Andrea Fuller's frustration. Ten minutes after that, he was about ready to throttle himself with the phone cord. At the conclusion of his umpteenth fruitless conversation with the owner of a guesthouse, during which the closest he'd got to anyone matching Draper's description was one individual who 'looked a bit shifty' and another who'd 'nicked a kettle', Miller looked up to see Xiu standing at his desk.

'I was thinking about this briefcase,' she said.

For the next few seconds, Miller pretended to be busy with something and tried not to appear nervous. He knew that his failure to tell Draper exactly where the briefcase was (far beyond his reach in some evidence locker) could not possibly have been lost on Xiu. He was grateful that she had thus far not mentioned it to him or – as far as he knew – anyone else. Of course, if his decision backfired and Draper's hunt for a case he was never going to find resulted in any more deaths, Xiu might not be quite so magnanimous, but as of now he had to believe he was getting away with it.

'What about it?'

'I don't see why Draper would still be looking for it.'

So, maybe he hadn't got away with it at all. Maybe Xiu was about to give him an even stiffer dressing down than the one Alex had given him the night before. The one he'd given himself.

'What makes you say that?'

'It's been what . . . a week since he chopped those hands off? Maybe more, because we don't actually know when he . . . '

'Did the chopping.'

'Right. So, those hands will be in an advanced state of decomposition by now. Reeking to high heaven I would have thought.'

'OK, so we've got a briefcase with stinky hands in.'

'Seriously smelly.'

'I still don't get your point.'

Xiu perched on the edge of his desk. 'Draper thinks that Bagnall gave the case to someone else, right?'

'Which he did,' Miller said.

'Of course, but Draper doesn't know that someone was you. He doesn't know the police have got it.'

Only because I chose not to tell him. 'Go on.'

'He's got to presume that whoever's in possession of the case has opened it, and that any normal person, as soon as they'd done that, would go straight to the police. Once they'd been sick, obviously.'

'Unless Draper believes that Bagnall told this fictitious someone *not* to open the case. Told them to stash it somewhere.'

'Yes, that's a possibility ... except that this case, which in your scenario Draper believes has been hidden under a bed or on top of a wardrobe or wherever, would be stinking the place out by now. Right?'

'Right. Eww ... stinky. I think we've established that.'

'So, who the hell would be holding on to *that*? Surely Draper can't be thinking it's an actual case he's looking for any more. Or even the hands.'

Miller thought about it. What Xiu was saying made sense, but that was no great surprise because it usually did. 'Personally, I'm not convinced that Dennis Draper is quite as concerned with putrefaction and the unpleasant odours resulting therefrom as you are. He probably hasn't even thought about it. But let's say he has ... '

'If he has, he's thinking that he's stuffed,' Xiu said. 'Cutler isn't going to hand over the money without George Panaides's hands, is he?'

'They weren't actually Panaides's hands.'

'That's irrelevant. What matters is that Draper's proof's gone for a burton.'

'You're forgetting about the rings,' Miller said.

'Of *course* I haven't forgotten about the rings.' Xiu looked horrified at the suggestion and stood up. 'That's my whole flipping point. The rings is where I've been trying to get to all along.'

'So why go round the houses with all this rotting hands business?'

'I was putting things in context.'

'Oh, fair enough.'

'Anyway, my point is, I reckon Draper's thinking that even if those hands have been chucked in a skip somewhere, someone will still be holding on to the rings. So that's what he'll be going after.'

Miller nodded and raised a hand. 'Right, just so I'm clear, because frankly you've made all this a bit complicated with the whole Schrödinger's rancid hands conundrum. Dennis Draper either thinks the case *is* still around, with or without severed hands in, or he *doesn't* but he thinks that maybe the rings are. Is that the gist of it?'

'More or less,' Xiu said.

'*Or* he's decided the whole thing is a waste of time, thought "sod this for a game of soldiers" and got the hell out of Dodge.'

'Which we both know is the least likely option.'

'Agreed.'

'And which would be a shame, because it would mean we're unlikely to ever catch him.' Xiu stepped away then turned and winked. Or perhaps it was a twitch. It was hard to tell sometimes. 'That said, it would get certain people off the hook . . . '

Miller watched her walk back to her own desk. He thanked a few of those deities he had any real faith in (Loki, the Norse trickster god, the Lord of the Dance, John Lennon) for partnering him with Sara Xiu, then picked up the phone again and called the next guesthouse on his list.

The Seaview (there were thirty-seven of them).

Opened: 1998. Six Rooms. Two Stars. Proprietor: Mrs Kathleen Trimble.

'Oh, good morning, Mrs Trimble, this is Detective Sergeant Miller from Lancashire Police. I'm terribly sorry to bother you, but as you don't appear to have replied to the urgent email we recently sent you, I was wondering if you had anyone currently residing at your establishment who, in your expert opinion and based on your considerable experience in the town's hospitality industry, looked like they might be capable of murdering someone then cutting their hands off ... '

He couldn't be arsed beating around the bush.

THIRTY-THREE

Isla Duddridge had no truck whatsoever with those tired old jokes about randy seaside landladies. It was just a stupid cliché she remembered from old comedy shows where fat, bald men rolled around with buxom, sex-starved widows in skimpy negligees, or winked and made saucy comments about rooms with 'extras' and testing mattresses and all that carry on. A load of sexist old nonsense, that's what it was! Isla was friends with a great many other landladies (though these days they preferred to call themselves proprietresses) and the truth was that most of them were far too knackered after running around all day cooking and cleaning to even think about you know what.

To suggest otherwise was ridiculous and frankly offensive. All that said though, a single woman had needs.

Since her old man had run off with a ticket seller from the Tower a few years back, Isla might have entertained a harmless fantasy or two and, yes, perhaps there had been one or two . . . dalliances with attractive men who were taking advantage of all the facilities available. Men she reckoned could count themselves seriously bloody lucky and who (with one unfortunate exception) always left glowing reviews. The miserable buggers who rated establishments such as hers might only ever have seen fit to give the Sandy Shores two and a half poxy stars, but what Isla had very occasionally chosen to offer a handful of specially selected guests was very much a five- star experience.

A hands on, personal service.

And a full English breakfast.

There had been a few enjoyable nights the year before with an electrical engineer who'd been working at the Pleasure Beach, an athletic weekend with a comedian who was bottom of the bill at the Winter Gardens (not funny, good stamina) and a less than successful encounter with a bathroom fitter who, having failed to rise to the occasion, had the cheek to leave a snarky review on Tripadvisor.

If Isla had a real weakness, though, it was for a tall dark type with a sexy foreign accent.

She smoothed down her new blouse as she climbed the stairs, then checked herself out in the mirror on the first-floor landing before knocking softly on the door of number three. She could hear the sounds of the TV from inside the room. She spoke slowly and clearly, because that was only polite with the continentals.

'Hola, Señor Diaz? It's Mrs Duddridge.' She smiled to herself. 'Isla. I was wondering if you fancied joining me for a drink. I've got a nice bottle of Rioja in and I bought some tapas from M&S. I thought it might make you feel at home.' She leaned a little closer to the door. 'Señor Diaz . . . ?'

'I'm busy.'

'Well, I don't mean now this minute. I was thinking a bit later on, you know. We could make a night of it, if—'

'I'm going out tonight.'

'Oh. Righto, love. Just a thought . . . '

Isla stepped away and slunk back towards the stairs. Sod him. It was his loss, and tapas was a waste of bloody time anyway.

Stupid little portions, wouldn't feed a cat.

Draper groaned into his pillow, then turned the TV up a little louder.

He was properly annoyed, because he'd planned a night in. He'd already chosen the pizza he was going to have delivered (the Mighty Meaty Monster) and, having checked, found there was a cracking episode of *Hetty Wainthropp Investigates* on Alibi. It was no *Midsomer Murders*, but he'd been looking forward to it. Now, he'd have to go out because that's what he'd told the landlady and he didn't want to upset her. He didn't want to have sex with her either, *God* no, but it wasn't her fault that she plainly found him irresistible.

The heart wanted what it wanted, right?

It was a pain in the backside, but Draper was sure he could find something useful to do. There were a couple of addresses he could do with checking out anyway because it always paid to get the lie of the land. For a minute or two he considered paying Wayne Cutler a visit, just to remind him that they had unfinished business, before deciding it would be . . . unwise, aside from which Cutler was probably looking for *him*. No, the next time he wanted to see Cutler was when the arsehole was handing over the ten grand he was owed, though, having been put to so much bloody trouble, he quite fancied seeing him again sometime after that. Popping by one day when Mr Cutler was least expecting it.

A visit from Sudden De'Ath . . .

All in all, he supposed that it couldn't hurt to get out and about again; to go back to work and do what he was there for. He'd been lying low since the near miss a few nights earlier, partly because it seemed sensible with the police all fired up and buzzing about, but also because that business at Slack's place had slightly discombobulated him.

What the hell had that weirdo been thinking? Chatting away in that kitchen, all nice and casual like they were discussing the weather or something, then chasing him out into the garden without so much as a water pistol when Draper was brandishing a knife.

Detective Sergeant Miller was someone Draper would have to think carefully about.

Even more worrying was why he hadn't done what he'd fully intended to do and *used* the bloody knife? He'd legged it, when there'd been plenty of time to carve the little sod up and still get away. So, why hadn't he? It had been the same with the homeless girl, some scary and ridiculous impulse to be – he could hardly believe he was even *thinking* the word – merciful.

Was he getting tired, maybe? Or old ...?

God forbid he was getting *soft*.

He shuddered a little at the thought and, to calm himself down, he took out his notebook and lay back to compose a nice, reassuring list.

HEROES (NO PARTICULAR ORDER)

1. John Nettles as DCI Tom Barnaby.
2. Jeremy Clarkson.
3. Princess Diana.
4. Iron Man.
5. Mum.

He drew a heart next to 'Mum' and, happy with that, he turned to the page containing his current work-related list and made a few amendments.

So, Bagnall hadn't had the briefcase. His mate Slack hadn't had it and neither had Bagnall's homeless friend. Somebody did, though, and whatever state the case and its contents were in by now, Draper needed to get hold of enough to convince Wayne Cutler that he'd done the job he was contracted for. So he could get paid and get gone.

Draper thought back to that note he'd found in Bagnall's flat. There was one more obvious place to go looking.

THIRTY-FOUR

'Cheer up, mate,' Miller said. 'This is great, isn't it?'

Imran grunted. 'It's my lunch hour.'

'This is the only time I could get away and you invited me, remember?'

'Because I'm an idiot.'

Miller was already pressed against Imran in the small cabin, but leaned harder into his shoulder. 'Because you're a deeply caring and thoughtful person.' He clapped his hands excitedly like a kid. 'More importantly, you *know* how much I love going on the big mower.'

Imran grunted again then leaned forward to adjust the settings. He was, as always, eager to ensure that the grass was given all necessary help to conserve water. The correct length of cut during each stage of the mow would also improve turf density and colour, promote deep digging roots and prevent diseases. 'Yeah, but it's my lunch hour.'

In order to facilitate any kind of conversation, Imran had

dispensed with the ear-protectors he would normally have worn, but they still needed to speak loudly to be heard above the noise of the engine and the blades.

'Stop moaning,' Miller said. 'I brought sandwiches, didn't I?'

Happy as Larry (Miller had no idea who Larry was or what he'd always been so bloody cheerful about) he stared out at the trees as they moved slowly past, the all-weather sports pitch beyond and the black and grey roofs of the industrial estate beyond that. 'To be fair, your hours *are* more flexible than mine,' he said. 'And there may even be one or two people who might suggest that my job's a little bit more important than yours. Now, that's not *my* opinion you understand, I'm just putting it out there.' He held out his palms and then moved them up and down as if weighing one thing against another. 'Murder or mowing, mowing or murder? It's a tough call . . . '

Imran glanced across and gave Miller the finger.

The mower trundled up and down the medium-sized field. As usual, Imran was wearing grubby overalls emblazoned with the Lancashire Parks Department logo beneath a high-vis jacket. Next to him, Miller wore his borrowed high-vis along with the ill-fitting plastic helmet upon which Imran always insisted. Miller would never argue with his friend about such things, but he did think it was a little bit 'health and safety gone mad'. They were progressing at a stately seven miles an hour in an 18-kilowatt single-speed ride-on rotary mower and not tearing around Brands Hatch in an F1 super-car. Realistically, there was little chance of Miller ending up in a tangle of twisted metal or being catapulted out of his seat into the mowing mechanism.

Still, Imran's park, Imran's rules.

'I did a stupid thing,' Miller said.

Imran didn't blink. 'You've done lots of stupid things.'

'Right, thanks, but—'

'Remember when you sent that condolence card and put LOL at the end because you thought it meant *lots of love*? Or there was the time you called that bouncer at Brannigans a knob-jockey?'

'Yes, I take your point—'

'Who can forget the night you had six cans of Stella and tried to defrost a freezer with a chisel? Now, that was expensive.'

'Have you finished?' Miller waited until he was sure that Imran had exhausted his supply of stories and told him about the conversation with Dennis Draper. The crucial fact he'd neglected to mention.

Imran nodded, thinking about it. 'Sometimes the stupid thing turns out to be the right thing?'

'I suppose.' Miller could only hope so.

Imran slowly turned the mower round and they headed back the way they'd come, mowing a parallel track. 'Course, sometimes it's just stupid.'

'Deeply profound as always,' Miller said.

'You're welcome.'

'He hurt Finn.' Miller watched Imran turn quickly to look at him and raised a hand. 'She's OK. A few bruises.'

'Was that because you didn't tell him about the briefcase?'

'No, it was before. Before I ... didn't tell him.'

'Good, because if you doing something stupid had led to Finn getting hurt, I might have had to give you a slap.'

'Sounds fair,' Miller said.

'As it is, it's just *him* I need to ... have a word with.' Imran leaned closer and lowered his voice. 'So once you've caught this bloke, see if you can organise a walk in the park, yeah? Give me ten minutes in the equipment shed with him.'

'Have a suspect bailed to your equipment shed?'

'Everybody needs a bit of fresh air, right? You take him for a nice afternoon in the park, a slushie maybe, or feeding the ducks, and then he accidentally wanders into my shed. It could happen.'

Miller shrugged. 'It might take a bit of wangling, but I'm happy to give it a bash ... '

Ten minutes later they were sitting on their favourite bench, the one with *Your Nan Is a Slag* carved into it. Miller had made Imran promise never to get rid of it, because it always made him smile.

They ate their sandwiches, after which Imran lit a cigarette and they sat staring out at the familiar surroundings. Nominally the chief groundskeeper at Claremont Park, Imran Mirza had become responsible for all the public areas – the children's playground, the various playing fields and gardens, the small café and even (on the three days a year it was open) the ice cream kiosk. The local authority employed specialist horticultural consultants and once or twice a month someone from the 'pond management team' showed up to moan about herons nicking the fish, but they all answered to Imran, officially or not.

'I was thinking about you this morning,' Miller said.

'Pervert.'

'Not long before you rang actually. I was thinking about school. About Graham Trotter and his gang.'

Imran said nothing for a minute or so, just carried on smoking. Finally, he said, 'I saw him in the pub once. Stood next to me at the bar. Bastard didn't even recognise me.' He smoked for a while longer then nodded towards the putting green, the condition of which was a matter of enormous pride and where he and Miller engaged in a winner-take-all competition once a month or so. The 'all' in question consisted of a five-pound note which invariably ended up in the pocket of Imran's overalls. 'A bunch of lads nicked all the flags the other day. Like that wasn't enough, one of them took a shit in the final hole. I mean, *right* in the hole.'

Miller shook his head in disgust. 'You never caught Tiger Woods doing that,' he said. 'Not even when he missed that sitter on the eighteenth in the World Match Play. What year was that?'

Imran clearly didn't care. 'I know who they were,' he said. 'Those lads. I called the police, but they didn't even bother coming.'

'Have you tried mentioning my name?'

Imran looked at him.

'Yeah, you're right. They'd probably have just hung up straight away.'

'I want to be planting trees,' Imran said. 'Taking care of the shrubberies and borders, keeping the grass looking good, but I spend most of my time picking up used noddies, empty nitrous bottles and dozens of them disposable vapes which are *never* disposed of in *any* of the six different litter bins.' He sighed out a stream of smoke. 'I just watch them chucking all this stuff on the floor.'

'Can't you do something about it?'

'Yeah, I tell them to stop. I offer to show them where the bins are, and they just laugh at me. I'm not going to get heavy about it, am I? Some of these lads are carrying knives.'

'Most of them, I reckon,' Miller said.

Imran dropped his butt, ground it out beneath his boot then bent to pick it up. 'It wasn't a barrel of laughs at school,' he said. 'Graham Trotter and all that . . . but I still think it's harder for kids now than it was for us.' He looked at Miller. 'I wouldn't want to be sixteen, mate.'

They watched a woman walk past, her mobile jammed to her ear and a pug they presumed she owned mooching along behind her. The dog was wearing a fluorescent green coat and looked suitably embarrassed.

'Mary's brought a new woman into the group,' Miller announced.

'Your dance group?'

'Yeah.'

Imran nodded, carefully considering this nugget of new information. 'Is she hot?'

Miller stared at him.

'OK, probably not appropriate. So . . . what do you think about it? This new woman.'

'To be honest, it's not so much about what *I* think as what Alex would think.'

'What would she think?'

'I sometimes wonder which would upset her more,' Miller said. 'Me being with someone else, you know, in every sense . . . or me *dancing* with someone else.' He looked over and saw that Imran was waiting for the answer. 'Oh, the dancing, no question.'

'In which case my first question is still valid,' Imran said.

'I'm just going to ignore you now . . . '

They rode back on the mower to the large equipment shed where all Imran's gear was stored. Miller took off his helmet and high-vis jacket and handed them back to Imran. He thanked him and said that the next time they went putting, that fiver was definitely coming his way. 'I presume you *have* cleaned the final hole out?'

Imran uncoiled a hose and began spraying the mower down. 'You'll catch him,' he said. 'That bloke you didn't tell about the briefcase.'

'You think?'

'You usually do.'

THIRTY-FIVE

The launch of the 'Bardsley's Bangers' range three days before had gone more or less as well as could be expected. Better than Frank had thought it would, considering that he'd been so distracted by Maureen's foul mood and therefore unable to give his bangers the attention they deserved. On and on at him she'd been, for bloody days now. She kept insisting that he wasn't giving her enough time or consideration even when he tried to tell her that these weren't exactly normal circumstances. Trying to keep his temper, he'd explained that right now he was having to *consider* if he'd ordered sufficient sausage meat and *consider* why a huge shipment of brioche baguettes was currently sitting in the back of a truck at Dover; all this on top of a horrendous situation in Blackburn where there seemed to be a calamitous shortage of ketchup *and* mustard.

'I don't give a tuppenny stuff about your ketchup,' she'd said. 'Or your mustard.' This was a few minutes ago in the kitchen.

'Please, Maureen.'

'Am I not more important to you than a bit of bloody sausage meat?'

'It's more than a bit, love—'

'I've had enough, Frank . . . I've had it up to here.' Maureen had slumped against the worktop and begun sniffling and no amount of comforting or reassurance from Frank had seemed to make any difference.

Eventually she'd begun shouting again, and when Frank tried to tell her that they could definitely go away together – somewhere luxurious for at least a couple of weeks – just as soon as the condiments situation had sorted itself out, Maureen had lost it altogether. Things might have got even nastier had his phone not rung while Maureen was ranting about playing second fiddle to an oversized hot dog, and Frank had discovered who was calling.

He'd immediately slapped his hand across the handset. 'I really need to take this.'

His wife was still shouting about sausages as Frank hurried away down the corridor, closed his office door behind him and sat down to focus on his phone conversation.

'I'm all yours, Mr Cutler.'

'Call me Wayne for God's sake,' Cutler said, chuckling. 'We can dispense with formalities, can't we? Things being as they are.'

'You sound a bit . . . echoey,' Frank said. 'Are you in a toilet?'

'Certainly not.'

'Good, because I'm not sure I'd be comfortable with that.'

'I just thought we should have a quick natter—'

'You're not recording this, are you?'

'I've got you on speaker, Frank,' Cutler said. 'That's all.'

'Fair enough.' Frank leaned forward to straighten the 'Lancashire's Best Burger' award which he'd now won three years on the bounce and which had his name engraved on the faux-marble plinth. It wasn't the prettiest trophy he'd ever seen, but he was fiercely proud of it. 'What did you mean, "things being as they are"?'

Cutler laughed again. 'Oh, come on, Frank. The Panaides business. I know you think I was responsible for what happened to him.'

'You're not seriously going to deny it, are you?'

'Well, I'm hardly going to admit it, am I? For all I know *you* might be the one recording this conversation.'

'I know all about Dennis Draper,' Frank said.

'Never heard of him,' Cutler said. 'At the same time, I'm impressed that you know his name.'

'You're not the only one with a few talkative coppers in his pocket, Wayne, so I'm well aware he's the one that killed George and that you were the one who hired him to do it.'

Frank could hear Cutler sigh, a bit wheezily. 'You remember when we talked on the phone a while back?'

'I do.'

'When you first opened up in my town?'

'Well, I don't think that strictly speaking it's *your* town,' Frank said. 'I'm sure the Unitary Authority would have an opinion about it for a kick-off, but be that as it may—'

'You assured me I had nothing to worry about in terms of competition or what have you. "Burgers are my business", that's what you said.'

'And they are.' Frank leaned forward again to wipe a line of dust from the silver-plated replica of his signature quarter-pounder. 'I'm looking at a trophy which proves it.'

'Your mate had other ideas though. That was the problem.'

'Yeah, George were a bit misguided, I can't argue with that, but all the same, I'm not sure he deserved what you decided he should get and I just couldn't look myself in the eye if I didn't do something about it. See, I need to balance the equation, because now it's all gone to cock.'

'I'm not with you, mate.'

'Come on, Wayne, I know you're not *that* thick. It's basic sums at the end of the day. I've lost one of mine, so things have to be . . . balanced up.'

Cutler lowered his voice which Frank supposed was an attempt to be menacing. 'With one of mine, that what you're on about?'

'That's about the size of it, but don't get your knickers in a knot, because I'm only talking about Draper and he's not *actually* one of yours, is he? He's more of a . . . freelance, so I reckon you should count yourself lucky, all in all.'

'Oh, is that right?' Cutler scoffed. 'I'd best nip out and get myself a couple of scratch cards; you know, seeing as my luck's in.'

'Aye, it can't hurt . . . ' Frank paused, seeing a text message pop up on his phone: an update on the Blackburn sauce drought. 'On top of which I'm doing you a favour. With all the other stuff this feller's been up to and the information he could pass on should the police get hold of him, I'm guessing you're as keen to get Draper out of the way as I am.'

While Cutler considered his response, Frank checked his text message and was relieved to see that an emergency consignment of ketchup was on its way from Chorley. It was a small piece of welcome news.

'You're telling me you've taken steps, are you?' Cutler asked, eventually.

'I've had a quiet word with someone,' Frank said. 'Stumped up a few quid.' It reminded him that he needed to put a call in sharpish to Torchy Molineux and find out just what the money he'd doled out was actually buying him; when that spanky new bit of welding kit Frank had paid for was going to be put to some use.

'Right you are then, as long as you understand that if anyone *I've* had a quiet word with comes across Draper before whoever it is that *you've* had a quiet word with, we might save you the bother.'

'Well, I'd *rather* it was my bloke, seeing as George and me go back a long way, but . . . fair dos. I won't make a fuss.'

'That's good,' Cutler said. 'Nobody likes a fuss, do they?'

'Not if they're sensible,' Frank said.

'It's been good to catch up,' Cutler said. 'Oh, I meant to say, my wife had one of your burgers the other day. She said it was very tasty.'

'That's nice to hear.' Frank tapped his trophy and smiled. 'Tell her to mention my name next time. I'm sure we can chuck in some free onion rings or what have you.'

'That's very kind,' Cutler said. 'But I think it was probably a one-off.'

Jacqui Cutler crept away from the door of her husband's office and started up the stairs. She waited until she'd closed the bedroom door behind her before swearing as loudly as she needed to.

God, Wayne was so full of . . .

She'd only told him she'd been into a Bardsley's to wind him up and she'd certainly never said anything about the burger being 'tasty'. It tasted like dog-meat, for heaven's sake! She'd taken one bite and binned it, yet here was Wayne using her name willy-nilly to butter up a business rival. No, it wasn't the worst thing her husband had ever done, not by a long chalk, but it was a measure of the man. He lied without thinking. He committed acts of violence because he enjoyed them and he continually put his own family in danger.

And he *still* hadn't apologised for the Creme Egg incident.

Once she'd calmed down a little, she opened the notebook she kept at the back of her make-up drawer and scribbled down a few of the things she'd overheard. The latest snippets of ammunition.

Of course she hadn't gone to Bardsley's dog-meat emporium because she was hungry. She'd popped into Booths and picked up a smoked salmon sandwich on the way there, for pity's sake. No, she'd just gone along to put out a few feelers or what have you. As it turned out, there'd been some kind of promotion on and there, propped up on the counter, was a stand-up postcard thingy with a picture of the boss himself – brandishing a sausage and grinning like he'd just had it off.

An arm around the shoulder of his smiling wife.

So, Jacqui had ordered a burger and fallen into conversation with the young girl dishing up the dog-meat.

'Oh, they're such a lovely couple, Frank and his wife. What's her name again . . . ?'

Downstairs, Wayne would doubtless be thinking about that phone call and about the best way to handle Frank Bardsley. Now, sitting at her make-up table and re-applying her lipstick, Jacqui was thinking about the best way to handle Wayne. It hadn't become any less scary, the prospect of making a big change, and Jacqui had decided that it wasn't one she was brave enough to make without a little help. Without a partner . . .

It was hard to imagine that any other woman in her position (certainly not one with two kids at home) would feel very differently. A woman with a husband for whom business had become everything; whose efforts to maintain his position now meant that murder was as much part of his daily business practice as negotiating a wholesale price on frozen meat patties.

She might be barking up the wrong tree, of course. There might not even *be* a tree. Maureen Bardsley might be every bit as happy as Jacqui was miserable, but there was only one way to find out.

What was the harm?

Jacqui stared at herself in the mirror and thought about that film from years back, where the two women decided to change their lives and drove off the cliff together at the end. She smiled when she remembered what it was called.

A good Lancashire name, Thelma.

THIRTY-SIX

His hour or so in the park with Imran (and riding on the big mower, obviously) had lifted Miller's spirits considerably. It usually did. Back in the office, he picked stray bits of grass from his jacket while he caught up with Xiu over a coffee. He checked out the latest slew of messages from Mary on the 'dance buddies' WhatsApp group (she was making 'solid progress' in her attempts to poach Alan, the community choir's pianist) and had a conversation with Tony Clough that could even have been described as 'pleasant'. He was as close to . . . perky as he was likely to get – all things considered – when he sat down to tackle an afternoon on the phone to some of Blackpool's least desirable guesthouses, the prospect of which would otherwise have filled him with dread.

None of them had any current residents that so much as resembled Dennis Draper, but even once that had been quickly established, Miller resisted the temptation to hang up immediately. He didn't waste time, but found just enough of it to take in a litany of complaints from one or two of the more bolshy proprietors. Helping the police with their enquiries was all well and good, but what about having to deal with vomit in the waste-paper basket, towels stained with hair dye and greedy guests pilfering from the breakfast buffet?

'Never mind your chuffing suspect, this bleeder was helping himself to half a dozen ketchup sachets at a time,' said Mrs Irene Williams of the Sunnyside Inn. 'Stuffing his pockets with hard-boiled eggs!'

That might have been the one time Miller was less than polite.

Had he been asked, he might have claimed it was a simple desire to see justice done – though it was probably just guilt – that saw him still at his desk nearly an hour after going-home time. Sitting in an almost empty office, he'd finally decided to knock it on the head for the day and had just stood to gather his stuff together when he got a call from DCI Bob Perks.

Miller seized the opportunity to vent his frustration.

'It's just bloody endless ... there's more beds for rent in Blackpool than there are in London, did you know that? And for all we know, Draper's kipping in a tent somewhere or sleeping in his car. He might not even be around any more.'

'Maybe I can help,' Perks said.

'You going to come down here and get on the phones, are you, Bob? Listen to landladies banging on about hard-boiled eggs—?'

'We know who those hands belonged to.'

'Oh, finally.' Miller sat down again. 'You found a body?'

'We don't need to, because we got a DNA match.'

'That's handy. In every sense.'

'Too right it is, and between you, me and the Police Conduct Authority, now we know whose body it is I don't think we'll be pulling out all the stops to find it.'

'So, not the local vicar then?'

'A rotten little shitehawk named Gordon Pickering. Known to have supplied assorted weapons including at least one surface-to-air missile to a variety of dodgy characters across the north-west. My guess is that Draper had bought guns off him at some point.'

'So why kill him?' Miller asked.

'Don't know, don't much care,' Perks said. 'Maybe they'd fallen out or Draper owed him money or something, so he thought he'd kill two birds with one stone. He didn't want to look very far because he needed those hands in a hurry, remember?'

Miller nodded. 'Maybe Amazon were out of stock.'

'Here's the important thing, though. Pickering has a brother. *Craig* Pickering – another upstanding citizen – is three years into a seven-year sentence for GBH. Just up the road as it happens, in HMP Preston. Now, other than being sure Draper killed Gordon Pickering and chopped his hands off, we don't know the full extent of their previous relationship.'

Miller had a stab at where this was going. 'But if they *did* know each other before, there's a strong possibility his brother knew Draper as well.'

'Spot on.'

'Well enough to steer us in the right direction, maybe.'

'Worth a punt, I reckon.'

Andrea Fuller – who had also been working late – waved as she passed Miller's desk on the way out. Miller waved back. 'It might be nice to pay him a visit.' He stood up and pulled on his jacket, his phone wedged between his shoulder and his chin. 'Tell poor old Craig about his brother.'

'That's exactly what I thought,' Perks said. 'Which is why I've sorted a visiting order for you tomorrow morning.'

Miller picked up his crash helmet and followed Fuller towards the door.

'Should I take him a bit of cake, d'you think? I find that a nice slice of Battenberg always goes down well when you're breaking bad news.'

Once Miller had treated Fred and Ginger to some fruit salad and put paid to the mushroom risotto he'd picked up from Gemelli's on the way home, he sat down to watch the video again. He'd lost count of the times he'd watched it now, but each time he opened his laptop, he did so in the hope that whatever was nagging at him about it – about what the man was doing after he'd handed Alex the envelope – might transform itself from a niggle into a full-blown, case-breaking revelation, so that Miller would never have to watch the damn thing again.

It didn't.

He snatched up his guitar and sat on the sofa for a while, noodling at a few of his favourite Beatles tunes. He played McCartney's 'Here There and Everywhere' then Lennon's 'In My Life'. To prevent the mood from becoming too soppy, he started to play 'Rocky Racoon', and when he glanced up he could see Alex watching him from the doorway.

He nodded at her and she nodded back.

It was clearly not a night for conversation, jokey or otherwise, and Miller knew that was because he was still thinking about what he'd just been watching. The unexplained encounter. Miller knew well enough by now that Alex could only ever answer questions he already knew the answers to.

When he was flailing around in the dark, she had nothing to say.

He found himself starting to play a lesser-known Beatles song called 'Not Guilty' but for whatever reason the chords wouldn't come, so he set his guitar aside and picked up his phone instead.

'Hey, Finn ... '

'Hey, Miller ... '

Miller was thrown and, for a few moments, he wasn't sure what to say. He'd been calling and leaving messages several times a day since Finn had walked out of Howard and Mary's place, but this was the first time she'd picked up.

'It's me,' he said.

'I know,' she said. 'Your name came up on my phone. It's why I just said, "Hey, Miller".'

'All right, smartarse. I'm just surprised you answered, that's all.'

'Yeah, sorry,' she said. 'I've been a bit busy.'

Miller swallowed back all the obvious questions about how busy someone who sat in a doorway most of the day could possibly be. Actually of course, they were ridiculous questions, because he knew very well she did other stuff. Most importantly, however easily he was able to imagine the things Finn got up to – and Miller wished more than anything that he wasn't – he did not need to be told in any detail what those things actually were.

He looked across again, but Alex had gone.

'I was just ... checking in, really,' Miller said. 'How's the face?'

'Yeah, it's OK.'

Miller could hear the hum of traffic close to her, the sounds of an argument somewhere nearby. 'Has the bruising gone down?'

'Well, I won't be launching a thousand ships any time soon, but I don't look too scary.'

'That's a relief.'

'It's been quite good for business, as it goes. People feeling a bit more sorry for me than normal, you know?'

'Oh well . . . swings and roundabouts.' Miller thought about those stairs at work and Dennis Draper smacking his head into every one of them as he fell.

'Have you caught him yet?' Finn asked. 'The bloke who did it, the one who killed Andy.'

The answer was easy enough, obviously, but Miller didn't really want to get too far into it. The close calls and the stupid decisions. 'No, but Imran says I will.'

'Oh, well that's all right then.'

They said nothing for a long few moments. The argument close by grew a little more heated. Someone was a *useless tosser* and someone else was *sick of being treated like scum.*

'Sorry for being a cow the other night,' Finn said.

'Now you're just being daft,' Miller said. 'You were upset.'

'All the same.'

'Well, you can always make it up to me by coming round for dinner or something. We can get a takeaway.'

'Maybe.'

'Have you got enough warm clothes, by the way? I know it was a bit nicer today, but it'll get cold again soon enough.'

'I can go to a charity shop if I have to,' Finn said. 'You don't need to worry.'

'I know I don't *need* to—'

'Listen, I've got to be somewhere, but will you say thanks to Howard and Mary for me?'

'No problem,' Miller said.

'You know, next time you and them are tripping the light fantastic or whatever.' There was an intake of breath and a papery crackle; it sounded like she was smoking. 'And you, obviously.'

'Me, what?'

'Thanks. I mean . . . I probably don't say it enough.'

'Don't be soft—' She'd hung up before Miller could say anything else, but it didn't matter. He knew that she wouldn't come round any time soon and it was annoying because he had any number of old coats and sweaters he could give her.

But that single, muttered *Thanks* would last him a good long while.

THIRTY-SEVEN

His favoured mode of transport was not allowed on the motorway, which Miller considered to be a heinous and discriminatory piece of legislation, but after a pleasant enough forty-five-minute pootle along the A583 – through Little Plumpton, Kirkham and Ribble – he parked the moped next to an HMP Preston 'meat wagon' and submitted himself to the purgatory of gaining entrance to the prison.

The routine of searches, property confiscation and X-ray machines took more than fifteen minutes and was one from which Miller's warrant card did not excuse him. He was fine with it, because he'd gone through the process a good many times before. He cheerfully parted with his rucksack (not a big deal), his mobile phone (far too big for any prisoner to shove up his backside, but hey ho) and only became a little chopsy when the hatchet-faced officer on duty demanded that Miller hand in his crash helmet.

'That's a bit over the top, isn't it?'

'It's a potential weapon that, sir.' The officer smacked the helmet into his palm and nodded. 'You could brain someone with that.'

'If I was so inclined,' Miller said. 'However, *were* anything to kick off in there, don't you think my having a crash helmet might actually help?'

Hatchet-Face just stared, so Miller didn't press the point.

The walk from reception took him through several areas of the prison where inmates were milling about. He was escorted at all times, of course, but this remained a journey that one or two of his colleagues might have found a little daunting. The merest sniff of a copper would elicit abuse if you were lucky or something far nastier if you weren't. On one occasion a year or so back, Tony Clough had been the target for a nicely aimed turd, the memory of which had cheered Miller up many a time.

'Morning . . . nice day for it . . . how's it going?'

Miller smiled and gave a thumbs-up as he was led past an eclectic group of prisoners gathered at the far end of the wing. He wasn't overly concerned about any possible reaction. Yes, there was always a slim chance that he might actually be recognised but he couldn't recall having banged anyone up in this particular prison and, that possibility aside, he knew very well that he didn't look like most people's idea of a detective.

The prisoners stared blankly back at him. Miller knew that most of them would think he was there to check stock in the prison library or teach a pottery class.

Half an hour after arriving, he was finally seated in the visits area, watching as Craig Pickering was shown in and pointed across to the table where Miller was waiting.

Miller raised a hand to wave.

Pickering slunk across and slid into the chair opposite Miller like he had nothing better to do. He was short but

wiry-looking, the predictable prison pallor contrasting nicely
with dark hair that hung down across his forehead like spider's
legs. He didn't appear to have a great many teeth.

Miller introduced himself.

Pickering just stared, looking bemused and apprehensive at
the same time, which Miller thought was a good trick.

'I've got one a bit like that.' Miller pointed at the regulation
prison tabard that Pickering was wearing. 'It's yellow, though,
so other drivers can see me when I'm on my moped. Actually,
I was wearing one yesterday when I was on a big mower, but
that one was green . . .'

'What you on about, mate?'

'Oh, sorry. I was just trying to make conversation really,'
Miller said. 'Keeping it light, you know, because I'm afraid
that I've come with some rather upsetting news.'

Now, Pickering just looked apprehensive.

'It's about your brother. Gordon. Thinking about it, maybe
I didn't need to say his name because obviously you know
who your brother is. But yeah, it's about him.' Miller waited,
hoping that Pickering would say, 'He's dead, isn't he?' like
people did on TV, but he didn't.

'He's dead,' Miller said. 'No easy way to say it, I'm afraid.'
He was aware there were probably easier ways to say it than
that, but he didn't have all day.

'Right,' Pickering said. He looked down at the metal tabletop and when he looked up again a minute or so later, there
was a film of tears across his eyes. 'Right, then.'

'I'm sorry for your loss,' Miller said.

Pickering nodded. 'So, what happened?'

Miller sucked his teeth and shook his head, because now
they were straying into slightly trickier territory. 'Well, I can't
tell you that with any real certainty because we don't actually

have your brother's body or indeed have any idea at all where it is. But I can promise you that he's dead. He's very dead.' Miller nodded. 'That much we *do* know.'

'How can you know for *definite*, though?'

'How do we know he's *dead*?'

'If you haven't got his body?'

'You sure you want to get into that? It's a bit grisly.'

'Tell me . . .'

Miller did as he was asked and, when he'd finished, Pickering sat staring helplessly down at his own hands, both thankfully still attached to the end of his arms. 'So yeah, that's how we know he was murdered and – in a roundabout way that I don't really need to go into – it's also how we know who murdered him.'

'I'm listening.' Pickering looked up, both his hands now clenched into fists. 'Who was it?'

'A contract killer who we believe your brother occasionally did some business with. A man named Dennis Draper . . . ?' Miller could see immediately that Perks's instinct had been right and that Craig Pickering knew exactly who Miller was talking about.

'Him?' Pickering barked out a bitter laugh. 'Yeah, well that's not his real name for starters.'

'No, we're aware of that,' Miller said. 'But as you and I are pals now, maybe we can start with you telling me what his real name *is*.'

'I'm not your pal.'

'Come on, Craig, I think we're definitely heading in that direction, so why don't you tell me anyway?'

'How do you reckon he murdered him?'

'Excuse me?'

'How did Draper kill Gordon?'

It was another awkward question. Dennis Draper had used a plastic bag to suffocate Andrew Bagnall and had most recently been seen brandishing a kitchen knife, but Miller's hunch was that he'd killed Gordon Pickering the same way he'd killed George Panaides. 'It's hard to be sure because, as I've already explained, we don't know where Gordon's body is, but my best guess, and it *is* only a guess, would be a bullet to the back of the head. That's definitely one of Draper's favourites.'

Pickering let out a long sigh.

'Would have been quick, though. If that's any comfort.'

'Not really.'

Miller leaned forward. 'Now, if we're going to get justice for your brother . . . for Gordon, which I'm sure is what *you* want too, we're going to need a bit of help. So, tell me about Draper.'

Pickering sat back and shook his head slowly. 'I'm telling you nowt.'

'Nowt?' Miller stared. Nowt was of no use to him at all.

'You heard me. I don't tell coppers nowt.'

'Yes, I heard you and I fully appreciate the ideological stance you appear to be taking here, but . . . he *killed your brother.*' Miller helpfully shaped his fingers into a gun and pulled the 'trigger' in case Pickering required a visual aid. 'He killed him and chopped his bloody hands off.'

'I don't care,' Pickering said. 'I'm not a grass.'

Miller sat back and sighed. 'Well, I can't say I'm not disappointed, Craig, because I am.' He reached into his pocket for a card and slid it across the table. 'Maybe you need a bit of time to reflect on things, though, so I'm going to leave you with that. It's got my number on, in case you change your mind.' He waved at the officer in the corner to let him know he was ready to leave. 'Just to say that were you to reconsider, and I can't promise anything, but there might be a little more enthusiasm when it comes to locating your brother's remains. Which would be nice.'

Pickering looked at him; sniffed.

'I'll leave you to chew on that then, shall I?' Miller stood up then pointed down to Pickering's mouth, which most definitely contained fewer than the recommended number of teeth. 'Presuming you can chew on *anything* ...'

THIRTY-EIGHT

The last dance of the evening's session was an up-tempo, full-on team extravaganza.

Mary had put together a short and energetic routine based around a basic swing, but with a few fancy moves of her own invention thrown in that she'd decided would stretch 'certain members of the group'. Those she felt (she was trying hard not to look at Nathan and Ransford when she said it) needed a 'bit of a push'. Miller suspected that Mary – who moved between the couples delivering instructions and shouting encourage-ment – was just keen to impress the newest member of the group with her skills as a choreographer and, while he didn't think ballroom aficionados would be getting too excited, he couldn't deny that she'd made a decent job of it.

Craig Revel Horwood might even have cracked a smile.

With his knee still a bit iffy and with negotiations with Alan from the community choir 'ongoing', Miller was once again happy to provide accompaniment for the evening. With the choice of suitable swing music down to him, he played 'Got to Get You Into My Life' – singing along with himself, parping out the horn parts for his own amusement and choosing to ignore the odd disapproving glance from the choreographer.

Miller decided he wouldn't tell her that he was playing what was famously Paul McCartney's 'love song' to marijuana.

He turned at the piano to watch them, relishing the glee on Ransford's face as he spun Gloria around, Nathan's rictus of concentration as he tried not to trip Veronica up and Mary's beatific smile as she counted out the steps and marshalled her troops. It was bittersweet, of course, Miller's joy tempered only by knowing how very much Alex would have enjoyed it.

How she would have *nailed* Mary's routine.

A few minutes later, they were all getting changed and making plans to repair to the Bull, as usual. Veronica had just announced that she would be coming along – if that was all right with everyone – and that the first round was on her, when the door at the back of the hall creaked open and Miller turned with the rest of them to see a familiar figure step in and wave.

'Who's that?' Nathan asked.

'Never you mind,' Howard said. He and Mary knew exactly who the man in the scarlet trousers and soft leather jacket was. Ralph Massey had just been beginning to make a name for himself during their last few years on the force.

While Miller hung back, the rest of the gang filed past their visitor on the way out. At the door, Howard gave Massey a good hard look, shouting back to let Miller know that there'd be a pint with his name on waiting for him at the pub.

Massey smiled and bowed.

'It's lovely to see you back with your little troupe again,' Massey said, once he and Miller were alone. He fashioned a sad face. 'Can't be quite the same though, can it? Not now—'

'Don't,' Miller said, an edge to his voice he hoped was obvious.

Massey shrugged and moved further into the hall. He wandered around, tut-tutting at the faded floorboards and cracked paintwork and grimacing as he fingered the dust on window ledges. 'You know, I'd be very happy to organise a space for you all at the Majestic. Far cleaner and better equipped than this hole.' He smiled. 'Mates' rates, obviously.'

'What do you want?' Miller asked.

'Well, as an entrepreneur for whom dance is, to say the least, fundamental to his business, I do like to keep abreast of what's happening in the community. The moves being made, as it were. It's heartening that there's so much genuine enthusiasm among the amateurs.'

Miller asked the question again.

'I was just wondering how it was going, that's all,' Massey said. 'Your *investigations*. I'm understandably keen to know if you and your colleagues have made any progress. I'm referring of course to your laudable efforts to rid our town of the one individual whose nefarious activities continually drag it down into the gutter.'

'The *one* individual?'

Massey smiled and sat down at the piano. He began to slowly play some tune which was probably meant to convey a message, but Miller didn't recognise it. He waited, fighting the temptation to smash the lid of the piano down on to Massey's perfectly manicured fingers.

Massey finished playing and looked up. 'Well? Is Wayne Cutler going to get what he deserves any time soon?'

'Since when do I or anyone I work with report to you?'

'You don't, obviously.'

'As long as you understand that.'

'Let me put it another way.' Massey took a few seconds.

'How adjacent are we to those theoretical circumstances we discussed last time we spoke?'

For a drag queen turned gangster, whose reading habits didn't go much beyond a subscription to *OK!*, Massey's habit of speaking as though he were far more erudite and sophisticated than he actually was remained as annoying as ever, but Miller understood him well enough.

You put Cutler away, I tell you what I know about your wife's murder.

The thought of doing anything that would further Ralph Massey's twisted ambitions was a deeply unpleasant one, but Miller knew he didn't have a lot of choice. He said, 'I'm ... hopeful.'

'Hopeful's good,' Massey said, beaming. 'Hopeful makes me happy.'

'I couldn't be more thrilled,' Miller said. 'Now, I've got friends waiting.' He took a few steps towards the door, then stopped and turned. 'Just before I go, though, a nice long prison sentence for Wayne Cutler is good news for ... well, the whole of humanity, that's a given. But what guarantee have I got that my life's going to get any easier when the only villain I've got to worry about is you?'

Massey laughed. 'Oh, I'm *much* nicer than Wayne Cutler,' he said, mock-outraged. 'And even if I wasn't ...' He held out his arms towards Miller and gave him the full 'jazz hands'. 'At least I can dance!'

Walking away towards the door, Miller heard Massey picking out another melody on the piano behind him, and this time the message was clear enough.

The *Strictly* theme tune.

Alex's ringtone.

*

Miller was quiet in the pub afterwards, but nobody questioned him about it. He guessed they'd been advised by Mary and Howard not to, for which he was extremely grateful; content to listen to the rest of them talk about promenades, basic passes and triple steps, while he sat and drank and thought about what Massey had said.

Those theoretical circumstances.

Maybe he was naïve or just being an idiot but, unlike DCI Lindsey Forgeham, Miller chose to believe that Massey *did* have information about what had happened to Alex and that, if Miller was able to put Wayne Cutler away, the owner of the Majestic would stick to his part of the bargain.

What other options did Miller have?

The only fly in this uncomfortable ointment was that his best shot at putting Cutler away was catching Dennis Draper and they were no nearer doing that than they were when he and Massey had first talked about things. Draper remained a ghost. One with bad hair and a propensity for chopping people's hands off, but a ghost nonetheless.

Right now, Miller's best – *only* – hope was that some dopey guesthouse owner might get round to looking at Draper's picture and recognise him as one of their guests. Or that Craig Pickering might reconsider his fierce commitment to saying 'nowt'.

It wasn't much to cling on to.

'I loved that song you were playing,' Veronica said, suddenly.

'Yeah, that was a banger,' Nathan said.

'It's actually about … weed, isn't it? Or have I got that wrong?'

Miller turned to her. 'You a Beatles fan?'

'Who isn't? Veronica said.

'Well, *you* can stay.'

Mary was looking horrified. 'That can't be right, can it, Declan? The song was about *drugs*?'

Miller nodded. 'So Paul McCartney says.'

She sighed sadly, shaking her head at the parlous state of the world, and when she looked at Howard he did exactly the same. 'You'll be telling me next that "Yesterday" is about heroin.'

'Don't be daft, Mary,' Miller said. 'But I can't make any promises about "Day Tripper" ... '

THIRTY-NINE

The next day finally delivered the brass-monkey weather that Miller had known was coming. It sent Finn hurrying to Barnardo's to buy a fleece and, with frost glittering on the park's footpaths, Imran was forced to pull his towable gritter from the equipment shed, but the sudden drop in temperature also heralded a change in Miller's luck.

Up to a point.

He arrived at work within a few seconds of Sara Xiu. She pulled up next to him on the motorbike that always made Miller's moped seem a little ridiculous, though he'd long given up rising to her comments about glorified mobility scooters or hairdryers on wheels. She'd once amazed him with a *very* out of character joke about his moped being like Kurt Cobain or Amy Winehouse because it couldn't quite make it to thirty, but he'd chosen not to dignify it with a response.

Though he had left an extremely realistic rubber rat on her desk later on.

They walked into the station together.

'Good night?' Miller asked.

'Yeah, all right . . . '

Her failure to look at him when she'd answered told Miller that, in all likelihood, his partner had spent another evening in the room above the King's Arms, and the night with whichever metalhead had taken her fancy. He was trying not to judge Xiu for what some might describe as a reckless approach to dating, but he *was* starting to get seriously worried about the damage she was doing to her eardrums.

'You?'

'Dance group,' Miller said.

'Nice.'

They pushed through the doors to the incident room together; nodded to those of their colleagues who were already at their desks. 'Though it was slightly spoiled when Ralph Massey put in an appearance.'

'Massey's joined your dance group?'

'Remind me, are you actually a detective?'

'Sorry, I just thought—'

'He came to ask how we were getting on with our mission to finally nail Wayne Cutler. Like we're his private police force or something.' Miller dropped his rucksack next to his chair and set his crash helmet down. 'I quite wanted to slap him with a dance pump.'

Xiu dropped off her own belongings at her desk then walked straight back to Miller's. 'Is he still making promises about your wife's case?'

Miller nodded.

'Promises he won't keep. You do know that, right?'

'You might be right, but if I've got to choose between what Massey *might* know and the things Forgeham and her team definitely *don't*, I think that, as of now, my money's on the former Miss Coco Popz.'

Xiu shrugged, like she couldn't be bothered arguing about it. 'Well, we'd better catch Draper then, hadn't we?'

'Right, so Draper can spill his guts about Cutler.'

'And Massey can screw you over.'

Miller raised a hand. He was already wondering where he could get hold of another rubber rat. 'You've made your point, Posh, all right? Just promise me you won't say "I told you so".'

Xiu thought about it. 'Only once.'

'Fair enough,' Miller said.

Xiu wandered away when Miller's phone began to ring, but as soon as he'd recognised the voice at the other end he waved her back over so that she could hear the conversation.

'Did you mean it?' Craig Pickering asked. 'About looking for Gordon's body?'

'We'll have shovels at the ready, Craig.' Miller checked himself in case he was sounding insensitive. 'I say that, but we might not actually *need* shovels. Depending on how we get on and where he actually *is*, we might end up using a heat-seeking helicopter or you know ... underwater search teams, but whatever it takes to find him, we'll have the appropriate equipment standing by.'

Xiu was listening in and looking excited. Miller had told her about his conversation with Craig Pickering when he'd got back from Preston the previous afternoon. The deal he'd offered him.

'It would mean a lot to our mum,' Pickering said. 'If we could get Gordon back.'

'Course it would,' Miller said. 'And I reckon we can give you his hands back an' all, eventually. We might need to hang on to them for a *bit* ... if there's a court case or what have you, but after that for sure.'

'Yeah, that'd be good.'

'So, tell me about Dennis Draper ...'

Ten minutes later, Miller was standing alongside Xiu and other key members of the team in front of Tim Sullivan's desk.

'OK, you ready for this, because it's really quite shocking? Dennis Draper's real name is actually, da-da-da-da-da-da-daaaa ... Dudley Driscoll.'

Sullivan stared. *'Dudley?'*

'It's where he's from, apparently, and the lack of imagination shown by his parents is clearly hereditary, because Mr Driscoll only ever uses aliases with the same initials. DD.'

'Double D.' Clough smirked and held his hands in front of his chest as though he was in possession of basketball-sized breasts. 'A bit ironic, considering that he ... you know ... doesn't like women.'

Xiu and Fuller both threw him their filthiest looks.

'Always the same two letters?' Sullivan asked.

'That's right, sir,' Xiu said. 'Even if he's sometimes pretend-ing not to be English. According to Craig Pickering, he's been Duncan Dunbar from Glasgow and he once pretended to be a Welshman called Dafydd Dafis.'

Sullivan reached for a pen. 'How are we spelling that?'

'I'm not sure it's relevant,' Miller said. 'But the bloke's clearly an evil genius.'

'Donald Duck,' Fuller said, apropos of nothing whatsoever.

'Danny Dyer,' Xiu said, joining in.

'Derek Dick!' Clough said.

Sullivan glared. 'Now you're just being stupid, DC Clough.'

'It's the real name of the singer from Marillion, sir.' Clough sounded a little hurt. 'Fish or whatever he's called.'

'I never had you down as a prog-rock fan,' Miller said.

Clough shrugged, reddening slightly though clearly pleased to have said something that had impressed Miller. 'It was in a pub quiz.'

'Right.' Sullivan stood up, ready to take charge. 'Now we're cooking, so let's get back on those phones, pronto. This should narrow things down a bit . . .'

FORTY

Miller and Xiu were snatching a quick lunch in the Deadly Duck and this time Xiu had very wisely decided to steer well clear of the rissoles. While Miller devoured a plate of chips and a pork pie that had thankfully not been prepared on the premises, she tucked happily into a cheese roll that even a chef with the limited ability of Janet's husband would have struggled to make a mess of.

'Good choice,' Miller said. 'Best to keep it simple.'

Xiu nodded, chewing. 'It's really nice, actually.'

Miller glanced across to see Janet eyeing them from behind the bar. She was smiling at the rare spectacle of a customer enjoying her lunch, but it quickly became a scowl when she saw that Miller was looking at her.

Miller grinned, his mood as good as it had been in several days, and Janet gave him two fingers.

All was as it should be.

'I know I might be straying into somewhat delicate territory here,' Miller said, 'but I'm not quite as convinced that some of your . . . other choices are equally sensible.'

Xiu put down her roll and waited. The look on her face made it clear that she knew what was coming and that Miller had massively misjudged his level of privilege within their relationship. It was instantly apparent that she might start twitching like a maniac if he went any further.

He couldn't help himself.

'I'm just saying . . . look, far be it from me to pass judgement on anyone's private life, least of all yours—'

'So don't then,' Xiu said. 'Stop now.'

'Right, got it.' Miller sat back and reached for a chip. He was on the verge of popping it into his mouth when he sat forward again. 'I just think there are better ways to . . . find someone, you know? That's all.' Once more he moved to eat the chip then decided against it and waved it around for emphasis instead. 'Come on, who the hell chooses a sexual partner based on their ability to play air guitar?'

Xiu managed a fast, thin smile, clearly trying not to get any more annoyed. She brushed crumbs from her shirt and calmly said, 'It's really none of your business, Miller.'

'You're right, Posh, it's not. I know it's not.' *Now* he ate the chip and sat back, shaking his head. 'Look, it's probably just because I don't have a love life of my own any more, so I'm taking what's obviously an unwelcome interest in yours. I'm sorry, but I can't help being worried. Never mind headbang-ers, some of those people look like proper head*cases*.'

'How would you know?'

Miller shrugged and looked down at his plate of chips. 'I might have put my head round the door, one night a couple of weeks back. Just to see, you know?' He sighed in disbelief at the state of things, in much the same way Mary had done the night before in the pub. 'I still can't find the right word to describe it . . . it was like hell, only instead of sulphur it stank of testosterone and Carling and all the demons had Iron Maiden tattoos.'

'It's just heavy metal, Miller. Well, death metal if you want to be specific—'

'It was bloody terrifying.'

Xiu's expression softened a little. 'Look, you don't need to worry, all right? I can look after myself, besides which I don't mind the smell of spilt lager and I *am* one of those headcases.'

'Fine,' Miller said. 'I'll shut up.'

They ate in silence for half a minute, then Xiu leaned tentatively towards him. 'Look, when it comes to relationships, some of us aren't quite as lucky as you.'

'*Lucky?*'

'What you had with Alex, I mean. Before. It's what most of us want if we're being honest, but it's rare, you know?'

Miller nodded. He didn't quite know what to say, though he imagined that Alex herself might have a few things to contribute the next time they talked.

'*Rare? You want to talk about "rare"? Let's talk about how many times you put the sodding bins out . . .*'

'Also, it's not going to be for ever, is it?'

'What isn't?'

'You not having a love life.' Xiu checked herself. '*Is* it?'

Miller opened his mouth but managed no more than a helpless squeak.

'I don't mean like *now*,' she said. 'Or next week or whatever . . . but maybe one day you'll meet someone else. You know, when you least expect it. I'm not saying you won't always be madly in love with your wife or that you'll ever forget her or anything, of course I'm not, but life goes on, doesn't it?' Xiu was reddening a little and starting to gabble; looking like she wished she hadn't gone down this iffy conversational road every bit as much as Miller had a few minutes earlier. 'Obviously I've never been in your position. I've never lost anyone close to me, which means I don't really know what I'm talking about . . . so maybe now it's my turn to shut up.' She sat back, breathing heavily. 'I'll shut up.'

This time, Miller *really* had nothing to say.

It wasn't as though the situation Xiu was talking about had never crossed his mind. A few times in the months since Alex had been killed he'd seen someone in the street, and once in this very pub, who – to use one of Alex's favourite expressions – he 'wouldn't have kicked out of bed for eating crisps' – but the notion had always been fleeting. It had felt horribly wrong and had quickly evaporated as soon as Miller had begun to imagine what Alex herself would have to say about it.

At the same time, though, he also knew that Xiu only had his best interests at heart and he was grateful for it. He guessed that what she was saying was right, generally speaking, and that the day might well come when such thoughts did not feel dirty or disloyal, but it still felt like a long way in the future.

'Listen, Sara . . . ' He stopped when he saw that Xiu was pointing and mouthing something. He hadn't even been aware that his phone was ringing.

Andrea Fuller sounded excited, which made Miller sit up straight immediately. When Xiu shuffled her chair forward, he set his phone on the table between them and put it on speaker.

'I think we've got him,' Fuller said. 'The Sandy Shores guesthouse on Freckleton Street. The initials are right and having seen the picture, the landlady reckons it's him.'

'Reckons?'

'Well, he's currently rocking a ponytail apparently, but she sounds pretty sure about it.'

'Good enough.'

'Oh yeah ... and he's Spanish.'

Miller stuffed the last of his pork pie into his mouth and reached for his jacket. 'Well, of course he is.' He waved a twenty-pound note so that Janet could see it, then tucked it beneath a glass.

'We'll be there in five minutes,' Xiu said.

'*Cinco minutos*,' Miller said, getting to his feet.

The two of them brainstormed Dudley Driscoll's likely aliases as they walked quickly towards the door.

'My money's on Domingo,' Miller said. 'I'm pretty *sure* that's Spanish.'

'What about Donatello?' Xiu said. 'Oh, wait, that's a Ninja Mutant Turtle ... '

Janet stepped from behind the bar as soon as they'd left. Having heard the conversation as Xiu and Miller were on their way out, she muttered to herself as she leaned down to clear away the dirty plates.

'He were a bloody sculptor.'

FORTY-ONE

Everything had been set up in the briefing room by the time ·
Miller and Xiu got back.

Tim Sullivan stood at the head of the table wearing a
headset that made him look like Madonna in a bad suit, his
phone already connected via Bluetooth to a large speaker
mounted on the wall. He looked to make sure the team
were seated and ready, reminded them all to pay very close
attention, then made the call. He cleared his throat when it
was answered and leaned forward to speak. His authoritative tone somewhat belied what little authority he actually
commanded.

'Mrs Duddridge? This is Detective Inspector Sullivan. I'm
here with my team to take you through a few key points in
advance of our operation later this afternoon.'

'You know, he's actually got quite a good voice for radio,'
Miller whispered to Xiu. 'Not to mention a great face for it.'

Xiu shushed him.

'Right you are,' Isla Duddridge said. She sounded a little

tinny through the speaker, but it was clear enough for everyone to hear.

'First of all, madam, thank you for your co-operation. It's
very much appreciated.'

'Welcome, I'm sure, though I must tell you that I'm still in
a bit of a state about the whole thing—'

'That's perfectly understandable—'

'Course, you never *really* know who you've got under
your roof, so the best you can do is take people at their
word, isn't it? I've been in this game a good few years and
up to now I've always been able to spot the bad eggs . . . you
know, get a read off them, but I suppose there's a first time
for everything.'

'Mrs Duddridge—'

'It's probably because he's foreign.'

'Can I ask where you are at this precise moment?'

'Well, I'm certainly not in the house, am I?'

'That's excellent.' Sullivan nodded, delighted that the first
of his pre-operational boxes had been ticked.

'I'm just across the road, outside the dry cleaners.'

'Could I please ask that you *not* return to your property until
we tell you that it's safe to do so?'

'Fair enough . . . but it's seriously parky out here and I only
thought to bring a thin jacket.'

'Is there not somewhere nearby you could go for a few
hours?' Sullivan asked. 'A café or something?'

The woman thought about it for a few seconds while the
sounds of screaming seagulls filled the room. Miller had seen
one the size of a Labrador a few days earlier and, until she
spoke again, he wondered if the woman had been plucked from
the pavement and carried off. 'I suppose I could pop in and
see Linda at the Tropic Delight. She's actually a competitor,

but we're friendly enough most of the time and she's usually got a bottle of something on the go.'

'Tropic *what*?' Miller leaned across to Xiu. 'She knows she's in Blackpool, right?'

'That sounds ideal,' Sullivan said.

'Hang on, I can see her coming now . . . '

'Please, Mrs Duddridge . . . '

Now, all Sullivan and the rest of them could do was sit back and listen to an impromptu conversation between the rival guesthouse owners.

'*I can't really talk now, Linda. I'm on the phone to the police.*'

'*The police? What's that all about, then, Isla?*'

'*Well, I can't say too much. I'll be across in a bit and we'll have a proper natter then . . .*' She came back to Sullivan. 'Sorry about that.'

'Madam, I must insist that you keep the details of what's happening to yourself. Otherwise you risk compromising our entire operation.'

The woman sounded more than a little offended. 'I'm not stupid, am I? Don't worry, I'll just tell her it was about my gnomes getting vandalised in the summer. I did report it, but bugger all was done, same as usual.'

Sullivan took a deep breath. 'Now, can I ask you to confirm that the individual you have registered as Diego Diaz is still inside the property?'

'I can't say as I've heard him go out,' she said. 'But I don't always because I stay in my lounge most of the time and I've not really had a lot to do with this bloke. Keeps himself to himself, you know what I mean?'

'That's fine,' Sullivan said. 'We'll find out soon enough. And he's in room number three, correct?'

'That's correct, yes. On the first floor.'

'What about your other guests?'

'Well, if I'm honest we're not exactly heaving at the moment. It's off-season, so I've only got two other rooms occupied. There's a gentleman from Wolverhampton and a nice young couple who've come down from Scotland to see the illuminations. They might be in their rooms or they might not. They're usually down at the Pleasure Beach this time of day, but what with it being so cold ...'

'That's not a problem, Mrs Duddridge. Obviously it would be better if they were out, but my officers are highly trained so even if they are in residence, they won't be in any danger.'

'Danger?'

'I know you've already been informed that our suspect is highly dangerous, so you must understand that this will be an armed operation.'

'Oh, blimey,' Isla said.

'That's about everything we need,' Sullivan said. 'I just have to ask again if there is any possibility that you could send us a floorplan of your property.'

She sighed. 'I already explained to the woman I spoke to before. My husband dealt with all that. I'm sure there *was* a floorplan or what have you, but since Brian did his moonlight flit I've no idea where all that stuff is.'

'There is a back door though, is that right?'

'Out to the patio area, yes. A couple of chairs and one of those outdoor heater things. For the smokers.'

'Understood. I'll have officers stationed at the rear of the property should our suspect try to leave that way.'

'What if he jumps out the window?'

'Don't worry, my officers will be on hand to pick him up and take him to hospital.' Sullivan looked quite pleased with his quip and looked up as though expecting a polite round of applause. 'Right, madam, thank you again for being so help-ful. I think I can let you go—'

'Mrs Duddridge?'

Sullivan looked up, not best pleased that Miller had broken into the conversation.

'Have you got a spare key?'

'I've got loads of spare keys, love. I run a guesthouse.'

'Great stuff,' Miller said. 'We can pick one up from you before everything kicks off. Saves us having to smash your front door in.'

'Yes, I was just going to suggest that.' Sullivan leaned down to the phone again as though re-taking possession of it. 'It's always best to go in quietly when possible.'

'What's he supposed to have done, anyway?'

Sullivan hesitated.

'I know you said Señor Diaz is dangerous, but what's that mean? I think I've got a right to know exactly what one of my guests has been up to.'

'I'm afraid I can't go into details at this stage. Suffice it to say—'

'I'm guessing it's some kind of human smuggling thing, because I read that a lot of them traffickers go through Spain. Presumably you're working with Interpol or whatever they're called, because—'

'Mrs Duddridge.' Miller again. 'You do know he's not actu-ally Spanish, right?'

'*How's* that?'

'He's from Dudley.'

'Oh, for God's sake.' The woman sounded annoyed. 'I needn't have wasted money buying that bloody tapas.'

As soon as he'd hung up, Sullivan leaned forward, his arms braced against the table to address his troops. 'OK, there's

an armed unit waiting for me to brief them, so I'll leave you
to familiarise yourselves with the details. I've got a couple
of officers already watching the property, front and back, in
case he leaves before we get there, but presuming that doesn't
happen, we'll wait until it's starting to get dark.'

He sniffed and looked at each of them in turn, eyes narrowed. 'Right, so let's get this done.'

There were nods and a few assertive 'sir's. Clough slapped
his hand on the table then stood up with his fists clenched
and his teeth firmly gritted, like a porky Henry V in some
low-budget student film.

Xiu looked at Miller.

'I'm a coiled spring,' he said.

'You don't seem overly excited,' Xiu said as they were
walking out.

Miller said nothing. In truth he was apprehensive, because
he needed this to work out for all sorts of reasons and the
fact that it was being organised by Tim Sullivan made him
extremely nervous.

Xiu made it clear she knew exactly what those reasons were.

'I thought you would be a bit more fired up,' she said.
'That's all. Catching Driscoll means we clear up two murders ... at *least* two. That's good for everyone and for you
more than most, right? Your gamble in not telling him about
the briefcase pays off, and maybe you get some ammunition
to go after Cutler ... and *maybe* Ralph Massey makes good on
his promise about Alex.'

She wasn't helping.

'Oh, I'm keen as mustard,' Miller said. 'The proper yellow
stuff. It's just that having to listen to "Alan Partridge with a
SWAT team" back there and seeing how much he gets off on

it tempers my excitement ever so slightly.' He nodded to where Sullivan was deep in conversation with the commander of the firearms unit. 'Did you see him do that funny crouching thing after he made his big speech at the end? I reckon he had a semi on.'

'Miller!' She looked disapprovingly at him, but couldn't suppress a smile for very long. 'I think you're probably . . . half right.'

FORTY-TWO

It was freezing in the car and Miller was wishing he'd been to the toilet before they left the station. There was a healthy degree of tension, obviously, and Miller knew that the dozen or more officers on tenterhooks in nearby vehicles or with weapons already trained on the Sandy Shores guesthouse would be buzzing with nervous excitement. It didn't make the waiting any less tedious, though.

'I suppose a quick game of I Spy's out of the question?'

Xiu turned, all set to let him know that it most certainly was—

'All units from TFC. State Amber. Repeat, state Amber. Stand by . . . '

The authoritative, yet nicely modulated voice of the Tactical Firearms Commander rang out from both their radios at the same time.

Miller nodded, impressed. 'Now, *he'd* be even better than Sullivan, I reckon.'

'Better at what?'

'On the radio.' He dropped into a smooth DJ voice. '"Hello and welcome to Firearms Hour here on Magic FM. I'll be keeping you company for the next sixty minutes, with soothing conversation about weaponry and a selection of classic songs to shoot by."' He looked to Xiu for a reaction.

'What's the *matter* with you?'

He'd been hoping for more.

Miller turned away to stare at the dark Skoda parked a hundred yards ahead on the opposite side of the road. With only the light from a nearby lamppost available, he couldn't make out the occupants clearly but knew that this was where the TFC was broadcasting from and that Tim Sullivan was sitting next to him. Behind them, Clough and Fuller waited in another vehicle, while the unmarked van from which six officers from the Firearms Operations Unit had just begun to emerge sat right around the corner.

'Roger. State Amber received. Standing by on Red . . . '

In the Skoda, while Sullivan sat twiddling his thumbs, the firearms commander would be studying a laptop, monitoring the separate feeds from the helmet-mounted cameras of his officers, who were already moving into position.

'How pissed off d'you think he is?'

'Who?'

'Sullivan. At not being the one who gets to give the "go". At having to sit there like a spare part while the bloke with the all the techy gear and the cool initials calls the shots. On a scale of one to ten, how much is that ticking him off, do you think?'

Xiu sat staring down at her radio, waiting. 'I've no idea . . . '

'I'm going for . . . a hundred and forty-seven—'

'State Red.' The TFC gave the order. *'Repeat, state Red. Go when you're ready . . . '*

Miller and Xiu watched as the firearms team crept along the

pavement to the guesthouse and took up their positions outside
the front door. He saw the drivers of passing cars slow down to
gawp and get quickly waved on, the decision having been made
not to close off the road in case the absence of traffic made
Driscoll suspicious. They watched the team leader produce
the key they'd collected earlier from Isla Duddridge and use
it to open the front door. They heard him announce that they
had gained entry before leading his officers into the property.

Then everything went quiet.

Had this been a TV drama or the climactic scene in some
unimaginative thriller, the radios in the various vehicles would
have immediately begun transmitting a series of chaotic
crashes and shouts: Armed police! Room clear! We've got
guns, you bastard!

That kind of thing . . .

As it was, all that screaming and kicking in of doors would
be little more than showing off when you already had a key.
Having guns certainly gave you an edge, but Miller knew
that stealth was a far more effective method of surprising and
hopefully apprehending a dangerous suspect. Moving like
a disciplined team of ninjas, the officers inside the property
would by now be employing a series of well-rehearsed hand
signals to communicate with one another as they made careful, *silent* progress through the house.

The team leader would point to his own eyes then point
again to indicate the direction of search. A thumb raised or
pressed to the tip of an index finger. A flat palm held above
the head to denote cover and a clenched fist telling an officer
to stop immediately.

'Do you think they ever get tempted to have a bit of fun with
it?' Miller began waving his hands about. 'All this signalling
business.'

Xiu looked at him. '*Fun?*'

'Maybe a nice game of charades or something.'

Once again, whatever withering comment Xiu was on the verge of delivering was cut off by the radio.

'*FOU team leader. The property is secure and room number three is empty. Repeat, suspect's room is empty . . .*'

Miller groaned in frustration and slapped his hand against the dashboard.

'We'd better get in there,' Xiu said.

'Can I just stay here and have a *little* cry first?'

'It's not the end of the world, Miller. There may well be something in there that *will* help us catch him, so—'

'I know that,' Miller said, wincing. 'I hurt my hand . . .'

He climbed out of the car and followed Xiu across the road to the guesthouse. He saw Clough and Fuller – in rather more of a hurry than he was – enter the building before him, and by the time he finally arrived at the front door, several of the armed officers were already on their way out.

Miller approached one who had just removed his helmet. As the officer began taking off his body armour, Miller placed his palms together then slowly opened them out. The officer stared at him.

'Come on . . . it's a *book*.' Miller sighed. 'A book, OK?' He held up three fingers. 'Three words. *First* word—'

The officer shook his head and swore at Miller under his breath. Xiu turned back and saw the mock-horror on her partner's face.

'What did he call you?'

'One word,' Miller said. 'One syllable.'

In the lobby, Tony Clough and Andrea Fuller were taking statements from the Scottish couple who had obviously been in residence and who'd evidently found the experience of having armed police knocking on their door rather more thrilling than the illuminations.

'Nothing this exciting ever happens in Cumbernauld,' the woman said.

At the foot of the stairs, the TFC was debriefing his team leader, while DI Tim Sullivan looked on with a face like a grief-stricken mullet. He'd been collared by Isla Duddridge who had hurried back in and was urgently demanding to know (a) when she could have her keys back, (b) if she was legally obliged to give the couple from Cumbernauld any kind of trauma-related refund and most importantly (c) to whom she should complain if any of those 'big ugly' guns had scraped her new wallpaper.

Miller and Xiu moved through the crowded lobby and climbed the stairs to the first floor.

The door to room number six was wide open.

'Looks lovely,' Miller said, peering in.

Xiu snapped on a pair of nitrile gloves. 'Twenty-four quid a night including breakfast, I think it could be a lot worse.'

Miller shrugged and pulled his own gloves on. 'Expensive hotels are more trouble than they're worth, anyway. Sometimes the towels are so fluffy you can't get your suitcase closed.'

Xiu was still trying to work it out as Miller pushed past her into the room, so she gave up trying.

They began to poke around, opening drawers and bending to look under the bed, which yielded nothing but a mouldy bible and a shocking amount of dust. Xiu picked up an old takeaway menu from the bedside table; a message scribbled on the back which had clearly been written by Andrew Bagnall just before he died. She showed it to Miller before sliding it into a plastic evidence bag.

Miller now knew how Driscoll/Draper had found Finn.

He was thinking about those stairs at the station again when he opened the small cupboard to discover several identical black shirts on wire hangers; socks, pants and T-shirts all neatly folded and a pair of training shoes that appeared brand new. He was frankly a little surprised that the man they were after was so particular about his wardrobe, but he lost interest when Xiu beckoned him over, having clearly discovered something a lot more interesting.

'Look at this.'

She was perched on the edge of the bed. Miller sat down next to her and watched her flicking slowly through a spiral-bound notebook. Judging by her expression as she handed it across for Miller to look at, Xiu clearly found a good deal of what she'd read hugely distasteful.

'He likes making lists,' she said.

Miller started turning the pages himself. 'Well, nobody likes a disorganised psychopath.'

He stopped at one of Driscoll's more recent entries.

He said, 'Oh, bloody hell . . . '

Fascinated as Miller was by their suspect's favourite tipples or the most memorable dying words of those he'd dispatched, this was a list that demanded rather more urgent attention. He was already on his feet and moving towards the door as he shoved the notebook into a plastic bag.

WHO'S GOT THE BRIEFCASE?

1. ~~Andy Bagnall.~~
2. ~~Keith Slack.~~
3. ~~Homeless girl.~~
4. ⋆Natalie Bagnall⋆

FORTY-THREE

Dudley Driscoll as was – *still* was somewhere deep down or if he was talking to his mother – who had spent the last few weeks as Dennis Draper, and more recently Diego Diaz, had been watching the comings and goings at the Sandy Shores guesthouse for the previous couple of hours.

Quite the spectacle the coppers had laid on.

He'd got out of there well before that of course, as soon as he'd clocked that something was amiss with the randy land-lady. He'd seen her scuttle away into the lounge when he'd come down to pick up a paper and the alarm bells had started ringing, because why would a woman who'd been all over him like a rash (which is quite probably what he'd have ended up with if she'd had her way) suddenly be avoiding him?

It wasn't hard to figure out what was happening.

He wasn't daft.

With no way of knowing when the boys and girls in blue would show up, he'd had little choice but to get out of there straight away. There hadn't even been time to chuck a few bits and pieces into a bag. It was annoying, having to leave all his stuff behind, but he'd done the same thing plenty of times before. In his game, you had to be ready to move on sharpish if things looked dodgy.

Not that he'd be moving on, as such. Not quite yet.

To start with, he'd hung around at the bus stop for a while and watched the unmarked vehicles parking up nearby. They'd be waiting until it was dark, he reckoned, one or two armed officers taking up their positions at the back of the house while their plain-clothes colleagues had eyes on the front, blah-di-blah. None of them were very hard to spot, however inconspicuous they tried to be, because Driscoll could smell a copper a mile away, and not just because so many of them stank of cheap aftershave and kebabs. One of them had actually walked right past him. They'd exchanged nods! He was far better at being inconspicuous than any chuffing copper, especially when he'd be the last person they were expecting to see so close to all the action and the cold weather had given him every reason to be wearing a long coat and a woolly hat.

After a while, he'd wandered along to a bench on the corner and sat there watching from behind a paper. Obviously he hadn't been reading it very closely, but it was still nice to see that his mug wasn't plastered across the front page any more. Even the murder of that lad Bagnall had been relegated to page five, but that wasn't really a surprise.

It was how things went, wasn't it?

People were around until they weren't and, even if Driscoll had helped a fair few of them on their way, life moved on.

With one eye on a report of Blackpool getting twonked three-nil at home to Huddersfield, he watched as the lads with the guns moved in. Creeping along the pavement, getting set. He guessed that one or two of the more gung-ho among them would already have their fingers poised on triggers, hoping that they might get a chance to do the job they'd been trained for. Watching them swarm through the front door into the guesthouse and knowing that they'd be getting no more shots away than Blackpool's centre forward, he almost felt sorry for them.

For obvious reasons, it had all been a bit of an anticlimax after that.

A few minutes later, he'd spotted that copper he'd last seen in the alleyway behind Slack's back garden. The strange one, Miller, getting out of a car and ambling across the road with his hands in his pockets, like he couldn't really be arsed, having already been told that he wouldn't be arresting anyone today. Ten minutes after that, he'd come tearing out of the house looking a damned sight keener than he had when he'd gone in and it wasn't hard to figure out why.

Yeah, it cheesed him right off that he'd had to leave his notebook behind, but it wasn't the end of the world. He could always write other lists. A more pressing concern was that now the Feds would have a pretty good read on where he'd be going next and, more specifically, who he'd be going after. They'd make it difficult for him, he knew that, but a challenge was good, because it kept him on his toes. He'd need to up his game, but that was no bad thing because it never did to be complacent.

If he hadn't been complacent in those bloody toilets a week and a bit before, none of this would be happening. He'd be long gone. He'd have genitals that were one hundred per cent functional and he'd be cheerfully spending Wayne Cutler's ten grand by now.

Not for the first time, Driscoll asked himself why he was even bothering, why he was still here and risking so much for ten poxy grand. The answer was vaguely depressing, but straightforward enough. Demand for his services had dropped off significantly during the pandemic, when people hadn't seemed so keen on having their enemies or business rivals bumped off. Maybe they thought Covid might do the job for them, but whatever the reason, his income had taken a serious hit. He hadn't got any sort of nest egg and it wasn't like people in his line of work had been at the head of the queue to be furloughed, so the sad fact was that ten grand was no longer an amount he could afford to sniff at.

On top of which, there was a principle at stake.

You did a job, you got paid for it, simple as that.

What the hell had happened to *fairness*?

Most important of all, there was his reputation to think about.

If word got around that he was the sort of bloke who would let himself get stiffed on payment, where would it end? He'd be a laughing stock. He'd be yesterday's hitman and he wasn't about to allow that to happen.

So, whatever the risks might be, he wasn't just going to scarper.

Walking away towards the seafront, Driscoll was already making plans. If he wanted to get his hands on that briefcase and the payoff that would come once he finally did, he'd need to be cautious and he'd definitely need to be clever. He'd have to think outside the box a bit, but he wasn't worried overly much.

Not when he thought about what and who he was up against.

Miller was clearly a cut above the rest of them, but he was no Tom Barnaby.

FORTY-FOUR

It seemed profoundly unfair to Miller that a day which had been positively bursting with promise could have left him feeling like he'd lost a pound and found a penny. He'd hoped that, by now, Driscoll or Draper or whatever his sodding name was would be sweating in an interview room, or better yet have been charged already and be curled into a foetal position, whimpering in a remand cell somewhere. But no, the fates had conspired to urinate fulsomely all over Miller's chips and ensure that neither of those things had happened. As it was, less-than-cuddly Dudley was still at liberty to enjoy the many and varied delights the town had to offer while breezily working out the best way to stalk and quite possibly kill the next seasider on his list.

Brilliant . . .

The drive home had been painfully slow because the moped was far from reliable on icy roads, but puttering through the freezing dark Miller had been able to console himself with the thought that things couldn't get any worse. Surely not.

He knew better than most that fate could be a vicious bastard, but piling agony on top of misery would be cruel and unusual punishment; like the re-election of Boris Johnson or an encore at a Queen concert.

Miller had arrived home looking forward to tinned sardines on toast, an hour or two in front of the telly and then, best of all, a cosy chinwag with a dead wife who would make everything better and reassure him that things weren't really as bad as all that.

It would be a decent end to the day, at least.

Before he'd had a chance to take his coat off or cuddle a rat, the phone had rung and Miller had known immediately there was unpleasantness coming his way. If he'd had even a smidgen of good fortune left to draw on it would have been a Nigerian prince promising a windfall or a breathy pervert demanding to know what Miller was wearing. He'd have settled for something work related: a mass shooting in KFC, say, or a routine pile-up on the M55.

No such luck.

'Hey, bro, it's me.'

His younger brother, Ross.

Miller couldn't decide which part of the cheery greeting was the most annoying. The 'bro', like his brother had joined a street gang, or the cheesy 'it's me' which suggested an easy familiarity and affection that Miller doubted he'd ever feel for his brother again. He felt closer to Tony Clough than he did to his brother. He was a lot fonder of his local newsagent, come to that, a friendly spud who he thought would be far more likely to donate a kidney, should Miller ever need one, than his brother.

'You there, Dec ... ?'

'Yeah, sorry. Just walked through the door.'

'Another hard day keeping the streets safe for the rest of us?'

'Something like that,' Miller said.

'So, I just called to let you know that I went to see Mum today.'

Right, Miller thought. You *just* called to let me know that, did you? To kindly let me know that you'd been to visit our mother while – and this was the important bit – I hadn't. 'How was she?'

'Oh, the same, you know. They're taking good care of her in there, though. Worth every penny, that place.'

'Good to know.'

'She was asking after you.'

Miller knew his brother was almost certainly lying. When Miller had last been to see his mum, she'd thought he was his father. 'That's good.'

'When was the last time you went to visit?'

And there it was, the real reason his jumped-up flashy little tit of a brother had called. To score a few more precious points. To nudge himself even further ahead in a competition Miller knew he could never win.

Because it was Ross who paid for the care home in Manchester.

Ross, who therefore loved their mother more than Miller did.

Ross, with his *very* successful property-management company, his nice house in the Ribble Valley, two lovely kids and a wife who was still alive.

'Not for a while, actually,' Miller said.

'That's all right.'

I know it's all right, you sanctimonious arse-biscuit. Miller tried to work it out and realised that he hadn't been to visit the care home for nearly two months. He'd only been once in fact

since Alex's funeral, which had also been the last time he'd
seen Ross. 'Work's been pretty full on,' he said.

'Course it has.'

It was no excuse, but it was all he had. He certainly wasn't
going to tell his brother how terrible the visits made him feel.
How sometimes he was grateful when work commitments got
in the way and how that, in turn, made him feel ashamed.

'Any news on the old man?' Ross asked, moving on like he
was working through an agenda.

Now, here was where Miller *did* have an advantage. He
hadn't seen his father since he'd arrested him five years before,
but he was able to track his movements via the Police National
Computer. Charlie Miller had most recently surfaced a few
months back in Wigan, where he'd been arrested after trying
to scam an old woman out of her life savings for some dodgy
roofing work.

'Not heard a peep,' Miller said.

'Probably best.'

'Listen, I need to crack on.'

'That's a shame.'

'I *know*, but I've got two rats looking up at me who need
cleaning out.'

'Right, so picking up a few rat turds is more important than
talking to your brother?'

'Oh, much more important,' Miller said. 'Catch you later,
bro . . . '

Miller hung up, then turned to see Alex leaning back
against the front door. It looked like she'd just got in from work
and, however many times they'd spoken since her death, the
sight of her still stopped Miller's breath for a moment.

'Your brother's not stopped being a massive dick, then.'

Miller was grinning as he took off his coat. 'There I

was thinking I couldn't possibly love you any more than I do,' he said.

'You might want to reconsider that in a minute.'

'Uh-oh . . . '

'Just . . . I was thinking that maybe it's time to build some bridges.'

'With my brother?'

'Why not? It wouldn't hurt to call *him* once in a while . . . and be honest for a change.'

Miller grunted as he trudged across to the cage, then grunted again when he knelt down to open the door.

'Tell him how you really feel whenever you visit your mum and how pissed off you are when he insists on letting you know how much it's costing him. Reach out, Miller. Be the bigger man.'

'Can you believe I was actually looking forward to this conversation?'

'Well, I can't help that, can I?'

'This was supposed to make me feel better.' Miller gently placed Fred and Ginger into their plastic roll-about balls and began clearing out their soiled bedding. 'I'm starting to think I should just gatecrash a funeral, cheer myself up a bit.'

Alex sighed and wandered over to the sofa. 'Fine. If it helps, the fact that Driscoll is still out there isn't your fault, so don't beat yourself up about it. Well maybe just a slap or two because you didn't tell him *you know what* about the *you know what*. What matters is you've still got more chance of catching him than anyone else and, most importantly, because *you* moved quickly Natalie Bagnall is safe and well for now.'

Miller looked up. 'For *now*?'

'OK, I could have phrased that better, but you see my point. Basically, get over yourself, you miserable bugger.'

Miller got slowly to his feet. 'Did you never think of volunteering for the Samaritans?'

Fifteen minutes later, once Miller and the rats had eaten, he and Alex lay sprawled on the sofa, eating crisps and watching *The Repair Shop*. Alex wiped her eyes after an old man's worm-ridden harmonium had been restored to its former glory. Miller quickly wiped his own, then sat up and turned the TV off.

'Ralph Massey came to see me last night,' he said.

Alex waited.

'Turned up after dance practice.'

'I'm guessing he wasn't there to check out your foxtrot.'

'No, he wasn't.'

'Because he'd have been sadly disappointed—'

'He came to remind me that he and I could still do ... business. That he had information to trade in return for Wayne Cutler getting put away.'

'You putting him away.'

'Well, I'm certainly the best chance Massey's got.'

'Which is why catching Driscoll matters to you so much.'

'It's one of the reasons,' Miller said.

'You think he's being straight with you?'

'There's a first time for everything.'

'Xiu doesn't think so.'

'Yeah, well, she's not always the best judge of things.' Miller reached across to softly brush crisp crumbs from her blouse. 'She ordered rissoles in the Deadly Duck.'

'I hope she's wrong,' Alex said. 'I hope Massey's as good as his word and you get the information you need.'

'Really?'

She took a few seconds then gave the smallest of nods.

'Well, that's good to hear, but I have to say I'm surprised.

You're normally a bit tight-lipped when it comes to certain touchy issues. You know, like your murder.'

This time the pause before she spoke was even longer. 'I want it to be over,' she said. 'Whatever it is you find out.'

'What happens then?' Miller asked.

Alex shrugged and turned away. Miller saw her raise a hand to wipe her eyes again, but told himself it was because she was still thinking about that old boy's harmonium.

FORTY-FIVE

Wayne Cutler stood at the bottom of the stairs and listened.

Clutching his phone, he was all set to make a call he could seriously do without making, but he didn't think it would hurt to put it off a few minutes longer, on top of which he couldn't shake the nagging suspicion that his wife was playing away. He didn't have what you might call hard evidence, but Jacqui had been funny with him for a while and it was a bit late for social calls. All the same, here she was up in her bedroom with the door shut, talking dead quietly like she didn't want to be overheard.

There was laughing, too ... giggling, even. Dead quiet giggling.

He listened for a few more seconds, then turned away towards his office, shaking his head. He was being ridiculous. What was it some actor had said when he was asked if he'd ever been unfaithful? Something about going out for burgers when there was steak at home. Or maybe it was going out for McDonald's when you had burgers at home ...

it didn't really matter. In the end he reassured himself with the one unassailable fact that meant he'd never have to think about it again.

She wouldn't bloody dare.

He closed the office door behind him and stalked across to his chair, deciding that he didn't want to think about burgers any more than he had to. If it wasn't for sodding burgers he wouldn't be making this sodding call for a kick-off. There was a growl in his throat as he stabbed angrily at the number on his phone; the one he'd got stored under '*HANDS*'.

'Mr Cutler . . . !'

There was surprise in his voice, definitely, but Dennis Draper didn't sound unhappy to be hearing from him. 'I wasn't sure this number would still be working,' Cutler said.

'Why wouldn't it be?'

'Heard you had to change locations in a hurry, that's all.'

'Got my phone, got my wallet. I'm sound.'

'You were lucky today, mate.'

'You're very well informed, Mr Cutler.'

'That's because I pay people to keep me informed.'

'Coppers, you mean?'

'Among other people. Now, listen—'

'Strikes me you were the one who got lucky,' Draper said.

'How's that?'

'Well, I seriously doubt you *want* me arrested. I'm taking a wild stab in the dark here, but a bloke such as yourself doesn't need the likes of me making statements, do you?'

Cutler remembered his conversation with that jumped-up burger flipper Bardsley. 'Funny, but people keep telling me how lucky I am.' There was a lot of background noise – traffic and wind – because Draper was clearly outside, but Cutler thought he heard a chuckle. Was the shit-stain actually *laughing* at him? 'Listen, why don't we stop messing about and get this thing sorted out?'

'Fine with me,' Draper said.

'Now I'm fairly sure you don't want to be hanging around here any longer than you've already had to and you're right, I wouldn't be broken-hearted if you slung your hook. So, because I'm feeling generous, I'm willing to forget all about the proof you agreed to provide and pay you five grand so as you can get on your way. How's that sound?' He heard Draper hawk something up and spit it out. 'Blimey, do you *have* to?'

'It sounds like an insult,' Draper said. 'The job was for ten, the job I *did*, so why should you get it for half price?'

'I'm trying to speed things along, that's all. Up to you.'

'I'm not in the business of doing discounts,' Draper said. 'I'll get you what I promised, you'll pay me what I'm owed and *then* we can speed things along.'

Cutler sighed and sat back, a headache brewing. Why the hell hadn't he just asked one of his own team to sort George Panaides out? It would have been simple enough. Why had he decided to outsource the job? A lesson, that's what it was. 'I've said my bit, Draper, so there you are.'

'Said mine, too.'

'Right then, we're done. Be lucky, yeah?'

'You be lucky too, Mr Cutler . . . '

Cutler put the phone down and walked out of the office to take up his position again at the foot of the stairs. He could still hear his wife's mysterious murmurings coming from the bedroom.

He shouted up. 'I'm making a cuppa, Jaq . . . you want one?'

There was a pause, a few more murmurs telling whoever she had on the other end of the phone to hang on. Then the bedroom door opened. 'Yeah, thanks, love. That'd be nice.'

Cutler wandered away towards the kitchen. He shouted again. 'You fancy a bit of chocolate to go with it? KitKat Chunky or something.'

'No ta, not for me.' The bedroom door closed again, but she carried on shouting. 'But I think there's a Creme Egg left in the cupboard if you want one . . . '

FORTY-SIX

The formal debrief on the previous evening's operation at the Sandy Shores guesthouse had taken place first thing. *No,* Sullivan had been keen to stress, the end result might *not* have been absolutely ideal, but it was important to focus on the *positives.* They had come away with what might prove to be game-changing information, not to mention the fact that every member of the team had carried out their job perfectly.

'Pretty much faultless,' Sullivan had said.

'Right, save for the fact that we don't actually have a suspect in custody.' Miller looked around. 'Unless I've missed something.'

'Yes, well.' Sullivan had gifted his team a smile clearly designed to suggest a calm wisdom. 'Personally, I favour a "glass half full" approach.'

'Remind me never to drink in the same pub as you,' Miller had said.

Now, half an hour later, a few of the core team sat together in Susan Akers's office. The DCI had decided that a more free-flowing and creative discussion might be the best way forward with the case, so had gathered those officers she most trusted to provide constructive ideas and genuine insight.

Also, Tim Sullivan.

Akers began by briefly echoing Sullivan's comments about how efficiently the operation at the guesthouse had been carried out. Miller cut in before she got to the 'but' that was intended to move the discussion along.

'I personally wanted to commend the DI on his delicate handling of Mrs Duddridge at the ... tail end of the operation,' Miller said. He shook his head in awe and wonder. 'The way he handled that woman's query about muddy boot-prints on her shagpile was a genuine masterclass in sensitive community policing.'

'Shut up, Miller.' Sullivan was clearly still riled that once boots – muddy or otherwise – were on the ground the night before, he hadn't been given something rather more important to do.

'I'm serious, Tim. You're obviously wasted in Homicide—'

Akers raised a hand. 'Yes, please shut up, DS Miller.'

'Of course, ma'am.' Miller winked at Sullivan. 'Seeing as you've asked so nicely.'

'Right, then.' Akers looked around. 'What do we think our suspect's next move is?'

'Well, we know what he'd like it to be.' Xiu shuddered, remembering some of the things she'd seen in Driscoll's notebook. 'Those lists ...'

'Horrible,' Miller said. '*Beyond* horrible.'

Akers and Sullivan both nodded.

'Who in their right mind doesn't have Ribena Sparkling Blackcurrant on a list of favourite drinks? The man's obviously more of a monster than we thought, and don't get me started on his list of things we'd all be better off without.' He saw the look Akers was giving him so chose *not* to get started. It was an effective shorthand, developed between them over many productive years working together, which had certainly resulted in fewer disciplinary hearings than would otherwise have been the case.

'Natalie Bagnall is safe though, correct?'

'Absolutely,' Sullivan said. 'She's at her parents' address and we've got a squad car parked permanently outside, as well as officers stationed on foot at the back of the property and patrolling the surrounding streets.'

'I still think she should be in a safe house,' Miller said.

'We gave her that option.' Sullivan looked to Akers. 'She chose not to take it, ma'am.'

'We can't make her,' Akers said.

'I'm going to have another word with her,' Miller said. 'Soon as we're done here.'

'Where's Driscoll going to go now?' Xiu asked.

'I'm not sure he'd risk another guesthouse,' Sullivan said.

'Sleeping rough then, maybe?' Xiu looked around, but nobody appeared to have a better suggestion. 'Well, we didn't find a wallet in his room, so I don't think he's helpless.'

'He's definitely not helpless,' Miller said. 'More importantly, he'll know what we *did* find in his room. So he knows that we know who his next target is. He won't do anything daft.'

'Do you think he knew we were coming last night?' Xiu asked.

'Maybe,' Miller said. 'Not sure it makes any difference.'

'Yeah, but if he *did* . . . isn't there a chance that he deliberately left that notebook to send us on a wild goose chase?'

'Good point,' Miller said. 'I see now that it might actually make a *massive* difference.' He thought about it for a few seconds. 'No, I'm still not convinced. We know the note he took from Andy Bagnall's flat was genuine, and that's where he got the idea that Bagnall's sister might have the case.' He looked across at Akers. 'Unless there's something we're not seeing or there's a list we didn't find, Natalie's the only option he's got left.'

'I still don't get it,' Xiu said.

Miller raised an eyebrow. 'Only on heavy metal night.'

Xiu glared, but it was clear the comment was lost on everyone else. 'I know that, for obvious reasons, Wayne Cutler's the last person Driscoll would want to run into, but if he wants his money so badly, why mess about chasing this stupid briefcase? Why doesn't he just try and catch Cutler off guard and take it?'

'It would be a brave man who tried that,' Akers said.

'He's barmy enough, though, right?' Nobody was arguing with her. 'So maybe desperate enough . . . ?'

'Let's hope he doesn't get *that* desperate,' Miller said. 'For everyone's sake.'

Finn was waiting for them in the car park, leaning against the wall, smoking. Miller marched across, surprised but happy to see her, though his expression hardened a little when he got close enough to see her face. The bruising around her nose and eyes had purpled, orange at the edges.

'Like I told you,' she said. 'Not launching any ships.'

Miller reached out, but she leaned away. 'Not unless they were launched *with* your face.'

'Is everything OK?' Xiu asked.

Finn rummaged in her pocket for a sheet of paper which she quickly began to unfold. 'We've found him.' She held up a black and white picture of Driscoll blown up from the local paper. It looked like it had been photocopied.

'What?' Xiu took the paper from her. 'Found him where?'

'Who's *we*?' Miller asked.

'Me and a few mates,' Finn said. 'Other people on the streets that I knock around with, you know? We handed this picture round and everyone kept an eye out. They were angry, after what he did.'

Xiu asked her question again.

'There's a row of derelict arches,' Finn said. 'On that bit of waste ground, behind the Vic.'

Miller and Xiu exchanged a look. The Victoria was the hospital in which both Wayne Cutler and Driscoll himself had been treated after the incident at the station. More significantly, it was where Natalie Bagnall worked.

'The lad who spotted him reckons he was sleeping there last night.'

Xiu reached immediately for her radio.

'Don't bother,' Finn said. 'He's not there any more.'

They looked at her.

'We checked.'

Miller began walking quickly away towards the car, Xiu a step or two behind him. 'He was never going anywhere near her parents' house.'

Xiu nodded her agreement. 'He's planning to go for her at work.'

'Aren't you going to tell someone?' Finn was hurrying to keep up with them. 'He might still be around there somewhere.'

'We'll call it in on the way,' Miller said.

'Where are you going?'

Xiu keyed the fob to unlock the car. 'To see Natalie Bagnall.'

Finn chucked her fag end away and thrust her hands into the pockets of her hoodie. 'That's Andy's sister, right?'

Miller stopped and turned to look at her. With everything that had happened since Finn had first called him asking for help, he'd almost forgotten that she and Andrew Bagnall had been friends. 'Yeah, his sister.'

'Can I come?'

'I'm sorry,' Xiu said. 'That really wouldn't be appropriate, because—'

Miller opened the back door. 'Hop in . . . '

FORTY-SEVEN

There was a degree of awkwardness when Natalie Bagnall's father opened the front door and introductions were made. Perhaps it was because the young woman accompanying the two detectives – aside from having serious facial bruising – was obviously not a police officer. It may just have been because Finn looked like . . . Finn. Mr Bagnall was clearly too polite to ask any questions and Miller, Xiu and Finn were welcomed inside and ushered through to a living room where Natalie and her mother were sitting together.

They both looked exhausted and empty.

Introductions were made again and this time, when eyes finally turned to her, Finn took the initiative. 'I was a friend of Andy's,' she said.

Miller was relieved. Though he had instinctively felt that her being there would be no bad thing, he still hadn't quite decided how he was going to account for the presence of a homeless drug addict in the home of a victim's family. He hoped her simple explanation would do.

Natalie stood up, walked across and pulled Finn into a hug.

'Have you caught him yet?' Natalie's father might have been polite, but he was blunt enough when he needed to be.

'I'm afraid not, sir,' Xiu said.

Mr Bagnall turned away, shaking his head.

'But we do have some important new information, which—'

'We need a quick word with Natalie,' Miller said.

Mr Bagnall turned back. 'Anything you've got to say to our Natalie concerns us, too.'

'I understand that,' Miller said.

'I'll be fine, Dad,' Natalie said.

'Why don't I make us all some tea?' Mrs Bagnall stood up quickly and walked towards the kitchen. 'Do you want to give me a hand, love?' She stopped and waited for her husband. Once he'd moved, somewhat reluctantly, across to join her, she took his hand, then looked back to Miller and the others. 'There's biscuits, if anyone fancies them.'

Miller thought that cheering would be inappropriate and suppressed the urge to punch the air. 'That would be smashing, ta.'

The four of them sat down.

'So what's this important information, then?' Natalie asked.

Officers had been dispatched to the house the previous evening. A marked car had been stationed outside ever since and beat officers were patrolling the surrounding streets. Natalie and her parents had been informed that there was reason to be concerned about their well-being, but had refused the offer of a safe house. Now, without going into too much detail (avoiding any mention of the list they'd found at the guesthouse) Xiu explained to Natalie that she was almost certainly in more danger than they'd first thought. They needed to seriously consider taking further steps to ensure her safety, Xiu said, until such time as any threat had been eliminated.

As nobody had told her *not* to be, Finn was a little more in-your-face about the situation. 'He thinks you've got the briefcase,' she said. 'So he's coming after you.'

Natalie just stared.

Realising that this was the first time Natalie had heard about any briefcase and was unaware of its significance, Miller did his best to explain. Once again he left out some of the more grisly details (severed and by now rotting hands) while at the same time stressing the lengths to which the man they were after was willing to go to get hold of it.

'I really think you should let us transfer you to a safe house,' he said. 'You and your parents.'

Natalie shook her head. 'We talked about this last night.'

'I know, but it's still the sensible thing to do.'

'I don't understand. There's coppers everywhere, so it's not like he's going to come knocking on our door, is it?'

'We just want to be sure,' Miller said.

The young woman thought about it. 'So, what happens if I'm shut up somewhere safe and sound for God knows how long?' She looked at Miller and Xiu. 'What happens to *him*?'

'Hopefully he gives up,' Xiu said. 'Once he realises he's not going to get to you.'

'And then what? He disappears?'

'Possibly ... '

Now, Finn was staring at Xiu and Miller. 'But don't you want to *catch* him?'

Miller knew that, as per the strictly enforced protocols regarding civilian involvement in police business, he should tell Finn to keep her thoughts and observations to herself. He didn't. 'Well, yes, obviously, but—'

'Right.' Natalie nodded at Finn. 'Isn't catching him the most important thing?'

'No it isn't,' Xiu said. 'Not when there's a substantial and documented threat to human life.'

Natalie looked down for a few moments, taking that in, but if Xiu thought that laying the situation out in rather starker language would change the woman's mind, she was mistaken. 'No, I'm not having that.' Natalie raised her head and shook it. 'I'm not going to hide and give this animal a chance to walk away. Besides which, all of us need to get on with our lives.' There were tears in her eyes, but she did not wipe them away and her voice didn't crack or waver. 'We want to be able to remember Andy without knowing that the man who killed him is still out there, doing God knows what to someone else. My mum and dad want to have some kind of . . . peace. They deserve that. I want to get back to work.'

'That's where he's going to come after you,' Finn said.

Xiu tried to cut her off. 'Hang on—'

'He was spotted near the hospital last night, and it makes sense, when you think about it. He's already sussed out that he can't get to you at home, not with coppers all over the show, so the hospital's his best bet.' She looked at Miller. 'Right?'

Xiu was looking at Miller too, glaring, as she waited for him to put a stop to Finn doing . . . whatever she was doing. Miller could see the sense in Xiu's objections, but he was inclined to ignore them. He was beginning to see where the conversation might be headed, the direction in which Finn was steering it, and he wasn't altogether sure it was a bad thing.

'Yeah, that makes sense,' he said.

Finn stood up and nodded to Natalie. 'Like she said, this bloke's an animal and he needs to pay for what he did to Andy. He should pay for . . . everything he's done.'

Now, Natalie stood up, too and walked slowly across to Finn. She raised a hand to gently touch Finn's face and Finn let her do it. 'He did that, right?'

'I'm fine,' Finn said. 'It's nothing.'

Natalie turned to Miller and Xiu. 'I'm safe here, yeah? With half the Lancashire constabulary hanging about outside.'

Miller couldn't say that she *wasn't*. A safe house would still have been his preferred option, but this location was about as secure as they could make it.

'OK, great,' Natalie said. 'So ... if he can't actually get to me, what's the harm in letting him try?'

Xiu was starting to look seriously uncomfortable. 'What's the *harm*?'

'He thinks I might have this briefcase, so why not convince him that I have and let him come and get it?'

'I'm sorry,' Xiu said. 'The idea that you volunteer yourself as some kind of ... bait to catch this individual is not one that we can possibly condone or approve. Is it, DS Miller?'

Miller stood up, trying to ignore the look from Finn; the hope all too clear in her expression, despite the bruises. 'Well, it's certainly thinking outside the box.'

'*Thinking outside the box?*' Xiu got quickly to her feet, waving her hands around like a referee trying to call a halt to a fight and stammering her protest. 'No, no, no, if the box was *here*, that thinking would be in—'

'Aberdeen?' Finn suggested.

'No, much further,' Miller said. 'More like somewhere in New Zealand.'

'You can't actually stop me though, can you?' Natalie said. 'That's the thing. Say if I was to leave for work, and I just happened to be carrying a briefcase like the one he's after and he just happened to see it . . . there's not a lot you can do about that, is there?'

Finn reached to take hold of Natalie's hand.

Miller thought about the briefcase under the bed at home that was an *awful* lot like the one Dudley Driscoll was after. He chose to ignore the look of horror on Xiu's face, focusing instead on the determination on Natalie Bagnall's, the urgent nod of encouragement from Finn.

'Bugger all,' he said.

FORTY-EIGHT

They met at a small country pub just off the A585 near Thistleton and took a table in the otherwise unoccupied conservatory at the back. There was a desultory children's playground on the grass beyond the big windows. A small pond with a few depressed-looking geese.

'It's nice.'

'It's *quiet*...'

They ordered a bottle of Sancerre as soon as they sat down and told the waitress that they'd need a few minutes with the menu. They each poured themselves a large glass and touched it to their companion's. They both laughed a little nervously.

'I was a bit surprised when you rang,' Maureen Bardsley said.

'I surprised myself by ringing.'

'More than a bit, tell you the truth. You're the last person . . . you know.'

Jacqui Cutler nodded. 'I called quite a few times actually.' She swallowed a seriously large mouthful of wine. 'I hung up if it was your old man that answered.'

With the waitress hovering, they consulted their menus and ordered. Pâté and lamb for Jacqui and a chicken Caesar salad for Maureen who quietly confessed, once the waitress had left, that she was trying to lose a few pounds.

'It's bloody daft, don't you reckon?' Jacqui said.

'Yeah, I know, but Frank's talking about a holiday and it would be great not to have to wear a one-piece swimsuit, so—'

'No, I meant what's going on between your Frank and my Wayne. It's daft and it needs to stop.'

'Oh ... yeah, but that's easier said than done, isn't it? You got any bright ideas?'

'One or two,' Jacqui said.

Maureen stared into her glass and shook her head. 'I say he's talking about a holiday, but that's probably all it is. Talk. Frank's just saying what he thinks I want to hear, whatever he thinks might make me happy.'

'You not happy, then?'

Maureen fiddled with her napkin.

'I don't mean to pry—'

'It's fine.' Maureen downed what was left in her glass and reached immediately for the bottle. 'I've been ... happier.'

Ten minutes later, as Maureen sat hungrily watching Jacqui Cutler eating the starter she'd denied herself, she leaned forward suddenly. 'There was a man I was close to,' she said.

Jacqui raised an eyebrow, chewing. 'Close to?'

'You know. Anyway, he was killed not long ago and I'm really not trying to spoil our lunch, because this is nice and it's lovely to get out of the house, but your old man was ... involved.'

'Oh, that's awkward.' Jacqui was spreading pâté onto a chunk of bread when the penny dropped. 'Wait ... Panaides?'

Maureen nodded. 'Like I say, I don't want to put a

dampener on lunch, and besides it was Frank's fault at the end of the day. It was his fault that George and I ended up getting close, because Frank was paying more attention to his burgers than he was to me.'

'Business always comes first, right?'

'Always,' Maureen said. 'So even if it was your old man who had George killed, it's ultimately Frank I blame for it, because he wouldn't let George spread his wings and George was the one with real ambition. The whole Bardsley's Bangers thing was his idea. He wanted to do chilli as well as curry sauce with the chips. George had . . . vision.' She shook her head sadly. 'In the end he had to start using the shops to shift a bit of whizz and a few tabs of Molly because he was so frustrated.'

'That's really bloody sad,' Jacqui said.

Maureen shrugged and took a healthy mouthful of Sancerre. 'The life we've both chosen.'

'Doesn't have to be for ever though, does it?'

Half an hour later, by the time the remains of their main courses were being cleared away, the two women had talked about all sorts of things. They had shared war stories and discussed a variety of ways in which their lives might be rather more fulfilling than they currently were. They had even hatched a plan or two, including a time and place for another lunch.

'Would you ladies like to see the dessert menu?'

Both women announced that they were stuffed, and even if Maureen Bardsley wasn't quite as stuffed as she might have been she still had that swimsuit to think about.

'We *could* order another bottle of wine though,' Jacqui said.

'Fine with me,' Maureen said. 'I got a taxi, but aren't you driving?'

Jacqui Cutler smiled. 'It's not a problem. I know most of the traffic officers round here, or rather they know me.'

'Who you're married to, you mean.'

Jacqui mock-shuddered and waved a hand to summon the waitress back over. 'There's got to be some perks, right?'

FORTY-NINE

From the car he'd rented under the name Denzil Dawson, he watched the house where Natalie Bagnall's mum and dad lived. The rental company had needed ID of course, but happily there'd still been a couple of fake driving licences in his wallet when he'd left the Sandy Shores. They'd been supplied by the same reasonably priced craftsman in West Bromwich who'd sorted him out with that fake police ID as well as the other bits of bogus documentation he'd needed over the years.

Moody passports, counterfeit bank cards, birth certificates, all sorts.

Driscoll was watching from a distance, using the binoculars he'd bought from GO Outdoors (which used to be Millets), and took care not to get too close and to keep changing location. There were more coppers knocking around than he'd seen at that guesthouse the night before, so he had to be a bit careful.

No, taking risks like this was not ideal, but what else could he do? There was still a decent payday at stake (when Wayne

Cutler coughed up) so until a better plan presented itself, watching the house where Natalie Bagnall was holed up seemed like the best worst option.

That briefcase might well be in there somewhere.

He was still properly browned off about Cutler trying to stiff him for half his fee. It had been a far dodgier offer than that, of course. He knew very well that if he *had* agreed to take the five grand Cutler was offering, there'd have been 'arrangements' to collect it which would doubtless have ended up with Driscoll dead in a ditch somewhere or chained to a cement block and feeding fish under the pier.

Did Cutler think he was born yesterday?

He raised the binoculars again, but there wasn't a fat lot happening. A couple of uniforms nattering next to a car, drinking tea. He'd seen Miller and his partner come and go half an hour before. It wasn't much of a surprise that they'd shown up because by now they'd seen his list, so they knew that Bagnall's sister was who he'd got pegged for having the briefcase, but for the life of him Driscoll couldn't work out why they'd brought that homeless girl with them.

He was still trying to get his head round that.

The car had been cheap to rent, but wasn't bad, as it happened. No, a Volkswagen Polo did not feature on his list of 'Cars I'd Like to Own' (the invisible car from *Die Another Day* was number one, obviously) but it would do for the time being. It was inconspicuous, it was nippy enough if he needed to get gone in a hurry and it was comfortable. That was one of the most important things, because he might very well be sleeping in it until this briefcase business was done and dusted. Until he could get the hell out of sodding Blackpool.

He had another look through the binoculars.

The house where Natalie Bagnall's parents lived was

actually a lot nicer than he'd thought it would be. Based on the scuzzy flat their kids had been sharing, he hadn't been expecting much, but then again he had no idea what the Bagnalls did for a living. Where their money had come from. Had they retired? They might still be in their fifties, so he couldn't take it for granted, but it started Driscoll thinking about when *he* might call it a day and put his feet up. It wasn't going to happen any time soon because, even with the 10K from the Panaides job, he wouldn't have enough stashed away, but all the same it was fun to think about the things he'd have more time to do once he was out of the game.

The places he'd visit (Rio de Janeiro, Venice, the pencil museum in Keswick) and the old TV shows he'd be able to binge.

With nothing much to write home about happening at the Bagnall house, he reached into the glove compartment for something to scribble on (the back of the Polo's handbook), took out a pen and began to formalise his wish-list of top motors.

CARS I'D LIKE TO OWN

1. James Bond's invisible Aston Martin.
2. A Ferrari (red or white).
3. The three-wheeler from *Only Fools and Horses*.
4. A silver Rolls-Royce.
5. *Midsomer Murders* ?????

He spent the next few minutes trying to decide between the Rover 75 that DCI Tom Barnaby (John Nettles) had originally driven, the Jaguar X-type he was driving from series nine onwards and the Magic Blue Volvo S80 he drove after that. It was difficult to pick one but, while he was thinking about it, he did at least make one firm decision.

He hadn't killed Keith Slack and he hadn't killed that homeless girl when he'd had the chance. He still didn't understand why, but he was starting to worry that his enthusiasm for the job might fade away completely before he even got the *chance* to retire.

Well, he wasn't about to let that happen.

Dudley Driscoll needed to get back to doing what he did best, the one thing he did better than anyone else. Same as with any other job really. You had a knack for something, you had to keep your hand in.

Briefcase or no bloody briefcase, Natalie Bagnall was going to die.

FIFTY

'Denzil Dawson?' Nathan was shaking his head. 'What kind of an idiot is this bloke, anyway?'

'He's obviously not *that* much of an idiot,' Howard said.

Mary was nodding. 'Or Declan would have caught him already.'

They were sitting in the Bull as usual, after a session during which Miller had once again spent all his time at the piano, providing the ideal accompaniment for a nifty quickstep and a half-decent American Smooth, while taking great care to avoid any songs that Mary might object to on the grounds of their drug associations.

It had taken his mind off the forthcoming operation, the thought of which was still making him very nervous.

'Well at least you know he's watching,' Veronica said.

Miller sipped his beer.

'It sounds like that's what you want.'

It was, but Miller knew that if he was unlucky and fate decided to do its business in his kettle, getting what he wanted could also see him back pounding the beat, talking to school-kids about knife-crime or chucking drunks into a meat wagon outside Brannigans.

He wondered if that bouncer Imran had mentioned was still around.

Miller and the team now knew that Driscoll had been watching the Bagnall house that morning because all vehicles in the surrounding streets had been run through the Automatic Number Plate Recognition system. A white VW Polo which had come back as being registered to a local car-hire company had been rented the night before. The renter's details had been checked out immediately and, once the only other Denzil Dawsons in the country had turned out to be a school caretaker in Aberystwyth, a retired plasterer from Leicester who'd recently died, and a butcher in Torquay, it seemed like a fair bet that the car in question was currently being driven by the man they were all after.

'I think it's a sound enough plan,' Howard said. 'Risky, obviously.'

'Everything's risky,' Mary said. 'I get a bit concerned just watching you put your socks on in the morning.'

Howard pulled a face, then joined in when everyone else laughed.

'Natalie is obviously a very brave young woman,' Ransford said.

'Yeah, she is,' Miller said, though he knew there were other words he could have used.

'Gloria and I would be very happy to send her a beautiful arrangement of flowers when all this is over.'

'We'll make something special,' Gloria said.

'That's nice of you.' Miller smiled at the couple, despite the flutter in his stomach when he thought about the chunk of their floristry business that involved the making of wreaths.

Ransford and Gloria had provided all the flowers for Alex's funeral.

Howard was right, of course. The plan *was* risky, but following lengthy discussions about just what those risks might be and how they could best be mitigated, Susan Akers had eventually given it the green light. The fact that it was Natalie Bagnall's idea had played well with the DCI, though Miller had chosen to leave out the encouragement she'd received from Finn.

Neither Miller nor Xiu had even mentioned Finn being there.

'It's like *Ocean's Eleven* or something,' Nathan said.

'Is it?' Miller stared at him, tearing open a new pack of pork scratchings.

'Well, yeah, like ... it's a sting, right?'

Ruth grinned. 'That makes you George Clooney, Dec.'

'I'll be sitting in the back of a van and quite possibly urinating in an empty pop bottle,' Miller said. 'If everything goes to plan I won't even be getting out. Not what I'd call a blockbuster.'

'Oh, I don't know.' Mary was halfway through her third gin. 'You can get up to all sorts in the back of a van.' She nudged Howard. 'Remember that Christmas we broke down on the A59?'

'Not really,' Howard said.

'Course you do. On the way to that jive competition in Southport.'

'All right, love,' Howard muttered, and stared into his glass.

'Well, we had to do *something* to keep warm ...'

Ruth began to giggle. 'Sounds like it was a straightforward survival issue.'

Miller wasn't really listening. He was thinking about things going to plan and hoping that Dudley Driscoll had still been watching the Bagnall house that afternoon. Hoping that he'd witnessed the humble piece of street theatre they'd laid on for his entertainment.

The decoy briefcase that Miller had purchased a week or so before had been smuggled into the Bagnall house inside a holdall. A few minutes later, Natalie Bagnall had stepped out of the house carrying it, looked around nervously, then locked it in the boot of her car. Ten minutes after that, she'd retrieved it and taken it back inside, having decided (or so they hoped it would appear to Driscoll) that the briefcase was far safer inside the house.

All that mattered was that Driscoll had seen it and was now convinced that the final person on his list was the one he'd been after all along.

That was phase one, and although Natalie Bagnall had showed some hitherto unheralded acting chops, Miller seriously doubted it was the most scintillating of openings to a sting movie. He was pretty sure that George Clooney would have demanded a rewrite.

'Well, I still think it's exciting,' Nathan said. 'If I was a copper it's the kind of op I'd love to get stuck into.' He saw Ruth smiling. 'It's short for operation.'

Miller decided now was not the time to mention Nathan's iffy bladder and its propensity to let him down at stressful moments. He thought about giving him a hard look instead, to remind him of their conversation about the harsh realities of policing, but decided even that might be tempting fate. So instead he asked if anyone else wanted a drink.

Mary cut in quickly before anyone could place their orders. 'In other news, Alan, the pianist from Thistleton, has let me know that he's available from next week.'

'Now, that's some *proper* excitement,' Miller said. 'Who needs George Clooney when you've got Alan from Thistleton?'

'I couldn't agree more,' Mary said. 'So provided your knee's not still playing you up, we can finally get you back on the floor, Declan.'

Miller shrugged like he wasn't bothered either way, though secretly he was quite pleased. He was keen to start dancing again. 'Right then, drinks . . . '

It was the same again, all round, though Nathan decided to switch from WKD to lager top. Perhaps he wanted to demonstrate that he was edgy and unpredictable; a good candidate for a detective post maybe or just someone that Ruth should be a little more interested in than she actually was. Either way, he was clearly still worked up about the operation Miller had been telling them all about.

'So, when's it happening then?' he asked before Miller could head to the bar. 'The sting.'

Miller felt that flutter again. He blinked away images of wreaths and thoughts of tedious days on beat patrol. He said, 'Natalie's going back to work tomorrow night.'

FIFTY-ONE

'I'm sitting here with two furry friends on my lap,' Miller said, when Xiu answered the phone. He was relieved that he couldn't hear the clatter of drums or the deafening scream of guitars, though it wasn't quite silence that followed the slight whimper at his mention of the rats. 'Doesn't sound like you're at home.'

'Doesn't it?'

'Doesn't sound like you're out playing headbanger Tinder either, so that's got to be good.'

'Let's not get into that again,' Xiu said.

'Perish the thought.' Miller tickled Fred's ears and the rat rolled on to her back. 'I just called to say thanks, really. For not saying anything to Akers about Finn.'

'I'm still not sure I was doing anybody any favours.'

'All the same.'

'Well, thanks for saying thanks,' Xiu said. 'I know it's one of those words you have a problem with. Like *sorry*.'

'Yeah, I'm very much with Elton John on that one,' Miller

said. 'Though if I was being picky, I'd point out to Mr John that it's not really the *hardest* word. I think floccinaucinihilip-ilification's a trifle trickier, but that said, I'm not sure it would work quite as well in the song.' Ginger was looking jealous, so Miller began to tickle her ears too. 'How are you feeling about Operation Bastard?'

'Operation *what*?'

'That's just what I'm calling it,' Miller said. 'I think it needs a name that's a bit snappier, you know?' He'd pointed out to Tim Sullivan that, as names for these things went, Operation Victoria was a little on the pedestrian side and of course he'd been happy to offer up alternatives. Bearing in mind the location of the op, he'd been quite pleased with Operation *Operation*, but Sullivan had been predictably resistant.

'I'm . . . apprehensive,' Xiu said. 'Aren't you?'

'No, I'm right as ninepence,' Miller said. 'I think we've got all the bases covered.'

'Let's hope so.'

'Look, Driscoll knows that *we* know he's after Natalie, but he doesn't know we know he's targeting the hospital. We're ahead of the game for once.'

'So why doesn't it feel like it?'

Miller had no answer that was going to sound convincing. He said, 'We should both get early nights, Posh. It's going to be a late one tomorrow.'

'OK.'

'I'll see you first thing.'

'If you're coming in on your moped you should probably leave now.'

'Is that another *joke*?'

'Not really.'

'Do you want to say "night-night" to the rats?'

'Sleep well, Miller . . . '

A few minutes after he'd hung up and had safely deposited Fred and Ginger in their beds, he turned to see Alex, or at least her blurry reflection in a TV screen that seriously needed dusting.

'You're not fooling anyone, you know,' she said. 'Least of all Xiu.'.

'I'm not trying to fool anyone.'

'Not even yourself? All that "right as ninepence" nonsense.'

'Well, there's no point making everyone nervous, is there?'

'They're already nervous and they've got every right to be, because it's a stupid idea.'

'To be fair, it was Natalie Bagnall's stupid idea.'

'Which you could have easily overruled,' Alex said. 'Every bit as easily as you could have told Driscoll that the police already had his precious briefcase, but yet again you failed to use what little common sense you've got and chose to keep your gob shut.'

'I might be misremembering,' Miller said. 'You know, being as I'm consumed with grief and all that, but I'm pretty sure you used to *tell* me to keep my gob shut. Like, several times a day.'

'Yes, because ninety-nine times out of a hundred it's what you should do, but there's a time and a place, Miller. Remember how guilty you felt after not telling Driscoll the truth? How worried you were that your decision had put people in danger? Just imagine how you'll feel if this goes tits-up.'

Miller knew it was supremely idiotic to get irritated with someone who was (a) dead and (b) imaginary, but he couldn't help himself. 'I'm going to call Finn,' he said.

As he'd guessed would be the case, that did the trick. He reached for his phone, and when he glanced back at the TV again all he could see was a distorted reflection of himself. Yes, the screen was filthy, but he guessed that the image was not wholly inaccurate, because he was starting to feel seriously blurry.

'Hey, Miller.'

'Hey, Finn.'

'You calling to give me a bollocking?'

'Well, obviously I should be,' Miller said. 'Yes, it was my fault for bringing you along in the first place, but you seriously overstepped the mark this morning. Egging Natalie Bagnall on like that, to the point where she's volunteered to use herself as bait to catch a very dangerous man. To put herself, quite possibly, in harm's way.'

'You could have put a stop to it,' Finn said.

'Yeah, I know—'

'But you didn't.'

Alex wasn't around any more, but that didn't mean Miller couldn't hear her laughing.

'So, was that the actual bollocking?' Finn asked. 'Or would that have been the bollocking that you should have given me, but aren't?'

She'd asked like she already knew the answer, because she understood Miller better than almost anybody.

He knew that she'd seen it in his face.

Two young women who were victims of Dudley Driscoll in very different ways, but were both equally determined to see him brought to justice, had come together. That morning in the living room of the Bagnalls' house – doing little to intervene as Natalie Bagnall had fed off Finn's anger and been fired up by it – Miller had been annoyed with the girl who was his daughter in everything but name, yet also fiercely proud of her.

Every bit as proud as he knew her mother would have been. 'OK, I'll consider myself well and truly bollocked,' she said. 'Now I need to crack on, because I'm bloody starving.'

'Talking of which, why don't you come round and I'll I cook you dinner when this is all over?' Miller was talking quickly before she had a chance to make an excuse. 'Nothing fancy, just a pie or something, and I promise it won't take long, like an hour and a half max, because I know you don't really like being here. We don't even have to talk much if you don't feel like it, or even at all. Not a dickie bird. We can do the whole thing in complete silence if that's what you want, like Trappist monks or mime artists. You just come over, say hello to the rats, eat and bugger off again.'

Miller spent half a minute listening to the evocative soundtrack of the town at night – the shush of the sea, the plaintive cry of distant gulls and the insistent beeping of a bin lorry reversing nearby – until Finn finally spoke again.

'What kind of pie?'

Fifteen minutes later, when Miller walked into the bedroom, Alex was lying on her usual side of the bed, thumbing through a copy of *Dancing Times*. She glanced up to see Miller watching her.

'Don't even think about it.'

'Well, obviously I'm *thinking* about it.' Miller got undressed and slipped into bed beside her. He yawned and stared at the ceiling for a while.

Alex didn't even look up from her magazine. 'She won't come, you know.'

'Have a bit of faith,' Miller said.

'I tried that once,' she said. 'Remember?'

Miller leaned across and turned the radio on, but he couldn't summon the energy to shout at any of the callers.

Not even the loon insisting that JFK had been shot by at least three different aliens. He was fast asleep before the bloke had finished ranting.

FIFTY-TWO

Much as she'd given him a hard time about it, because it really *wasn't* any of his beeswax, Xiu was reluctantly willing to concede that Miller had a point. Picking up people at a low-rent death-metal night in a room above a grotty pub was probably not the best way to meet someone she was likely to have any kind of long-term relationship with.

Long-term, in this case, meaning more than one night.

She'd tried telling herself that didn't really matter, because it was just a physical thing anyway, but it wasn't even as though that was always great. More often than not it was anything but great, because she and whoever she ended up with were both usually trollied and far too exhausted after several hours droning on about Metallica and throwing themselves around to get up to anything very interesting. One bloke had fallen asleep in the taxi back to her place and a woman who'd made some very exciting promises during an extended drum solo was spark out and snoring before they'd had so much as a snog.

Plus – and she hated to admit that Miller had been right

about this – the smell wasn't much of a turn-on either. There was nothing wrong with enjoying a drink when you were letting your hair down or the sultry glow of perspiration after you'd been dancing a while, but stale beer on sweat-soaked denim was hardly Chanel No 5.

So no, it was not ideal, but it wasn't like she had much alternative.

The problem was, she rarely actually met *anyone*. Well, that wasn't strictly true because she met people all the time, but most of them were in handcuffs which was hardly a dream start to any relationship and certainly not one with a rosy future. Offenders aside, she knocked around with plenty of fellow coppers of course, but she certainly didn't want to get into anything serious with one of *them*. Yes, she'd like to spend quality time with a partner and yes, she was lonely sometimes, but she wasn't a maniac.

On any list of suitable matches among those people she most associated with, coppers came a notch below violent criminals and a fair few of them (certainly some she'd known back in the Met) were not a great deal more honest or law-abiding.

Something had to change, though; she knew that.

She'd always thought that online dating was for saddos, but perhaps it was time to admit she *was* a saddo and take the plunge.

She was still thinking about it when she heard the applause and started to walk back upstairs. The interval was over. Asscrack were about to start their second set and there was a woman with a Freddy Krueger tattoo that Xiu quite liked the look of.

FIFTY-THREE

The dirty white van they were using as the mobile comms base was parked around the side of the hospital from which the operation took its name. The hospital where Natalie Bagnall worked. Being unable to park at the front wasn't a major issue as they were in communication with plenty of officers who had eyes on the main entrance, and staying hidden was the main priority. Yes, it would have been nice to have a direct view of the entrance, but they would have stuck out a mile. The operation could quite possibly end up lasting days and the van being parked near the entrance for anything more than an hour or two would have made them horribly conspicuous.

Nobody could afford the cost of a hospital car park for that long.

It was almost ten p.m. and Miller and Xiu had already been sitting in the back of the van for three hours when Tony Clough – who was in the front, cosied up next to Tim Sullivan – turned to give them a thumbs-up.

'So far, so good.'

Miller leaned forward. 'What, because everyone involved is still alive, as far as we know? Because the hospital hasn't blown up or been hit by an asteroid? Because you haven't broken wind yet? You might need to be a bit more specific, Tony.'

Nerves were possibly making Miller even tetchier than normal and, in fairness, so far so good was about the best they could hope for considering some of the people involved. Of course there were weak links in any chain, but when you had the likes of Sullivan and Clough on the team, it was as if several links on one of those ten-tonne chains they used to anchor ships had been removed and replaced by spaghetti hoops.

The hoop-in-chief had been predictably bumptious at the morning briefing.

'This is the big one,' Sullivan had said. And 'Let's bring this one home.'

The DI had clearly been very excited at the prospect of an operation that was likely to be the turning point of the investigation. He was ready and he was rising to the occasion, even if he was a little blasé when it came to the seriousness of the operation itself. While not *completely* ignoring the risks inherent in what they were doing, he seemed happy enough to play down the possibility of that turning point involving demotions or disciplinary hearings or – if things went spectacularly pear-shaped – the death of an innocent member of the public. Perhaps his head had been turned by the fact that, although there'd be a firearms commander on site to whom he would have to defer should the need arise, at least he wouldn't end up having to answer to a stroppy landlady.

'This is the big one,' he said, when they'd finished, right before he'd shaken his head, cross with himself when he remembered that he'd said it already.

The rest of the day had been taken up with logistics in and around the hospital. A technical team had gone in to check that the Vic's CCTV cameras were all working (at least half of them hadn't been) and to ensure that live feeds from the hospital's security system could be patched through to all mobile units. Floorplans were studied so that officers could be best positioned inside the hospital, observation posts were established close to all the entrances and the firearms unit took key decisions about where to best deploy their teams.

At lunchtime, while Miller and Xiu were grabbing a toasted sandwich, Xiu had said, 'Well, I'm not sure if it's *the* big one. Like Sullivan said.'

'Twice.'

'But it's definitely *a* big one. Biggest operation I've ever been involved with.'

'You look tired,' Miller had said.

Xiu had focused on her sandwich after that.

The first part of operation Victoria – which Sullivan had actually referred to as 'setting the trap' – had begun when Natalie Bagnall left for work. She'd carried the briefcase out to her car at 7.15 p.m., placed it in the boot, then set off on a nice steady drive which would see her arrive in good time to change into her uniform and be stepping into A&E by 7.45.

'Good girl,' Sullivan had cooed softly into his radio, broadcasting to all units. 'Good girl . . . '

In the unmarked car directly behind her, Miller had turned to Xiu. 'That's how I talk to Fred and Ginger.'

There were other unmarked vehicles in front of Natalie's Kia Picanto, a radio on the passenger seat in case of emergencies and all units watching out for Draper/Driscoll/Dawson's VW Polo, which had not been spotted anywhere since the previous afternoon.

'Nice and easy . . . just driving to work, nice and normal . . . *good* girl.'

'For the love of God,' Miller said. 'Make it stop.'

Carrying the briefcase and looking for all the world like she didn't have a care, Natalie had eventually walked across the darkened car park, briefcase in hand, and in through the hospital's main entrance bang on time. Plain-clothes officers, while maintaining an appropriate distance, had moved with her, monitoring every step of her progress until she'd arrived in Accident and Emergency. From that point on, all any of them could do was wait for Driscoll to make his move.

'Game on,' Tim Sullivan had announced.

'Oh, do put a sock in it,' Miller had said.

Now, four hours after that, Miller was still sitting alongside Xiu in the back of the comms van and wondering how it was possible to be nervous and unutterably bored at the same time. He stared at the as yet unused empty pop bottle and thought about having a bash, just to give himself something to do. He wondered what practical arrangements Xiu had made, urination-wise. It would need to be something with a wider access point. A paper cup maybe or a small Tupperware container.

He thought about asking her, then decided against it.

Xiu sniffed and rolled her head around.

'You *do* look tired,' he said.

She ignored him.

He leaned over to tap the shoulder of the civilian technician who was sitting in front of a row of video monitors. 'I don't suppose you can get Channel Four on any of those, can you? I think *Naked Attraction* might be on.' The technician said nothing. 'No? Just a thought . . .'

He reached for his phone when a text message alert sounded, unable to contain his excitement.

It was a message from Bob Perks.

How's Victoria going?

Bastard.

What???

Sorry. That's just what I call it.

Well, good luck. If you catch him, can I sit in on the interview?

If you bring biscuits.

Deal.

No, cake—

Miller stopped typing when the radio suddenly crackled into life and the voice of an officer rang around the van.

'Unknown male approaching the entrance to A&E. Looks like our man.'

Sullivan turned from the front seat and raised a hand, like everyone wasn't already frozen and paying attention. They all stared at the monitors.

'Approaching camera location now.'

Miller leaned towards the screen, holding his breath as he waited for a close-up shot of the suspect.

'Oh, for God's sake, *I* look more like Driscoll than he does.' Miller leaned even closer. 'He looks like that bloke off *Antiques Roadshow*. The one who does the Oriental ceramics.'

'All units stand down.' Sullivan barked into his radio. 'Repeat, stand down.'

'You're a thundering twatbadger,' Miller muttered as he reached for his phone to finish the SMS conversation with Bob Perks. 'Repeat, twatbadger.'

You still there? Perks had asked. Then, Everything all right?

Miller let his head fall back against the side of the van and stabbed out a reply.

So far, so good.

FIFTY-FOUR

The man who answered the phone did not sound best pleased. 'You got any idea what time it is?'

'Yeah, and I'm wide awake,' Cutler said.

'Well, so am I now.'

'Tough tits.'

'What do you want?'

Cutler had given up on trying to sleep and with Jacqui already dead to the world (and quite possibly dreaming about whoever she'd been whispering to on the phone a couple of nights before) he'd climbed out of bed and stalked downstairs to his office. Now, he was slumped in an armchair in the corner, with his phone in one hand and a tumbler of Bell's in the other. He was wearing pyjamas beneath the monogrammed dressing gown Jacqui had bought him for his fortieth – which he suspected made him look a bit of a ponce – and wondering if the bloke with whom he was trying not to lose his temper was more of a liability than an asset.

He'd give him one last chance to prove it, either way.

'Have a guess why I couldn't sleep?' he asked.

'Cheese?'

'*What?*'

'Did you eat cheese before bedtime?'

'Are you trying to wind me up?'

'Chocolate can do it as well ... the caffeine, yeah? And crisps because of all the salt—'

'What are your lot up to?' Cutler asked the question with just enough menace to make it abundantly clear that he had not called in the early hours of the morning to discuss chocolate or chuffing cheese.

'How d'you mean?'

'This Driscoll business.' Cutler knew Dennis Draper's real name by now along with the fact that he hadn't been caught in the raid at the guesthouse. The men and women Cutler paid to pass on such nuggets of intelligence had provided plenty of helpful information, but he was hoping this particular source might be able to provide a rather more practical service. 'The big operation at the hospital.'

'Well, I'm not part of that team, so—'

'I don't care what bloody team you're part of, pal. I want to know what's happening.'

'I might be able to make a call.'

'Yeah well, that'd be a start.'

'A start?'

Cutler took a sip of whisky and rubbed his chest. He'd popped a couple of Gaviscon before bed, but the heartburn hadn't gone away and he could still taste the chicken tikka masala he'd had for dinner. 'You do know I don't particularly want Driscoll arrested, don't you, Christopher? You do understand that, right?'

'I can see why it might be awkward.'

'*Awkward?*'

'Yeah, yeah . . . I get it, OK. I'll try and find out what's happening, but if it's an ongoing op, that might not be until it's all done and dusted.'

'Right, but I'm guessing that, in this instance, my idea of done and dusted is not quite the same as yours.' Cutler grimaced and this time it wasn't the heartburn. 'Or Detective Sergeant Miller's. See, Driscoll being arrested and then gobbing off in an interview room is obviously what some of your more diligent and less bent colleagues are hoping for, but on a magic island, I'd prefer him out of the picture rather more permanently.'

'There's not a lot I can do about that.'

'Isn't there?'

'Well, no, not really.'

'That surprises me, because it's not like you haven't got form, is it?'

'*Once,*' the man said. 'It was once.'

'Right, because on that occasion you were the one at risk and I'm telling you that if this doesn't go the way I want it to, you might find yourself at risk again.'

'Is that a threat, Mr Cutler?'

Cutler rolled his eyes because . . . how thick could you be? 'Yes, *obviously.*'

'I honestly don't know what you think I can do.'

'I'm sure you can work something out. Easier to deal with the situation now, I would have thought, than trying to get to Driscoll once he's in custody.'

'This is all hypothetical anyway, because with a bit of luck Miller and the rest of those clowns'll cock it up and Driscoll won't get nicked.'

'I'd rather not take that chance,' Cutler said.

'You're asking a lot.'

Cutler stretched out his legs and wiggled his feet. There was a small hole in one of his slippers, which *really* annoyed him because Wayne Cutler was not a man who should have holes in his slippers. The bloody things needed chucking and maybe this idiot who thought he was 'asking a lot' needed chucking, too.

Under a bus, off a tower block, into the Irish sea, whatever.

He said, 'You know, maybe *you* should be the one who's paying *me*.'

'Because ... ?'

'Oh, I don't know.' Cutler was starting to get angry. 'The stuff I've got on you. A few bits and pieces which some of your colleagues might be very interested in.'

'Why would you do that?'

'Because I've got a slipper with a hole in it and right this minute I reckon it's a damn sight more use to me than you are!'

'I'm useful, Mr Cutler, you know I am—'

Cutler was up and out of his chair fast enough to slop whisky all over the rug. 'Well, *make* yourself bloody useful pronto, and do something about Dudley Driscoll.'

FIFTY-FIVE

It was just shy of one o'clock in the morning and, in the back of the van, while the atmosphere was still unquestionably thick with tension, Miller was still bored and coming up with increasingly ridiculous ways of coping with the tedium. He repeated various words over and over in his head until they sounded ridiculous: tickle, spatula, custard. He blinked frantically then closed his eyes to enjoy the lightshow and made himself feel a bit sick. He tried, using only the power of his mind, to get Tony Clough to spill coffee in Tim Sullivan's lap.

He counted specks of dandruff on the computer technician's shoulders.

He tried to picture rats dancing.

He emitted a low and steady hum for several minutes, until Xiu told him to shut up.

'I'm not sure I'm cut out for long periods of surveillance,' he said.

'You think?'

'I need to be *out* there, you know? I need to be on the front line, where the action is and where real coppers find out what they're made of. I need to feel the blood pumping and the adrenalin fizzing. I need—'

Xiu told him to shut up again.

He sighed and stared down at the pop bottle which he'd put to good use half an hour previously. He wondered what he'd do if he needed to use it again and decided it definitely hadn't been a good idea to drink all the pop *in* the bottle before getting into the van. To the tune of an old Police hit, he quietly began to sing, 'Wee-wee in a bottle . . .' then stopped when Xiu stared as though she might be about to pick the bottle up and assault him with it.

'Are we being stupid?' he asked her. 'You think Driscoll's coming?'

'Yeah, I think he might,' she said.

'Any time soon, you reckon?'

'Like you said, he's not going to go after Natalie at the house, and he doesn't know he was spotted near the hospital. So yes, if Driscoll's seen the dummy briefcase, there's every chance he'll show up, but I can't promise you that'll be before the end of tonight's shift. Or before I massively lose it and taser you.'

'Fair enough,' Miller said. He nodded, thoughtful, then smacked his lips a few times. 'So, *not* soon, then?'

Natalie couldn't remember any shift on A&E – and certainly not a night shift – that hadn't been stressful, but for very obvious reasons this one was a little bit more nerve-racking than it would otherwise have been. She was sitting in a side room and bandaging up an old woman's knee, but there could be a fleet of ambulances on its way to the Vic with the seriously injured victims of a motorway pile-up and she'd have been less stressed out than she was at that moment.

She told herself she was being ridiculous, and not just because a fleet of ambulances was a little fanciful these days, not to mention that if there were any available ambulances at all, her imaginary RTA victims would have been waiting for several hours on the hard shoulder.

She was being ridiculous because she was safe.

Of course she was. There were plain-clothes coppers all around her, there were cameras everywhere and she had that radio in her pocket so she could let them know if she was worried about anything. She'd followed all their instructions to the letter and everything was where it should be. Thinking about it, she was probably a lot safer than she'd be on a normal shift, with drunks and nutcases tipping up on a regular basis and kicking off if they didn't get seen fast enough.

She wasn't in any danger.

'You OK ... ?'

Natalie told the old woman that she was fine, but however much she tried to think reassuring thoughts, she couldn't stop asking herself why she'd been daft enough to open her gob in the first place. To make out she was brave and suggest something as stupid as this. *Bait*, for crying out loud, like she was in some stupid thriller and the man they were after wasn't the dangerous psychopath who'd killed her brother.

She was a nurse, for God's sake, not that woman out of *The Silence of the Lambs*.

'Only you look a bit peaky.'

Natalie tried to smile and to stop her hand from shaking as she wrapped the bandage.

The old woman sucked in a breath. 'That's a bit tight, love ... '

Natalie told herself to try and stay calm, to just keep doing what she was doing until all this was over. She could go on her break in ten minutes or so, and she'd feel better after a coffee and a couple of quick fags. Yeah, course it was stupid, but sometimes you had to do the stupid thing and step up.

She was doing this for Andy.

Dudley Driscoll sat at a table outside Costa sipping a hot chocolate and picking at a fair-to-middling blueberry muffin. All things considered, he was feeling pretty chipper. He'd had a quite a lot of good luck so far – which evened things out, he reckoned, because this whole silly caper had started with a spot of extremely *bad* luck in those station toilets – and he knew that with just a little bit more he'd have that briefcase soon enough.

Then it would just be a question of making sure that Wayne Cutler did the decent thing. He couldn't count on that, obviously, because the likes of Cutler rarely did the decent thing, prided themselves on the fact that they were anything *but* decent, but Driscoll wasn't overly worried. He had a whole variety of ways to make people do things they were not inclined to, especially when they owed him money.

Part of him hoped that Cutler would need a bit of persuading.

He swept the muffin crumbs from the table into his palm and tossed them into his mouth, then he looked at his watch.

It was about time he made a move.

It looked to Miller as though Tony Clough had nodded off again. More than once he'd seen the DC's big, boiled-potato head begin to loll, then finally drop, before jerking upright the moment Sullivan had barked instructions into his radio.

'All units, status update ... Alpha team please report ...'

There'd been plenty of that.

Once or twice, on being so suddenly roused from his much-needed beauty sleep, Clough had actually let out an involuntary cry.

Miller was beginning to get jumpy himself. For no good reason, the boredom had given way to a bizarre hyper-vigilance; an alertness that was uncomfortably close to feeling scared. In the last few minutes, he'd gone from hoping that something would happen to feeling dread at the thought that it might be just about to.

He was dry-mouthed and shivery. There was a funny whistle when he breathed and, most annoyingly, he couldn't keep his leg still.

'Miller!' Xiu reached down to grab Miller's foot, which was moving quickly backwards and forwards across the metal floor of the van, as though he was trying out for a one-man version of *Riverdance*.

Miller keyed his radio. 'All units at the rear of the building ... give all those fire doors another once-over, would you?' He knew that officers had eyes on all the entrances and exits and that Driscoll would be spotted if he tried to get in through Maternity, Cardiac, Occupational Health or any of the other dozen or so departments that offered a way in. He also knew that there were smaller doors at the back which were opened many times a day by both hospital staff and patients who wanted to smoke. Doors that were often left open. 'Just to be sure, yeah ... because if you're regularly nipping out for a sneaky Marlboro or a vape or whatever, you might prop the door open with a bucket or something and forget to close it when you'd finished. So, can you check and let me know ... ?'

He stared at the radio, waiting for confirmation.

'Calm down, Miller,' Xiu said.

'I'm perfectly calm.'

'Really?' She nodded down to where she still had a firm hold of his foot to stop it thrashing around. 'I think I preferred it when you were humming or singing songs about urine—'

'Why hasn't Driscoll shown up?'

Xiu shrugged.

'He must have seen the briefcase, right? We know he'd been watching the house.'

'Well, we presume so.'

'So what's he waiting for?'

'I don't know,' Xiu said. 'Maybe he's just biding his time.'

'He hasn't done any "biding" up to now, has he? He killed Andy Bagnall the same day the briefcase went missing and he didn't mess about going after Finn or Slack. He's someone who acts quickly, so what's he up to?'

'How should I know?'

'Where the hell *is* he, Posh?'

'Look, we've done everything we can. It's all in place, so we just need to be patient. Simple as that. We just—' Xiu stopped, seeing a look of horror creep across Miller's face. 'What?'

'Oh, Christ alive . . .'

'*What?*'

'What you just said.' Miller stood up fast, ducking at the last moment to avoid hitting his head on the roof of the van. '*Patient.*' As soon as Xiu had said the word, the horrific explanation for Driscoll's no-show had popped into Miller's head and, sure as eggs were eggs and Miller couldn't dance a decent foxtrot, he'd known that he was right. 'That's exactly what Driscoll *is* . . . a patient. Well, what he *was*, anyway, when they were sewing his wedding tackle back together. Remember? Easy enough for him to waltz back into A&E *any* time he fancied and give them some old granny about the wound not healing up or some infection or something. Once he's in there, hanging around in triage or wherever, he just wanders off into the hospital and disappears.'

Miller looked at Xiu who was now on her feet herself, and at Sullivan and Clough who had turned from the front seats. He pointed to the hospital, the lights shining in all parts of the vast building.

'We're sitting around in this stupid van like lemons, waiting for Driscoll to turn up, and he's already in there!'

FIFTY-SIX

Driscoll was quite convinced he wasn't the only person hiding out in the hospital. Since he'd first arrived the evening before – a short walk from A&E to the Diabetic Resource Centre, from there to the X-ray department, then through the stroke ward and away – he'd spotted several people he was sure were homeless or just skint and making good use of the free facilities. It made perfect sense when you thought about how pricey it was to live anywhere a bit more conventional.

The cost of heating and lighting, all that.

You could wander around happily undisturbed in a nice warm hospital for days, he reckoned. Weeks even, considering how massive the place was, the variety of excellent services on offer and (thankfully) how few security guards he'd encountered since he'd been there.

A skeleton staff, one of them had told him when he'd enquired. 'Cutbacks and shortages, mate. Welcome to the NHS.'

'It's a disgrace,' Driscoll had said.

God bless the government.

No, it wasn't quite a leisure centre, but there were miles of corridors if you fancied some exercise. There was no shortage of places to grab a couple of hours' sleep when you needed it (he'd made very good use of several different waiting areas), there were toilets all over the shop (many with showers) and he had no complaints about the food. The first-floor restaurant did a cracking gammon, egg and chips and there was a very decent café by the cardiac unit. It had all been very pleasant really. Obviously he knew there were cameras everywhere and coppers knocking about – they'd have to be stupid not to work out that he'd end up at the hospital eventually and he knew Miller wasn't stupid – but they weren't watching out for someone who looked like him.

He was now rocking short hair – courtesy of Gazza's Chop Shop the previous afternoon – and a pair of Boots' reading glasses. He was wearing scrubs he'd grabbed from a laundry hamper and, crucially, sporting a nice blue NHS lanyard. The attached ID card (supplied by his mate in West Bromwich) was tucked into the top pocket of the scrubs, because obviously you wouldn't want it dangling and getting in the way if you were doing important medical stuff and also because it hid the photograph of a doctor that wasn't him.

He'd actually spent most of the time sitting around in Main Reception.

They'd even given him a staff discount at the Costa!

Driscoll checked his watch again, nodding to some poor old soul on crutches as he walked past the pharmacy then the chapel and the toilets he'd sat in with a newspaper for a couple of hours that morning; ambling back in the direction of A&E. Towards the nurses' lounge and the locker room just behind it.

Natalie Bagnall would be taking her break in a few minutes.

*

Ignoring Sullivan's command to stay exactly where he was, Miller opened the back doors of the van, jumped down and charged towards the hospital. Xiu was similarly insubordinate. They ran for the back entrance which was signposted Gastroenterology, past the bewildered officers on watch and in through the double doors.

Miller shouted into his radio as he ran. 'We need to secure the building *now*. Driscoll's inside the hospital. Everyone got that? Driscoll's inside the hospital so just . . . close all the sodding doors.'

Xiu was right behind him as they tore through the respiratory ward and out into the corridor, past a number of startled staff and several plain-clothes officers who were standing around panic-stricken, as though they were waiting for someone to tell them what to do.

On cue, Sullivan's voice rang out through all the radios, finally confirming the order to seal the hospital up.

'Nobody in, nobody out. Repeat . . . '

Miller and Xiu stopped and looked around, unsure suddenly which way to go. Miller had been inside the Vic plenty of times but had always come in through the main entrance and he'd momentarily lost his bearings. He collared a passing porter and shouted, 'Accident and Emergency.'

'You're in the wrong place.'

'Which way?' Miller stepped closer to the porter as though the accident in question might be about to happen to him. 'Where's A and bloody E?'

The porter went pale, then pointed.

Miller and Xiu could see other officers converging on the corridor as they all ran hell for leather towards Natalie Bagnall's department.

*

She usually had a crafty cigarette midway through a shift, but she couldn't remember the last time she'd needed one quite so much. It had been a pretty standard night so far, quieter than normal, in fact – a few broken bones, a handful of post-pub punch-up injuries, two serious knife wounds and a drug overdose – but the effort of trying to do her job, of staying calm while knowing she was being stalked by the man who'd killed her brother, had left Natalie feeling utterly exhausted.

Trudging into the locker room, she was tearful and about ready to collapse.

Her friend Emma was just on her way out and, seeing that Natalie was having a tough time, hung back for a moment to comfort her. With no idea of the real reason, she put Natalie's distress down to the fact that she was still grieving, and stepped across to give her a hug.

'Listen, Nat, nobody's going to bat an eyelid if you want to knock off early. It's understandable.'

Natalie assured her friend that she was fine and they arranged to get breakfast together at the end of the shift.

'If you're sure,' Emma said. 'I don't want to be treating *you* later on.'

Natalie leaned back against her locker and heard the door shut as Emma left. She closed her eyes and tried to breathe normally, and she'd no idea how long she'd been standing there when she heard a noise and turned to nod at the doctor who'd obviously just come in.

She tried to place him and had just decided that she couldn't remember seeing him before when she noticed the small, silenced gun in his hand and understood why.

Natalie froze.

'Let's not do anything silly, OK, love?'

The hair was a lot different and now he had glasses on,

but she still recognised the man she'd seen on the front of the newspaper and in the TV reports. She didn't take her eyes off the gun as she quietly slid her hand into the pocket of her scrubs.

Driscoll saw her staring at the gun and held it up. 'Yeah, dinky little thing this, isn't it? Bought it off a mate of mine. I say mate . . . I mean he *was* until I shot him in the head and chopped his hands off. We had a bit of a falling out, you know?'

'How did you get in here?' Natalie asked. She was trying to keep the tremor from her voice because, silly as it was, she didn't want to let this man see that she was afraid. She felt for the radio in her pocket and pressed what she hoped was the right button. 'The locker room's got a passcode.'

'Oh, I just came in when that other nurse was coming out.'

'Lucky,' Natalie said. Emma had probably held the door open for him. They'd certainly have something to talk about at breakfast, she thought.

Or they would have done . . .

'I do *know* the passcode though. I stood behind someone when they were using it last night.' He took a step towards her, the gun still hanging loose from his hand, then used it to point at her locker. 'Briefcase in there then, is it?'

Natalie nodded.

'Well, we haven't got time to mess about,' he said. 'So let's have it open, shall we?'

FIFTY-SEVEN

'*The locker room's got a passcode . . .*'

Now, thanks to Natalie's quick-thinking in keying her radio, Miller knew exactly where she was. Where, unfortunately, she and Driscoll *both* were. Provided she was able to keep her finger on the button, their conversation would now be being broadcast to every radio unit.

'*Oh, I just came in when that other nurse was coming out.*'

'*Lucky.*'

He and Xiu were still tearing along corridors, following signs to A&E. He shouted at a woman in scrubs as she stared at them running past. 'Where's the staff locker room?'

The woman shouted back. 'Depends which one you're looking for.'

Xiu looked at him.

'*I do know the passcode though. I stood behind someone when they were using it last night. Briefcase in there then, is it?*'

Miller stopped and ran back, the woman moving away from him as he got closer to her, until she was pressed against a wall.

He knew he looked a little crazed, but he couldn't be fagged digging out his warrant card, so was trying very hard not to sound like someone who'd absconded from the psych ward. 'What do you mean, which one?'

'There's over five hundred medical staff working here, so there's more than one locker room.'

'Well, we haven't got time to mess about. So, let's have it open, shall we?'

Suddenly there was just the hiss of static, then silence. Natalie had taken her finger off the button.

'The nearest one's right behind A&E,' the woman said. 'Just around that—'

Miller and Xiu were already running.

Driscoll moved to stand close to Natalie as she fiddled awkwardly with the padlock, her fingers sweaty and shaking.

'Don't be nervous,' he said.

As she twisted the dials, trying to line up the correct sequence of numbers, Natalie wondered if this monstrous moron had any idea how ridiculous he sounded. Yeah, sorry if the fact that you're already wanted for God knows how many murders and you've got a gun is making me a touch jumpy.

The padlock opened and she reached for the door.

'Nice and slow.' Driscoll stepped back and raised the gun.

'Just take the stupid briefcase and go,' Natalie said.

'We'll see,' Driscoll said.

She reached up to the shelf where she'd placed the briefcase when she'd arrived at work. She slid it slowly out at an angle so that Driscoll could see the case coming, while the hand that was hidden by the door reached carefully for the other, somewhat smaller object she'd stashed in the locker a few hours before.

Something Xiu had given her before she'd left for work.

'Don't worry, you're not going to need it,' Xiu had said. 'I've got a spare, that's all, and it never hurts to have one around.'

'Finally,' Driscoll said, when the case had emerged. 'You wouldn't believe the bloody trouble that thing's caused me.'

Natalie held the case up for him to take. She had one hand wrapped around the handle, the rage bubbling up as she offered Andy's killer what he'd come for. As she realised that the *trouble* he was moaning about included him having to beat her little brother half to death before suffocating him.

The trouble . . .

Driscoll lowered the gun as he reached forward to take the case. He smiled, which was when Natalie shoved the briefcase hard into his chest and produced the small can of pepper spray she had taken from her locker and hidden behind it. She shouted as she let him have it full in the face; swore and kicked out as she kept on letting him have it, even when he was writhing on the floor and screaming.

Then Natalie stepped over him and ran.

Miller had given up being subtle or asking politely. Now he simply sprinted through the crowded A&E waiting area shouting 'Locker room' and following the pointed fingers of alarmed-looking members of staff. As he and Xiu burst through the doors and into the triage room, he could hear the sweary complaints of those who'd already been waiting hours and thought he was queue-jumping. He heard somebody close behind him calling for security.

'You really can't be here.'

'Police.'

'Yes, we've already called them.'

'We *are* the chuffing police, now where's the locker room?'

They charged past a seemingly endless row of curtained-off cubicles, past several patients on trolleys and a few lying stretched out on benches, until they reached a dead end. There were doors to the left and right of them with corridors beyond. Signs on both that read *Staff Only*.

'Pick one,' Miller said.

Xiu hesitated for just a second, then pointed, and they barrelled through a set of doors which had not even closed behind them before they ran straight into a hysterical Natalie Bagnall.

'He was in there,' she screamed. 'He was in there . . .'

Miller wrapped his arms around her and squeezed. He shushed and rubbed her back as she sobbed into his shoulder, but he was staring beyond her into the corridor. Looking for Driscoll.

They were quickly surrounded by a gaggle of other officers looking determined and chuntering into radios. Even Sullivan and Clough finally put in an appearance. Xiu stepped forward to take over comforting duties and, more importantly, to make sure Natalie wasn't injured.

'Do you need any medical treatment?' she asked.

Natalie managed to confirm that she was unhurt.

'Are you sure?' Xiu held the young woman's face in her hands and smiled. 'Because we're definitely in the right place if you do.'

'I'm fine.' Natalie was still breathing heavily. 'I used what you gave me.'

'Nice work,' Xiu said.

'What's the passcode?' Miller asked. 'For the locker room.'

Natalie spluttered out the numbers and, half a minute later, Miller watched as a firearms officer slowly pushed the door open and went inside.

Miller waited. A tiny, vicious part of him – one that only

emerged whenever someone on a property show said 'the wow factor', and once during a seriously competitive dance-off in Rochdale – was half hoping that he'd hear a gunshot.

'Room clear,' the officer shouted.

Miller waited until the firearms officer had left, then stepped inside. His eyes began to sting immediately and he knew exactly what Xiu had given to Natalie Bagnall. Looking around, he couldn't help wishing that the girl had been given something that would do rather more serious damage, or at least have debilitated her attacker for a little longer.

The locker was still open, Miller's replica briefcase lay empty on the floor, and Dudley Driscoll had gone.

FIFTY-EIGHT

The time he'd spent hiding out in the hospital had given Driscoll a pretty good feel for the layout of the place, but now that was just about *all* he had. He staggered, blinded and screaming like a stuck pig as he crashed through a set of doors that he thought might lead out to a loading bay at the back of the hospital. He quickly discovered he was wrong and went blundering helplessly onwards in the hope that he might find some other way out.

He rubbed at his eyes which only made the pain worse, then almost immediately forgot that he'd done it and did it again.

He ran into one dead end and then another.

He turned around, yelling in pain and frustration.

He had to try and find an exit fast, and while he could barely see his hand in front of his face that was looking increasingly unlikely. It wasn't as if he could head towards somewhere a bit more crowded and ask for directions. He knew there were coppers everywhere and, if he couldn't get out of the hospital quickly, the only option he had left was to find somewhere to lie low. At least until he could see properly.

Christ on a bike, it felt like his eyes were actually *burning.*

He charged around a corner, panting as he felt his way along the walls before tripping and tumbling down what was a mercifully short flight of stairs. He picked himself up, cursing and turned to continue down a second much longer flight, and then a third . . .

Seemingly as far down as it was possible to go, he moved forward a little more cautiously, because wherever the hell he'd ended up, it was starting to feel a little strange. The temperature had dropped and the noises he was still making, the gasps and the moans, sounded echoey. Whatever this bit of the hospital was, he could sense it wasn't one that anyone used much any more.

It was some kind of storage area, he guessed, hidden away in the bowels of the place, or maybe the bit that housed the boilers and generators and what have you. There were probably all sorts of disused tunnels under places like this, for diverting waste away or maybe transporting bodies in the olden days.

Surely he could find somewhere to hide down here.

Driscoll was creeping forward now, goosepimply suddenly and it didn't matter that he couldn't see a great deal, because he could make out just enough to know that it was pretty much dark as night down here anyway. It didn't seem like there were any windows and, if there were lights, nobody had bothered turning them on.

It felt as if the corridor widened suddenly and he realised that he'd entered a large room or vault of some sort, with boxes or maybe machines lined up against the walls and a smell that made him think of school dinners. Something rotting somewhere.

For the first time in as long as he cared to remember, Dudley Driscoll felt afraid, but when he turned to go back the way he'd come, it was only to find himself squinting at a figure moving quickly across the room towards him. A man, or more accurately the shape of a man. Even in semi-darkness and with what minimal vision he had, Driscoll could tell what the man had in his hand, because the shape of a silenced pistol was one he'd become pretty familiar with over the years. It was ... distinctive.

It wasn't like the bloke was pointing a banana at him, was it?

His own gun had gone missing while he was playing silly buggers with Natalie Bagnall in that locker room, but even if he'd had it, he wasn't able to see well enough for a gun to be of any use. Right then, he couldn't hit a cow's arse with a banjo.

Even though he'd lost his bearings completely, there was only one thing he could do.

He spun around and ran, but only as far as the wall he smacked into, hard enough to wind himself and break his nose at the same time. The jolt of excruciating pain made him forget momentarily about the burning in his eyes, but even that only lasted as long as it took for the man to step up behind him and press the gun against the back of Driscoll's head.

The barrel clunking softly against his skull.

There wasn't exactly a lot of time – no more than a second or two before the trigger was pulled – so he was never going to come up with anything terribly memorable, but all the same Driscoll knew, even as he said them, that these were not likely to make anyone's list of famous last words.

'Oh, boll—'

FIFTY-NINE

Miller had already escorted Natalie out through a fire door and watched her smoke two cigarettes in quick succession. Now, he and Xiu sat with her in the nurses' break room, while she drank coffee from the vending machine and tried to stop shaking. They told her how brave she was, and how clever. Miller knew that they should probably be asking her questions, too, but it seemed a little too soon. There would be plenty of time later on for her to make a statement, and besides, she was the one with questions.

'How did he get in? You lot were everywhere ... all the cameras and stuff. How the hell did he get past you?'

'He was here before we were,' Miller said.

'I don't get it. How could he ... ?' She shook her head and gulped her coffee.

Xiu did her best to explain. 'We think Driscoll had been inside the hospital for a while. Hiding out, which is not that tricky given the size of this place. He might even have come in the night he was spotted by Finn's mates nearby, but we're fairly certain he was watching your house yesterday, so I'm betting he got here later after that day.'

'He was waiting for you to come to him,' Miller said.

Natalie stared blankly for half a minute, then turned and began looking frantically around.

'He's still here, right?'

'Don't worry,' Xiu said.

'Yeah, but he's still *here*, though. Somebody was saying all the exits had been closed off, so he must still be in the hospital.'

There were half a dozen officers – plain-clothes and uniform – in the room with them, but considering what idiots Driscoll had made of them all so far, Miller thought Natalie's concern was understandable. 'We'll find him,' he said.

'You promise?'

'We'll find him, Natalie.'

There was no way that Driscoll could have left the building between the incident in the locker room and the order to seal the hospital. The man had all manner of disturbing capabilities, but seeing as the power of invisibility wasn't one of them, Miller was almost as confident of finding him as he was trying to sound. The only fly in the ointment – and as flies went this was a sizeable and irritating one – was that Tim Sullivan was coordinating the search. Miller told himself that, though it had now been over an hour without any result, even Sullivan couldn't botch the search of a sealed building. He tried to banish the image of the DI simply wandering the hospital corridors with his hands cupped around his mouth, shouting, 'Come out, come out, wherever you are . . . '

'My mum and dad will be asleep,' Natalie said. 'But I need to let them know I'm OK.'

'We'll take care of it,' Xiu said. 'We've still got a car outside the house.'

'Thanks.' She'd begun shaking again.

'You need another fag?' Miller asked.

'No, I'm good.'

'Or something a bit stronger, maybe. There must be all sorts knocking around in some of these cupboards ... a nice bit of fentanyl or whatever. I know, what about a lovely drop of morphine?'

Natalie managed the first smile they'd seen since they'd found her.

There was a sudden burst of radio chatter after which a uniform came hurrying across. Miller stood up and moved to meet him, keen to have the conversation out of Natalie Bagnall's earshot.

'Sounds like they've found him, sir.'

'Where?'

'Apparently, there's a kitchen in the basement and he was in there.'

'Well, you've got to admire the man's composure,' Miller said. 'Half the Lancashire Constabulary looking for him and he nips down to make himself an omelette.'

'No, it sounds like it's disused. Just full of old cookers and freezers and what have you, so he wasn't—' The officer stopped when he saw the look on Miller's face that made it clear he'd been joking. 'Oh, I see. Well, anyway, I don't think he'll be making himself anything any more.'

Miller tried not to let the disappointment show on his face. While Dudley Driscoll being brown bread was unlikely to keep too many people awake at night and was, by any objective measure, a major boon for all humanity, it was not good news for him.

'They found him on a fridge, apparently.'

'I presume you mean *in* a fridge.' Miller never ceased to

be amazed at the stupidity of certain people, even when under extreme pressure. How could a killer as obviously smart as Driscoll have chosen such a stupid and dangerous hiding place?

The copper shook his head. 'I think they definitely said *on*, sir . . .'

Either the uniformed officer was right and this kitchen was no longer being used or the NHS was in a lot more trouble than Miller had thought. Certainly, if there *was* still any food coming out of this damp and dingy hellhole, the Vic would be killing rather more patients than it saved.

There were unlabelled cans spilling from rotten cardboard boxes, a rack of metal shelves piled high with old pots and pans and crockery, and an industrial-sized sink that was coated in something Miller didn't really want to think about for too long. A row of hulking, blackened cookers ran along one wall, while another was lined with sixties-style fridges and freezers, coated in dust and connected by cobwebs. The room, lit only by a single bare bulb, was largely in shadow and would have been positively spooky were it not for the gaggle of coppers peering at the body, nattering cheerfully as they waited for the CSIs to arrive and trampling all over what was most definitely a crime scene.

Miller walked across and stared down at the dead man. The bloodstained scrubs were clearly the result of having his nose forcefully repositioned, and he appeared to be slumped casually against one of the fridges.

'Oh, *I* see what he was talking about.'

'What who was talking about?' asked the nearest uniform.

There was a trickle of blood from one ear and, when Miller leaned down to get a closer look, he could see the small tip of metal buried deep inside Driscoll's lughole. 'That must have smarted,' he said.

'Nail gun, if you ask me,' the uniform said. 'Right up close to the side of his head and ... pffft.'

Miller had not asked but was nevertheless impressed by the officer's mime and most especially the accompanying sound effect. He was about to say as much when he spotted yet more blood matted in the hair at the back of the man's head. He asked for a pair of nitrile gloves, snapped them on, then leaned down to carefully move Driscoll's head forward.

The PC whistled as if he was impressed. 'Well, bugger me.'

'Yes, that *is* a bit weird.' Miller stared down at what was clearly a gunshot wound.

'It's like he was killed twice,' the uniformed officer said. 'Once with a nail gun and once with a ... gun gun.'

'Possibly,' Miller said.

'Whoever did it obviously wanted to make very sure he was dead.'

Miller wasn't convinced, but right then there was another peculiarity that he found rather more interesting. Whatever the officer thought about the cause or causes of death, being on the receiving end of two wounds – each of which would almost certainly have been fatal – was far from the strangest thing that had happened to Dudley Driscoll.

A metal collar, perhaps three inches thick, had been fastened tight around Driscoll's neck – post-mortem would have been the practical option – and then ... attached to the metal door behind him.

'Some kind of hand-held welding tool, I reckon.' The officer pointed at several molten blobs on the floor around the body. 'Look, you can see the spatter.'

Miller had been present at what could only be described as

some pretty outré crime scenes in his time. He'd seen what was left of someone killed when a firework had exploded, having been inserted somewhere a firework was definitely *not* designed to go. Some years ago, he'd attended the death of a lad with a fatal nut allergy, who'd been force-fed Revels by a killer playing a deadly, if unorthodox, game of Russian roulette. He'd seen the body of one poor sod that had been completely shaved and another on which the killer had (rather helpfully) drawn a self-portrait in felt-tip pen, but this was the first time he'd come across a body welded to a fridge.

He waited, looking expectantly at the helpful uniform. 'You not got a sound effect for that?'

The officer thought about it, then shook his head.

'Frankly,' Miller said, 'I'm disappointed.'

By the time Miller and the rest of the team arrived back at base, he'd not slept for nearly twenty-four hours and doubted very much that he'd manage to stay awake too much longer. He'd be out like a light once Tim Sullivan had begun what was sure to be a complicated debrief.

Leaving the hospital, Miller had tried to hide his profound disappointment at the way things had turned out. He couldn't quite bring himself to smile, but he did his best to make all the right noises and tried not to look too miserable when others talked about the 'right result' or made jokes about a job 'weld done'.

Xiu had seen through it, of course. Only she knew that Dudley Driscoll's death – a more than solid blow to their hopes that he would name certain names – had robbed Miller of the single piece of leverage he had with Ralph Massey. With nobody willing or able to implicate Wayne Cutler in the contract killing of George Panaides, Miller had lost his one chance to get key information about Alex's death.

Xiu caught up with him as they walked into the station.

'We can get him another way,' she said. 'It might take a bit more time, but we can still give Massey what he wants.'

'You think?' Miller appreciated the effort, but he was in no mood to be cheered up.

'Course we can.' She put a hand on his arm. 'He's going to slip up eventually.'

'Yeah, obviously he is,' Miller said. 'And Blackpool are going to win the Champions League . . . and I'm going to win *Strictly*.'

The desk sergeant waved as Miller walked past and held out a scrap of paper. 'Somebody called for you.'

Miller snatched the note and stared down at it. The desk sergeant was not perhaps the most diligent of officers and certainly not what you might call a 'details' kind of guy. The scribbled information consisted solely of a time, a name and the most perfunctory of messages.

It was enough to stop Miller in his tracks, though.

7.45 p.m.
Cutler
Will call back

STEP THREE

CLICKETY-CLICK

SIXTY

Miller had already informed the group that he needed to leave as soon as the session was finished, so – while acknowledging how much he would miss the banter, the beer and the pork scratchings – he would sadly be unable to join them all in the pub afterwards. Howard said he was disappointed, but that it must be something important, and Miller assured him that it was. It also meant, crucially, that the conversation they were all (especially Nathan) desperate to have could only take place during the tea break.

It had been three days since the operation at the Victoria Hospital.

They had a lot to talk about.

Before that, while tea was being poured and biscuits snaffled, Mary had a few words of congratulation and encouragement vis-à-vis the actual dancing. Ransford and Gloria's mambo had been passable if not quite perfect, she said. Nathan and Ruth's quickstep was *perhaps* a little on the stodgy side. Howard had not disgraced himself during their lindy hop – well, only a little – and she was sure her toes would be right as rain if she used the footbath when she got home. She saved the highest praise for Miller's foxtrot with Veronica. His knee had recovered sufficiently for him to dance again, so while Alan from Thistleton took over at the piano (not too shabby Miller thought, but where were the Beatles tunes?) Miller had ventured back out onto the floor. He was understandably a little alarmed when Mary had insisted on a foxtrot, and while he had initially questioned the wisdom of her decision – 'Seriously?' 'It never hurts to get straight back in at the deep end, Declan.' 'Well, it does if you drown', etc. – he was happily surprised now to hear her words of approval.

'Maybe I've finally cracked it,' he said.

Mary bit delicately into a Bourbon. 'I wouldn't go that far.'

Nathan was necking his tea and clearly growing impatient. 'Come on, mate, let's hear it then.' Miller had already teased them with a few details and some had clearly seized Nathan's interest more than others. 'A flipping nail gun?'

Miller took them through the highlights of the operation; from the moment in the van when he'd realised what Driscoll was up to, to the discovery of his body in the disused kitchen. He left out the unimportant stuff like his 'wee in a bottle' song and getting lost trying to find A&E, and he even managed a half-decent reproduction of the uniformed officer's nail-gun impression.

Nathan had a bash himself and continued to try and perfect it.

'That girl was incredibly brave,' Ransford said.

'Pfffft-shtoof,' Nathan said.

'And pressing the button on the radio like that, when she was face to face with him.' Gloria shook her head in admiration. 'So clever. She will be getting the very best floral arrangement we do.'

'And balloons,' Ransford said.

'Yes, with her name on.'

'So, who killed Driscoll then?' Ruth asked.

Miller had obviously asked himself the same question, one that was currently being posed on a somewhat larger scale by those leading the new murder investigation. 'Well, I don't know specifically, but presuming only one individual was responsible for Driscoll's death, and that's a big presumption, he's obviously someone who's comfortable working with tools . . .'

'Shhhuh-dooft,' Nathan said.

Miller threw him a look to let him know he could stop now. ' . . . as opposed to just dancing with them. So . . . there *are* a couple of obvious candidates who would have *wanted* Driscoll killed, and my guess is that one of them organised it.' The truth was that Miller didn't much care who had killed Driscoll. What he did know was that the killer had probably been able to escape from the hospital fairly quickly. It had been impossible to keep the Vic sealed for very long, what with emergency patients arriving and the necessity to allow in extra police and forensic teams, so it would have been relatively simple for whoever had done it to sneak out.

Not that Miller imagined him slipping unseen out of a back door, not with the amount of gear he'd have been carrying. With his nail gun and his portable welding equipment to hump around, he'd have needed a hand trolley at the very least.

Pushing one of those things and wearing a high-vis jacket, nobody would have looked at him twice.

'My money's on Frank Bardsley.' Mary was still nibbling at her biscuit.

'Not a bad shout,' Miller said.

'Because he had a score to settle.'

Howard nodded. 'Or Wayne Cutler, of course. To prevent Driscoll grassing him up.'

Miller smiled at the two ex-coppers sipping tea and vicariously working the case. They'd almost certainly solved it between them, but the mention of Cutler's name had started Miller thinking about that phone call he'd missed while he was at the hospital.

Or more specifically, the call-back the following morning.

He'd had very little in the way of good fortune, Miller reckoned, at least not when it came to Alex's murder, but things had finally changed. Just when he'd thought that his one shot at getting crucial new intelligence had been stymied, help had fallen into his lap from the unlikeliest of sources.

'I'd been thinking of doing a pottery class or something,' Veronica announced suddenly. 'That or "Upholstery for Beginners", but I have to say that I'm *so* glad I signed up for this. Dancing and murder. What's not to like?'

'Plus the odd bit of welding,' Miller said. 'For variety.'

Veronica grinned. 'Absolutely.'

Nathan put his hands together, pleading. 'Can I please have *one* more go at the nail-gun noise? I reckon I've got it now.'

Everyone immediately turned to object, but Ruth was quickest, stepping across and waving a shortbread finger at him in an unfeasibly threatening fashion. 'Only if you want me to go out and get an *actual* nail gun, then use it to nail your feet to the floor.'

Miller nodded, wincing, because it looked like she meant it.

'Well, it couldn't make his dancing a lot worse,' Mary said.

SIXTY-ONE

For all its flashing lights, bright colours and the tinny music which Miller supposed was current, it was clear that the arcade hadn't been done up since the '60s. Miller took his place on a sticky vinyl stool, looked around, and decided he'd best make that the *1860s*. There was a line of one-armed bandits along one wall that looked every bit as knackered and ancient as anything he'd seen in the Vic's basement kitchen. There was a whack-a-mole which he was betting hadn't been whacked in a while and a battered mechanical giraffe on which parents could dump their kids while they blew all their spare change. There were old-fashioned pinball tables (*Fishy Tales* and *The Flintstones*), a 20p coin pusher and *three* different crane grabbers crammed with faded soft toys, which had probably been disappointing children and gullible adults since the end of the Second World War.

It was the bingo they all came for, though.

The consoles ran in a semicircle around the large platform which took up most of the arcade's available space. Twenty or more spots giving each player the chance to play several games at once, sliding small plastic doors across their numbers whenever they were called out. Good, old-fashioned fun. All the excitement of gambling, but cheap and cheerful enough at 10p a game (or twelve games for a quid) to ensure that nobody was likely to lose their house. Miller reckoned there'd be one or two bingo maniacs who spent enough time in the place to have lost some of the things *in* their house, and that they'd be the punters who kept the place afloat.

Not that there were many of them around tonight.

Miller was seated two stools along from an angry-looking woman eating chips, who – when she wasn't triumphantly flicking across those little bits of plastic – was muttering to herself or scowling at the bingo caller. An old man two places along from her looked like he was asleep, though he could just as easily have been dead. Around the corner from him sat a young couple who might have been giggling because the whole set-up was vaguely comical, but more likely were doing so because they were high as kites.

The only other player was the fashionably dressed man on the stool next to Miller's. The man he had come here to see.

'You want to play?' Massey asked. 'On me.'

'I don't think I could stand the excitement,' Miller said. 'Why are *you* playing?'

'You win a game, you get a ticket.' Massey held up the bunch of tickets he had already amassed. 'You get fifty tickets, you can pick one of *those* babies.' He pointed towards the somewhat random array of tatty-looking prizes, spotlit on a table next to the bingo caller.

A dartboard, a lava lamp, a matching set of bright pink suitcases.

'Oh, right, I get it now,' Miller said.

'To be truthful, I actually find it quite relaxing.' Massey leaned a little closer. He clearly did not want to raise his voice, but it was hard to be heard above the *clunk*s and *ting-ting-ting*s from the various machines. 'A nice, harmless way to unwind after a stressful day at the ballroom.'

Miller looked across to where Massey's tame twin skinheads, Pixie and Dixie, were feeding coins into one of the fruit machines. 'Ah, it's nice to see you've brought your nephews along for a treat. You think they'd like a go on the mechanical giraffe?'

Massey refused to rise to the bait. One of his numbers was called out and he flicked it shut. 'Besides which, I own the place, so whatever I spend in here ends up in my pocket anyway. I win, I win. I lose ... I win.'

Miller nodded like he was impressed. 'You can never have enough pink plastic suitcases.' He looked around, keen to get into the conversation he was there for, but not wanting to push it. If he knew one thing about Ralph Massey, aside from his propensity for shiny trousers and casual violence, it was that he could be capricious. He did not want to appear over-eager, only for Massey to change his mind about their arrangement at the last minute because he wasn't in the right mood.

He stared at the young woman who was calling out the numbers as they appeared on a monitor in front of her. She spoke into her cheap microphone in a rapid yet dreary monotone that made it sound as if she was unutterably bored.

'Twelve ... thirty-five ... forty-six ...' She sighed. 'Seven ... twenty-three ...'

Miller understood that in the interests of making money they needed to get through games as quickly as possible, but all the same she wasn't putting on much of a show.

'I know you're only paying that poor girl minimum wage.'

He nodded towards the young woman. 'But don't you think there could be a little more ... theatre? Jazz it up a bit?'

Massey shook his head. 'Jazz it up?'

'Well, not literally. I'm not talking about scat singing and tuneless saxophones, but come on, Ralph, you're an ex-performer yourself, so you know what I mean. What happened to all that normal bingo stuff? Two fat horses ... sixty-six. Key of the door, number twelve, whatever.'

Massey turned back to his numbers. He was waiting for just one, his finger hovering expectantly over the plastic slider, only for the angry woman with the chips to beat him to it.

'House!'

Massey watched the caller hand the woman a ticket and glared at both of them in turn. The caller shrugged like there was nothing she could do, but Massey obviously thought there ought to have been. He took a deep breath, cleared his board and focused as the next game was announced. 'You said on the phone that there was news.'

'Yes, there is definitely news,' Miller said.

'I'm all ears.'

'We're on.'

'On, as in ... ?'

'As in time finally being up for our mutual friend.'

'Fourteen ...' droned the caller.

Massey hissed out a victorious 'Yes', flipped his slider and glanced at Miller. 'And that's a definite, is it? You're not making promises you can't keep, are you, Detective Miller?'

'Tomorrow,' Miller said. 'Wayne Cutler's last day as a free man.'

'Now, that *is* exciting.'

'There's no way he can slide out from under this one.'

'You're sure? Because he is awfully slippery.'

'We have awfully powerful testimony,' Miller said.

Massey covered another number and rapidly clapped his hands together, seemingly as delighted at his steady progress towards one of the prizes as he was at Miller's news. 'You've made an old drag artiste very happy and I thank you for it.'

Miller wasn't prepared to wait any longer. 'So, let's hear it then. What is it you know about what happened to Alex?'

'What?' Massey stared.

Miller stared back.

'I'm not sure I know what you mean—'

Miller smacked a hand across Massey's console and leaned in. 'Do not mess me about, Ralph, because I swear—'

'I'm *joking*!' Massey shook his head. 'Honestly, some people have no sense of humour. I'm just trying to build the tension a bit.' He saw the look on Miller's face and sighed. 'Fine. So, here it is. You could do a drumroll, if you wanted.'

'Tell me,' Miller hissed.

Massey shrugged, then spoke nice and quietly. 'Your wife was murdered by a fellow police officer,' he said. 'By one of yours, and . . . that's it.' He held up a hand to head off Miller's next question. 'There's no point asking me for a name, because I haven't got one and that's the God's honest truth, but I do have a fair idea what happened and why.'

Miller could not find the words, still trying to process what he'd just been told. He nodded for Massey to go on, then listened as the man who would soon be the most powerful underworld figure in town explained exactly why Alex had been killed.

Who had said what and to who.

Where money had been hidden.

What Miller had been watching on that video.

'And that's just about all she wrote,' Massey said. 'Now, I'm one ticket away from that fabulous lava lamp, so I'd very much like to get back to my game.'

Miller stood up and drifted slowly towards the door, his mind still turning faster than any machine in the place. He was vaguely aware of the woman shouting 'House' again somewhere behind him and of Massey standing up and shouting, any pretence of sophistication gone. 'Right, that's your lot, love. You're *barred*.'

'You can't do that.'

'I'm a man who can do whatever he bloody well likes, darling. Now, on your way before I stick them chips where the sun don't shine.'

SIXTY-TWO

Miller was buzzing, but painfully distracted; wired and desperate to do something, yet unable to decide precisely *what* he should be doing that didn't involve smashing the nearest available object or just shouting out of the window. He put two slices of bread into the toaster and promptly forgot about them. He opened the fridge then stared into it for a while, not really sure what he'd opened it for.

'Butter, maybe?'

He closed the door and turned to see Alex at the kitchen table. 'Yeah, sounds feasible.'

'Oh, I meant to say, well done on the hospital job. A very nice result . . . not for Mr Driscoll, obviously, but that's not going to keep anyone awake at night.' She sighed and leaned forward to run her hands across the tabletop. 'I've been trying to think of a few more welding jokes, but it is quite . . . niche.'

Miller did not want to talk about Dudley Driscoll. He sat down opposite Alex and told her what he did want to talk about.

'Massey made good on his promise, then?'

'Strangely, I always thought he would.'

'His one good deed for the year,' Alex said. 'Maybe the twisted old stick insect's dying, which wouldn't be the worst news I've heard lately.'

'He's got ulterior motives.'

'Well, come on then.' She sat back and folded her arms. 'I mean obviously I *know*, but our strange little chinwags are bound by certain conventions, so spit it out.'

'You were killed by a copper.'

Alex shook her head. 'Right, and you're surprised, are you?'

'Yeah, a bit,' Miller said. 'Though I do get why I shouldn't be.' The Lancashire Constabulary was not yet in *quite* the same parlous state as the Met, but the notion that police officers were paragons of virtue, or could even be trusted to do what was in their basic job description and uphold law and order, had certainly taken a kicking. Trust in coppers was at an all-time low, thanks to those serving officers all over the country who had recently been convicted of a shocking range of criminal offences.

Murder, rape, GBH, ABH, drug smuggling ... Miller was just waiting for one to get sent down for genocide and that would pretty much be the full set.

'It's why you were watching this copper in particular.'

'Yeah, he's a very bad lad,' Alex said. 'If I'd known quite *how* bad, I might have been a bit more careful. I probably got a bit cocky.'

'Don't even *try* and suggest it was your fault.'

'OK, then I won't.' She smiled at Miller and leaned over to touch his hand. 'That's a relief.'

'So ...' Miller stood and began pacing around the kitchen, as he outlined the details of Alex's murder and finally got to tell her some of the things she *didn't* know. 'You won't be amazed to hear that both Massey and Cutler were keeping tabs on you, because they knew you were keeping tabs on *them*. The copper in question, the one who eventually . . . you know . . . was in Cutler's pocket, obviously.'

Alex nodded. 'We found out he'd been taking money off Wayne Cutler for a couple of years. Feeding him information and warning him if any of our colleagues were getting too close.'

It was exactly what Massey had told him. 'So you let it be known that you might be tempted to have a bit of what he was having. That you could be turned.'

Alex nodded again and gave Miller her best Darth Vader impression. 'To the Dark Side, Luke.'

'Right, so . . . you accept the odd bit of money and feed this bloke some bogus intelligence while you're gathering enough evidence to put him away. Once he trusts you, he goes to Cutler and lets him know he might have found another officer happy to join the payroll. Good news all round, right? Because what self-respecting gangster wouldn't want another bent copper on the payroll? But Cutler's been watching you, so he breaks the bad news and tells this copper exactly who his new recruit really is.'

Alex smiled a little sadly and pointed at herself. 'Ta-daaaa!'

'That's when our bent copper decides there's only one way to keep himself safe.' Miller faltered a little as the memories of the last time he'd seen Alex alive began to crowd in. Vivid and unbearable. 'He was the one who called you that night . . .'

She smiled, but now she was having to make as much effort as Miller was. 'Yeah, and we'd have won that sodding competition if it wasn't for him. My tango was *flawless*.'

'I'm not arguing,' Miller said.

'You wouldn't dare.'

'But don't you think this is a bit more important?'

'I'm dead, Miller. There isn't much that's hugely important.' She looked across at him, still smiling even though the tears had started. 'But yes, obviously ...'

'He arranges to meet you somewhere, only this time he's got a gun, and ...' Miller bit back a sob. 'You *can* chip in here, you know?'

'Is there any point?'

'I suppose not. It's not like anything you can add is going to be admissible in court, is it?' He laughed, then sobbed, then laughed again. He clutched at the lapels of an imaginary robe and declaimed in the voice of a posh defence barrister, 'Call Alexandra Miller!'

Alex laughed right along, wiping a sleeve across her face before she joined in. It was the kind of silly skit they'd acted out in this very room together many times, making one another laugh over a bottle of wine at the end of a horrible day. She was a good mimic, so her grumpy and officious judge was spot on. 'Correct me if I'm wrong, but isn't "Alexandra Miller" the name of the *victim* in this case?'

Miller's prosecution barrister took his cue. 'Absolutely, m'lud. I think m'learned friend is losing his marbles!'

Their laughter died slowly away. Miller leaned back against the worktop and looked at her. Perhaps it was just the tears making her eyes shine, but he couldn't remember ever seeing her look so beautiful.

'So, why didn't Massey tell you any of this before?' Alex asked. 'If it was all about getting ammunition to nail Cutler that he could then pass on to you, surely he had enough.'

'He obviously didn't think so,' Miller said. 'There was no guarantee that Cutler couldn't make it all disappear, and besides, there's no way this copper would have given any evidence against him. It certainly wouldn't have made any difference to his sentence, not if he was going down for murdering a fellow police officer. On top of which, if he did spill his guts, any time spent in prison would be a lot less ... comfortable. It's tough enough for coppers inside as it is, but with friends of Wayne Cutler in there with him, he'd have been shanked in the showers before you could say "vulnerable prisoners wing".'

'I can't help wishing that's what had happened,' Alex said. 'If only because I never got to dance my tango.'

'So, Massey let the ammunition build up and waited until he was sure Cutler was going down anyway. I reckon he knew Chesshead would give me those photos, which is the reason that copper killed the poor sod, and when they weren't enough, he sent me the video.' Miller pushed himself away from the worktop. 'Talking of which ... '

'Really? *Again?*'

Miller marched into the living room, sat down in front of his laptop and called the video up. He looked across to see Alex watching TV, flicking idly through the channels.

'That'll be the one hundred and thirty-seventh time you've watched the stupid thing,' she said. 'I've counted.'

'Yeah, but now I know something I didn't know before,' Miller said.

'Ooh, *First Dates* is on ... '

He pressed play and leaned close to the screen. Alex, the man in the shadows, the envelope stuffed with what he now *knew* to be cash. When it had finished, he went back to the beginning and played it again.

And again.

That niggle was even stronger now. Something the bent

copper was doing while he was waiting for Alex to count the money. Something weird with his hands . . .

'It's the one where that builder keeps winking while he's telling the woman all about his big drill. Remember, Miller?'

'*Yes!*'

'Right, and she calls her mate when she's in the toilet and tells her what a plonker he is.'

'No, the' – Miller pointed frantically at the laptop – 'the bloke in the video, for crying out loud. The one who *killed* you.'

Alex was still transfixed by the cheeky builder. 'Oh yeah?'

'I know who he is.'

Miller let the video play through one more time to be sure, and by the end of it, he was. Now he knew exactly what had been bothering him about the man's hands, or more specifically what the man was doing with them.

He knew because he'd only recently watched him doing it.

He sat back and stared across at Alex. 'Seriously, though? It's *him*?'

She didn't take her eyes off the TV screen. 'Well, d'uh!'

SIXTY-THREE

'Big day,' Miller said.

Xiu nodded. 'They don't come much bigger.'

They were leaving the station after the pre-operational briefing, during which Tim Sullivan had said much the same thing. Despite having spent most of the time imagining the DI as his plums were fed slowly into a mangle – much like the one his Auntie Bridget still used – for once Miller could not disagree with him.

'Have you thought about how many murder cases we could close today?' Xiu asked.

'At least half a dozen,' Miller said.

'Maybe more.'

'All being well.'

They were walking across the car park towards one of the three vehicles that would be involved in the operation, and clearly Xiu could not help but notice the spring in Miller's step. 'You're very chipper today,' she said. 'Considering what's at stake.'

'What can I tell you? I'm a man who rises to the occasion.'

Xiu did not look convinced. 'You don't look even a *bit* nervous. I was half expecting that irritating humming business again.'

'Well, the first thing is we won't be sitting in the back of a van all bloody day.'

'Right. And?' Xiu waited. 'What's the second thing?'

'Sorry, I forgot to say . . . I know who murdered Alex.'

Xiu stopped. Two steps later, Miller did the same and walked cheerfully backwards to join her.

'*What*? *How*? No, no, *who* . . . ?'

They were in something of a hurry, so Miller provided the answers to all her questions as succinctly as possible, then threw in the answer to one she hadn't asked. He wasn't even convinced that she was ever going to ask, but he'd been meaning to tell her for a while. 'Oh, and Finn is Alex's daughter, by the way.'

Xiu just stared.

'It's a long story.'

Eventually Xiu managed to get some words out. 'OK, well, we can circle back to *that*, but . . . what about the other thing? The officer who killed your wife, I mean?'

'Yeah, it's a shocker, isn't it?'

'A *shocker*? For God's sake, Miller . . . when are you going to talk to Forgeham?'

'Well, not today,' Miller said. 'Obviously we're going to be a bit tied up anyway, but more importantly, I need to go in there with solid evidence. I want this bloke bang to rights.'

'Yes, of course.'

'Banger than bang to rights. The big bang of bang to rights.'

'You thought about how you're going to get it?'

'Thought about it and taken steps.' Miller nodded, smiling. 'You may rest assured that steps have most definitely been taken.

I've got two possible streams of evidence, one from a source who's mad keen to help me and is already on the case. The other one, maybe not so much ... but let's see what today brings, shall we?' He pointed towards the car and they began moving again.

Xiu was still shaking her head and muttering. Several times she opened her mouth to say something, then appeared to change her mind. She raised her arms, then let them drop again, as if completely banjaxed by the turn the day had taken, though she did seem to have calmed herself down a little by the time they got to the car.

'I already knew about Finn,' she said as they were getting in. 'Just so you know.'

'No flies on you, are there, Posh?'

'The way you were that first time I saw you together, I knew it wasn't just because you felt sorry for her.'

'Right, even though I am a deeply compassionate person.'

'Then I saw a picture of your wife,' Xiu said. 'It wasn't rocket science.'

As the car pulled away and Xiu put her foot down, Miller began chuntering to himself. 'People always say that, don't they? Like rocket science is the hardest thing in the world and it's really not. I'm not saying *I* could do it, just that I'd like to see some of these so-called rocket scientists have a bash at something that's properly difficult. Like trying to put a key on a brand-new keyring or opening a carton of milk without it exploding all over the floor. Let's see them try to find the end on a roll of Sellotape or bath a cat or dance a half-decent bloody foxtrot, come to that ...'

Xiu waited until Miller had taken a breath. 'They're both gorgeous, by the way.'

Miller looked at her.

'Finn and Alex.'

SIXTY-FOUR

'You can stop laughing now,' Bardsley said.

'Sorry, I just think it's hilarious.' Cutler cut into his steak. 'A bloke who spends his whole life working with meat, even if some of it is a bit dubious, then comes out and orders . . . what the hell is it, again?'

Bardsley looked down at his main course with distaste. 'It's a mushroom and lentil nut roast.' He pushed a fork through it, as though that might somehow magically transform it into a plate of lamb chops. 'Mrs Bardsley thinks I should eat a few more veggies and suchlike. Cholesterol and what have you.'

'Well, at least Mrs Bardsley still cares,' Cutler said.

They'd agreed to meet midway between Blackpool and Preston because that seemed fair and had settled finally on a gastropub just off the A583 outside Kirkham. 'Place has got some decent reviews,' Cutler had told Bardsley on the phone. 'Two courses each for thirty quid a pop and it's out of the way.'

'I wish I was eating what my driver's got,' Bardsley said. The man in question was sitting in a Lexus outside and was probably already tucking into the pasty he'd bought from the nearby garage. Cutler's driver, parked up next to him in a Range Rover, had thought ahead and brought a packed lunch.

'Think about how much healthier you'll be.' Cutler popped a chunk of steak into his mouth and took a glug of the extremely cheeky Malbec he'd ordered to go with it. He swallowed and looked at Bardsley. 'A damn sight healthier than Dudley Driscoll, that's for bloody sure.'

'Yeah, well. Had to be done, didn't it?'

'I didn't expect it to be done like *that*,' Cutler said. 'Apparently, they needed special lifting gear to get the body out. Because the fridge had to come with it, you know?'

'What can I say?' Bardsley took a tentative mouthful of food. 'The individual in question is very ... creative. Got to take my hat off to him though, especially considering that Driscoll was already dead when he found him.'

Cutler shook his head, though he didn't look particularly shocked. 'Was he?'

Bardsley wasn't surprised that Cutler wasn't surprised. 'Yeah. Shot in the head, apparently. But you know, if you've gone to the trouble of bringing a nail gun and welding gear along, it seems a shame not to use it.'

'Well, it never hurts to make sure, does it?'

'Torchy's always been a belt and braces kind of bloke.'

'Who the hell is he, anyway?'

'No names, no pack-drill, right?'

'OK, it's just that I might be able to put a bit more work his way. You know, if he fancies it.'

'Let's just say he was a lad I was at school with. He was an old mate of George's as well, so I think he enjoyed himself.'

'Fair enough,' Cutler said. 'Whatever lights your candle.

Or in this case, your welding torch. Fact is, I wish I'd never hired that moron Driscoll anyway, all the arse-ache it caused.'

'A bit more than "arse-ache" for George.'

'Agreed, and I'm sorry for your loss, but you've got to admit that Panaides had to be dealt with.'

Bardsley sighed. 'Yeah, I take your point. He did get a bit above himself.' He waved the waiter across and held up his plate. 'Could you take this away and bring me gammon, egg and chips?'

Cutler grinned as the waiter sloped back towards the kitchen. 'So, Driscoll for Panaides evens things up then.'

'Absolutely,' Bardsley said. 'A mathematical equilibrium has been restored.'

'Equi . . . what?'

'We're all square, Wayne.' Bardsley sipped his mineral water. He was wishing it was a pint of Old Mill which he'd noticed the place had on tap, but Maureen had told him he needed to cut down on the beer a bit as well. 'So, we can move forward knowing that there are no grudges.'

'Certainly not from me,' Cutler said. 'I won't even kick up a fuss if you want to open another place or two in Blackpool.'

'That's very reasonable of you.'

'Long as nobody else gets above themselves.'

'They won't.'

'Because I don't want to be spending money to have another one of your lot taken out any time soon. Prices for decent hitmen have gone through the roof since Brexit.'

'I'll see to it,' Bardsley said.

Cutler sat back, chewing. 'Good, and in the spirit of co-operation, I might even expand a bit and start shifting some of my merchandise in your neck of the woods. You're all right with that, aren't you?'

'Well, hang on ... I'm not sure that having more drugs around would be awfully good for my business. The only reason folk *want* a burger or a nice battered sausage is because they've had a skinful in the pub. That's my whole thing. They don't want to eat fast food after they've had the kind of stuff *your* lads'll be selling.'

'Well, not with coke, maybe, but I was thinking weed would be more the way to go. You never heard of the munchies, Frank? A few extra stoners hanging around on Fishergate, you'll be quids in.'

Bardsley considered it, then shrugged. 'OK ... yeah, I suppose that makes sense. Some Cutler cannabis and a Bardsley's Banger sounds like a reasonable night out.'

Cutler raised his glass and leaned across to touch it to Bardsley's. 'To hands across Lancashire.'

The waiter arrived with Bardsley's gammon, and he glanced up to see the couple coming from around the bar just before he proceeded to get happily stuck in. 'Now, *that's* more like it.'

'Afternoon, Wayne.'

Bardsley may not have recognised the couple who had now arrived at the table, but Cutler certainly did and looked less than delighted to see them. He laid down his cutlery. 'I was really looking forward to that.' He nodded down at his half-eaten steak. 'Now you've gone and put me right off.'

Bardsley looked up. 'Friends of yours, Wayne?'

'Detective Sergeant Miller and Detective Sergeant ...' Cutler shook his head at Xiu and smiled sadly. 'Sorry, I'm rubbish at remembering names.'

The mention of the word 'detective' had been more than enough to get Bardsley's attention. He'd quickly lost interest in his gammon and was staring at their visitors.

'Oh, that's right,' Miller said. 'And the concussion didn't

really help, did it? You couldn't remember the name of the bloke who'd killed George Panaides, but miraculously it seems to have come back to you now. The bloke that caused you all that ... how did you so delicately put it a few minutes ago? Arse-ache.'

Cutler looked across at Bardsley; a flicker of concern.

'My colleague's name is Detective Sergeant Xiu, by the way. That's *Xiu*, not spelled how it sounds, and I've got a feeling that you won't forget it again any time soon.' He pointed to the all but untouched gammon on Bardsley's plate. 'That looks tasty.' He looked at Xiu. 'Don't you think that looks tasty?'

'It does. But their nut roast is excellent, too.'

'So everyone says.'

'You seem to know a lot about it,' Cutler said. 'Been here before, have you?'

'We know all sorts about all sorts,' Miller said. 'Thanks largely, and I must say somewhat surprisingly, to your wife.'

'*What?*'

Miller looked at Bardsley. 'And yours. Yeah, Jacqui and Maureen told us all manner of things, not least of which was the time and the place you'd be having this nice romantic lunch.' He leaned down towards Cutler. 'She even predicted what you'd order.'

Xiu smiled at Bardsley. 'Your wife will be pleased to hear that you at least gave that nut roast a try.'

'Have you finished, Miller?' Cutler glared at him.

'Well, it was more of a dramatic pause, really, but if you're itching to say something, don't let me stop you.'

'I don't know what it is you *think* you've got, but by the time our lawyers have finished pulling it to pieces, it's going to amount to the square root of sweet FA.' He took a sip of wine then picked up his cutlery again. 'So why don't you both bugger off and leave us in peace?'

'Tricky,' Xiu said.

'Yes, tricky,' Miller said. 'I mean we *would*, but because your better halves – I like to call them Jax and Mo – gave us plenty of time to set things up, we've now got all these flipping recordings to wade through, you see?'

'All these *what*?' Bardsley asked.

Cutler looked at Bardsley again and shook his head.

They were both as pale as the napkins.

'There's all these cameras for a start . . . look!' Miller pointed up at the cameras in the corners of the ceiling. 'There's those two, plus the ones set up at the bar and by the door and there's microphones all over the shop, including one just . . .' he pointed down to the arrangement of dried flowers next to the salt and pepper, '*there*, hidden away in that rather nice table arrangement.' He leaned down towards it and said, 'Hello? Testing, testing . . . so, there you are, lots to watch and listen to later on. I might even end up having to miss *The One Show*, which is, well, an arse-ache, but what can you do?'

'Swings and roundabouts,' Xiu said.

Miller nodded. 'That's exactly what it is.' He looked back at Cutler and Bardsley, who by now were staring down at the table, each with a good deal to think about. 'Oh, and obviously you're both nicked. Don't mind us, though, you go ahead and finish your lunch.'

SIXTY-FIVE

The lawyer – who Cutler had confidently predicted would be pulling Miller's case apart – looked as though he couldn't pull the skin off a rice pudding. With a sickly expression and hair almost as thin as the rest of him, he sat next to Cutler in the interview room staring at the wall or shuffling his highly polished brogues. For the first few minutes, things had ticked along nicely with his most important client doing just as instructed and parroting a succession of 'no comments' of which any villain worth his salt could be rightfully proud. Unfortunately for his soon-to-be-exasperated brief, Cutler was not the kind of villain who had ever been able to keep his gob shut for very long. This, together with a mountain of evidence that would give Ranulph Fiennes a nosebleed, left the lawyer in no doubt that *he* was the one with sweet FA and little to do but stare at his nails and think about how best to spend his two hundred and fifty quid an hour.

A year's supply of Hobnobs, an electric guitar like John Lennon's and perhaps a jaunty hat, Miller thought. *That's how* I'd *spend it.*

'I'm very glad you've decided to be a bit more chatty, Wayne,' Miller said. 'All that "no comment" stuff really builds the tension on a cop show but it's *so* bloody tedious. I honestly thought I was going to drop off at one point, and just think about the poor sod who has to type all this up!'

'Who's watching?' Cutler nodded towards the camera in the corner. It was far from being his first rodeo, so he knew that the interview was currently being viewed by many others in the station.

'Oh. Well, Detective Sergeant Xiu, obviously . . . remember her? DI Sullivan and DCI Akers and maybe even one or two senior to *her*. For all I know, the Chief Constable or the Home Secretary might be up there tuning in. You're quite the draw.'

'Well, course I am.' Cutler looked up at the camera and raised two fingers to everyone watching.

'For the benefit of the audio recording,' Miller said, 'Mr Cutler has just gestured somewhat offensively to Detective Inspector Sullivan.' He sat back, anticipating the pleasure he would get later on, picturing the DI's reaction. 'I swear, you could have knocked me down with a feather,' he said. 'When I got that call. The message was waiting for me after that business at the hospital – you know, when things got a bit unfortunate for the man you paid to have George Panaides killed, right before he got up close and personal with a fridge. You see, it just said "Cutler" on the note, so I presumed it was you. Yes, I did think it was a bit strange, because it's not like you're ringing me up for a natter every week, but all the same, I was gobsmacked when it turned out to be the fragrant Jacqui.'

'Don't.'

'What, is she not particularly fragrant?'

'Don't mention her name.'

'That's not going to be easy,' Miller said. 'Considering

she's the one who's provided so much of the evidence we have against you. Oh, I see, don't mention her name because it's unbearably painful to think that your own wife's going to be responsible for you spending the rest of your life in prison. Yeah, I can see that would be quite a tough gig for your average marriage guidance counsellor.'

Miller shook his head at how terribly sad it all wasn't, then looked down at his notes and began to read from Jacqui Cutler's statement. *"'I overheard my husband talking to the man I now know was Dudley Driscoll several times. He called him Draper back then. They talked about how much money it would cost to handle George Panaides. Then later, after Panaides was dead, he was offering him half that much.'"* Miller looked across the table at Cutler. 'Yeah, well you can't blame a bloke for negotiating, can you?' He went back to the statement. *"'I also heard him talking about the murder to Frank Bardsley. 'We might save you the bother,' he said. He was talking about the contract that was then out on Driscoll.'"*

Cutler swore quietly, then more loudly at his lawyer when the man leaned across as if to offer some advice. The lawyer quickly leaned away again.

'If it makes you feel any better, even if Jacqui hadn't decided to speed up the process, you were always going to end up in prison eventually and the truth is I really don't think she would have waited for you. To be honest, she was giving *me* the eye last time I was round at your place, which only goes to show how desperate she was.'

The look of disgust on Cutler's face made it clear that Miller's words really hadn't helped him feel better at all.

'As it is, Wayne, Mrs Cutler has told us about a great many other conversations she overheard and about which she kept meticulous records. Discussions about major drug deals, extortion involving at least three different town councillors, and several other murders. Now, we'll need to talk about them at some point, because she also claims to know exactly where many of those victims' bodies ended up, but let's start with Panaides, shall we?'

'Bardsley's wife did the dirty on him as well, did she?'

'Mrs Bardsley was equally forthcoming, yes.'

Cutler sighed and shook his head.

'He's currently being questioned in Preston,' Miller said. 'There are a few unexplained fires and several serious assaults he needs to talk to us about, as well as the whole "conspiracy to murder" thing. But even once he's given us the real name of the man he calls "Torchy" I doubt very much he'll go down for quite as long as you. A bit of a lightweight, really.'

Cutler was still shaking his head, as though unable to take it all in.

'Now that I mention it – conspiracy to murder, I mean – did you pay Dudley Driscoll to kill George Panaides?' Miller waited, while the lawyer looked hard at Cutler as though willing him to keep his trap shut. 'Did you agree to pay him ten thousand pounds in exchange for proof that the killing had been carried out, namely the victim's severed hands complete with distinctive signet rings? Did you—?'

'It beggars belief,' Cutler said. 'Don't you think so?'

'That you had Panaides killed? Don't be ridiculous, Wayne, it's eminently believable. Now, if you were asking me to believe that Snoop Dogg had him bumped off or that the Abominable Snowman was responsible—'

'That she'd do *that*. That the mother of my children would turn on me after everything I've done for her.'

'What can I tell you, mate? Relationships are tricky beasts.'

'Vipers, that's what these women are. A nest of chuffing

vipers.' Cutler sat forward quickly, red-faced and snarling. 'Vipers in our ... what-d'you-call-'em ...? Bosoms!' He scowled at Miller. 'That's *funny*, is it?'

Miller put a hand across his mouth to hide the smirk. 'Sorry, but yeah, it is a bit. You know, when you say it like that. In the plural.' He looked down at Jacqui Cutler's statement again. 'Now, if we could go back to what your wife overheard—'

The lawyer was about to say something, but Cutler didn't give him the chance. 'Yes, of *course* I had that jumped-up little toe-rag killed.'

'Oh! Well, that's extremely helpful, Mr Cutler, thank you.' Miller looked over at the lawyer and was unable to resist winking.

'What else was I supposed to do? I've got a position to maintain in this poxy town, haven't I? You heard what Frank Bardsley said yesterday. Even he admitted that his mate got above himself, so he needed bringing down a peg or two. I decided to do it permanently, that's all. People would have *expected* me to have George Panaides killed, so how would it have looked if I'd let it go? You tell me, how would it have looked?'

'Well, call me a big wet libtard,' Miller said. 'But I don't think killing people is a *great* look. That might just be me.'

'You do your thing and I'll do mine,' Cutler said.

Miller nodded and sat back, knowing that with a confession secured, in a room on the floor above Susan Akers and the rest of them would be punching the air. Sullivan would already be accepting the handshakes by now. 'OK, let's talk about Driscoll. When did you first meet him?'

It was if Cutler suddenly remembered that he *had* a lawyer sitting next to him. He looked across at the man and nodded, then turned back to Miller.

'No comment.'

'What, seriously?' Miller asked.

The lawyer blinked slowly and stared at his client with an expression that said, *It's a bit bloody late now, pal.*

'OK, well that seems like as good a time as any to take a quick break. Interview suspended at ... twelve forty-seven p.m.' Miller turned off the recording equipment, but made no move to leave.

'Are we done?' the lawyer asked.

'I think you probably are.'

The lawyer looked to Cutler for an OK, then scuttled from the room as soon as the nod was given, looking very much as if he was considering a career change. Hairdressing maybe, or something in the theatre.

Cutler sat staring at Miller. Defiant but evidently intrigued.

'It's just a quick one really,' Miller said, quietly. 'Off the record ... for the time being anyway. I get that it's a big ask, considering where we are and what the outcome's very likely to be. Bearing that in mind though, it strikes me that you might just think ... sod it, why the hell not do something *helpful* for a change? So, here's the thing, Wayne. There was one more murder I was hoping you might be able to give me a hand with ...'

SIXTY-SIX

What with it being the middle of the day and there being an interview yet to be completed and them being highly responsible police officers and suchlike, there hadn't been any bottles cracked open in celebration. Well, not that Miller could see. There was certainly a party atmosphere in the place though, and he did suspect that one or two of the mugs being cradled by all and sundry might contain something a little stronger than tea.

'You're a star, mate,' Clough shouted, raising his mug in salute. 'An absolute bloody star.'

Yeah, maybe tea with a shot of whatever Tony Clough kept in his bottom drawer along with a variety of emergency pies.

For the second time in as many weeks, Miller had been greeted like a conquering hero. As per his rescue of Keith Slack, a round of applause had broken out as soon as he'd walked into the incident room and, were it not for the other things on his mind, Miller's reaction would definitely have been a bit ... showier. On any other occasion he might have gone as far as a contained but triumphant lap of honour. He might even have clambered up on to his desk to conduct the songs being bellowed in tribute to one of the finest pieces of detective work in the history of the force.

He would have returned a few high-fives at the very least.

As it was, Miller stood quietly at the back of the small crowd and listened as Susan Akers made a short and heartfelt speech. He proffered a thumbs-up when she mentioned his name. He glanced at his watch when nobody was looking and, with what appeared to be uncharacteristic humility, he just shrugged when she talked about a successful operation that she could safely say had made the streets of their town a whole lot safer.

Then everyone – even Tim Sullivan – began to clap again and someone shouted, 'Speech!'

Miller took another quick look at his watch, slapped a hand to his breast and started to gabble. 'OK ... well I can't tell you how much this means to me. I didn't prepare anything, but I have *so* many people to thank, obviously. My family for always telling me to believe in myself and teaching me how to stay grounded. My therapist, my agent, my therapist's agent and my agent's therapist—' He looked across and saw Akers frowning. 'Er ... right, well, it's not every day you get to put away someone like Wayne Cutler.'

'And Frank Bardsley,' Akers added.

'Brank Fardsley,' Clough shouted, leading Miller to believe that whatever was in the DC's Mr Men mug, very little of it was actually tea.

'Yeah, him as well. But it's a team effort, so we should *all* be patting ourselves on the back, because this is a good day.' Miller looked around at the smiling faces and produced a grin of his own. The day was far from being over and, if the next half an hour or so of it went according to plan, it would certainly end up being the best he'd had for a very long time. 'So anyway, that's it. Onwards and upwards and ... enjoy your tea.'

There was another smattering of applause as people coalesced into smaller groups and a few of the more dedicated officers drifted back towards their desks. Miller turned towards the door, ready to leave, but Susan Akers intercepted him.

'What can I say, Dec? That was quite the job you did on Cutler in there. Though I'm not sure your interview technique would make any force teaching seminars.'

'If it did, I'd change it,' Miller said.

'I meant what I said. Getting that man put away is seriously good news for everyone. Well, with the possible exception of Serious and Organised of course, whose noses might be a little out of joint. You've not so much done them a favour as done their job for them.' She smiled as she touched her mug to his. 'I have to say, I'm *very* much looking forward to the "congrats" phone call from DCI Perks.'

Miller knew that word had already reached the top floor, because he'd received a text from Bob Perks within two minutes of leaving the interview room. If the man thought his toes *had* been trodden on, he did not sound awfully displeased about it.

We're all on the same team, Dec. Alex would have been very proud. Bob.

It was time for Miller to leave and when Tim Sullivan slid across to bask in the DCI's praise for *his* team's efforts, Miller grabbed the chance to move away.

He found Sara Xiu standing between him and the door.

'Well, this is pretty great, isn't it?'

'It's absolutely fantastic,' Miller said. 'Hugely moving. In fact, the whole thing's been a treat from start to finish. Now if you'll excuse me . . .'

He moved to step round her, and she moved to stand in his way.

'Where are you going?'

'I need to head off.'

'You can't go yet,' Xiu said. 'I hate to spoil the surprise, but for once there's actually going to be cake.'

Miller looked round. 'Where?'

'I think they sent a uniform down to the shops for one.'

'OK, well that's a shame, because, you know . . . cake, but there's somewhere I really need to be.' He looked at her then nodded meaningfully upwards. 'Someone I need to see and something I cannot bloody *wait* to do.'

Xiu's eyes widened the moment she understood. 'Right now?'

'Oh yes,' Miller said. 'It's showtime, Posh.'

She stepped closer to him, then whispered urgently, 'I know you won't need any help with this, but if you do just shout. I'll be straight up there with everything I can lay my hands on. Taser, telescopic baton, whatever you need.'

'I'll bear it in mind.'

'I mean it,' she said. 'Anything.'

Miller reached across to squeeze her shoulder. 'Thanks. I know you do, but don't worry, I've already laid on some support.' He stepped towards the door, then turned to issue vital last-minute instructions. 'I hope I don't need to tell you that if it's a Colin the Caterpillar cake—'

Xiu nodded, serious. 'You want the face.'

'Yes, *obviously*.'

SIXTY-SEVEN

This time, Miller had called ahead to avoid being ducked or otherwise fobbed off. He needn't have bothered, though. If the fact that he wasn't glared at *too* much as he walked through the squad room hadn't made it plain enough, he could tell by the unexpected warmth of DCI Lindsey Forgeham's welcome – a smile, the offer of a seat and a hot drink – that news of Cutler's confession had preceded him.

He felt like a reality TV star who'd actually *done* something.

'Sounds like someone had quite the morning,' Forgeham said.

'Well, I can't speak for anyone else,' Miller said. 'But I certainly started the day off in very fine style with *the* most sublime boiled egg. I mean, they're harder to get perfect than people think, but this one was just magnificent.'

'What are you talking about?' Forgeham shook her head. 'No, *why* are you talking about it?'

'I had Marmite soldiers, too.' Miller blew a chef's kiss.

Forgeham's second smile was not perhaps as warm as her first. 'You're definitely something of an oddball, DS Miller—'

'None taken—'

'—and I think that's putting it kindly. I have to say, I'm not altogether sure you'd last very long on my team, but there's no denying that you get the job done.'

'Oh, I'm all job, me, ma'am. Job, job, job, twenty-four-seven.'

'Yes, well, if we can move on from your breakfast, the result you've had today is certainly a very big one.'

'Imagine if I got *two*,' Miller said.

'Sorry?'

'Two big results, on the same day. Just imagine if I somehow managed to put another killer away in ... I don't know, the next twenty minutes, say. What d'you reckon the odds on that would be?'

'I really have no idea.'

'They'd be astronomical,' Miller said. 'I think you'd get shorter odds on Ant or Dec becoming the next pope. Personally, I'd plump for Ant, because I think the robes would really suit him, but I can see why that might be a controversial choice. Long odds, that's essentially my point. Long odds on me collaring another murderer.' He leaned towards her. 'But if Ladbrokes would be willing to take your money, I'd get yourself down there pronto, because I'm telling you, it'd be a seriously canny bet.'

The DCI sat back and narrowed her eyes, as though she was starting to regret welcoming Miller into her office at all. 'And this hypothetical second individual, is he or she a suspect in a case I'd be familiar with?'

'He,' Miller said. 'And he's rather more than a suspect.'

'The question still stands.'

'Well, I didn't get lost and stumble in here by accident, did I?'

'Why *are* you here?'

Miller began to tell her, but he'd got no further than

explaining to Lindsey Forgeham exactly why she'd be *very* familiar with the case when she raised a hand to stop him.

'I really don't like where this is going,' she said.

'Well, I can't help that, and trust me, it's going exactly where you think it's going. It makes perfect sense, don't you think? All that time, there I was suggesting that your investigation was proceeding rather more slowly than might have been expected, when really it wasn't proceeding at all.'

'We had this conversation last time you were here, DS Miller.'

'Yes we did, and I'm as convinced now as I was then that your own conduct has been unimpeachable, ma'am. How could I think otherwise when, as I'm sure you remember, I'm madly in love with you?'

'Let's not start that nonsense again.'

'Sadly, I can't say the same for everyone on your team,' Miller said. 'The unimpeachable thing, not the madly in love thing—'

'Are you actually going to name this individual you're talking about?'

'Oh, abso-bloody-lutely I am.' Miller could see that Forgeham was running out of patience. 'I'm guessing you'd like me to talk you through the evidence as well.'

Forgeham stared at him, steely. 'It never hurts, does it?'

Miller began to lay it all out again, but aside from the name and what he'd seen on his laptop, he didn't get much further than he had the first time. He stopped, more than a little irritated, when he saw Forgeham shaking her head. 'You're not really letting me get into my stride here.'

'No, and I've got no intention of letting you go any further.' Forgeham got to her feet. 'You really think you can come waltzing in here and accuse one of my officers of murder based on nothing more than something you saw on a grainy bit of video? Something you *think* you saw.'

'Oh, I definitely saw it,' Miller said. 'But you're right, it's still a bit . . . flimsy . . . and if that was the only evidence I had, I wouldn't have come waltzing in here at all. As it is, I would have been perfectly happy to come into your office doing a bloody tango, and, bearing in mind the circumstances of my wife's death, I'm sure you can appreciate how ironic that would have been. Because no, I'm not accusing your officer based solely on his actions in that video. There's also the small matter of the regular payments he received from Wayne Cutler which he's been hiding in an offshore account under a false name.'

Forgeham blinked. 'Can I ask how you know about this?'

'You can ask, but you'll have to forgive me if I'd rather not reveal my sources at this point.' It was a shame, because Miller knew how much Nathan would have loved to get the credit, and how disappointed he was when he'd found out that the results of his totally illegal hacking efforts were not admissible in court. Miller had already promised him free drinks in the Bull's Head for six months and he'd be sure to let everyone (especially Ruth) know what a sterling job Nathan had done on his behalf. 'I'll let you have the details, obviously. You can check it all out through more official channels and you'll be able to confirm that the financial evidence against this man is very much waltz-worthy.'

Forgeham said nothing.

'There was definitely one other thing.' Miller began to count off on his fingers, as though the piece of information he'd deliberately saved until the end had temporarily slipped his mind. 'The video . . . the payments into his iffy bank account and . . . oh yes, Wayne Cutler named him about an hour ago.' He saw the shock on Forgeham's face. 'I *know*. Who would have thought that someone as uniquely horrible as Cutler had it in him to do the right thing? You live and learn, right, ma'am?'

Miller stood and walked towards the door.

'Where are you going?'

'Well, based on all that evidence we've just been discussing, I rather thought I'd go and arrest the bastard.'

Forgeham walked smartly around her desk. 'Now, hang on a second, DS Miller. When it comes to the distance you must maintain from this investigation, I'm afraid that nothing has changed.'

Miller shrugged. 'Of course. I know that my relationship with this man's victim – or to be more accurate, *one* of his victims – makes my involvement a tad problematic. I understand that I can't be directly involved, and that once he's been arrested, I probably won't see him again until he's in the dock and I'm in the witness box.' He stared towards the incident room and squared his shoulders. 'But I would advise you or anyone else who doesn't believe I should be the one to put this man in handcuffs to think twice before they try and stop me.'

Forgeham said nothing.

Miller opened the door. 'Oh, and you probably won't make it down to Ladbrokes in time, but if you're quick you might still be able to get that bet down online.'

SIXTY-EIGHT

There were even more people staring in Miller's direction when he came out of Forgeham's office than there had been when he'd gone in and he wondered if any of their conversation might have been overheard. He didn't think he'd raised his voice, but it was certainly possible. He was as focused as he'd ever been, as single-minded, but that didn't mean he hadn't lost control for a moment or two or said something stupid, because it never did.

He didn't always remember, not immediately anyway.

Hadn't Alex told him often enough?

Miller was perfectly capable of saying something he shouldn't have at almost any time.

It was funny – funny enough to make Miller actually smile – that the only person who wasn't looking at him, or looking while pretending not to, was the man he was there to have a few quiet words with. To take one last good look at, before that man was frog-marched down to the booking area and from there to a cell.

MARK BILLINGHAM

'*I want it to be over. Whatever it is you find out.*'

'*What happens then?*'

This, Miller thought. *This is what happens . . .*

He was sitting at a desk with his back to the door of Forgeham's office and, even if Miller hadn't quite crept up on him, he guessed it was the noise that finally made Detective Constable Christopher Palmer turn round.

'What the hell are you doing?'

Miller was trying to click all four of his fingers in quick succession, passing the tips of them rapidly across the top of his thumb to make a sound like very quiet castanets. 'I'm not quite as good at it as you are,' Miller said, trying again.

'*What?*'

'Maybe if there'd been any sound on that video I'd have worked it out quicker. I got there eventually though, right? That's what counts.'

Palmer laughed as he held out his arms and looked to several of his colleagues who were sitting close by. 'Has anyone got the first idea what this nutter's on about?'

'It's a thing you do when you're impatient,' Miller said. 'Waiting for something, you know? It's an idiosyncrasy. You might not even be aware you're doing it, but you *were* doing it in a video I got sent: clicking your fingers while you stood waiting for my wife to count the money in an envelope you gave her. Does that ring any bells? I couldn't work out what it was before, but then once I'd found out that you were a copper, I watched the video again and I remembered seeing you do it *here*. A couple of weeks back, when I came up to see your boss and you were waiting for her to sign your paperwork off. Remember?' Miller tried the thing with his fingers again. 'Oh, that wasn't bad,' he said. 'I think I've cracked it now.'

Palmer stood up.

Now everyone in the incident room was watching.

'I'm guessing you were going to take early retirement at some point anyway. Why wouldn't you, because you've got quite a tidy sum stashed away in that bank account in Singapore. Alex reckoned you'd been taking bungs from Wayne Cutler for at least a couple of years, so what's that . . . a few grand a month? What were you planning to do when you knocked the Job on the head? Open a pub? Maybe go into private security or something, that's always a popular choice.'

'Are you listening to yourself?' Palmer asked.

'I try not to,' Miller said.

'If you think I had anything to do with your wife's murder, you're even madder than everyone says.'

'I don't *think* anything,' Miller said. 'I know you killed her, same as I know you killed Gary Pope. Poor old Chesshead had already sent me the photos by the way, so that really wasn't necessary. Oh, and the post-mortem on Dudley Driscoll confirms that it was the gun gun that killed him, as opposed to the nail gun.'

'Nail gun?' For the first time, Palmer looked genuinely confused.

'Oh, sorry, I was forgetting that happened after you left, but it doesn't matter. What *does* matter is that we've also had the ballistics report back which tells us conclusively that Driscoll was shot at the hospital with the same weapon that was used to kill Alex and Gary Pope. So now we know that one was down to you, as well. Probably just a favour for Wayne Cutler, right, to make sure Driscoll never got a chance to talk? He had you over a barrel when you think about it.'

Palmer laughed again, though it was not altogether convincing. 'Listen, mate, maybe you're the one who needs to think about what they'll be doing when they've handed in

the warrant card, because as soon as word of this panto-
mime gets round, you'll be out on your ear.' He tapped the
side of his head. 'Enforced "medical retirement", something
like that.'

Miller nodded. 'I can understand why you're in such a bad
mood, Chris.'

'Can you now?'

'Absolutely. Thirty-odd grand a year's a decent wedge by
anyone's standards, so I'm guessing you were at least a *bit*
worried when you heard that Wayne Cutler was in custody.
You must have been gutted when you found out he'd actually
confessed and you'd be waving bye-bye to that nice steady
source of tax-free income. I mean, if I lost that sort of dosh I'd
be seriously cheesed off.'

'I haven't lost anything, pal.'

'And as if that wasn't bad enough . . . '

Palmer looked at him, swallowing hard.

'Oh yes, sorry to be the bearer of bad news, but I'm afraid
Wayne's rather thrown you under the bus. Under a big lovely
bus with "compelling testimony" plastered all over it. He
was a bit stressed at the time, admittedly, but he was only too
happy to confirm my wife's suspicions. It's quite funny as it
goes, because he actually told me you weren't even worth the
money he was paying you. So, if it's any consolation, I reckon
you were going to get sacked anyway.'

Palmer took a step back and wrapped his hands around the
edge of the desk.

'I know,' Miller said. 'Some days everything just goes tits
up, doesn't it?' He clocked the pair of uniformed officers as
they appeared in the doorway. He'd tapped the two of them up
first thing and they'd been only too eager to help. They were
big lads and, more importantly, they'd both known Alex, so

Miller guessed that they wouldn't be too gentle with Palmer if he tried to resist arrest.

Or even if he didn't.

There was only one way to find out.

'Christopher Palmer, I'm arresting you for the murders of Alexandra Miller, Gary Pope and Dudley Driscoll. You do not have to say anything, but it may harm your defence if you do not mention when questioned something which you later rely on in court. Anything you do say may be given in evidence.'

The two uniforms had begun walking across as soon as Miller had commenced the caution. The larger of the two handed him a set of handcuffs and nodded, while his partner spun Palmer around. Miller fastened the cuffs until Palmer winced and didn't bother loosening them, before turning him back round until they were face to face. Now that Miller had said the things he was duty-bound to say in front of a great many witnesses, he decided to improvise a little.

'No, you don't *have* to say anything, but now's more or less your last chance. To say something about my wife. Maybe just a few words about what you did to her that might make me talk these two lads out of accidentally dropping you on your head on the way down the stairs.'

Palmer sniffed, like he was thinking about it, then smiled when he'd come up with something that pleased him. 'You think she was good at her job, yeah? Your saintly missus. Well, I don't mind admitting that I was certainly fooled, Miller, but maybe she was fooling the lot of you. Because if you ask me, the best way to convince someone you're happy to go on the take is because you actually are.'

Later, at the inevitable but mercifully brief disciplinary hearing, Miller would claim it was the look on Palmer's face as much as what he'd said that led to the attempted assault on a prisoner who was already in handcuffs. If he was being honest, it was probably a bit of both. Either way, this was when Miller did something he hadn't done since the unfortunate incident outside Brannigans over twenty years before, and tried to throw a punch.

It was ill-advised to say the least.

He could hear Alex telling him as much.

'For God's sake, Miller. I can throw a better right hook than you ...'

Back then, the bouncer at Brannigans had simply told Miller he was a pissed-up pillock and shoved him up against a Ford Fiesta. Now, Palmer just turned his head while one officer grabbed Miller's arm and several others attempted to pull him away and then, after some sweary and ungainly pushing and shoving, Miller toppled backwards over an office chair and broke several small bones in his wrist.

SIXTY-NINE

Within two minutes of the lights going up, the bar at the Winter Gardens Opera House was already three or four deep with thirsty customers and Jacqui and Maureen were very glad they'd pre-ordered their interval drinks. They collected them from the bar, handed the barman a ten pound tip and carried their glasses across to a corner.

'Enjoying it?' Maureen asked.

Jacqui pulled a face. 'I could do with a bit more gin and a bit less tonic.'

'The show, I mean.'

'Oh yeah, it's great.' She looked around at the smiling faces, listened to the excited chatter for a few seconds. 'This was a nice idea. Thanks.'

Maureen touched her own glass to Jacqui's. 'Life goes on, right?'

'If I'm honest . . . I did think that comedian who was on first was a bit crude.'

'I thought he was funny.'

'Yeah, he was ... but it's supposed to be a family show, isn't it?'

'It's sixteen-plus.'

'I'm just saying some of it was a bit near the knuckle. That joke about the horse ... '

Maureen sniggered, muttered the punchline to herself and sniggered again.

Jacqui had never considered herself a prude. Far from it. She was well aware that, having spent the best part of thirty years married to someone whose idea of an entertaining night out involved duct tape and an electric drill, it was somewhat ironic that she should be offended by a bit of harmless smut. All the same, though ... a horse? 'The impressionist was pretty good though,' she said. 'His Bruce Forsyth was spot on.'

They drank and people-watched while other audience members hurried to get served. A thick-set herbert in a football shirt tried to push past them on his way to the Gents, then thought better of it and moved quickly away when Jacqui fixed him with a hard stare.

'Crikey,' Maureen said. 'That was a bit fierce.'

Jacqui shrugged. 'Wayne taught me how to do it. It's all about making your eyes go dead.'

'Can you show me?'

'Yeah, course. It comes in handy when someone tries to get ahead of you at the checkout in Sainsburys.'

'Ta very much.' Maureen leaned a little closer. 'You been in to see him?'

'He doesn't want me to.' Jacqui sniffed and brushed hair back from her face. 'Suits me fine, tell you the truth. I talked to him on the phone just after he was sent down on remand, but he wasn't making a lot of sense. Just swearing at me and ranting about vipers.' She stared into what was left of her G&T. 'You seen Frank?'

Maureen nodded. 'Day before yesterday.'

'How did that go?'

'He says he forgives me.'

'*What?*'

'Oh, he doesn't mean it.' Maureen smiled. 'He's just playing nice because he thinks I won't come after him for as much as I would if he was being nasty.'

'And will you?'

'Oh God, yes. Don't get me wrong, I'm not looking to clean him out, anything like that. A few years inside is going to be tough enough for him as it is, especially when you're a good-looking man like my Frank.'

Jacqui did her best not to guffaw, but thankfully Maureen wasn't looking at her anyway.

'I certainly don't want anything to do with the business.' Maureen looked as though she'd swallowed something unpleasant. A slice of lemon perhaps, or one of her husband's sausages. 'I've had quite enough of meat, thank you very much. So, he can keep all his burger joints and vans and what have you and carry on running all that from inside. All I want is the money I know very well he's got stashed away ... and the house, obviously.'

'Of course.'

'And the holiday cottage in Prestatyn.'

'It's no more than you deserve,' Jacqui said.

'I'm just thinking about what's best for the kids,' Maureen said. 'For Archie and Francesca.' She downed the last of her rosé. 'What about you? What's your plan ... going forward, like?'

'Nice and simple,' Jacqui said. 'Divorce. Whether the

divorce will be nice and simple is a different question. I don't think Wayne will want to play nice, but maybe it happens automatically after he's been inside for a few years. You got any idea how that works?'

'Not a clue,' Maureen said. 'I reckon you've got pretty decent grounds though. Mental cruelty and whatnot.'

'Oh yeah, there was plenty of that.'

'So what are you going to sting him for?'

'Nothing stupid,' Jacqui said. 'Just half of everything, which I think is only fair, and you never know, maybe I could start running a bit of the business. I know every bit as much about it as Wayne ever did.'

Maureen looked at her.

'Not the really dodgy stuff. Nothing where people get hurt.'

'Oh, OK . . . '

'Not seriously hurt, anyway. Besides, I reckon DS Miller and his mates might well be inclined to look the other way, don't you? The favour I've done for them.'

'I was thinking more about what Wayne would think,' Maureen said. 'I can't see him being thrilled about it.'

'Nor me, but by the time he gets out he'll be too old and knackered to do much about it. Or he'll be in a box. Personally, I don't really mind which.'

'Sounds like you've thought it through,' Maureen said.

Jacqui drained her glass. 'Oh, I've been thinking about it for quite a while. A few years to get myself and the kids properly set up, then I'm buggering off to the sunshine.'

'I've always fancied Torquay,' Maureen said.

'I was thinking more like the Maldives,' Jacqui said.

'Oh, fair enough.'

The bell rang to signal that the second half was about to begin, so they pushed their way back towards the auditorium.

'So, what's in the second half then?' Jacqui asked.

Maureen took the programme from her handbag and began leafing through it. 'So, there's a few dancers to kick us off, then another comedian who I've never heard of ... and a singer to finish.' She held out the programme as they moved towards their seats, so that Jacqui could see the singer's picture. 'Looks like a bit of an Elvis tribute.'

'I really hope he sings "Jailhouse Rock",' Jacqui said.

They were still chuckling a few minutes later when the lights went down.

SEVENTY

'I think you did it on purpose,' Finn said. 'Just so I'd have to do all the work.'

Miller was sitting at the kitchen table, watching her. He pushed a fork into the plaster cast on his wrist in an effort to scratch the itch that had been driving him mad for hours. 'Yeah, you got me.' With him having only one working hand, the lion's share of the cooking had indeed fallen to Finn, though to call it 'cooking' was something of a stretch, consisting merely, as it did, of sticking a couple of M&S pies into the oven (one steak, one cauliflower and leek), opening a bag of frozen chips and emptying a tin of beans into a saucepan.

'I'm knackered already.' Finn leaned back against the worktop and folded her arms.

Miller grinned, but fought the urge to say anything sarky. He knew that her normal regime of food preparation involved half an hour's begging followed by a short walk to Greggs and the delicate removal of a vegan sausage roll from its paper bag. Having grafted for at least ten minutes in Miller's kitchen – following careful instructions to open a few packets and fill a pan with water – she was probably feeling like she'd spent several hours being shouted at by Gordon Ramsay.

'You're doing a great job,' Miller said. He was still working the fork under the edge of the plaster and moaned with pleasure when he finally hit the spot. 'Oh, yes, that's good.'

Finn grimaced. 'Please don't, Miller.'

'Please don't what?'

'You're making . . . sex noises,' she said. 'It's cringey.'

'Firstly, I'm just scratching, so chill out, sister and secondly, *that's* not my go-to sexy noise anyway. *This* is—'

'No!' Finn clapped her hands across her ears and kept them there until Miller waved to let her know he wasn't going to make any further noises.

Then he made the noise again.

'You're disgusting,' Finn said, laughing. 'So I'm going in there to play with the rats.' She stopped at the sound of a motorbike outside, then turned a few seconds later when the doorbell rang. 'Who's that?'

'Well, it might be Jehovah's Witnesses,' Miller said. 'In which case we can just invite them in for a quick natter, then tell them to bugger off when dinner's ready.'

'Miller . . .'

'Look, I knew you were a bit nervous about coming over, so I thought a bit more company might make things easier, that's all. Take the pressure off a bit.'

'What kind of company?'

'Why don't you go and find out?' Miller stood up as Finn headed a little reluctantly for the front door. He opened the oven to check on the pies and, by the time he walked into the living room, Finn was greeting their guests.

He could tell immediately that he'd made a good decision.

Finn was smiling as she took Sara Xiu's crash helmet from her, then closed her eyes and held on tight when she was pulled into a hug by Natalie Bagnall.

Natalie stepped back to look at her. 'That's better.'

Finn nodded, a little embarrassed at being the centre of attention.

The bruising on Finn's face had all but disappeared, though Miller knew there were still plenty of scars that nobody could see. He was also well aware that Natalie Bagnall had plenty of her own.

'How's the wrist?' she asked.

'Itchy,' Miller said.

Finn nudged Xiu, who was eyeing Fred and Ginger's cage warily. 'When he scratches, it's like a porn movie.'

Natalie had put the cast on Miller's wrist herself, three days before at the Vic. She looked confused when she reached to re-examine her handiwork, only for Miller to pull away and hide it behind his back. 'What's the matter?'

'I've got some very juvenile friends.' Miller sighed and held out his arm to her. 'So I apologise in advance.'

Natalie looked down at the plaster cast which was already looking a little tired, though not quite grubby enough to disguise what Imran had drawn on it in black felt-tip pen. She nodded, impressed. 'Well, I can't argue with the anatomical detail,' she said. 'Though they're usually a bit smaller than that.'

Finn and Xiu laughed.

'Right then.' Miller rubbed his hands together, forgetting that one of them wasn't really working properly and wincing a little. 'Who's up for getting hammered?'

'If you absolutely insist,' Finn said.

'I'd better not,' Xiu said, nodding towards her crash helmet.

'Well, I'm only on the *back* of the bike,' Natalie said.

Xiu looked disapproving. 'You could still fall off.'

'I've got some bungee cords,' Miller said. 'We can tie you on if we have to.'

Natalie took her jacket off. 'Happy days ... '

Dinner was demolished in short order and, though nothing had been previously discussed, there was no talk about the murders that had brought them together. The victims, living or dead. There was no mention of hired killers with a penchant for alliterative aliases, of severed hands in briefcases, pepper spray or welding.

There was plenty of chat though, and Miller was happy enough to sit and listen.

Natalie told a story about a man who'd come into A&E with a Kinder Egg wedged up his bum and Xiu described an incident when a woman had rung 999 because her local McDonald's had run out of McNuggets. They raved about TV shows they loved and slagged off those they hated and, when they were discussing music and Natalie confessed to Xiu that she was a big heavy metal fan, Miller almost spat out a mouthful of steak pie.

Everyone, especially Finn, laughed a lot.

Once everything had been cleared away, Finn went outside to smoke and Natalie and Xiu generously volunteered to do the washing up. Miller politely asked the smart speaker to play *Abbey Road* and walked across to the window.

Staring out, he could see the distant lights from Wales ... or perhaps it was the Isle of Man. Miller was never quite sure. The sea was just an undulating mass of blackness, but in the wash from the necklace of streetlamps he could just make out the figure walking slowly down the hill towards it.

Alex.

It might have been anyone, of course, but Miller recognised the swing of her arms as she moved and the orange Blackpool FC hat she'd bought outside Bloomfield Road one Saturday afternoon. She hadn't been a football fan. She just liked the colour, she'd said. Miller watched, holding his breath, because it was the first time he'd seen her outside the house and he wondered what it meant.

He could not take his eyes off her as she walked for another half a minute or so, moving in and out of the shadows before stopping and turning. She stared back at the house, back at him.

She raised a hand.

Miller didn't hear Finn come back in and only knew she was standing next to him when he felt her hand slide into his.

'That was nice,' she said.

They stared out together into the darkness for another minute or so and it felt perfectly comfortable, perfectly normal, even though Miller knew she wasn't seeing what he was.

'I think I just said goodbye to your mother.'

Finn didn't seem thrown at all and just let out a soft breath. 'I said goodbye to her a long time ago.'

'No, you didn't.' Miller squeezed her hand. 'And she certainly never said goodbye to you.' He watched as the shape of his wife began to blur until he could barely make it out. He touched the fingers of his damaged hand to the glass and said, 'I love you,' wondering why, after all the conversations they'd had since her death, he'd waited until now to say it.

Finn turned to look at him, unaware that the words had not been meant for her, or that they might just as well have been. 'Don't be soft,' she said.

Miller turned away from the window and gave her a

look, because he didn't want her to feel awkward. Because wasn't he just a big daft idiot who was always saying the wrong thing?

'Sorry . . .'

ACKNOWLEDGEMENTS

I am delighted (not to say enormously relieved) that Declan Miller's first outing in *The Last Dance* seems to have gone down well with the majority of readers. As you are someone who has just read the second book in the series, I can only assume that you are one of those. So, thank you. Of course, you might be one of those weirdos who turn to the last page first (trust me, they exist) so you may not actually have read it yet, but either way, you've paid good money for a copy, so my 'thank you' still applies. If you've stolen/borrowed/illegally downloaded it, I'm not *quite* so grateful, but a reader's a reader, right?

Even if they're light-fingered or 'careful with money'.

This is my twenty-third full-length crime novel and, as always, I am indebted to a huge number of people for getting it across the line. The team at Little, Brown have been as supportive and encouraging as always, despite the jokes (sorry/not sorry) and left me free to wander off in all manner of strange directions, confident that, from start to finish, *The*

Wrong Hands was in the right hands. So, a massive thank you – once again – to David Shelley, Charlie King, Catherine Burke, Robert Manser, Callum Kenney, Tamsin Kitson, Jon Appleton, Tom Webster, Sean Garrehy, Hannah Methuen, Gemma Shelley and Sarah Shrubb. Outside of LB, I am yet again thankful for the forensic and life-saving attentions of Wendy Lee and Nancy Webber.

All of the above are amazing, but special thanks are due to my editor Ed Wood, my agent Sarah Lutyens and the best publicist in the business, Laura Sherlock for putting up with me. They are, without doubt, the best one man/two women trio of superstars since Boney M.

My thanks are also winging their way across the pond to the Miller posse in the US, more specifically, the team at Inkwell and at my US publisher Grove Atlantic. I'm hugely grateful to Morgan Entrekin, my editor Joe Brosnan, my publicist Jenny Choi and my agent David Forrer for keeping the faith and pretending to get jokes about saveloys, *Homes Under the Hammer* and that bloke from the Go Compare adverts.

Fist-bumps and hugs to my fellow Fun Lovin' Crime Writers – Luca Veste, Doug Johnstone, Chris Brookmyre, Stuart Neville and Val McDermid – for the rock, the roll and all the laughter this year. The best gang there is, with a fried egg on top.

And I'll say it again, but the most heartfelt thanks of all are due to you – dear, *dear*, wonderful, wise, highly attractive and, above all, discerning reader. Thank you for welcoming Declan Miller so warmly and I hope his sophomore appearance in print has only increased your tolerance to his antics.

Oh, and in true James Bond fashion and in response to a good few emails of late, Tom Thorne will return next year in ...

Finally, before anyone fires off an email using capital letters to signify their outrage, I'm well aware that there haven't been any peanuts in a bag of Revels for ages. That's why the incident described took place a good while ago, besides which, why should cold hard facts get in the way of a good joke?